GRASS

A FOUNDATION BOOK / DOUBLEDAY

New York   London   Toronto   Sydney   Auckland

GRASS

Sheri S. Tepper

A Foundation Book
Published by Doubleday, a division of
Bantam Doubleday Dell Publishing Group, Inc.
666 Fifth Avenue, New York, New York 10103
Foundation, Doubleday, and the portrayal of the
letter F are trademarks of
Doubleday, a division of Bantam Doubleday Dell
Publishing Group, Inc.

Library of Congress Cataloging-in-Publication Data
Tepper, Sheri S.
Grass / Sheri S. Tepper.—1st ed.
p. cm.
ISBN 0-385-26012-1
I. Title.
PS3570.E673G7   1989
813'.54—dc19   89-30105
CIP

Book Design by Claire M. Naylon

A voice says, "Cry!"
And I said, "What shall I cry?"
All flesh is grass....
Isaiah 40—6

1

Grass!

Millions of square miles of it; numberless wind-whipped tsunamis of grass, a thousand sun-lulled caribbeans of grass, a hundred rippling oceans, every ripple a gleam of scarlet or amber, emerald or turquoise, multicolored as rainbows, the colors shivering over the prairies in stripes and blotches, the grasses—some high, some low, some feathered, some straight—making their own geography as they grow. There are grass hills where the great plumes tower in masses the height of ten tall men; grass valleys where the turf is like moss, soft under the feet, where maidens pillow their heads thinking of their lovers, where husbands lie down and think of their mistresses; grass groves where old men and women sit quiet at the end of the day, dreaming of things that might have been, perhaps once were. Commoners all, of course. No aristocrat would sit in the wild grass to dream. Aristocrats have gardens for that, if they dream at all.

Grass. Ruby ridges, blood-colored highlands, wine-shaded glades. Sapphire seas of grass with dark islands of grass bearing great plumy green trees which are grass again. Interminable meadows of silver hay where the great grazing beasts move in slanted lines like mowing machines, leaving the stubble behind them to spring up again in trackless wildernesses of rippling argent.

Orange highlands burning against the sunsets. Apricot ranges glowing in the dawns. Seed plumes sparkling like sequin stars. Blossom heads like the fragile lace old women take out of trunks to show their granddaughters.

"Lace made by nuns in the long-ago time."

"What are nuns, Grandma?"

Here, there, wide-scattered across the limitless veldts, are the villages, walled about to keep the grass at bay, with small, thick-walled houses, each with its stout doors and heavy shutters. The minuscule fields and tiny orchards are full of homely crops and familiar fruits, while outside the walls the grass hovers like some enormous planet-wide bird, ready to stoop across the wall and eat it all, every apple and every turnip and every old woman at the well, too, along with her grandchildren.

"This is a parsnip, child. From long ago."

"When was long ago, Grandma?"

Here, there, as wide-scattered as the villages, the estancias of the aristocrats: bon Damfels' place, bon Maukerden's place, all the places of the other bons, tall thatched houses set in gardens of grass among grass fountains and grass courtyards, with their own high walls— these pierced with gates for the hunters to go out of and for the hunters to return through again. Those who return.

And here, there, nosing among the grass roots, will come the hounds, muzzles wrinkling, ears dangling, one foot before another in a slow pace to find it, the inevitable it, the nighttime horror, the eater of young. And look, there behind them on the tall mounts, there will come the riders in their red coats, silent as shadows they will come riding, riding over the grass: the Huntsman with his horn; the whippers-in with their whips; the field, some with red coats and some with black, their round hats pressed hard upon their heads, eyes fixed forward toward the hounds—riding, riding.

Among them today will be Diamante bon Damfels—young daughter Dimity—eyes tight shut to keep out the sight of the hounds, hands clenched pale upon the reins, neck as fragile as a flower stem in the high, white cylinder of the hunting tie, black boots glistening with polish, black coat well brushed, black hat tight on the little head, riding, riding, for the first time ever, riding to the hounds.

And there, somewhere, in the direction they are going, high in a tree perhaps, for there are copses of trees here and there upon the vast prairies, will be the fox. The mighty fox. The implacable fox. The fox who knows they are coming.

2

It was said among the bon Damfels that whenever the Hunt was hosted by the bon Damfels estancia the weather was perfect. The family took credit for this personally, though it could as properly have been ascribed to the Hunt rotation, which brought the Hunt to the bon Damfels early in the fall. The weather was usually perfect at that time of the year. And early in the spring, of course, when the rotation brought the Hunt back again.

Stavenger, Obermun bon Damfels, had once been informed by a dignitary from Semling—one who fancied himself an authority on a wide variety of irrelevant topics—that historically speaking, riding to the hounds was a winter sport.

Stavenger's reply was completely typical of himself and of the Grassian aristocracy in general. "Here on Grass," he had said, "we do it properly. In spring and fall."

The visitor had had better sense than to comment further upon the sport as practiced on Grass. He had taken copious notes, however, and after returning to Semling he had written a scholarly monograph contrasting Grassian and historic customs regarding blood sports. Of the dozen copies printed, only one survived, buried in the files of the Department of Comparative Anthropology, University of Semling at Semling Prime.

That had been half a long lifetime ago. By now the author had almost forgotten about the subject, and Stavenger bon Damfels had never thought of it again. What foreigners did or said was both incomprehensible and contemptible so far as Stavenger was concerned, and no one should have allowed the fellow to observe the Hunt in the first place. This was the bon Damfels' entire opinion on the matter.

The bon Damfels estancia was called Klive after a revered ancestor on the maternal side. It was said among the bon Damfels that the gardens had been written of as one of the seventy wonders of the allwhere. Snipopean—the *great* Snipopean—had written so, and his book was in the library of the estancia, that vast and towering hall smelling of leather and paper and the chemicals the librarians used to prevent the one from parting company with the other. No one among the current bon Damfels had read the account or could have found the book among all those volumes, most of them unopened since they had been delivered. Why should they read of the grass gardens of Klive when those gardens were all around them?

It was in that part of all grass gardens known as the first surface that the Hunt always assembled. As host, Stavenger bon Damfels was Master of the Hunt. Before this first Hunt of the fall season—as before the first Hunt of each spring and fall—he had picked three members of the vast and ramified family as Huntsman and first and second whippers-in. To the Huntsman he had entrusted the bon Damfels horn, an elaborately curled and engraved instrument capable only of muted though silvery sounds. To the whippers-in he had given the whips—tiny, fragile things one had to take care not to break, ornaments really, like medals for valor, having no utilitarian purpose whatsoever. No one would have dared to use a whip on a hound or a mount; and as for sounding a horn near a mount's ear or even within hearing except for the ritual summons and when the Hunt had ended, no one would have thought of it. No one asked how it had been done elsewhere all that time ago or even currently. Quite frankly, no one of the bons cared in the least how it was done elsewhere. Elsewhere, so far as the bons were concerned, had stopped existing when their ancestors had left it.

On this first day of the fall hunt, Diamante bon Damfels, Stavenger's youngest daughter, stood among those slowly gathering on the first surface, all murmurous and sleepy-eyed, as though they had lain wakeful in the night listening for a sound that had not come. Among the still figures of the hunters, servant women from the nearby village skimmed, seemingly legless under the long white bells of their skirts, hair hidden beneath the complicated folds of their brightly embroidered headdresses, bearing bright trays covered with glasses no larger than thimbles.

Close between Emeraude and Amethyste (called Emmy and Amy by the family and "the Mistresses bon Damfels" by everyone else), Dimity was polished and brushed to a fare-thee-well, immaculately turned out in her hunting garb, and with a headache already from hair drawn back severely to fit beneath the round black cap. The older girls had red lapels on their coats, showing they had ridden long enough to become members of the Hunt. Dimity's collar was black, as black as the shadows lying at the back of her eyes, shadows her sisters saw well enough but pretended not to notice. One couldn't indulge oneself. One couldn't allow malingering or cowardice in oneself or in members of the family.

"Don't worry," drawled Emeraude, the best advice she could offer. "You'll get your Hunt colors very soon. Just remember what the riding master told you." At the corner of her jaw a little muscle leapt and leapt again, like a shackled frog.

Dimity shivered, the shadows writhing, not wanting to say and yet unable to keep from saying, "Emmy, Mummy said I didn't have to. . . ."

Amethyste laughed, a tiny shiver of unamusement, emotionless as glass. "Well of course you don't have to, silly. None of us *had* to. Even Sylvan and Shevlok didn't *have* to."

Sylvan bon Damfels, hearing his name, turned to look across the first surface at his sisters, his face darkening perceptibly as he saw that Dimity was with the older girls. With a word of excuse to his companions, he turned to come swiftly over the circle of pale gray turf, skirting the scarlet and amber fountaingrasses at its center. "What are you doing here?" he demanded, glaring at the girl.

"The riding master told Mummy . . ."

"You're not nearly ready. Not nearly!" This was Sylvan, who spoke his mind even when it was unpopular—some said *because* it was unpopular—somewhat enjoying the attention this attracted, though if challenged he would have denied it. To Sylvan truth was truth and all else was black heresy, though on occasion he had the very human difficulty of deciding which was which.

"Oh, Sylvan," Amethyste said, pouting prettily and pursing lips she had been told were fruitlike in their ripeness. "Don't be so harsh. If it were up to you, nobody but you would ever ride."

He snarled at her. "Amy, if it were up to me, nobody would ride, including me. What is Mother thinking of?"

"It was Daddy," Dimity offered. "He thought it would be nice if I got my colors soon. I'm already older than Amy and Emmy were." She glanced across the first surface to the place where Stavenger stood watching her broodingly from among the elder Huntsmen, his lean and bony figure motionless, the great hook of his nose hanging over his lipless mouth.

Sylvan laid his hand on her shoulder. "For heaven's sake, Dim, why didn't you just tell him you aren't ready?"

"I couldn't do that, Syl. Daddy asked the riding master, and the riding master told him I'm as ready as I ever will be."

"He didn't mean—"

"I know what he meant, for heaven's sake. I'm not stupid. He meant I'm not very good and that I'm not going to get any better."

"You're not that bad," Emeraude soothed. "I was lots worse."

"You were lots worse when you were a child," Sylvan agreed. "But by the time you were Dim's age, you were lots better. So were the rest of us. But that doesn't mean Dim has to—"

"Will everybody just quit telling me I don't have to?" Dimity cried now, the tears spilling down her cheeks. "Half my family says I don't have to and the other half says I'm ready now."

Sylvan was stopped in mid-bellow, stopped and stilled and turned suddenly soft. He loved her, this littlest one. It was he who had first called her Dimity, he who had held her when she had had the colic, who had carried her against his shoulder and patted her while he strode up and down the corridors of Klive, the thirteen-year-old boy cuddling the infant and yearning over her. Now the twenty-eight-year-old yearned no less over the fifteen-year-old girl, seeing the infant still. "What do you want to do?" he asked tenderly, reaching out to touch the moist little forehead under the brim of the black cap. With her hair scraped back and tightly bound she looked like a scared little boy. "What do you want to do, Dim?"

"I'm hungry and I'm thirsty and I'm tired. I want to go back in the house and have breakfast and study my language lesson for this week," she cried through gritted teeth. "I want to go to a summer ball and flirt with Jason bon Haunser. I want to take a nice hot bath and then sit in the rosegrass-court and watch the flick birds."

"Well then," he started to say, his words cut off by the sound of the Huntsman's horn from beside the Kennel Gate. Ta-wa, ta-wa, softly-so-softly, to alert the riders without offending the hounds. "The hounds," he whispered, turning away. "God, Dim, you've left it too late."

He stumbled away from them, suddenly quiet. All around them conversations ceased, silence fell. Faces became blank and empty. Eyes became fixed. Dimity looked around her at all the others ready to ride to the hounds, and shivered. Her father's eyes slid across her like a cold wind, not seeing her at all. Even Emmy and Amy had become remote and untouchable. Only Sylvan, staring at her from his place among his companions, seemed to see her, see her and grieve over her as he had so many times.

Now the riders arranged themselves on the first surface in a subtle order, longtime riders at the west side of the circle, younger riders at the east. The servants had skimmed away at the sound of the horn, so many white blossoms blowing across the gray grass. Dimity was left standing almost by herself at the east edge of the turf, looking across it to the path where the wall of the estancia was pierced by a massive gate. "Watch the Kennel Gate," she admonished herself unnecessarily. "Watch the Kennel Gate."

Everyone watched the Kennel Gate as it opened slowly and the hounds came through, couple on couple of them, ears dangling, tongues lolling between strong ivory teeth, tails straight behind them. They moved down the Hounds' Way, a broad path of low, patterned velvetgrass which circled the first surface and ran westward through the Hunt Gate in the opposite wall and out into the wider gardens. As each pair of hounds approached the first surface, one hound went left, the other right, two files of them circling the hunters, watching the hunters, examining them with red, steaming hot-coal eyes before the files met one another to stalk on toward the Hunt Gate, paired as before.

Dimity felt the heat of their eyes like a blow. She looked down at her hands, gripping one another, white at the knuckles, and tried to think of nothing at all.

As the last couple joined one another and the hunters moved to follow, Sylvan left his place and ran to whisper in her ear, "You can just stay here, Dim. No one will even look back. No one will know until later. Just stay here."

Dimity shook her head. Her face was very white, her eyes huge and dark and full of a fear she was only for the first time admitting to herself, but she would not let herself stay. Shaking his head, Sylvan ran to regain his place. Slowly, reluctantly, her feet took her after him as the hunters followed the hounds through the Hunt Gate. From beyond the wall came the sound of hooves upon the sod. The mounts were waiting.

From the balcony outside her bedroom window, Rowena, the Obermum bon Damfels, let her troubled gaze settle on the back of her youngest daughter's head. Above the high, white circle of her hunting tie, Dimity's neck looked thin and defenseless. She's a little budling, Rowena thought, remembering pictures of nodding blossoms in the fairy books she had read as a child. "Snowdrops," she recited to herself. "Fringed tulips. Bluebells. And peonies." She had once had a whole book about the glamorous and terrible fairies who lived in flowers. She wondered where the book was now. Gone, probably. One of those "foreign" things Stavenger was forever inveighing against. As though a few fairy tales could hurt anything.

"Dimity looks so tiny," said the maidservant, Salla. "So tiny. So young. Trailing along there behind them all...." Salla had cared for all the children when they were babies. Dimity, being youngest, had stayed a baby longer than the others.

"She's as old as Amethyste was when she rode for the first time. She's older than Emmy was." Try though she might, Rowena could not keep her voice from sounding defensive. "She's not that young."

"But her eyes, mistress," Salla murmured. "Like a little girl. She doesn't understand about this Hunt business. None of it. None of it at all."

"Of course she understands." Rowena had to assert this, had to believe it. That's what all the training was for; to be sure that the young riders understood. It was all perfectly manageable, provided one had proper training first. "She understands," Rowena repeated stubbornly, placing herself before the mirror, fiddling with the arrangement of her thick, dark hair. Her own gray eyes stared back at her accusingly, and she pinched her lips into an unlovely line.

"Doesn't," said Salla as stubbornly, quickly turning away to avoid the slap Rowena might have given her if she could have done it without moving. "She's like you, mistress. Not made for it."

Rowena tired of looking at herself and chose to change her ground. "Her father says she must!"

Salla did not contradict this. There would have been no point. "She's not made for it. No more than you were. And he doesn't make you."

Oh, but he did, Rowena thought, remembering pain. Made me do so many things I didn't want to. Let me quit riding, yes, but only when I was pregnant with the seven children he made me have when I only wanted one or two. Made me ride right up until the time I got old, with lines around my eyes. Made me bring the children up to the Hunt, when I didn't want to. Made them all like him, all the way he is—except Sylvan. No matter what Stavenger does, Sylvan stays Sylvan. Not that Syl lets on what he really thinks. Sylvan just roars about everything. Clever Syl, to hide his true beliefs among all that bluster. And Dimity stays Dimity as well, of course—but poor Dim —Dim couldn't hide anything. Would she be able to hide her feelings this morning?

Rowena went back to the balcony and craned her neck to look over the top of the wall. She could see the movements of the waiting mounts, tossing heads, switching tails. She could hear the clicking of hooves, the *hruffing* sound of a breath suddenly expelled. It was too quiet. Always too quiet when the riders mounted. She had always felt there should be talk, people calling to one another, greeting one another. There should be . . . something. Something besides this silence.

Outside the Hunt Gate the hounds circled and the mounts waited, shifting impatiently from foot to foot, tails lashing, necks arching as they pawed the ground, all quietly as in a dream where things move but make no sound. The air was warm with their steamy breath, full of the haylike smell of them, the sweaty stench. Stavenger's mount came forward first, as was proper, and then others, one by one, coming for the Huntsman and for the whippers-in, and then for the riders of the field, the oldest riders first. Dimity stood behind Emeraude and Amethyste, shivering slightly as first one, then the other vaulted up onto the backs of waiting mounts. Soon she was the only one left unmounted. Then, just as she decided that there was no mount for her, that she could slip back through the gate, the mount was there before her, within reach of her hand.

It stared at her as it extended a front leg and crouched slightly so that she could put one foot on the brindled leg, grasp the reins, and leap upward, all as she had done time after time on the simulator, no different except for the smell and the heaving breath which spread the vast ribs between her legs, wider than the machine had ever done. Her toes hunted desperately for the notches between the third and fourth rib that should be there, finding them at last far forward of where she thought they should be. She slipped the pointed toes of her boots in, locking herself on. Then it was only a matter of hanging onto the reins and keeping her spurs dug in and her legs tight while the great creature beneath her turned high on its rear legs to follow the others away, west. She had worn her padded breeches for hours on the simulator, so they were properly broken in. She had had nothing to drink since early the previous evening and nothing to eat since noon yesterday. She wished fleetingly that Sylvan could ride beside her, but he was far ahead. Emeraude and Amethyste were lost in the welter. She could see Stavenger's red coat, the line of his back as straight as a stem of polegrass. There was no turning back now. It was almost a relief to know that she couldn't do anything but what she was doing. Nothing else at all, not until the Hunt returned. At last there was sound, a drumming of feet which filled all the space there was to hold it, a resonant thunder coming up from the ground beneath them.

From her balcony above them, Rowena heard the sound and put her hands over her ears until it faded into silence. Gradually the small sounds of insect and bird and grass peeper, which had ceased when the hounds arrived, began once more.

"Too young," brooded Salla. "Oh, mistress."

Rowena did not slap her maidservant but turned to her with tears in her eyes instead. "I know," she said. She turned to see the end of the line of riders as it fled away down the garden trail toward the west. Riding out, she said to herself. Riding out. And they'll ride back again. Back again. Saying it over and over like a litany. Back again.

"She'll be back," said Salla. "She'll be back, wanting a nice hot bath."

Then both of them stood staring into the west, not seeing anything there except the grass.

Down the wide hallway from Rowena's suite of rooms, in the mostly unused library of Klive, certain nonhunting members of the aristocracy had assembled to consider a matter of continuing irritation to them all. Second leader at Klive was Stavenger's younger brother, Figor. Some years ago, following one of the many hunting accidents which occurred every season, Figor had stopped riding to the hounds. This left him free during hunting seasons to take upon himself many of the responsibilities of the estancia while Stavenger was otherwise engaged. Today Figor met with Eric bon Haunser, Gerold bon Laupmon, and Gustave bon Smaerlok. Gustave was the Obermun bon Smaerlok, head of the Smaerlok family still, despite his disability; but both Eric bon Haunser and Gerold bon Laupmon were younger siblings of the family leaders, men who were also hunting today.

The quartet assembled around a large square table in one corner of the dimly lit room, passing among themselves the document which had occasioned their meeting. It was a brief document, headed with the cursive arabesques which spelled out the names and attributes of Sanctity, laden with seals and ribbons and signed by the Hierarch himself. This same group of aristocrats had responded to similar documents in both the remote and recent past, and Gustave bon Smaerlok betrayed considerable impatience at having to do so yet again.

"This office of Sanctity is becoming importunate," the Obermun said now from the wheeled half-person he had occupied for the last twenty years. "Dimoth bon Maukerden says so. I asked him and he went into a rage over this business. And Yalph bon Bindersen. I asked him, too. Haven't had a chance to get over to bon Tanlig's place yet, but Dimoth and Yalph and I are agreed that whatever this Sanctity wants, it has nothing to do with us, and we won't have their damned *fragras* here. Our people came to Grass to get away from Sanctity— now let Sanctity stay away from us. It's enough we let them stay on digging up the Arbai city, enough that those Green Brothers make mud pies with their little shovels up there in the north. Let *elsewhere* stay *elsewhere* and Grass stay Grass. So we all agree. Let's tell them so, once and for all. It's Hunt season, for heaven's sake. We haven't time for all this nonsense." Though Gustave no longer rode, he was an avid follower of the Hunt, watching the pursuit from a silent, propeller-driven balloon-car whenever the weather would allow.

"Easy, Gustave," murmured Figor, the fingers of his right hand massaging his left arm at the point where the flesh and the prosthesis joined, feeling the pain pulse beneath his fingers, a constant accompaniment to existence, even after two years. It made him irritable, and he guarded against expressing the irritation, knowing it arose from the body rather than the mind. "We don't need to make an open revolt out of it. No need to rub Sanctity's fur the wrong way."

"Revolt!" the older man bellowed. "Since when does this *fragras* Sanctity rule on Grass?" Though the word *fragras* meant simply "foreign," he used it as it was usually used on Grass, as the ultimate insult.

"Shhh." Figor made allowances for Gustave. Gustave was in pain also and was undoubtedly made irritable thereby. "I didn't mean that kind of revolt, and you know it. Even though we have no religious allegiance to Sanctity, we pay it lip service for other things. Sanctity is headquartered upon Terra. We acknowledge Terra as the center of diplomatic intercourse. Maintainer of our cultural heritage. Eternal cradle of mankind. Blah and blah." He sighed, massaging again. Gustave snorted but did not interrupt as Figor went on. "Many take our history seriously, Gustave. Even we don't entirely ignore it. We use the old language during conferences; we teach Terran to our children. We don't all use the same language in our estancias, but we consider speaking Terran among ourselves the mark of cultured men, no? We calculate our age in Sanctity years, still. Most of our food crops are Terran crops from our ancestors' time. Why run afoul of Sanctity—and all those who might come roaring to her defense—when we don't need to?"

"You want their damn what-are-they here? Prodding and poking. You want their nasty little researchers upsetting things?"

There was a moment's silence while they considered things that might be upset. At this time of the year only the Hunt could be upset, for it was the only important thing going on. During the winter, of course, no one went anywhere, and during the summer months it was too hot to travel except at night, when the summer balls were held. Still, "research" had an awkward sound to it. People asking questions. People demanding answers to things.

"We don't have to let them upset anything," Figor said doubtfully.

"They've told us why they want to come. There's some plague or other and Sanctity's setting up missions here and there, looking for a cure." He rubbed his arm again, scowling.

"But why here?" blurted Gerold bon Laupmon.

"Why not here as well as anywhere? Sanctity knows little or nothing about Grass and it's grasping at straws."

They considered this for a time. It was true that Sanctity knew little or nothing about Grass except what it could learn from the Green Brothers. Foreigners came and went in Commoner Town, allowed to stay there only so long as it took to get the next ship out and not allowed to come into the grass country at all. Semling had tried to maintain an embassy on Grass, unsuccessfully. Now there was no diplomatic contact with "elsewhere." Though the word was often used to mean Sanctity or Terra, it was also used in a more general sense: Grass was Grass; what was not Grass was elsewhere.

Eric broke the silence. "Last time Sanctity said something about someone having come here with the disease and departed without it." He rose awkwardly on his artificial legs, wishing he could so easily depart, without his disability.

"Foolishness," Gustave barked. "They couldn't even tell us who it was, or when. Some crewman, they said. Off a ship. What ship, they didn't know. It was only a rumor. Maybe this plague doesn't even exist," he growled. "Maybe it's all an excuse to start proselytizing us, snipping at us with their little punches, taking tissue samples for their damned banks." Even though the bon Smaerloks had come to Grass long ago, the family history was replete with accounts of the religious tyranny they had fled from.

"No," said Figor. "I believe the plague exists. We've heard of it from other sources. And they're upset about it, which is understandable. They're running about doing this and that, not to much purpose. Well, they will find a cure for their plague. Give them time. One thing you can say for Sanctity, it does find answers eventually. So why not give them time to find the answer somewhere else, without saying no and without upsetting ourselves? We'll tell this Hierarch we don't take kindly to being studied, blah and blah, right of cultural privacy—he'll have to accept that, since it's one of the covenants Sanctity agreed to at the time of dispersion—but we'll say we're sensible people, willing to talk about it, so why not send us an ambassador to discuss the matter." Figor made an expansive gesture. "Then we can discuss and discuss for a few years until the question becomes moot."

"Until they all die?" Gerold bon Laupmon asked—meaning, Figor supposed, everyone of human origin not upon Grass.

Figor sighed. One was never certain with Gerold that he quite understood what was going on. "No. Until they find a cure. Which they will."

Gustave snorted. "I'll give that to the Sanctified, Gerold. They're clever." He said it in the tone of one who did not think much of cleverness.

There was a pause while they considered it. Eric bon Haunser urged at last, "It has the advantage of making us look perfectly reasonable."

Gustave snorted again. "To who? Who is it looking at us? Who has the right?" He pounded on the arm of his chair, scowling, turning red in the face. Ever since the accident which had cut short Gustave's riding career, he had been irascible and difficult, and Figor moved to calm him.

"Anyone can, Gustave, whether they have the right or not. Anyone can look. Anyone can have an opinion, whether we want them to or not. And if we should ever want something from Sanctity, we'd be in a good position to ask that the favor be returned."

Eric nodded, seeing that Gustave was about to object. "Maybe we'll never want anything, Gustave. Probably we won't. But if we did, by chance, we'd be in a good position. Aren't you the one who always tells us not to give up an advantage until we have to?"

The older man simmered. "Then we have to be polite to whoever they send—bow, scrape, pretend he's our equal, some fool, some off-planeter, some foreigner."

"Well, yes. Since the ambassador will be from Sanctity, he'll probably be Terran, Gustave. Surely we could suffer that for a time. As I mentioned, most of us speak diplomatic."

"And this *fragras* will have a silly wife and a dozen bratlings, probably. And servants. And secretaries and aides. All asking questions."

"Put them someplace remote, where they can't ask many. Put them at Opal Hill." Eric named the site of the former Semling embassy with some relish, repeating it. "Opal Hill."

"Opal Hill, hah! Farther than nowhere! All the way across the swamp-forest to the southwest. That's why the people from Semling left. It gets lonely at Opal Hill."

"So, the man from Sanctity will get lonely and leave as well. But that will be his fault, not ours. Agreed? Yes?"

Evidently they were agreed. Figor waited for a time to see if anyone had any second thoughts or if Gustave was going to explode again, then rang for wine before leading his guests down into the grass gardens. Now, in early fall, the gardens were at their best, the feathery seed heads moving like dancers to the beat of the southern wind. Even Gustave would mellow after an hour in the gardens. Come to think of it, Opal Hill had very nice gardens as well, young but well designed. The Sanctified penitents expiating their sins here on Grass by digging up ruins and designing gardens—the ones who called themselves the Green Brothers—had spent considerable care upon the Opal Hill gardens. Nothing had disturbed the gardens since the people from Semling had left. Perhaps this ambassador person could be interested in gardening. Or his wife, if he had a wife. Or the dozen bratlings.

Afar from Klive, deep among the grasses, Dimity bon Damfels tried to exorcise the pain in her legs and back. Even after all those hours on the simulator, all the pain she had experienced there, this was different. This was intrusive, hateful, intimate.

"When you think the pain is unbearable," the riding instructor had said, "you can review the track of the Hunt in your mind. Distract yourself. Above all, do not think of the pain itself."

So she distracted herself, reviewing how they had come. They had ridden out along the Trail of Greens and Blues where the patterned turf along the path went from deepest indigo through all shades of turquoise and sapphire to dark forest green and bright emerald, upward to the ridge where tall plumes of aquamarine watergrass undulated in ceaseless waves. Beyond the ridge the watergrass filled a shallow basin dotted with islands of sandgrass, the whole making such a marvelously lifelike seascape that it was called the Ocean Garden. Dimity had once seen a picture of a real ocean when she went with Rowena to Commoner Town to pick up some imported fabric. It had been hanging on the fabric merchant's wall, a picture of a sea on Sanctity. She remembered saying at the time how much the imaged expanse of water looked like grass. Someone had laughed at this, saying it was the grass that looked like water. How would one know which looked like which? In fact, they looked like one another, were like one another, except that one could drown in water.

Musing on this, Dimity surprised herself with the thought that one might almost drown in grass as well. One might wish to drown. Her left knee was in agony. Little trails of fire crept from the knee upward toward her groin. Distract yourself, she repeated mentally. Distract yourself.

At the end of the Trail of Greens and Blues, the hounds had run silently into Thirty-shadows Forest, where giant black stems, thick as her body, grew tall, clucking hollowly far above as they collided in the small wind. Here velvet turfs were planted in mosslike clusters around hillocks of stonegrass, and here the mounts had followed as the trail led upward toward the Ruby Highlands.

On the Highlands the vistas were of amber and peach, apricot and rose, with veins of deepest red threaded through the paler colors to climax in bursts of skyrocketing bloodgrass, and here the trail turned aside from the gardens to run off into the untended gramineae of the surrounding veldt. It was tallgrass veldt, with nothing to see but the stems rushing by as her mount forced his way through, nothing to hear but the rustle of the plumy seed heads, nothing to think of but steeling herself against the blows of the blades, keeping her head down so those blows fell on the padded cap and not on her face.

Still, she could tell from the sun that they were running north, and Dimity concentrated upon this. The seven remaining estancias were separated from one another by at least an hour's air travel, and yet they occupied only a small part of the surface of Grass. What did she know about the land north of the Damfels estancia? There wasn't another estancia there. The nearest estancia was that of the bon Laupmons, but it was a great distance to the southeast. Directly east were the bon Haunsers. The Friary of the Green Brothers was north, but some ways east of the bon Damfels estancia. There were no other estancias to the north, no villages, nothing except more prairie and a long, shallow valley where there were many copses. "Many copses means many foxes," she quoted silently to herself. Undoubtedly they were riding toward the valley.

The pain was suddenly there again, moving in her other leg. "Better than distraction," the riding master had said, "is to let yourself fall into the rhythm of the ride and think of nothing." She tried not fighting the pain, not distracting herself, just going with it. "Above all, do not disturb the mount or attract the attention of the hounds." She would not attract their attention. She would just let it go, let it go, not thinking about anything.

On the simulator Dimity had never managed to think of nothing, and she was surprised to find how much easier it was here. Almost as though something was working inside her mind to wipe it clean. An eraser. Rub, rub, rub. She started to shake her head in annoyance, not liking the feel of it, remembering only just in time that one must not move, really must not move. The intrusion in her mind scraped at her. Deliberately, she went back to distraction, thinking of her newest ball gown, reviewing every flounce, each embroidered leaf and blossom, and after a time the hurtful feeling inside her head departed.

"Ride," she said silently to herself. "Ride, ride, ride." The repetition took the place of the emptiness, driving out the ball gown, and she simply held on, moving as the mount moved, shutting her eyes, not seeing anything else. Her backbone was a fused column of agony. Her throat was dry. She wanted desperately to scream, and fighting down the scream took all her strength.

Until suddenly they crested a long ridge and stopped. Her eyes popped open, almost against her will, and she looked down into the valley before them. It was not unlike the Ocean Garden, except that these waves were of tall grass in shades of amber and dun while the islands were actual trees, copses of trees, the only kinds of trees that existed on Grass. Swamp trees, growing wherever springs of water came to the surface. Fox trees. Haven for the toothed devils. Where they lived. Where they hid, when they weren't slinking among the grasses, killing the foals.

"Never say 'foals' where the mounts can hear you," the riding master had said. "That is our word. We merely assume there are foals, though we have never seen any, so don't say it. In fact, never say anything where the mounts can hear you."

So she was silent now, as all the riders were, their speculations kept entirely to themselves. Dimity saw the faces of the other riders, pale with concentration, unselfconsciously quiet. Dimity would not have believed Emeraude could be this quiet if she had not seen it. Mummy probably couldn't believe it at all. And Shevlok! How often did one see Shevlok without an imported cigar in his mouth—only the best Shafne tobacco would do for Shevlok—or his mouth open telling someone something. Except when Father was around, of course. When Stavenger was around, Shevlok was notable for sitting in corners and not attracting attention to himself, notable, one might say, for self-effacement.

As this Hunt was notable for quiet. Silent as the earth-closets in midwinter, when no one else was there and the frost lay deep. Dimity concentrated on breathing quietly. The eraser feeling was in her head again, and she fought it off, thinking about what she would have for dinner when the Hunt was over. Grass-hen fried in oil with imported spices on it. A fruit salad. No. Too early for fresh fruit. A dried fruit pie.

And then they were off, down into the valley toward one of the dark copses, Dimity reminding herself what the riding master had had to say about that. "The trees are extraordinary," he had said. "It will be difficult not to gasp or exclaim. You will do neither, of course. You will keep your mouth shut. You will not crane your neck or stare about or shift your weight." Besides, she had seen them on the simulator screens, a thousand hours' worth of them.

So she kept her mouth shut and her face front as the black towers loomed around her, their leafy burden shutting out the sky, the world suddenly full of the sound of water and of hooves moving in water, the squish and slide of it, the smell of it filling her nostrils in a way quite different from the smell of rain. This was not merely damp but sodden, a dank, fecund smell. Dimity opened her mouth very quietly and breathed through it, getting herself accustomed to the smell which made her want to sneeze or cough or gasp.

She felt the signal for the hounds, felt it without understanding it until the hounds lunged away, scattering outward in all directions, noses to earth. The sound of their scuffling scramble faded. There were historic words to go with this, the riding master had said. Into covert, her mind said. Into covert, my lads." As though anyone would really dare say "my lads," to hounds!

Somewhere a grass peeper shrilled and shrilled again, an ar-rhythmic pulse within the grove, repeating until it was almost but not quite a pattern, then silencing until she thought it had stopped, only to return once more. She caught a glimpse of a peeper out of the cor-ner of her eye, white and wriggly, squirming among the grass roots.

A hound bayed, a deep, bellowing *aroo* which made her heart falter as it went on and on. Then another joined, half a tone above, the sound of the two like a knife in her ears. Then all the pack, the tones of the voices lost in a vast cacophony, *aroo* and *aroo*, unmelodious and dissonant. The mounts screamed in answer and lunged deeper into the wood. They had found the fox, started the fox, would pursue the fox. Dim-ity shut her eyes and held on once more, biting her tongue, biting her cheeks, anything to stay conscious and upright, anything at all.

A thought came to her.

This is Darenfeld's Coppice, her mind told her. Darenfeld's Coppice which lay, once upon a time, within the bounds of Darenfeld's es-tancia. You are riding to hounds in Darenfeld's Coppice, where your friend Janetta bon Maukerden died. Dimity's mouth opened to shout, and her mind told her mouth to close itself once more. You will be still about it, she told herself. No one really said Janetta died here. No one said that. No one said anything except her name and then whispering, "Darenfeld's Coppice." And when Dimity asked, they said shush, shush, don't say, don't ask.

They know more than you do, she told herself. You can't tell them anything they don't know already.

The hounds were baying as they raced away, and the mount beneath her was dashing after them. She stayed on, eyes shut once more. It was all she could do to hold on. To stay where she was. Not to fall off. To be silent. To bear the pain. To go on with the Hunt.

The Hunt does go on. Time passes. The fox runs for hours. The riders pursue it for hours. Dimity forgets who she is or where she is. There is no yesterday, nor any tomorrow. There is only an everlasting now, full of the pound of feet on the turf, the rustle of grasses as they push their way through, the scream of the fox far ahead, the bay of the hounds. Hours gone. Days, perhaps. Perhaps they have ridden for days. She would not know.

There is nothing to mark the passage of time. Thirst, yes. Hunger, yes. Weariness, yes. Pain, yes. All of these have been there since early in the morning: burning thirst, gnawing hunger, aching bones, deep-set as a disease. Her mouth cannot be drier than it is, her stomach emptier. She cannot hurt more than she hurts. And now, at last, she gives up fighting against it. It will last forever. The thing in her head wipes out any concern about that. Nothing measures time. No before. No after. Nothing, nothing. Until the mount beneath her slows and stops and she unwillingly leaves the agonized daze she has fallen into and opens her eyes.

They are standing at the edge of another copse, moving slowly into it, into a grove, into the dusky cathedral shade of the trees. High above them the foliage opens to allow the sun to pierce the gloom in long radiant spears. One of them lights Stavenger where he stands upon his mount with the harpoon in his hands, ready to throw. From the tree branches above comes a scream of rage, then Stavenger's arm whips out and the line streaks behind the harpoon like a thread of purest gold.

A horrible scream again, this time of agony.

A hound leaps high to seize the line in his teeth. Other hounds as well. They have it. They are pulling the fox out of the tree, still howling, still screaming, never silent for an instant. Something huge and dark with glistening eyes and mighty fangs falls among them, and then there is only the sound of screaming mixed with the sound of teeth.

Dimity closes her eyes again, too late not to see the dark blood fountaining among the struggling bodies, and feels . . . feels a welling of pleasure so deeply intimate it makes her flush and draw her breath in, makes her legs quiver where they bestride the body beneath her, makes her whole body rock in a spasm of ecstatic sensation.

All around her other eyes are closed, other bodies quiver. Except for Sylvan. Sylvan sits erect, eyes fixed on the bloody tumult before him, teeth bared in a silent rage of defiance, his face quite blank. He can see Dimity from where he is, see her body thrashing, her eyes closed. In order not to see it, he turns his face away.

Dimity did not open her eyes again until they had come all the way back to Klive and had left the Dark Forest to enter upon the Trail of Greens and Blues. There the pain became too much to bear silently and she moaned without thinking, only a tiny sound. One of the hounds looked back at her, a great, violet-mottled hound, its eyes like flames. There was blood on it, blood all over it, its own blood or the blood of the fox. She was conscious in that moment that those same eyes had looked at her again and again during the hunt, that those same eyes had looked at her even when the fox fell from the tree into the middle of the pack, when she felt . . . that.

She looked down at her hands clenched upon the reins and did not raise her head again.

When they arrived at the Hunt Gate, she could not dismount by herself. Sylvan had to help her. He was at her side so quickly that she thought no one noticed how weak she was. No one but that same hound, his red eyes gleaming in the gathering dusk. Then he went away, all the hounds went away, the mounts went away, and the Huntsman sounded his horn softly at the gate, crying, "The Hunt is over. We have returned. Let us come in."

From the balcony, Rowena heard the muted horn call. It meant the creatures were gone and humans waited to be attended to. She leaned across the balustrade, hands clutching one another, mouth open, as a servant opened the Kennel Gate from inside and the weary hunters straggled through: the Master and the members of the Hunt in their red coats, the women in their black, their padded breeches making them look wide and froglike in the gloom. White breeches were sweat-stained now, and the pristine purity of the hunt ties had been sullied by dust and by chaff from the tall grasses. Male servants waited with goblets of water and bits of grilled meat on skewers. Baths were waiting, had been waiting for some hours, steaming from the heat of their own little furnaces, and the hunters, hands full of meat and drink, scattered toward their various rooms. Gasping, ready to cry out at last from the fear she had fought during the long day, Rowena sought among the riders until she found the slight figure of Diamante leaning on Sylvan's arm. Then the tears spilled over and she sought a voice she had almost lost in the conviction that Dimity had not returned.

"Dimity." Rowena leaned across the rail, not wishing to be overheard by Stavenger or one of the other aristocratic old guard. When the girl looked up, Rowena beckoned, and Sylvan nodded toward a side door. Within a few minutes Dimity was in her mother's room and Salla was greeting her with an exclamation of disgust.

"Dirty. Oh, you're filthy, girl. Filthy. Like a migerer mole creature. Covered all over. Take that coat off, and that tie. I'll get your robe and you can take off the rest of this filthy stuff."

"I'm dirty but I'm all right, Salla," said the girl, moon-pale, pushing weakly at Salla's busy hands.

"Dimity?"

"Mother."

"Give Salla your clothes, dear. Here, I'll help you with your boots." There was a brief, grunting interlude as the high black boots were tugged off. "You can have your bath in here while you tell me about the Hunt." She moved through the luxurious bedroom, beckoning, opening the door into the mosaic-tiled bath, where water had been already drawn and kept steaming by its own fires. "You can use my bath oil. You always liked that when you were tiny. Are you sore?"

Dimity tried to smile in response, failed. It was all she could do to keep her hands from shaking as she stripped her underclothes away, letting them fall in a pile on the bathroom floor. Only after she was neck deep in steaming water did Rowena say again, "Tell me about it."

The girl murmured, "I don't know. Nothing happened." The water was soaking away the pain. It hurt to move, and yet in the warm soothe of the water it had become almost pleasure to feel that ache, that deep, abiding agony of the bones. "Nothing happened."

Rowena stamped her foot, very softly, eyes bright with tears. "Did you have any trouble mounting?"

"No. Not really."

"Had you . . . had you seen the mount before?"

Dimity opened her eyes, suddenly aware, looking at her mother directly. "The mount? I think it's one I've seen before, grazing maybe, out near the shortgrass field where Syl and I used to play." Perhaps this meant something. She searched her mother's face, but Rowena only nodded. When Rowena had first ridden, her mount, too, had been one she had seen watching her when she was a child.

"Where did you go?"

"I think we drew a copse in Darenfeld's ... in the valley."

Rowena nodded again, remembering dark trees towering, shutting out the sky, the ground covered with small flowering mosses, a noise of running water under the mosses, under the roots. Remembering Dimity's friend, Shevlok's lover, Janetta. ...

"Did you start a fox?"

"Yes." She shut her eyes, unwilling to say more. She didn't want to talk about it. She wanted to forget it. Next time she would give in to the pain right away. Next time she wouldn't fight it. Through slitted lids she saw Rowena's face, still questioning, still demanding, wanting more. Sighing, Dimity said, "The hounds went in. Pretty soon they were all baying, and we went racing off. I seem to remember the hounds lost him three or four times, but they got him each time again. Maybe I only made that up. He just ran and ran forever, that's all. And then the hounds treed him away north somewhere."

"Did you kill?"

"Stavenger did. Daddy. I mean, the Master did. He only had to throw once. I couldn't see where the harpoon stuck, but they pulled the fox out of the tree and the hounds got him." She flushed then, deeply, the blood rising into her face in an unmistakable tide as she remembered what had followed.

Rowena saw the flush, interpreted it correctly, and turned aside in order not to confront what she saw there. Shame. Embarrassment. Mortified pudicity. Rowena sought for something, anything to say other than ... other than this. It had happened to her, too. It had always happened. She had never mentioned it to another soul. She had not known until now whether it was her guilty secret or a secret shared.

"You didn't really see the fox, then."

"I couldn't see anything except a blob in the tree. Then eyes, and teeth, and then it was all over."

"Ah." Rowena sighed, the tears now streaming, laughing at herself and her fears, shamed for Dimity's shame but relieved just the same.

"Mother! I'm all right. It's all right."

Rowena nodded, dabbing at her eyes. Of all the things that might have gone wrong, none had. Dimity had mounted, had ridden, hadn't fallen off, hadn't been attacked by the fox, hadn't done anything to upset the hounds.

"Mother." Softly, moved by the tears, offering something.

"Yes, Dimity."

"There was this one hound that kept watching me, all the time we were coming back. A kind of purplish mottled one. He just kept looking at me and looking at me. Every time I looked down, there he was."

"You didn't stare!"

"Of course not. I know better. I didn't even seem to notice, not that the hound could see. I just thought it was funny, that's all."

Rowena argued with herself. Say too little? Say too much? Say nothing? "Hounds are peculiar that way. Sometimes they watch us. Sometimes they don't look at us. Sometimes they seem to be amused by us. You know."

"I don't, really."

"Well, they need us, Dimity. They can't climb, so they can't kill the fox unless we bring him down."

"They only need one man for that, somebody with a strong arm to throw the harpoon."

"Oh, I think there's more to it than that. The hounds seem to enjoy the Hunt. The ritual of it."

"When we were riding back, I kept wondering how it ever got started. I know they ride to the hounds on Terra, back before Sanctity, before we left. That was in my history book, with pictures of the horses and dogs and the little furry thing—nothing like our fox at all. I couldn't figure out why they should have wanted to kill it, even. With our foxen, killing it is the only thing to do. But why do it this way?"

"One of the first settlers made friends with a young mount and learned to ride him, that's all there is to it," Rowena answered. "The settler taught some friends, and the young mount brought along some more of its kind, and gradually we had a Hunt again."

"And the hounds?"

"I don't know. My grandfather told me once that they were simply there one day, that's all. As though they knew we needed them to have a proper Hunt. They always show up on the proper day at the proper place, just like the mounts do. . . ."

"If we call them hounds when they aren't really hounds, how come we don't call the mounts horses?" Dimity asked, lying back until her head was half submerged, contented now to say nothing much, to talk, perhaps to have her mother wash her back.

Rowena was startled. "Oh, I don't think the Hippae would like that, not at all."

"But they don't mind being called mounts?"

"But my dear, we never call them even that where they can hear us. You know that. We never call them anything at all where they can hear us."

"It makes your head feel funny," said Dimity. "Doesn't it?"

"What?" asked Rowena, suddenly on her feet. "What does?"

"Hunting. Doesn't it make your head feel funny?"

Rowena said in a preoccupied tone, "It has a kind of hypnotic effect. It would really be rather boring otherwise." She put a folded towel within Dimity's reach, then left the room, closing the door behind her to keep the steamy warmth within.

One of the hounds watching Dimity? She bit her lip, frowned, acquired a suddenly haunted expression. She would have to speak to Sylvan about that. Right now he would be closeted with Figor about that Sanctity business, but perhaps he had noticed something. No one else would have noticed anything, but perhaps Sylvan had. Or perhaps it had all been in Dimity's mind. Weariness and hours of pain could do that.

Still it would be an odd thing to imagine. The hounds had killed, so they should have been in a good mood. There was no reason for one of them to have watched Dimity. There was no reason for Dimity even to have imagined it. Surely no one had ever said anything to her, about Janetta . . . about that side of things.

She would speak to Sylvan about it. As soon as she could. As soon as this silly matter of the scientific mission was decided and everyone could think about something else.

Grass.

Millions of square miles of prairie, with villages and estancias, with hunters and the hunted, where the wind walks and the stars shine on stalk and seed plume and where the sluglike peepers cry from the roots all day and all night, except when certain things call deep in the star-specked dark to make a stunning, eerie silence fall.

North, almost at the place where the shortgrass country begins, are the ruins of a city of the Arbai, not unlike the many other cities of the Arbai found among the settled worlds, except that here on Grass the inhabitants died of violence. Among the ruins the Green Brothers are intermittently occupied, digging trenches, listing artifacts, making copies of the volumes in the Arbai library. The Brothers are penitents, it is said, though no one else on Grass knows or cares what they are penitent about.

A little north of the dig, in the sprawling, vaulted Friary, other Green Brothers keep busy in their gardens, busy with their pigs and chickens, busy sky-crawling, busy walking out into grasses to preach to the Hippae perhaps, or to the foxen, who knows? All of them, too, are penitents, cast out of Sanctity to this far, lonely place. They were here, unwillingly, when the aristocrats arrived. Some of them lament that they will still be here, as unwillingly, when the aristocrats have gone.

And finally there is the port, and Commoner Town, both of them set down in the one place on Grass where little grass grows, a high, stone-based ridge surrounded by swamp forest—a long, slender ellipse, a hundred square miles or so given over to shipping and warehouses and hydroponic farms, to quarries and meadows and mines and all the other clutter and cacophony of human life and human business. Commoner Town, where strangers can come and go without bothering anyone, where foreigners can do their incomprehensible and, as the bon Damfels do say, contemptible business.

And there is the port, where fat ships fall, squatting on their fiery tails as they arrive from Shafne and Semling and the planet most call Sanctity until they are reminded that it is really named Terra, the first home of man. Men and women are on Grass in many guises: transients and merchants and craftsmen and ships' crews and preachers needing hotels and warehouses, shops and brothels and churches. Children, too, with their playing fields, and teachers with their schools.

Occasionally a small group of adventurous children or bored transients will leave the port or town behind them and walk the mile or two down the long slope to the place where the ground flattens out in marshy meadow. There is a kind of springiness in the mossy growth there, a resilient dampness at first, which, if they go on, rapidly turns to the kind of sogginess one might expect after days of rain. Walkers can get a bit farther on that ground, feeling their feet squelch deeply into it, though most draw back in fear that it will quake and give way, as indeed it does in a little space, becoming so boggy that stubborn explorers have to leap from tussock to tussock over braided streams gleaming in oily lights. There are huge blue-leafed clume trees in this bog, and flowers blooming like pale candles, and powder-winged moths the size and color of parrots and smelling of incense, and there are huge homely frogs whose forebears came with the first settlers long ago.

So much one can see on a casual walk from Commoner Town— so much, but no more, because just beyond the clume trees the bog deepens and the tussocks become jungly islets separated by twined rivers of dark water full of twisted roots and things that go squirming into the slime with ominous plopping sounds. There the trees have bluer leaves, and they grow taller the farther one goes, shutting out the light. To go on into the forest one would need a boat, a shallow skiff or punt with a long pole to push against the murky depths below, or maybe a paddle to dip silently into that smooth dark water, propelling one along the labyrinthine leafy halls.

Not that it hasn't been done. Some few heedless men have built themselves vessels of greater or lesser water-worthiness to carry them exploring; some few foolhardy commoner boys and maybe a girl or two have made themselves boats to slip between the great buttressed trunks of the trees and the reaching tentacles of vine and take themselves farther into the glimmering shadows of the swamp forest. Not many. There might have been more, except that of those who went in, a good many never came out. Grown men from off-planet have tried it, too, doughty men and strong, but they have been lost just as the boys and girls were lost.

And those who did come out again? What could they say about it except that it was wet and dark and full of things slithering and that it got wetter and darker and more slithery yet the farther one went? In fact, they have said very little. It is almost as though they could not remember what they might have seen, there in the dank depths of the swamp forest. As though they had gone in and come out again by accident, while sleeping, having seen or heard nothing at all.

And, after all, who cares? Who has any need to go in there? Nothing comes out of the mire and the viny trees to do anyone harm, and nothing has been seen in the swamp that anyone wants. From above, the great trees look like the restless billows of a miles-wide gray-green sea. From afar, they are a wall shutting Commoner Town inside and keeping the restless energies of its tradesmen and craftsmen from erupting. From inside, they are a wall against the inexorable grasses, keeping them at bay. North, south, east, and west, all sides of the town are closed off by the swamp forest. No road in, no road out, and the depths of the forest inviolable, the depths of its trees and waters unknown and unseen, though so wide and ramified that —even though no one has ever seen anything of the kind—everyone in Commoner Town believes there is a something there that will emerge, someday, to the astonishment of them all.

3

The streets of St. Magdalen's were, as usual, deep in mud. Marjorie Westriding Yrarier had to leave her hover at the hamlet gate, next to the population post, and go slogging through mire which came almost to her ankles as she went past the chapel and the soup kitchen to the hovel that had been assigned to Bellalou Benice and her children. One child now: Lily Anne. The two legal children had publicly repudiated their mother a month ago, so they were well out of it. The phrase set up an ugly resonance, and Marjorie flushed, angry at herself for being angry at the two almost adult Benices. "Well out of it" was accurate, and Bellalou herself had probably encouraged her offspring to execute the demeaning ceremony as soon as both were old enough. On Terra, both the planetary and most of the provincial governments claimed a Judeo-Christian heritage, but "honor thy father and thy mother" had no meaning for illegals or for their parents.

At the hovel Marjorie set her pack on the stoop while she scraped her boots on the step edge, kicking the gluey clods off into the morass. There was no excuse for this. It would take less money to pave the streets than it took to lay temporary sidewalks during the quarterly visitations by the board, but Marjorie was a minority voice on the Board of Governors, which had a "no frills" policy vis-à-vis its charitable endeavor. Most of the board members made their decisions about Breedertown without ever seeing the place or any of the people in it. Not that they didn't coo and flutter around Marjorie for being so "dedicated," so "brave." She had taken considerable satisfaction in that, once. Some time ago. Before she knew as much as she knew now.

The hovel door opened a crack, disclosing Bellalou's swollen face. Someone had hit her again. Not her putative husband. He'd been shot last year for illegal procreation.

"Ma'am," said Bellalou.

"Good morning, Bellalou." Marjorie smiled her visitation smile, carefully not patronizing. "How's Lily?"

"Fine," the woman said. "She's fine."

Lily Anne was not fine, of course. When Marjorie came into the slovenly room, the illegal glared at her out of a sullen face as bruised as her mother's. "You checkin' up on me agin."

"Trying to keep you alive until the ship goes, Lily."

"Maybe I'd rather be dead, you ever think of that?"

Marjorie nodded soberly. Oh, indeed. She had thought of that. Maybe Lily would rather be dead. Maybe most illegal people would rather be dead than shipped away to Repentance, where two thirds of them would die before they were thirty anyhow. Though Marjorie had undertaken this work out of the religious conviction that life at any price was worth living, that was before she had seen certain documentaries, read certain exposés. Even she was no longer sure Repentance was preferable to simple death.

"You don' mean that, Lily," Bellalou remonstrated.

"Fuck I don't."

Marjorie intervened, trying to convince herself as much as the girl. "Look at it this way, Lily. You can have all the babies you want on Repentance." That, at least, was true. Population was as much needed on Repentance as it was now rigidly controlled here on Terra. Babies born on Repentance would be citizens of that planet.

"Don't want babies there. Want my baby you took." It was the most recent plaint, since the abortion Marjorie had arranged, risking her own freedom and possibly her marriage in the process. Neither Rigo nor the local law would have looked kindly on that particular act of charity. Marjorie's confessor, Father Sandoval, wouldn't have been precisely cheery about it, either, had he known. Taking another step down a path she had prayed was not irreversible, Marjorie hadn't told him.

"Lady Wesridin' din take your baby, Lily. If you din have that abortion you'duh been shot by the pop'lation as soon as you showed, you know that." Bellalou looked pleadingly at her daughter. "Illegals can't do that." Only third and subsequent living children were actually illegal. Though Bellalou herself was not an illegal, her status made little difference. As the parent of one she had been stripped of her civil rights. She went on, as though to claim a future joy for her daughter, "It'll be better on Repentance."

"Don't want Repentance. Rather be shot," the girl cried.

Neither Marjorie nor Bellalou contradicted her. Marjorie found herself wondering why she simply hadn't let it happen. Poor little beast. Ignorant as a chicken. Half her teeth were falling out already and she couldn't read or write. No one was allowed to teach illegals anything or give them medical care. On her sixteenth birthday, Lily would be taken to the port to join a mob of other young illegals destined to live and die on the colony planet, and if it hadn't been for the recent abortion and the implant of a very illicit five-year contraceptive device, the poor little cow wouldn't have lasted until deportation. Planetary law said any illegal who came up pregnant got shot, along with whatever male illegal or de-righted person she claimed was responsible—if she cared to claim, which a surprising number of them did. Such claims made against certain respectable men, however, had caused some changes in the law. Now, only women served as guards in Breedertown. Only women were on the visitation committee.

"You get to have kids," Lily whined. "You rich people!"

"Two children," Marjorie said. "Only two, Lily. If I had a third child, it would be illegal, just like you. They'd take away my rights, just like they did your mother's. They'd make my older children repudiate me, just like your brother and sister did to Bellalou." She said it all wearily, not believing it. Rich people didn't get in that kind of mess. They never had. Only the poor got trapped: by ignorance, by religion, by self-righteous laws passed by people who broke them with impunity. Marjorie herself had an implant, imported from the Humanist Enclave on the coast. Another thing she hadn't told Father Sandoval. She hadn't told Rigo, either, but surely he suspected. Probably his mistress had one as well.

She brushed the wrinkles out of her trousers as she rose. "I brought some clothes for you to wear on the ship," she told the girl. "And some things you'll need on Repentance." She handed the package to Bellalou. "Lily will need these things, Bellalou. Don't let her trade them for euphies, please." Despite all efforts to keep them out, dealers in euphoriacs managed to do a good business in St. Magdalen's.

"Gimme," whined Lily, snatching at the package.

"Later," said her mother. "Later on, honey. I'll give it to you later on."

Her business with Bellalou finished, Marjorie returned to the clammy air and the mud, glad that one visit was over, not eager to go on to the half dozen other hovels she had scheduled for today. There was so little she could do. Food for hungry children. A few antiseptics and painkillers that weren't considered really "medical." The local province was populated largely by the Sanctified, which meant there were provincial laws against both contraception and abortion. Stack that up against the planetary population laws against more than two living children per mother and what did you get? St. Magdalen's Town. Breedertown. A charitable foundation set up by rich Old Catholics to shelter the unfortunate and unwise who followed either their inclination or their religion. As head of the Visitation Committee, Marjorie saw more of the place than most. Hands smoothing her disordered hair, she corrected herself: She saw more of it than any of them. They had been quick to admire her for her dedication but damned slow to emulate it.

All of which merely increased her doubts. The chairmen before her had been chairmen in name only, or they had been women no wealthier than Marjorie who hired others to do the visitations for them. Why did she insist on doing this herself?

"You've got visions of yourself as a saint," Rigo had sneered. "Being an Olympic gold medalist wasn't enough for you? Being my wife isn't enough? You also have to be Saint Marjorie, sacrificing herself for the poor?"

That had stung, though it hadn't been true, not really. The gold medal had been long ago, before they were married. Young Marjorie

Westriding had been a medalist, yes, but a lot of subjective opinior on the part of judges and officials went into deciding who got medal: One might take a great deal of pride without being at all certain of one's personal merit, at least so Marjorie had tried to explain to an unsympathetic Rigo, who barked laughter, pretended to disbelieve her even as he seized her in a passionate embrace. The truthful answer to his question would have been, no; the gold medal wasn't enough. Besides, it was a long time ago. She needed something comparable now, something uniquely her own, some perfect achievement. At one time she had thought it might be her family, her children, but seemingly that wasn't how it worked out. . . .

So she had tried this, and this wasn't working either. Gritting her teeth, she stepped down into the mud and started for the next hovel.

When she returned to the hover some hours later she was tired and filthy and sunk deep in depression. One of "her" girls had been executed that week by a population patrol. Two children in one family seemed to be dying, probably from something contagious which could have been prevented if immunizations were allowed for illegals, which they weren't. A thousand years ago the population of Breedertown could have been shipped off to Australia. A few hundred years ago, they might have been allowed to emigrate to wild colony planets. But with Sanctity meddling and threatening whenever people tried to spread out, there was no real colonization anymore. There wasn't anyplace to send excess people except Repentance, if they stayed alive long enough to get there.

But Repentance really could be worse than the alternative. Now that Marjorie had decided that was true, it seemed rather pointless to go on. So long as Sanctity ruled, there was no legal way to do anything significant. Every week there would be a new girl pregnant or about to be, on and on, forever. If Marjorie spent everything she had, money and blood, it would do no lasting good. Did it matter whether any of them individually escaped from Terra? Lily? Bets, from last month? Dephine, from the month before that? If one didn't get there, someone else would. What kind of life would they have, the ones who got there? Mired in ignorance and resentment, probably dying young. . . .

Marjorie gritted her teeth, forbidding herself to cry. She could quit, of course. There were dozens of excuses she could give the board, all of them acceptable. But she had taken on this duty, and it would be sinful, surely, just to lay it down. . . .

She shook her head violently, sending the hover into a sickening lurch. The blare of a warning siren from the console brought her back to herself. It would be better to think of something else. Of the children: Tony's aspirations. Stella's tantrums. She would think of anything else, even of Rigo and his mistress. Mistresses. Plural. Sequential.

The car slid across the boundary of the estate from the hoverway, and she lifted a hand to the head groom as she passed the stables, praying that Rigo wasn't home to fight with her about where she had been, what she had been doing. She was too tired and depressed to argue. She'd wanted to do something significant, an achievement, some fine gesture, and she'd failed, that's all. It hadn't been an unworthy desire, not one Rigo should challenge her about, insisting that she explain why, why, why. Especially now that she wasn't sure any longer.

Perhaps Rigo had been right in the first place. Perhaps she really had wanted to be a saint. And if that were true?

Wry laughter seized her; tears squeezed from her eyes as she parked the hover and sagged against the seat, wondering how one went about being a saint these days. She started to wipe her face and compose herself, remembering all at once that she didn't need to pretend composure, didn't need to pretend certainty, didn't need to pretend anything. This time, at least, she would not have to explain herself to Rigo. He would not be home until evening. This was the day Roderigo Yrarier, faithful Old Catholic and staunch son of the Church, had done the unthinkable. He had answered a summons to Sanctity.

One hundred golden angels stand on the tower spires of Sanctity, wings wide, trumpets lifted, lit by internal fires which make them shine like a century of suns. Sanctity's crystal towers mass against one another in a lofty and breathtaking bonfire of glittering surfaces against the dark of an empty sky. Both day and night they are a lighthouse, a guide—so Sanctity says—to the great diaspora of humanity clustered on the nearest possible worlds out there in the darkling seas of space.

They are also a beacon for tourships which hang in swarms the requisite fifty kilometers away, viewports clustered with spectators. The ships are allowed no closer for fear of some unspecified disaster.

They may come only near enough for the tourists to make out the huge angels on the summits of the towers and read the linked words picked out in mirrors and lights upon the highest walls.

Sanctity. Unity. Immortality.

Though it is impossible to see anything in detail from that distance with the naked eye, Sanctity is never observed at closer range. To all the worlds Sanctity stands forever upon the Terran horizon, perceivable yet remote, holy and unapproachable, fully accessible only to its chosen ones: the Hierophants, the servitors, the acolytes. If there is reason for a male outsider to come inside (women may not come at all), he must first obtain the proper papers. Then he must use those papers, after proving he is indeed male, to gain access to the well-guarded terminus far out in the surrounding countryside. If satisfied, the guards will allow him to enter a conveyance which will take him through silent tunnels to a reception area a respectful distance from Sanctity's protected heart.

That heart would be the subterranean quarters of the Hierarch himself, far below the angel-spiked towers and protected by half a mile of earth and stone from all possible harm. The Hierophants of exalted degrees occupy apartments nearby. The machines are above that, and then the chapels, and only then the terminus and reception area. In the lowest rooms of the towers are the suites of the servitors and clergy of moderate status. The farther up one is assigned to live, the lower down the organizational ladder one finds himself, or such is the conventional wisdom. The higher up, the longer it takes one to get down to the chapels and the tunnels where the ritual work of Sanctity is conducted. The higher up one lives, the less valued one is. At the top, communing with the clouds, are the eager converts with too little intellect to be good for anything much; the old, their anonymity fading into forgetfulness; the pledged acolytes, serving out their unwilling terms.

And it is there, in the highest floor of the highest tower, that Rillibee Chime spends his undutied hours, squatting in purported meditation in cloud-surrounded silence, sprawling through papery, celibate nights on his narrow bed, untinted by happy dream. It is here he rises in the morning and washes himself, here he dons his soft slippers, here he puts on a clean, colorless suit with its tight, anonymous hood and touches his face with powder to remove any unseemly color. As he does this, he watches birds going by in long, purposeful V-shaped lines, headed southward toward the warm lands, toward Rillibee's home. Sanctity is set upon the edge of the waste, both to separate itself from the humdrum daily affairs of the world and to avoid taking up room which nature needs for other things. Behind the glittering towers lie the arctic tundra and the ice and a cold uninterrupted for many centuries.

Though cold has no meaning in Sanctity. Within the towers the temperature never changes. Rain does not fall, nor snow intrude upon these quiet corridors. Nothing grows. Nothing is acknowledged to die. If Rillibee were to fall seriously ill, he would be spirited away and another acolyte would occupy his room, do his work, attend to his services. No one would care that one had gone and another had come. A message might be sent to his parents or guardians, if he had any such, but that is the only notice that would be taken. Though doctrine teaches that the immortality of the person is the sole reason for Sanctity's edificial existence, there is no personality allowed in its service—at least not at Rillibee's level. There are few names known in Sanctity: the Hierarch, Carlos Yrarier; the division chief for Missions, Sender O'Neil; the name of the Hierarch Elect. Rillibee's name will never be among them.

Sometimes he says his name to himself, over and over, silently, reminding himself who he is, clinging to himself, the self he had known, the self with memories and a past and people he loved once. Sometimes he stares out at a neighboring tower, trying to see through the sparkling surface to any person there, to someone else, someone with another name, fighting down the cries that threaten to break loose in his rigid throat.

"I am Rillibee Chime," he whispers to himself. "Born among the cactus of the deserts. Companion of birds and lizards." He summons up the memory of birds, lizards, of the lines of ducks overhead, of flat corncakes cooked on a hot griddle, the taste of savory beans, the memory of Miriam, Joshua, Songbird as they were, once, long ago. "Two more years," he whispers to himself. "Two more years."

Two more years of his term of service. Not that he had been pledged by his parents as the sons of the Sanctified were pledged. Not that he had been promised in order for his mother to receive permission to bear a son. It was only among the Sanctified that women had to pledge their boy children to years of service in Sanctity itself, and Rillibee's people had not been Sanctified. No, Rillibee had been taken, taken in, adopted, assigned to service because there had been no one left to keep the grasping minions of Sanctity at bay.

Two more years, Rillibee says to himself, if he can last that long. And if he cannot? Sometimes he asks himself that question, fearing what the answer is. What happens to those who cannot last out their terms? What happens to those who cannot choke the screams down, who gibber or shout or curse, as he wants to curse . . . ?

"Damn," the parrot had said, long ago, making Miriam laugh. "Damn. Shit."

"Damn," Rillibee whispers now.

"Let me die," the parrot had said. No one had laughed then.

"Let me die," Rillibee agrees, hands outstretched to the glowing six-winged seraphim on the towers.

Nothing happens. The angels, though constantly solicited, do not strike him down.

Each day he goes out of his cubicle to the drop chute and stands looking at it for a moment, wondering if he has the courage to leap into it. When he first came to Sanctity he was pushed into it, pushed into it time after time, feeling himself falling forever while his skin crawled and his stomach fought to get out through his nose. Ten years now, and he still screams mentally each time he thinks of dropping into the chute. He has found an acceptable alternative. Inside the bottomless well of the chutes are fat metal staple-shaped rungs, set there for men to climb upon when the chutes must be cleaned or repaired. A thousand feet down. A thousand feet up. Rillibee climbs them twice each day, rising early to be sure he has time.

After the climb, mess hall. He has come to mess hall for ten years now, every day since he was twelve, but he still fights down the urge to cough at the smell of breakfast. Mess hall. Full of the forever stink of nasty-tasting stuff. He does not stay to eat.

He goes climbing, down once more to duty hall, searching out his number from among a thousand others on the lighted board. RC–15–18809. Clerical duties for the Hierarch. Cleric-all required. Guide duty. Level three minus, Room 409, 1000 hours.

The Hierarch. Strange that they should appoint someone so young and uncommitted as Rillibee to attend the Hierarch. Or, perhaps, not strange. So far as Sanctity is concerned, he is merely a part, interchangeable with any other part. It takes no commitment to guide a visitor or operate a cleric-all.

His body will not be required for two hours. Time to do something. Time to go to Supply and check out a cleric-all. Time to go up to commissary level and buy something to eat that tastes like real food. Time to go to the library and pick out something for recreation. He is afraid to go where people are. Cries of loneliness and frustration are too close to the roots of his tongue. He swallows, trying to drive them down, but they stay there, rough greasy lumps of unswallowed and habitual grief.

Better to go where almost no one goes. One more climb down to chapel level and a slow walk along the corridor, passing chapel after chapel, hearing the mosquito whine of the speakers over each altar. Picking a chapel at random, Rillibee goes in and sits down, putting on the earphones which slow the mosquito whine to an understandable speed. A ponderous bass voice is chanting, "Artemus Jones. Favorella Biskop. Janice Pittorney." Rillibee slips the earphones off and watches the altar instead.

Each day an elder sits behind the altar, waiting for the anonymous acolyte to present a list of new enrollees. The elder nods his head and the acolyte begins, "On the world of Semling, a womanchild born to Martha and Henry Spike who has been named Alevia Spike. On Victory, a boychild born to Brown Brittle and Hard Lost Blue who has been named Broken Sound. On Repentance, a boychild to Domal and Susan Crasmere who has been named Domal Vincente II."

To each such intelligence the elder bows low, intoning words made nonsensical by overuse, words none of them in the towers hear any longer. "Sanctity. Unity. Immortality." Meaning doesn't matter. The mere utterance of these words opens the holy door. The mere syllabic mutter enters the name into the rolls of humanity. When the words have been intoned, the robed acolyte holds his forms and tissue samples for a moment in the sacred smoke before thrusting them into slots where they plunge down slanted surfaces of polished stone into a place this acolyte, like most short-term acolytes, will never see. There the name is put into the files and the cell sample is put into the tissue banks, both making an immortal place in the holy history for little red-wrinkled Alevia, for screaming infant Broke, for drowsy Dom.

Rillibee has been down in the clucking depths once or twice on records duty. The genealogy machines are down there, muttering to themselves as they assign numbers and make note of the genetic information in the cell samples, information which will serve, should the occasion arise, to resurrect the body of Alevia or Broke or Dom or this one or that one or anyone who has ever lived, uniquely himself or herself, distinguishable from all their human brethren alive or dead, emerging newborn from the clone machines. In body only, of course. No one has found a way yet to record memory or personality. Still, better body than nothing, so the Sanctified say as they drop their samples down. If the body lives, it will accumulate memory, and in time there will be a new creation not unlike the old. Who is to say the new Alevia will not, on strange occasions and with a sense of déjà vu, relive her former life? Who is to say that Dom will not look into the mirror and see there the ghost of a former self?

In the depths of Sanctity is the name of every man and woman who has ever lived in all of human history. Those for whom no written history could be found have been extrapolated by the humming machines back to the edge of the time when there was no mankind. There are men and women in the machines with names no historic person ever knew, names in languages that were spoken at the dawn of time. Never mind that no one alive can speak the language of Homo habilis; the machines know what it was and the names of those who spoke it. Adam, just down from the trees, is on the list, and Eve, scratching her butt with a splay-thumbed hand. Their genotypes are there as well, designed by the machines and assigned appropriate DNA sequences. Every person ever alive is there, in Sanctity/Unity/Immortality.

And all of it, every machine, every entry, every sample, all of it is guarded. There are guards everywhere, watching, noticing, reporting. Watching for those who may not conform to the ideal of S/U/I. Watching for acolytes who fall apart into gibbering madness. Watching for Moldies, members of that sect that has wearied of troublesome life and desires only the end, the ultimate destruction of Sanctity, of Terra, of a hundred worlds, of life itself—the end of all those men and women on the eternal list.

Every day, in each of a thousand chapels, parts of the list are read by the machines, read aloud, dawn to dusk, dusk to dawn. When the list has been read in its entirety, the machines start over. The mosquito whine of the reading has no end as it rehearses all of humanity from father Adam to little Dom, over and over again.

As it goes on Rillibee sits staring at the elder, half listening to the names put forward by the acolyte, lifting the mechanism back to his ear as the machine recitation goes on. "Violet Wilberforce. Nick En Ching. Herbard Guston." Everyone else who has ever lived, but not Rillibee Chime. He has never heard his name in that mechanical voice. Perhaps he will not be enrolled until he has completed his twelve years and gone. The earpieces are thick with dust. It has been a long time since anyone has come there to listen, a long time since anyone has cared about the litany.

In a little while he will pick up the cleric-all and report for duty to Room 409, level three minus. In a moment. For now, he will sit here very quietly, choking down his loneliness as he says *Rillibee Chime* to himself, carefully listening to the sound of it, words spoken aloud in a human voice in this empty hell where no one speaks his name.

As Rigo Yrarier stepped out of the conveyance pod in the reception area deep underground, he was not entirely surprised to find his skin crawling with superstitious revulsion. He hadn't wanted to come here. Uncle Carlos had sent a message begging him to come. Uncle Carlos, the family scandal. Carlos, a skeleton in the confessional, as it were. Apostate Uncle Carlos, long ago lapsed from the Old Catholic religion of his birth and now Hierarch of all this . . . *this*. Rigo looked around himself trying to define *this*. This hive. This unholy ant's nest. Outside the glass room in which he stood, identically suited and powdered figures scurried like so many anonymous insects.

Rigo had not wanted to come, not even on a mission of mercy, which is what Uncle Carlos had called it in his message. Missions of mercy were Marjorie's business, not Rigo's, and he was not even sympathetic with hers. Useless, all of it. One could not save people who were too stupid to save themselves, and the same thing applied to Sanctity, so far as Rigo was concerned. Then, surprisingly, Father Sandoval had urged Rigo to answer the plea. No doubt Father had reasons of his own. He would probably want a report; he would want to know all about Sanctity, what it looked like, what went on there. Old Catholic clergy were allowed to take tours of Sanctity about as often as Old Catholic clergy allowed the devil to assist at mass.

The superstitious revulsion Rigo felt was only part of his reluctance. There was a good deal of anger and hostility in him as well, which he recognized and tried to guard against showing as he looked about for someone who would tell him where to go next. The ghostly aspect of the suited and powdered nonentity who came through the hissing door and bowed in greeting did nothing to alleviate Rigo's sense that something was crawling on him. Neither did the long walk as he followed his guide down ramified corridors, past chapel after chapel, all of them empty, all of them buzzing with the shrill telling of names, endless lists of names.

It would be better, he thought, if they invented machines to listen as well as machines to speak, or simply let one machine rehearse the names quietly and eternally to itself. As much would be achieved, certainly, without this mosquito howl which made his skin itch and his head hurt. His own name was undoubtedly in that noise somewhere. His own and Marjorie's, and the children's. There was no escaping it, even though their families had filed the exemption forms saying they were of another faith, did not wish to be listed in Sanctity, did not wish their children to be listed, did not believe in the mechanical immortality and the hope of physical resurrection which was the best Sanctity could offer. Despite his father's passionate outbursts against Sanctity's arrogance and its pretensions, despite his mother's hysteria and Father Sandoval's gentle resentment, Sanctity would have done as it pleased. Everyone knew the exemption forms were a travesty. Filing them was merely a signal for one of the Sanctified missionaries to track the exempted ones down, to haunt them until the missionary could obtain a few living cells. Any crowded street or walkway would do. A quick punch was all it took. Like a pinch, a nip, a needle touch. They were like rats, those missionaries, a secret multitude, sneaking and prodding, bringing names and tissue samples here to become part of this . . . this.

This. Sanctity/Unity/Immortality. The words were on all sides of him, engraved in the floors, set into the walls, cast into the surfaces of doorknobs. Where there was not room for the words, the initial letters pocked every surface, S/U/I, S/U/I, S/U/I.

"Blasphemous fiction," Rigo muttered to himself, quoting Father Sandoval. He tried to take shorter steps so that he would not tread on the heels of his guide, wishing with every step that he hadn't come. Not for Uncle Carlos. Carlos the traitor. Bad enough he had been a heretic without having become Hierarch, a source of embarrassment for all Old Catholics everywhere.

The hooded escort stopped, gave Rigo a quick look as though to see if he was properly dressed, then knocked at a deeply recessed door before opening it and gesturing for Rigo to enter. It was a small, featureless room furnished with three chairs. The hooded acolyte came in to perch on one of them, anonymous as a new nail, fingers poised over a cleric-all. In another chair, one set apart near a slightly open door, an old man huddled, a waking corpse with dull, deep-sunk eyes. His bandaged hands shook and his voice quavered.

"Rigo?"

"Uncle?" Rigo asked, not sure. He had not seen the old man for decades. "Uncle Carlos?" There was a stench in the room, like a closed attic where something had died.

The shaking moved from arms to head, and Rigo interpreted this as a nod. The hand motioned slightly toward the empty chair, and Rigo sat down. He saw death before him, death too long delayed.

Despite himself, he felt pity. The acolyte on the other chair was preparing to take notes, already keying his cleric-all to record and transcribe.

"My boy," came the whisper. "We're asking you to do something. To go on a journey. For a time. It is important. It is a family matter, Rigo." He leaned back in the chair, coughing weakly.

"Uncle!" Damned if he would call him *Hierarch*. "You know we are not among the Sanctified. . . ."

"I am not asking that you do it for Sanctity, Rigo. I am asking for family. For your family. All families. I am dying. I am not important. We are all dying—" He was shaken by a paroxysm.

The door opened and two robed attendants boiled in, offering a cup, half snarling at one another in their eagerness to help.

Rigo reached out a hand. "Uncle!"

He received glares from fanatical faces, his hand was slapped away.

The aged man beat at them weakly. "Leave me, leave me, fools. Leave me," until they bubbled away from him and departed, reluctantly. "No strength to explain," he murmured, eyes almost closed. "O'Neil will explain. Ass. Not you. O'Neil. Ass. Don't write that down," this to the acolyte. "Take him to O'Neil." He turned to his nephew once again. "Please, Rigo."

"Uncle!"

The man drew himself together and fixed Rigo with a death's-head glare. "I know you don't believe in Sanctity. But you believe in God, Rigo. Please, Rigo. You must go. You and your wife and your children. All of you, Rigo. For mankind. Because of the horses." He began to cough once more.

This time the weak coughing did not stop, and the servitors came back with officious strength to bear the old man away. Rigo was left sitting there, staring at the powdered, anonymous figure across from him. After a moment, the acolyte put the strap of the cleric-all over his shoulder and beckoned for Rigo to follow him out. He led the way down a twisting hall to a wider corridor.

"What's your name?" Rigo had asked.

The acolyte's voice was hollow, inattentive. "We don't have—"

"I don't care about that. What's your name?"

"Rillibee Chime." The words fell softly into quiet, like rainwater into a pool.

"Is he dying?"

A moment's pause. Then, softly, as though to answer was difficult or forbidden. "The whispers say he is."

"What is it?"

"Everyone says . . . plague." The last word came as bile comes, choking. The anonymous face turned away. The anonymous person panted. It had been a hard word to say. It meant an end to time. It meant two years might not be long enough for him to get out of this place.

It was also a hard word to hear.

"Plague!" It came out of Rigo's belly like a grunt.

These days the word meant only one thing. A slow virus of the most insidious type and hideous aspect. A slow virus which emerged at last to make the body devour itself as in a spasm of biological self-hatred. Father Sandoval had insisted on showing Rigo a banned documentary made by a fellow priest, now dead, at an aid station where plague victims were treated and given whatever rites would comfort them. There had been bodies on all the cots, some of them still living. Rigo's eyes had slid across the picture, observing it without wanting to see it. The cube had made him see it. It had included sound and smell, and he had recoiled from the stench as he tried to shut out the guttural, agonized coughs, the mutilated bodies, the eyes sunk so deep they made the faces seem skull-like.

"Plague," he muttered again. The rumor was that it had moved from planet to planet, lying dormant for decades, only to emerge at last in place after place, giving no hint of its origin, subverting every attempt to stay it. The rumor was that science had proved helpless, able to isolate the monster but utterly incapable of stopping it once it had invaded a human host. The rumor had been circulating for over twenty years. If there really was plague, by now the victims must be numbered in the billions. So said rumor and rumor only, for Sanctity denied that there was plague, and what Sanctity denied, the human worlds denied—by and large.

"You mean my uncle?" Roderigo demanded.

"I didn't know he was your uncle until today. The Hierarch." The acolyte turned to stare at him with suddenly human eyes. "I'm not supposed to say anything to you, sir. Please, don't tell them I did. Here are the rooms of the division chief for Missions, sir. If you have questions, you must ask the division chief. You must ask Sender O'Neil."

The acolyte turned away, losing himself in the stream of anonymous acolytes, only at the turn of the corridor turning back to stare at Roderigo Yrarier, who still stood there before the door, his eyes down, an expression of loathing on his face.

"That acolyte should be disciplined," said a watcher. "Look at him, standing there, staring." The watcher himself was staring nearsightedly through the crack of a very slightly opened door, his age-spotted hand trembling on the wall beside it.

"He's only curious," said his companion from over his shoulder. "How often do you think he gets to see anyone except the Sanctified. Shut the door. Did you understand what the old man said, Hallers?"

"The Hierarch? He said his nephew had a chance of finding what we need because of the horses."

"And do you think Yrarier will succeed?"

"Well, Cory, he has a fine dramatic look to him, doesn't he? All that black hair and white skin and red, red lips. I suppose he has as good a chance as anyone."

The man addressed as Cory made a face. He, himself, had never been dramatic-looking, and he often regretted that fact. Now he looked simply old, with wispy hair frilling his ears and spiderwebs of wrinkles around his eyes. "He looks more dramatic than clever, but I hope he succeeds. We need him to succeed, Hallers. We need it."

"You don't need to tell me that, Cory. If we don't get a cure soon, we're dead. Everyone."

There was a pause. Hallers turned to see his lifelong companion staring at the floor, a thoughtful expression on his face. "Even if we get it very soon, I think it will be better if we let the dying go on, some places."

Hallers moved uncertainly toward his companion, his expression confused. "I don't understand what you mean."

"Well, Hallers, suppose we get the cure tomorrow. Why should we save everyone? Our own best people, of course, but why bother with everyone else? Why bother with some of the worlds, for example?"

Silence in the room while Hallers stared and Cory Strange watched for his reaction. Shock at first. Well, when Cory had first had the idea, he had been shocked at it too. But then Cory had realized what it could do for Sanctity. . . .

"You'd let them die? Whole worlds of men?"

The other shrugged elaborately, wincing as the shrug started a sudden pain in one arthritic shoulder. "In the long run, I think it would be best for Sanctity, don't you? Mankind is too widespread already. Sanctity has done what it can to stop exploration, but it does go on. A group here, a group there, sneaking out. Little frontier worlds, here and there. And what happens? A place like Shafne, for example, where we can't even get a decent foothold! No, men are spread far too widely for us to control well."

"That's certainly the current view of the Council of Elders, I agree, but—"

"In any case," the other interrupted, "we need to keep an eye on Yrarier so we know what he's up to. Didn't you tell me that Nods had been assigned to Grass? Head of Acceptable Doctrine with the penitents there, didn't you say? Or did someone else tell me?"

"It must have been someone else. You mean our old friend Noddingale?"

"Him, yes. Though he's adopted one of those strange Green Brother names. Jhamlees. Jhamlees Zoe."

"Jhamlees Zoe?" The other laughed breathlessly.

"Don't laugh. The Brothers are quite serious about their religious names. Stay a moment while I write a note. Have one of your youngsters pack it into something innocent-looking, cover it with a code note and a destruct-wrap, and send it on the ship that takes Yrarier."

He sat at his desk and began to write, "My dear old friend Nods ..." his hand forming the letters with some difficulty.

His equally ancient friend, leaning over his shoulder, interrupted him by venturing curiously, "The old Hierarch will be dead within hours everyone says. Will the new Hierarch feel the same way about this business, Cory? About consolidating and letting some of the worlds just ... well, just go?"

"The new Hierarch?" Cory laughed again, this time with real amusement as he turned his wide, fanatical eyes on his companion. "You mean you didn't know? That's right! You've been outside for a while. The Council of Elders met a week ago. The new Hierarch will be me."

4

"It looks as though it has been winter forever," Marjorie Westriding Yrarier remarked, careful to keep her voice level and without complaint. Complaint would not have been diplomatic, but her host and escort, Obermun Jerril bon Haunser, would not allow himself to take offense at a mere expression of opinion. Taking offense would be even more undiplomatic than giving it—certainly by someone who did not know her but whose business it undoubtedly was to get to know her as soon as possible. Looking at the angular planes of his long, powerful face, she wondered if he ever would. He had not the look of a man who cared much who others were or what they thought.

However, he set himself to attempt charm with an unaccustomed smile. "When summer comes," he said in the heavily accented Terran he used as diplomatic speech, "you will believe it has lasted forever also. All the seasons on Grass are eternal. Summer never ends, nor fall. And though you do not see it at this moment, spring is upon us."

"How would I know?" she asked, genuinely curious. From the window of the main house, which was set upon a slight rise, the landscape below her seemed an unending ocean of grayed pastels and palest gold, dried grasses moving like the waves of a shoreless sea, a surface broken only by scattered islands of broad and contorted trees, their tops so thickly twigged they appeared as solid masses inked blackly against the turbid sky. It was not like spring at home. It was not like any season at home, where she now desperately longed to be, despite the enthusiasm she had at first whipped up for this mission.

"How do you know it is spring?" she demanded, turning away from the window toward him.

They stood amid high, echoing walls in an arctic and empty chamber of what was to be the embassy. The distant ceiling curved in ivory traceries of plaster groins; tall glass doors opened through gelid arches onto a balustraded terrace; pale glowing floors reflected their movements as though from polished ice through a thin, cold film of dust. Though it was one of the main reception rooms of the estancia, it did not seem to require furnishings or curtains across the frigid glass. It seemed content with its numbing vacancy, as did the dozen other rooms they had visited, each as tall, wintery, and self-contained as this one.

The estancia, though conscientiously maintained, had been untenanted for some time, and Marjorie, Lady Westriding, had the feeling that the house preferred it that way. Furniture would be an intrusion in these rooms. They had accommodated themselves to doing without. Rejecting carpets and curtains in favor of this chill simplicity, they were content.

Unaware of her brief fantasy the Obermun suggested, "Look at the grasses along the stairs to the terrace. What do you see?"

She stared, convincing herself at last that the amethyst shadow she saw there was not merely an effect of the often very tricky light. "Purple?" she asked. "Purple grass?"

"We call that particular variety Cloak of Kings," he said. "There are hundreds of grasses on this world, of many shapes and sizes and of an unbelievable array of colors. We have no flowers in the sense some-

one from Sanctity would understand, but we do not lack for bloom."
He used the word "Sanctity," as did most of those they had encoun-
tered upon Grass, as a virtual synonym for Terra. As before, she longed
to correct him but did not. The time when Sanctity had been contained
on Terra was many generations past, but there was no denying its
ubiquity and virtual omnipotence on man's birthplace.

"I have read Snipopean's account of the Grass Gardens of Klive,"
she murmured, not mentioning it was almost the only thing she had
been able to read about Grass. Sanctity knew nothing. Terra knew
nothing. There was no diplomatic contact and no information could
be transmitted and returned much more quickly than the Yrariers
themselves could arrive—months after Sanctity had begged permission, months after permission for an ambassador had been given,
months after Roderigo's old uncle—now long since dead—had
begged them to come. All had happened as swiftly as possible, and
yet almost two Terran years had passed since these aristocrats had
said they would allow an embassy. Now the Yrariers must make up
for lost time. She went on calmly, "The Grass Gardens of Klive are
at the estancia of the Damfels, I believe?"

He acknowledged her slight interrogative tone with a nod. "Bon
Damfels," he said, emphasizing the honorific. "Stavenger and Rowena
bon Damfels would have been pleased to welcome you, but they are
in mourning just now."

"Ah?" she said in a questioning tone.

"They recently lost a daughter," he said, an expression of distaste
and embarrassment upon his face. "At the first spring Hunt. A hunting
accident."

"I sympathize with their sorrow." She paused for a moment, allowing her own face to reflect an appropriately assessed measure of
compassion. What could she say? Would too much sympathy be
effusive? Would curiosity be misplaced? A hunting accident? The
expression on the man's face indicated it would be safer to let more
information be given rather than ask for it. She waited long enough
for the Obermun to continue, and when he did not she returned to
the safety of the former subject. "What does it mean when the Cloak
of Kings shows purple along its bottom?"

"The color will be halfway up the stems in a matter of days, and
you will begin to see the flush of the gardens—rose and amber, turquoise and emerald. This estancia was named Opal Hill because of
the play of color each spring evokes. These gardens are young, but
well laid out. The flat place there at the bottom of the stairs is what

we call a first surface. All grass gardens have such an enclosed, flat area of low turf. It is the place from which all garden walks begin. From that place, trails lead from prospect to prospect. In a week, the winds will soften. We have entered upon the spring collect. By the end of the period—"

"A period being?"

"Sixty days. An arbitrary choice made by the earliest settlers. When a year extends over two thousand days, it is hard to make shorter lengths of time mean much. A period is sixty days, ten periods make a collect, four collects—one corresponding to each season—make a year. We reflect our Terran ancestry by dividing each period into four fifteen-day weeks, but there is no religious significance attached."

She nodded her understanding, risked saying, "No Sabbath."

"No planetary religious holidays of any kind. Which is not to say there is no religion, simply that matters of faith have been irrevocably removed from any civil support or recognition. Our ancestors, while all benefiting from noble blood, came from a variety of cultures. They wished to avoid conflict in such matters."

"We have much to learn," she said, fingering the limp leather of the little testament in her pocket. Before they left Terra, Father Sandoval had sent it to the Church in Exile to be blessed by the Pope. Father Sandoval, claiming to know her better than she knew herself, had said it would help reconcile her to the experience after her first enthusiasm wore off. So far she had noticed little reconciliation. "The authorities at Sanctity told us almost nothing about Grass."

"If you will forgive my saying so, Terrans know almost nothing about Grass. They have not, in the past, been particularly interested."

Again that confusion between Terra, the planet, and Sanctity, the religious empire. She nodded, accepting his not ungentle chiding. Either way, it was probably true enough. Terrans had not cared about Grass. Not about Semling, or The Pearly Gates, or Shafne, or Repentance, or any of the hundred human-settled planets far and adrift in the sea of space. What was left of human society on Terra had been too busy forcing its own population down and restoring an ecology virtually destroyed by the demands of an insatiable humanity to concern itself with those emigrations that had made its own salvation possible. Sanctity squatted on the doorstep of the north, regulating the behavior of its adherents wherever it could, while everyone else on Terra got on with trying to survive. Once each Terran year Sanctity celebrated with flags and speeches and off-planet visitors. The rest of the time Sanctity might as well have been somewhere else.

Sanctity was not Terra. Terra was home, and this was not. Though Marjorie wanted to say this loudly, with emotion, she restrained herself.

"Will you show me the stables?" she inquired. "I assume our horses have been revived and delivered?"

Until this moment she had seen nothing approaching real discomfort on the aristocrat's face. He had met them in the reception area of the revivatory at the port, seen to the collection of their belongings, provided them with two aircars to bring them to the estancia which they were to occupy—aircars they were to retain during their "visit," he had said. He had remained to guide her through the summer domestic quarters while her husband, Roderigo Yrarier, toured the winter quarters and the offices of the new embassy with Eric bon Haunser, a younger but no less dutiful member of the Grassian aristocracy. Throughout this not inconsiderable itinerary, Obermun bon Haunser had been smooth and proper to a fault, but the question of the horses made him uncomfortable. If he did not precisely lose countenance, something at the corners of his mouth let composure slip, though subtly and only momentarily.

Marjorie, whose Olympic gold medals had been in dressage, puissance jumping, and endurance events, was accustomed to reading such twitches of the skin. Horses communicated in this way. "Is something wrong?" she inquired gently, keeping herself strictly under control.

"We had not been . . ." He paused, searching for a way to say it. "We had not been advised in advance about the animals."

Animals? Since when were horses "animals"?

"Does it create a problem? Someone from Semling said the estancia has stables."

"No, not stables," he said. "There are some shelters nearby which were used by Hippae. Before this place was built, needless to say."

Why needless to say? And Hippae? That would be the horselike animal native to this planet. "Are they so different that our mounts can't occupy their stalls?"

"Hippae would not occupy stalls," he replied, seeming less than candid as he did so. He lost composure sufficiently to gnaw a thumbnail before continuing. "The shelter near Opal Hill is not being used by Hippae now, and it might serve to house your horses well enough, I suppose. However, at the time of your arrival we did not have available to us any suitable conveyance for large animals." Again, he attempted a smile. "Please excuse us, Lady Marjorie. We were set at a small contretemps that confused us for the moment. I am sure we will have solved the problem within a day or two."

"The horses have not been revived, then." Her voice was sharper than she had intended, edgy with outrage. Poor things! Left lying about in that cold, nightmarish nothingness.

"Not yet. Within the next few days."

She took control of herself once more. It would not do to lose her temper and appear at a disadvantage. "Would you like me to come to the port? Or to send one of the children? If you have no one accustomed to handling horses, Stella would be glad to go, or Anthony." Or I, she thought. Or Rigo. Any of us, man. For the love of heaven . . .

"Your son?"

He sounded so immediately relieved that she knew this had been part of the problem. Some diplomatic nicety, no doubt. It was possibly thought inappropriate for the ambassador or his wife to have to attend to such matters, and yet who else could? Well, let it pass. Show no anxiety. Don't risk eventual acceptance of the embassy over the matter of a day or two—this embassy that might almost have been an answer to her prayers, this opportunity to do something of significance. Don Quixote and El Dia Octavo could sleep that much longer, along with Her Majesty, Irish Lass, Millefiori, and Blue Star. "We are looking forward to riding to our first Hunt," she said; then, seeing his dismay, "Only as followers, of course."

Seemingly, even this was not appropriate. An expression of outright panic showed on the man's face. Good Lord, what had she said now?

"We have made arrangements," he said. "A balloon-car. Perhaps this first time, until you are more familiar."

"Whatever you think best," she said firmly, disabusing him of any notion he might have that she would make difficulties. "We are completely in your hands."

His face cleared. "Your cooperation is much appreciated, Lady Marjorie."

She forced herself to smile over the screaming impatience inside her. She had been testy ever since they had arrived. Testy and hungry. No matter how much she ate, it did not seem to quell the sick emptiness inside her. "Let us take up the matter of titles, Obermun bon Haunser."

He frowned. "I don't understand."

She decided to make the point she had been wanting to make about the difference between Sanctity and Terra. "At home, on planet

Terra, among those who once called themselves Saints and now identify themselves as the Sanctified, I would be addressed simply as Matron Yrarier. Men are either Boy or Husband. Women are either Girl, or (briefly) Bride, or Matron. Both sexes are at some pains to marry early and lose the titles of childhood. We—that is, our family—are not among the Sanctified. I do not regard any of Sanctity's female titles as pertaining to myself.

"I am, however, Terran. In my childhood home, the area called Lesser Britain, I am Marjorie, Lady Westriding, my widower father's eldest child. 'Lady Marjorie' would only be correct if I were a younger daughter. Also, I have the honor of being the Master of the Westriding Hunt. The position was offered me, I believe, because of my good fortune at the Olympics."

He looked interested but without comprehension. "Olympics?"

"A Terran contest of various athletic skills, including horsemanship," she said gently. If there was much the Yrariers did not know about Grass, there were many things the Grassians did not know about the Yrariers, as well. "I rode in what is called puissance jumping, in which the horse cannot see what is beyond the barrier, and that barrier is well over his head." He showed no comprehension. "You do not have that here, I see. Well, I did that, and dressage riding, which is a very gentle sport, and endurance riding, which is not. I was what is called a gold medalist. Roderigo was a medalist also. It is how we met." She smiled, making a deprecatory gesture. Obviously the poor man knew nothing about all this. "So, I might be called Lady Westriding or Madam Yrarier or Master, though the latter is appropriate only on the hunting field. Perhaps there is some title given to ambassadors or their wives here on Grass? It would be convenient for me to know what title would be considered acceptable."

Despite his initial ignorance, he had followed all of this closely. "Not, I think, Madam Yrarier," he mused. "Marital titles are not customary except between family leaders, that is in 'bon' families. Each family has one Obermun and one Obermum, almost always husband and wife, though it might be mother and son. There are seven aristocratic families currently, quite large families by now: Haunser, Damfels, Maukerden, Laupmon, Smaerlok, Bindersen, and Tanlig; and these families use the prefatory 'bon,' before their names. When a child results from a liaison between members of these families, it is given a surname by either the father or the mother, depending upon what family the child will be part of, and thereafter continues in that name whether later married or not."

"Ah," she mused. "So, in meeting a woman or child, I will not know—"

"You will not know the relationship. Not by the name, Lady Westriding. We are a country people, sparsely scattered upon a small part of our world. Long ago we fled the oppression of Sanctity and the crowding of Terra"—his raised brows told her he had taken her point—"and have had no wish to allow either upon Grass. Though some estancias have been lost, we have never added another estancia to the initial number—except for Opal Hill, of course, but we did not build that. We know one another and one another's grandfathers and grandmothers back to the time of settlement. We know who liaised with whom, and what child is the child of whom. It seems to me appropriate you should be called Marjorie Westriding or Lady Westriding. This places you upon the proper level in your own right. As for learning who everyone else is . . . you will need someone who knows. Perhaps I could recommend someone to you as secretary, some lateral family member, perhaps. . . ."

"Lateral?" She raised a quizzical eyebrow, shivering a little at the chill in the room.

He was instantly solicitous. "You are cold. Shall we return to the winter quarters? Though spring is imminent, it will still be more comfortable below for the next few weeks."

They left the high, cold room and the long, chill corridors to go down a long flight of stairs into the winter house, the cold weather house, into other rooms where the walls were warm with grass-cloth, cozy with firelight and lamps and soft, bright couches. Marjorie sank into one of these with a sigh of relief. "You were speaking of my hiring as secretary a 'lateral family member'?"

"Someone parented by a *bon*, but on one side only. Perhaps with the name, but without the *bon*."

"Ah. Does this represent a great handicap? This lack of a *bon*?" She smiled to show she meant it teasingly. Still, when he answered, it was with such a stiffness as to tell her it was no laughing matter.

"It means one has a commoner parent. Such a person would not live on an estancia except in a service capacity and would not attend the summer balls. One without the *bon* would not Hunt."

"Aha," she said to herself, wondering whether the Honorable Lord Roderigo Yrarier and his wife would be considered sufficiently *bon* to hunt or attend the summer balls. Perhaps this had been the reason for that business about the Hunt and the delay with the horses. Perhaps the status of the whole mission was somewhat in question.

Poor horses, lying there all cold and dead, no warm stable, no oats, dreaming, if horses dreamed, of a fence too high to jump and green grass always out of reach, unable even to twitch.

Aloud she said, "Obermun bon Haunser, I am extremely grateful for all your kindness. I shall send Anthony down to the port tomorrow in one of the fliers you have so thoughtfully provided. Perhaps you will have someone meet him there to assist him with the horses. Perhaps some kind of trailer or provisions truck can be obtained?"

"This was our dilemma, Lady Westriding. Our culture does not allow vehicle tracks across the grasses. Your animals must be airlifted here. One does not drive here and there on Grass. One flies. As quietly as possible. Except in the port area and Commoner Town, of course. Surrounded as it is by forest, roads are quite appropriate there."

"How interesting," she murmured. "However it is done, I am sure you will attend to it impeccably. Then, if you will be so gracious as to recommend one or two people who know the way things are done on Grass, perhaps I can begin furnishing the residence and making the acquaintance of some of our neighbors."

He bowed. "Certainly, Lady Westriding, certainly. We will requisition a cargo vehicle from the commoners. And in one week's time we have arranged for you to observe the Hunt at the bon Damfels estancia. It will give you the opportunity to meet many of your hosts." He bowed again, taking himself away, out the door and up the stairs to exit through that empty house. She heard his voice echoing there as he greeted the other bon and departed with him. "Hosts," he had said. Not neighbors. She, wondering if he had meant what the distinction implied, was very much aware of the difference.

"What was all that?" His voice came from behind her, from the corridor leading to the offices. Rigo.

"That was Obermun bon Haunser explaining that the horses have not yet been revived," she said, turning to confront her husband. He, lean and no less aristocratic than the man who had just left, was clad all in black except for the high red-and-purple-striped collar which identified him as an ambassador, sacrosanct, a person whose body and belongings were immune to seizure or prosecution, on penalty of retaliation from Sanctity—an organization both too far away and too distracted by recent internal events and current horror to do any retaliating at all. His face was set in what she called—though only to herself—his ugly mode, sullen at the mouth, the wide lips unenlivened by amusement, the black eyes overshadowed by heavy brows and wearied by too little sleep. When he was like this, darkness seemed to follow him, half hiding him from her. He, too, had confessed to feeling testy, and he looked irritated now. She sought something to interest him, something to blow the shadows away. "Do you know, Rigo, I'd be interested in finding out whether the children and I have diplomatic immunity on this planet."

"Why would you not?" His eyes blazed with anger at the idea. Roderigo had a great capacity for anger.

"Women do not take their husband's names here, and from something the Obermun said, I question whether they take status, either." Not that Roderigo's status was higher than her own. If it came to bloodlines, perhaps her own pedigree was a little better, not that she would ever mention it. "I'm not sure a diplomat's wife is anybody." Not that she had ever planned or wanted to be a diplomat's wife. Not that Rigo had ever been a diplomat before! So many things were not, she reflected. Not the way she would have had them, if she'd had the choice, though there was still the chance this whole business might turn out to be significant and worthwhile.

He smiled humorlessly. "Mark down one more thing we weren't informed of."

"I'm not sure I'm right."

"Your impressions are often the equal of others' certainties, Marjorie," he said in his gallant voice, the one he most often used with women, her no less than any other. "I'll put Asmir Tanlig to checking it."

"Asmir?"

"One of my Grassian men. I hired two this morning after I managed to shake off the Haunser." He scraped an extended finger down his palm, flicking it, ridding himself of something sticky, in mime.

"Is the Tanlig man you hired a *bon*?"

"Lord no. I shouldn't think so. A bastard son of a bon two generations back, perhaps."

"Lateral," she exclaimed, pleased with herself for knowing. "The Tanlig must be what they call a lateral."

"I hired a Mechanic, also."

This puzzled her. "You hired a mechanic?"

"His name is Mechanic. Philological successor to the ancient Smiths or Wrights. His name is Sebastian Mechanic, and he holds no blood with the aristos, as he was at some pains to tell me." He sank into a chair and rubbed the back of his neck. "Coldsleep makes me feel as though I'd been ill for weeks."

"It makes me feel dreamy and remote."

"My dear—" he began in the gallant voice, with only an undertone of hostility.

"I know. You think I'm always remote." She tried to laugh, tried not to show how that hurt. If Roderigo hadn't thought his wife remote, he wouldn't have needed Eugenie Le Fevre. If he hadn't had Eugenie, Marjorie might not be remote. Circle, and around once more, like a horse quadrille, change reins, pirouette, and on to the next figure.

Rigo, point made, changed the subject. "Make note, my dear. Asmir Tanlig. Sebastian Mechanic."

"What are they to be to you?" She inquired. "Representatives of the middle classes?"

"Little enough of that, except perhaps at Commoner Town. No, representatives of the peasantry, I'd say, who will circulate among the villagers and find out if anything is known. I may need others to find out about Commoner Town, though Tanlig would fit in well enough there, if he cared to. Mechanic, now, he's peasant through and through, and resentfully prideful about it."

"Hardly the type of servant to improve our reputation among the *bons*"

"The *bons* aren't to know anything about it. If we are to complete our mission here, we'll need access to all levels of society. Sebastian is my link to the people of the soil. He knows enough not to call himself to the aristocrats' attention. And if you want to know how I got on to the men without bon Haunser knowing, the Sanctity charge from Semling told me about them. I've already asked them the question."

"Ah." She waited, holding her breath.

"They say no."

"Ah," she said again, breathing. So there was hope. "No plague here."

"There is no unexplained illness that they know of. As we agreed, I told them we're making a survey."

"They might not have heard. . . ."

"Both of them have kin in Commoner Town. I think they would have heard of any strange sickness. But, it's early days. The aristocrats have putative control of ninety-nine percent of the planet's surface. There could be things going on here the commoners simply don't know of."

"It sounds as though you have things well in hand." She sighed, her weariness and hunger suddenly heavier than she could gracefully bear. "Would you have any idea where Anthony might be?"

"If he's where I told him to be, he's with Stella up in the summer quarters, making a rough floor plan of the place for me. We'll have to furnish it rather quickly, I'm afraid. Asmir tells me there's a craftsmen's area in Commoner Town. A place called, unimaginatively enough, Newroad. Lord knows where the old road was."

"Terra, maybe."

"Or any of half a hundred other places. Well, it doesn't matter where it was, so long as we know where this one is. According to Asmir, we can get very acceptable stuff built there within two or three weeks—long Grassian weeks—and he's already sent word on what he calls the *tell-me* for some kind of craftsmen's delegation to come call on us."

"By acceptable, does he mean to the bons, Rigo? I have a feeling everything we do will be measured and weighed by the bons. I think our poor horses were not revived because the bons did not know whether they would accept them or not, here on Grass. They have creatures of their own."

"Hippae."

"Exactly. Who are never kept in stalls, so the Obermun told me."

"Where in the devil are they kept, then?"

"I have serious question as to whether they are 'kept' at all, Rigo, though they live in something not called stables. Why don't we collect Anthony and Stella and go explore them together?"

The places not called stables were cavernous halls dug into the side of a hill, lined and pillared with stone. A rock-lined, spring-filled tank at the back cast a wavery luminescence across the low-arched ceiling. Half a dozen tall slits in the hillside were the only entrances.

"We could put the stallions and the mares in here and all their foals for the next hundred years," Stella observed with brooding annoyance, taking a large bite from the apple she had brought with her. "And it would still be blasted inconvenient." Stella, with her black hair and eyes and passionate disposition, resembled her father. Like him, she moved as a whip cracks, always seeming to arrive wherever she was going with considerable noise but without having bothered to travel the intervening distance. She shouted now, listening to the echo of her own voice as it rattled back into blackness among stout pillars. "Hallooooo," a hunting halloo, as one sighting a fox might cry. "Grass stinks!" she cried, with the echo coming back, *"ing, ing, ing, ing."*

Anthony made no comment but merely looked around himself with dismay, trying not to let it show through the calm demeanor he had determined upon as appropriate for the son of an ambassador. He had carefully thought out what his role should be, and prayed hourly for the fortitude to continue in it. He was the one who resembled Marjorie. He had her wheat-colored hair and hazel eyes, her cool, white skin, her sapling-slender body, her placid appearance and equable temperament. Like her, he was prey to a thousand inner doubts and horrors he never let show on the surface. Like her, he was thought beautiful, was passionately admired even by unlikely people. At nineteen he was almost of his father's height, though not yet of a man's bulk.

A stripling, his mother thought, admiring him.

A mere boy, his father thought to himself, wishing Tony were older so that he could be told why they had come, older so he could be of more help.

"A social problem of some dimension," Obermun bon Haunser was at that moment remarking to some of his fellow bons. "And so is the daughter, Stella. We'll have to warn off our own young ones," he said. Sooner or later the Yrariers would learn of this opinion, and he wondered what he would say then. He did not like the idea of being looked at angrily by Lady Westriding. Her look had a quality of knives about it. Knives which cut deeply.

Currently, however, Marjorie was cutting only into the structure of the stables, carving one part mentally from the whole. "We can partition this part of the cavern off," she offered. "Make half a dozen nice box stalls along this side with an opening from outside into each one and build a little paddock out there. Later, when winter comes . . ." She stopped in dismay, remembering what winters here were said to be like, wondering what they would do with the horses when winter came.

"We won't still be here, surely?" Anthony said, his own apprehension coming through. He heard it and amended himself more calmly. "Will the mission last that long?"

His father shook his head. "We don't know, Tony."

"What kind of horses can these Hippae be?" Marjorie mused, turning to look into the shadowy corners of the vast, low space. "This looks like some great burrow. Like the meeting hall of a badger's set."

"The meeting hall of a badger's set?" her daughter mocked. "Mother, you amaze me." She shook her hair over her shoulders, the depthless black silk of it flowing down over her back like lightless water. Her seventeen-year-old body was still slight, and the beauty which would be ravishing was only beginning to emerge. Now she smiled a siren's smile and sulked at her parents out of deeply fringed eyes. "When were you last in a badger's set?" It was not said lovingly. Stella had not wanted to come to Grass. They had insisted that she come, but they had been unable to tell her why. To Stella, the journey had been a violation of her person. With maximum drama, she likened it to rape and let them know it as often as possible. "In some other life?" she mocked now. "In some other time?"

"When I was a changeling," her mother answered firmly. "Long and long ago, when I was unconscious of my dignity. As I am about to be again. I am going to change into some nice old robe and become sedentary. I need food, a lot of food, and then some familiar book and sleep. There is too much that is strange here. Even the colors of things aren't right."

And they weren't. Her words brought it to all their attention as they left the caverns to walk through a pleached alley of imported trees toward the residence. The colors weren't right. The sky should be blue and was not. The prairie should be the color of dried grass, but their eyes insisted upon making it pale mauve and paler sapphire, as though under a stage-light moon.

"It's only that it's foreign to us," Tony said, trying to comfort her, wanting to be comforted himself. He had left things behind, too. A girl who mattered to him. Friends he cared about. Plans for education and life. He wanted the sacrifice to have been for something, for some reason, not merely to exist for a time in this chill discomfort amid strange colors. Tony had not been told why, either, but he trusted Marjorie when she told him it was important. It was Tony's nature to trust, as it had been Marjorie's at his age, when she married.

"We will ride to the Hunt," Rigo said firmly. "The horses will be recovered by then."

"No," Marjorie said, shaking her head. "Apparently we mustn't."

"Don't be ridiculous." He said it, as he often did, without thinking, and was immediately annoyed as he saw the pain in her face.

"Rigo, my dear, surely you don't think it's my idea not to ride." She laughed, a light little laugh which said in the only way she could that he was being obtuse and unpleasant. "Obermun bon Haunser almost came apart at his impeccable seams when I suggested we would merely join the field on horseback. Apparently arrangements have been made otherwise."

"Damn it, Marjorie. Why was I sent here? Why were you? Except for the horses?"

She didn't try to answer him. It was not a question which could be answered. He glared at her. Stella stared, giggling a little, enjoying this discord. Tony made uncomfortable little *hrnching* sounds in his throat as he did when caught in some seeming conflict between them. "Surely," he said softly, "surely . . ."

"I thought it was something important we were here for?" sneered Stella, unwittingly derailing her father's hostility toward Marjorie and bringing it upon herself.

"We would scarcely have come otherwise," he snapped angrily. "Our lives have been disrupted, too, and we are no fonder of Grass than you are. We, like you, would prefer to be at home, getting on with our lives." He lashed at an offending seed head with his whip. "What's this about not riding?"

Marjorie answered softly, trying to keep them all calm. "I don't know why we mustn't ride to the Hunt, but it is clear that we must not. My counsel, Ambassador, for what it is worth, is that we do what that stiff, awkward Haunser man has arranged for us until we find out what is going on here. We are not *bons*, after all, and Obermun bon Haunser took some pains to point out to me that neither Sanctity nor Terra know anything at all about Grass."

Rigo might have said something more, except that a sound interrupted him. Such a sound as a tormented soul might make, if such a one had the voice of the thunder and the cataract. It was a wholly natural sound, as a small world might make, being rent apart, and yet they did not doubt that it issued from a throat and lungs and a body of some indescribable sort. Something that a name could be put to if one only knew what it was. A cry of desperate loneliness.

"What?" breathed Rigo, unmoving, alert. "What was that?"

They waited, poised, perhaps to run. Nothing.

In the time ahead they were to hear the cry several times. Though they asked about it, no one knew what made it.

El Dia Octavo woke from evil dream to uncomfortable reality. His feet were not on the ground and he thrashed, though weakly. A voice came incomprehensibly through a veil of pained dryness. "Lower that sling, you fool, and put him down."

Hooves touched solid surface and the stallion stood trembling, head lowered. He could smell the others. They were somewhere near, but it was impossible to lift his head and look. He flared his nostrils instead, trying the odor for that complexity which would include them all. A hand ran along his side, his neck. Not *her* hand. A good hand, but not her hand. Not *his* hand, either. This was the male-one most like *her*, not the female-one most like *him*.

"Shhh, shhh," said Tony. "That's a good boy. Just stand there a little while. It'll come back to you. Shhh, shhh."

What came was the dream. Galloping with something after him. Something huge. Huge and fast. A threat from behind. A fleeing. He whickered, begging for reassurance, and the hand was there.

"Shhh, shhh."

He slept standing, the dream fading.

He woke enough to walk up a ramp into something that moved, then he slept again. When the thing stopped moving, he woke enough to walk down the ramp again and *she* was there.

"*She*," neighed Millefiori. "All right. *She*."

He nodded, making a sound in his throat, dragging his feet as he tried to follow *her*. Nothing smelled quite right. There were familiar sounds, but the smells were wrong. When he was inside the stall, lying on the grass there, it didn't smell right either.

There was noise outside. The other stallion screaming, making a fuss.

El Dia Octavo nickered at him, and so did the mares. In a moment Don Quixote quieted, making a sound of misery.

Then *she* came, patting, stroking, talking to them, saying, as Tony had, "Shhh, shhh," giving him water.

He drank, letting the water flow into that place of dry fear. After a time he slept again, dreamlessly, the dream gradually losing itself in the smell of the strange hay.

"Odd," murmured Marjorie, staring down at him.

"They seemed frightened," said Tony. "The whole time, they seemed scared to death but so lethargic they couldn't do anything about it."

"I had bad dreams when I first got here. And I woke up frightened all the time."

"So did I." Tony shuddered. "I wasn't going to say anything, but I had real nightmares."

"An effect of coldsleep?" Marjorie wondered.

"I asked around at the port. Nobody seems to think that's a usual thing after coldsleep."

"Odd," said Marjorie again. "Well, at least the stalls were finished on time."

"They did a good job. People from the village?"

"People from the village. It seems to be a reciprocal kind of arrangement. We give them employment and buy their produce, and they provide whatever help we need. They've been here for years, maintaining the place. I've picked a few of them to work with the horses. Perhaps we can find two or three grooms among them."

They left the stables and went back to the house, turning once or twice to look back as though to assure themselves the horses were all right, both of them thinking it strange that the animals gave every sign of sharing their own bad dreams. Marjorie swore to herself she would spend time with them over the next few days, until the trauma had passed.

Other matters intervened, however. Among them was the arrival of the craftsmen's committee for Newroad, who went through the summer rooms of Opal Hill making lists.

"You want it done in the local manner, don't you?" the spokesman of this delegation asked in trade lingua. He was a stocky, bald-headed man with froggy bags around his eyes and an engaging grin. His name was Roald Few. "You don't want anything that will make the bons' tongues clack, right?"

"Right," she had agreed, amazed, and amused at herself for being so. What had she expected? Poor ignorant fools like those in Breedertown? "You're very quick, Mr. Few. I thought we were the first embassy Grass has had."

"The only one now," he replied. "There've been a few. They can't winter it, you know. Can't stay. Too lonely. Semling had a man here for a while. Here, I mean. At Opal Hill. Semling built the estancia, you know."

"Why weren't the summer quarters furnished?"

"Because it was coming autumn by the time it was built, and by the time autumn was half gone, you know, so was the man from Semling. He never got to the good part of the year. So, what have you to tell me about colors and all that?"

"Can I depend upon you to make us look acceptable?" she asked. "If I can, there's a bonus in it for you. My husband likes warm colors, reds and ambers. I prefer the cooler ones. Blue. Soft gray. Sea green. Hah," she paused. "There is no sea on Grass, but you apprehend." He nodded. "Perhaps, if it is in keeping with local usage, you could give us a little variation?"

"Variety and make you look good," he said, pursing his lips as he noted it down. "Do my best, madam, and may I say you show good sense in leaving it to us. Us on the Newroad work well together, and we'll do you well who trusts us." He gave her a sharp look, meeting her open gaze with a frank nod of his own. "I'll tell you something, just me to you. You and the family come over the forest into commoner territory every now and then. Commoner Town, the aristos say, but we say Commons, meaning it's for all of us. We've got food there you'll never get out here, things we ship in for ourselves. It gets damned lonely out here if you're not all turned inside out like these bons. You might even decide you'd like to live in Commons during wintertime, if you're here that long. You've got animals, too, and they'll do better in Commons than they will out here. We're set up to winter animals there. There are hay barns we fill every summer, and cow barns down along our own quarters. All the villages close up, wintertime, and move into town. Among the aristos nobody'd know, did you or not. Anybody calls you on the tell-me, splice you through to Commons and who'll know you're not out here, sufferin' winter. Do you speak Grassan, by any chance."

"I thought Grassians spoke Terran or trade lingua," she replied, dismayed. "Obermun bon Haunser spoke diplomatic Terran to me."

"Oh, they'll do that if they like," he said with a nasty grin. "They'll speak diplo and some of them will even lower themselves to speak trade lingua, and then the next time they'll turn their backs to you and pretend they don't understand you at all. You'll get further with 'em if you know Grassan. Way I understand it, it's a mishmash of languages they all spoke when they came here, and then it's changed since. Each family speaks its own variety of it, kind of a family dialect, a game they have, but mostly that's a matter of family words and you can understand the sense if you know the language. You'll get further yet if they don't know you speak it until you speak it pretty good. I can send you a teacher."

"Do," she agreed, all at once trusting and liking him. "Send me a teacher and be very close-mouthed about it if you will, Mr. Few."

"Oh, I will." He snorted. "I'll send you a man in two days. And you call me Roald, like all the Commons do. Damn bons." The animosity seemed habitual rather than acute, and Marjorie did not inquire into it, merely making a note that Rigo should hear of it if he had not already learned of it for himself.

In addition to the commodious guest and servants' quarters in the main house, there were three small detached residences at Opal Hill available to members of the embassy staff. Given first choice, Rigo's faithful assistant Andrea Chapelside had picked the small house closest by, to be most readily available in case of need. Her sister Charlotte would live there with her. Father Sandoval and his companion priest, Father James, took the largest of the detached residences, intending to use part of it as a library and school for Stella and Tony and the largest room as a chapel for themselves and the embassy. This left the smallest house for Eugenie Le Fevre. It had a summer kitchen, living room, and bedroom above the ground and several cozy winter rooms below. Each of the houses was connected by a tunnel which led to the big house. Each opened upon a separate vista of the gardens.

When Roald Few finished his business with Marjorie, he called on each of the other residents of Opal Hill, getting their instructions for the furnishing of summer bedrooms and sitting rooms. The middle-aged women in the first house had pictures of what they wanted, things that looked like home. The men in the larger house wanted everything as plain as it could be, and one room they wanted untouched except for the provision of some little seats with kneeling stools in front of them and an altar kind of arrangement. The delicate-looking younger man had drawn a picture which the older stocky man nodded approval over. Both of them religious, Roald thought. Not dressed like Sanctified, though. These had funny little collars. Something different from the usual run.

"I hope this will not cause you too much trouble," the older of the two said in a steely voice which only seemed apologetic.

"No trouble at all, except one," said Roald with an engaging smile. "And that's knowing what the proper title is for you and the other gentleman. I know you're some sort of religious folk, and I wouldn't want to go astray with the lingo."

The delicate gentleman nodded. "We are Old Catholics. I'm Father Sandoval, and my companion is Father James. Father James' mother is sister to His Excellency, Roderigo Yrarier. We are usually called Father, if that wouldn't offend you." And if it would, his voice said, say it anyhow.

"I don't stay in business being easily offended," Roald assured them. "If you wanted me to call you uncle, I'd do that, too. I might balk at aunt, but uncle I could manage."

This brought a chuckle from the younger priest, and Roald nodded at him cheerfully as he left.

The smallest house was the most remote and the last on his list. It was there, in the empty summer quarter, that he met with Eugenie. He had not been with her for long before he knew everything about her. Everything, he thought to himself, that he needed to know.

"Pink," she said. "Soft pink. And rose shades, all warm, like the inside of a flower. I miss flowers. Curtains to shut out the night and the sight of that awful grass. Soft curtains that drape and blow in the wind. Wide couches with pillows." She moved her hands and her lips, sketching what she wanted on the compliant air, and he saw what she saw, a nest feathered in ivory and rose, sweet-scented as —so fable had it—a Terran morning. She was wearing a silky gown that flowed behind her on the air, fluttering with her movement as though she were accompanied by soft winds. Her hair was light brown, the great wealth of it piled high on her head with tiny curls escaping at her brow and the nape of her neck. Her eyes were an ageless blue, innocent of anything but pleasure and untroubled by thought.

Roald Few sighed, silently, knowing all about it. This lady looked like the little porcelain woman his wife kept on the table at home. Poor Lady Westriding. She had interested him enormously, and now he pitied her as well. What was it had gone wrong there? he wondered. So many things could happen. He would tell Kinny, his wife, all about it, how they looked, what they said, and Kinny would know. She would tell him the story over supper, how this Roderigo and this Lady Westriding had almost been true lovers, almost a natural pair, but this something else had happened, and now there was this pink lady for the Lord's bed while the cool blond woman was left all alone. Though perhaps he didn't leave her alone. There was that possibility, too.

"Rose pink," he said to Eugenie as he noted it down. "And lots of soft cushions."

When Roald returned home, his wife, Kinny, was waiting with supper ready to go on the table. Since Marthamay had married Alverd Bee and moved over to the other end of town, Roald and Kinny had been alone sporadically—that is, when none of the children had needed a baby-tender or a home-from-their-own following an argument with a spouse. Arguments with spouses, Roald had taken care to point out to each of his children, were as inevitable as winter but were not life-threatening provided one took a little care in advance. Such as making a habit of going on home to cool off for a day or so when needed, and no insult meant and none taken by either party. Just as spring followed winter, so better understanding followed a little cooling off.

Currently none of the children were fighting with their wives or husbands and none of the grandkids were in residence, so he and Kinny had the place to themselves, which pleased him considerably when it happened.

"I made goose with cabbage," Kinny told him. "Jandra Jellico slaughtered a few geese, and she got on the tell-me to let me know. I hurried right over to get a fat one."

Roald licked his lips. Spring goose with cabbage was one of his favorite dishes, and Kinny could make it like no one else. It was goose with cabbage had made him look at her in the first place, her with her round little arms and round little face, and it was goose with cabbage had happily punctuated all their seasons together since. Goose with cabbage generally meant a celebration of some kind.

"So, what good thing is going on?" he asked her.

"Marthamay's pregnant."

"Well, isn't that wonderful! There for a bit she was worried."

"She wasn't really. It was just her sisters teasing her when the time went by after she and Alverd married and nothing happened."

"Alverd getting ready to do a little digging, is he?"

"She says yes." Kinny smiled as she forked a mouthful of cabbage into her rosy mouth, thinking of tall, eager Alverd Bee slaving away down in the winter quarters, digging a new room as every new daddy did. Alverd was likely to be elected mayor of Commons in a week or two, and mayors had little time for such doings. Well and all, the brothers would help him, just as he'd helped them. "So, tell me all about the new people."

He told her, about the ambassador and about Marjorie and the other lady in her soon-to-be-pink nest.

"Ah," said Kinny, wrinkling her nose. "That's sad."

"So I thought," he agreed. "His wife's a lovely lady, but cool. Take a little wooing, that one."

"And him, I suppose he's too hot and impatient for that."

Roald chewed as he thought. Yes. As usual, Kinny had hit it right on the head. Too hot and impatient by far, Roderigo Yrarier. Hot and impatient enough to get himself into a mess of trouble, before he was through.

Not liking that idea, Roald changed the subject. "What does Marthamay think they'll name the baby?"

Marjorie's language instructor arrived two days later. He introduced himself as Persun Pollut. He sat beside her in what would become Marjorie's study, just inside a large window warmed by an orange sun, while craftsmen came and went with crates and cartons, tools and ladders in the hall just outside. Watching the workers, Marjorie spoke of the strangeness of needing both winter quarters and summer quarters separate from one another.

"Winter is long," he admitted, drooping his eyebrows at her. "It is so long we grow tired of looking at one another." Persun had exceptionally long and sinuous eyebrows. He was young, though not callow; supple, though not yielding; determined, though not rigid. Marjorie felt Roald Few had selected well, particularly as Persun had shown good sense in not advertising the purpose of his presence. He had taken a room in the nearby village and announced that he was there to carve some panels for "Her Ladyship's private study." Now, seated at his ease in that study, he continued his explanation.

"Winter is so long that one tires of thinking of it," he said. "We grow tired of breathing the air which is not only cold but hostile to us. We go under the ground, like the Hippae, and wait for spring. Sometimes we wish we could sleep like them."

"What on earth do you all do with yourselves?" Marjorie asked, thinking once more of what they would do with the horses during wintertime. If they were still on Grass. Anthony kept saying the Yrariers would be on their way home by then, but Anthony didn't know why they had come.

"In Commons we visit and have games and do our work, and have winter festivals of drama and poetry writing and things of that sort. We go visit the animals in the barns. We have an orchestra. People sing and dance and train animals to do tricks. We have a winter university where most of us learn things we would never learn if it weren't for winter. Sometimes we bring professors in from Semling for the cold season. We're better educated than the bons, you'll find, though we don't let them know that. There are so many tunnels and storage rooms and meeting rooms under Commons it is like living over a sponge. We come and go, here to there, without ever looking at the outside where the wind cuts to the bone and the cold mist hangs over everything, hiding the ice ghosts."

"But the bons stay on their estancias?"

"Out on the estancias they don't have our resources, so they pass the time less profitably. In the town we have some thousands of people to draw upon, more in the winter than are living there now. When winter comes, the villages empty themselves into Commons. The port remains open year round so there's visitors even during the cold time. The hotel has winter quarters, too, with tunnels to the port. On an estancia there may be only a hundred people, a hundred and a half maybe. On an estancia everyone grows very tired of everyone else."

There was silence for a moment, then she said tentatively, "Have you any charities on Grass?"

"Charities, ma'am?"

"Good works. Helping people." She shrugged, using the phrase Rigo often used. "Widows and orphans?"

He shook his head at her. "Well there's widows, right enough, and occasional an orphan, I suppose, though why they should need charity is beyond me. We commoners take care of our own, but that's not charity, it's just good sense. Is it something you did a lot of, back where you came from?"

She nodded soberly. Oh, yes, she had done a lot of it. But no one had thought it important enough to take her place. "I think there'll be a lot of empty time," she said in explanation. "The winters sound very long."

"Oh, they are long. The aristos have a saying in Grassan: *Prin g'los dem aufnet haudermach*. That is, 'Winter closeness is separated in spring.' Let's see, maybe you'd say it, 'Winter liaisons sunder in spring.' " He thought this over, wobbling his eyebrows. "No, perhaps a Terran would more likely say 'marriages': 'Spring loosens winter marriages.' "

"Yes, we would probably say marriages," she agreed somberly. "How did you learn to speak diplomatic?"

"We all speak it. Everyone in Commons does. The port's very busy. Shipments in, shipments out. We've got more brokers in Commons than you'd suspect. We order things from off-planet. We sell things. We need to send messages. We speak diplomatic and trade lingua and Sembla and half a dozen other languages, too. Grassan is very ponderous and uncertain. It's a language invented by the aristocrats. Like a private code. I will teach it to you, but don't expect it to make sense."

"I promise I won't. Do you make your living teaching Grassan?"

"Oh, by the marvelous migerers of the Hippae, no, Lady. Who would there be to teach it to? Everyone here knows it and who else cares? Hime Pollut the woodcarver is a friend to craftsmaster Roald Few, and I am Pollut the woodcarver's son, and he is making use of me during a slack season, that's all."

She could not hold back her laugh. "You *are* a woodcarver, then?"

His eyes went soft and dreamy. "Well, more that than anything else, since I haven't made my fortune yet." He paused, then sat up, bringing himself to attention. "Though I will. There's money to be made in Semling silks, take my word on it. But I will make some panels for your study, Lady, since we must have some reason for my being here if the Grassians are not to know that you are learning their language." Besides, since he had seen her, he had wanted to do something for her. Something quite surpassing.

"What shall I do when Obermun bon Haunser recommends a secretary for me?"

Persun nodded in thought. "Tell him you will consider it. Outside of Commons no one moves very quickly on Grass. So I have heard from a few people coming from off-planet who have to deal with the aristos. They get very impatient. So, let the Obermun wait. He will not be annoyed."

She reported all this to Rigo and sent the suggested reply in response to the Obermun's recommendation of a certain Admit Maukerden when, eventually, that recommendation arrived.

With one thing and another, several days passed before Marjorie had time to ride. Anthony and Rigo had gone out several times, and even Stella had been unwillingly forced into exercise duty. The day after the craftsmen departed, Marjorie went out with the men of the family. The morning was bright, clear, and warm, and she found herself wishing Stella would join them, though the girl had refused their invitation with a certain hauteur. Stella rode brilliantly, but she had made it clear that she would not enjoy riding on Grass, that she would not enjoy anything on Grass. Stella had left friends behind, one friend in particular. Marjorie had not been sorry. Perhaps Stella's ostentatious lack of enjoyment was to punish Marjorie for not caring, but Marjorie could not, knowing what she knew and Stella did not. The best she could do was wish that Stella were with them as they walked down the winding path to the newly built stables.

The stable hands had done what they had been told to do: They had cut grass of certain types and filled mangers with it, mucked out the newly built stalls, and provided locally grown grain of three or four types in small quantities in order to observe which were eaten. They watched as the Terrans saddled three of the horses, asking questions in trade lingua without embarrassment or shyness. "What is that for?" "Why are you doing that?"

"Don't the bons ride?" asked Tony. "Haven't you seen a saddle before?"

Silence fell while the two men and one woman looked at one another. It was evidently not a topic they felt comfortable discussing. Finally the woman said, almost in a whisper, "The Hippae would not . . . would not allow a saddle. The riders wear padding instead."

Well, well, well, said Marjorie to herself. Isn't that something. She caught Tony's eye and shook her head slightly just as her son was about to say something like, since when did a horse decide what it would allow.

"Our horses find the saddle more comfortable than they would our bony bottoms," she said evenly. "Perhaps the Hippae are constructed differently."

This seemed to smooth things over, and the hands went back to their questions. Marjorie noted which questions were most intelligent and which questioners most understanding.

"It is hard to cut the bluegrass," one of them said. "But the horses like it best."

"What are you using to cut it?" she asked. They showed her a sickle of inferior steel. "I'll give you better tools." She unlocked a tack box and gave them laser knives. "Be careful," she said, showing them how they were used. "You can lose an arm or a leg with these. Be sure no one is in the way of the blade."

She watched them experimenting with the knives, cutting armfuls of grass with single strokes, exclaiming in surprise and pleasure and giving her grateful looks. She would need a stud groom, and of necessity he would have to be drawn from among the villagers. Already these people were patting and stroking the horses much more than was absolutely necessary.

Sanctity had allowed them to bring only six animals. Considering how long their stay might be, they had chosen to bring breeding stock. Marjorie had volunteered to leave her favorite mount, the bay gelding Reliant, behind. Instead, she rode El Dia Octavo, a Barb stallion trained by a former Lippizaner rider. Rigo was mounted on

Don Quixote, an Arabian. Tony was riding Millefiori, one of the thoroughbred mares. Three of the mares were thoroughbreds and one, Irish Lass, was a draft animal, brought along for size. If they were stuck on this planet for a full Grassian year or more, at least they would have the amusement of building their own stud.

Tony led them along a low fold of ground which took them some half a mile toward a natural arena he had been using to exercise the horses, a level place of low, amber grass, almost circular in shape. Once there, they fell into the ritual of exercise, walk, trot, collected canter, trot, walk again, first in one direction then in the other, extending the trot, the canter, then stopping to dismount and examine the horses.

"Not even breathing hard," said Rigo. "They've been getting better every day." He sounded enthusiastic, and Marjorie knew that he was scheming. Rigo was always happiest when he had some kind of covert activity going on. What would it be? Something to astonish the natives? He went on bubbling about the horses. "Remarkable how quickly they've recovered."

"Like us," Marjorie offered. "A day or two feeling miserable and then we felt like ourselves. They haven't lost their muscle tone. Let's do a few minutes more and then walk them back. We'll do more tomorrow."

She mounted, again falling into the familiar rhythm. Half pass, tight circle, half pass again.

Something at the ridge line caught her eye, a darker shadow in the glare of spring sun. She looked up, puzzled, seeing the forms there, silhouetted against the light, so dazzled by the sun that she could not make them out clearly. Horses? An impression of arched necks and rounded haunches, only that. She couldn't tell how large they were or how far away.

El Dia Octavo stopped, staring where Marjorie stared, making a troubled noise in his throat, the skin over his shoulders quivering as at the assault of stinging flies. "Shhh," she said, patting him on the neck, troubled for his trouble. Something up there bothered him. She stared up at the sun-dazzle again, trying to get a good look. A cloud moved toward the sun, but just before the light dimmed, the dark silhouettes vanished from the ridge.

The watchers seemed to prefer to remain unobserved. She urged Octavo forward, wanting to ride to the ridge and see where they had gone, whatever they were.

The stallion quivered as though he were in pain, as though something were terribly wrong. He made a noise in his throat, precursor to a scream. Only her legs tight around him and her hand on his neck held him fast. He seemed barely able to stand, unable to advance.

Interesting, she thought with the surface of her mind, noticing the way Octavo's hide was trembling over his shoulders. She no longer urged him to move but concentrated only on calming him. "Shhh," she said again. "It's all right, it's all right."

Then, suddenly aware of the deep, causeless thrill of terror inside herself, she knew what the horse was feeling and that it was not all right.

5

The morning of the Hunt found all the Yrariers full of odd anxieties they were loath to show, much less share. Marjorie, sleepless through much of the night, rising early to walk through the connecting tunnel to the chapel, attending early mass, admitting her nervousness to Rigo when she found him in the dining room when she returned. He, pretending calm, inside himself as jittery as any pre-race jockey, full of mocking lizards squirming in his belly. Tony, lonely, that much evident from the eagerness with which he greeted them when he came into the room, bending over his mother with a hug that was slightly clinging. Stella, disdainful, expressing no affection at all, half dressed, full of angry invective and threats against the peace and tranquility of Grass.

"It'll be awful," she said. "Not riding, I mean. I have half a mind not to go. Why won't they—"

"Shh," said her mother. "We promised one another we wouldn't ask. We don't know enough yet. Eat your breakfast. We want to be ready when the thing comes." The thing. The vehicle. The not-horse which they were expected to ride within. All the Grassian vehicles seemed to be mechanical devices trying to look like something else: drawing room ornaments or lawn statuary or bits of baroque sculpture. The one that had brought the horses had looked like nothing so much as an aerial version of an ancient wine amphora, complete with stylized representations of dancers around its middle. Tony had told her it had been all he could do not to laugh when he saw it; and Marjorie, who had watched its laborious descent with disbelief, had turned aside to hide her amusement. Now she said again, "Eat your breakfast," wondering if she needed to warn Stella not to laugh. If she warned Stella not to, Stella would. If she didn't, Stella might not. Sighing, Marjorie fingered the prayer book in her pocket and left it to God.

They did eat their breakfast, all of them, ravenously, leaving very little of what had looked like a large repast for twice as many people. Marjorie ran her hand around her waistband, noting that it seemed loose. With everything she was eating she still seemed to be losing weight.

The aircar, when it arrived, was overly ornamental but not actually funny, a luxurious flier, engineered for vertical ascent. Once inside it with Obermun bon Haunser as their guide, they lowered themselves into deeply padded seats and were given cups of the local hot drink—which was called, though it did not resemble, coffee—while the silent (and apparently non-bon) driver set off toward an unseen destination. They flew to the northeast as the Obermun pointed out notable landmarks. "Crimson Ridge," he said, indicating a long rise deeply flushed with pink. "It will be blood-red in another week or two. Off to your right are the Sable Hills. I hope you feel somewhat privileged. You are among the very few non-Grassians who have ever seen anything of our planet except for Commoner Town, around the port."

"I wondered about Commoner Town," said Rigo. "On the maps it shows as a considerable area, some fifty miles long and two or three miles wide, completely surrounded by forest. I understand it is entirely given over to commerce or farming. When we arrived, I saw roads in and around Commoner Town, though there are none on the rest of the planet."

"As I have previously explained to your wife, Ambassador, there is no grassland around Commoner Town. When we speak of the town, we mean the whole area, everything right down to the edge of the swamp. Here on Grass, where swamp is, trees are, as you can see if you look to your left. That is the port-forest coming up below. Quite a different surface from the rest of the planet, is it not? It doesn't matter if they have roads in Commoner Town, because there is no grass to destroy, and they cannot get out through the swamp." Obermun bon Haunser pointed down at the billowing green centered with urban clutter, his nostrils flaring only very slightly in what was unmistakably an expression of contempt. He had spoken of the roads as though they were something malevolent, something seeking subtle egress, like serpents caged against their will.

Stella started to blurt something but held it in as she received the full force of a forbidding glare from her father.

"You prefer they not get out?" Anthony asked, with precisely the right tone of disingenuous interest. "The roads or the commoners? Why is that?"

The Obermun flushed. He had obviously said something spontaneous and unplanned which he now regretted. "The commoners have no wish to leave the town. I meant the roads, my boy. I cannot expect you to understand the horror we have of marring the grasses. We have no fear of harvesting them, you understand, or making use of them, but scarring them lastingly is abhorrent to us. There are no roads on Grass except for the narrow trails linking each estancia to its own village, and even these we regret."

"All exchanges between estancias, then, are by air?"

"All transport of persons or material, yes. The tell-me provides informational exchange. Information entered at your node at Opal Hill can be directed to specific recipients or to certain sets of recipients or used for correspondence with *elsewhere*. The tell-me links all the estancias and Commoner Town. All travel, however, all deliveries of imports or shipments of export material, are by air."

"Imports and exports? Consisting of what, mostly?" This was Stella, deciding to be a good child for the moment.

The Obermun hemmed and hawed. "Well, imports are mostly manufactured goods and some luxury products such as wines and fabrics.

For the most part, exports are what you might expect: various grass products. Grass exports grain and colored fiber. I am told by the commoners who attend to such matters that the larger grasses are much in demand for the construction of furniture. The merchants liken it to Terran bamboo. There is some export of seed, both as grain and for planting elsewhere. Some of the grasses thrive on other planets, I am told. Some which thrive only here yield valuable pharmaceutical products. Some are highly ornamental, as you have no doubt observed. It's all done by license to various commoner firms. We bons haven't the time or inclination to be directly involved with the business. I don't suppose it's very lucrative, but it is sufficient to support us and the town, which is to our advantage."

Rigo, remembering the huge warehouses and the thriving shipping he had seen at the port, suppressed any comment. "And do I understand correctly that the grasses aren't botanically related to Terran grasses? They're indigenous? Not imports?"

"No. They are not even similar on the genetic level. Almost all the varieties were here when we arrived. The Green Brothers have hybridized a few to get certain colors or effects. You will have heard of the Green Brothers?" It was not really a question, for the man stared out the window of the flier, the line of his jaw and mouth expressing discomfort. Whatever they had been talking about was something that upset him. "They were sent here long ago to dig up the ruins of the Arbai city, and they took up gardening as a sort of hobby."

Marjorie welcomed the change of subject. "I didn't know there was an Arbai ruin on Grass."

"Oh, yes. In the north. The Brothers have been digging away at it for a very long time. I am told it is like most such cities, flat and widespread, which makes it a long task to uncover. I have not seen it myself." He was manifestly uninterested.

Marjorie changed the subject again. "Will we have the opportunity to meet any members of your family today, Obermun?"

"Mine?" he started, surprised. "No, no. The Hunt is still at the bon Damfels'. It will be at the bon Damfels' all this period, before moving on to the bon Maukerdens'."

"Oh," Marjorie said, surprised into speaking without thought. "I thought you said the bon Damfels were in mourning."

"Of course," he said impatiently. "But that would not interrupt the Hunt."

Rigo threw her an admonitory glance which she pretended not

to see, persisting sweetly. "Will others be riding with the bon Damfels?"

"Two or three houses usually hunt together. Today the bon Damfels will be hunting with the bon Laupmons and the bon Haunsers."

"But not your family."

"Not my wife and children, no. The women and younger children usually ride only with the home Hunt." He set his jaw. She had happened upon a sensitive subject once more.

Marjorie sighed to herself. What subjects were not sensitive on this place?

"We will be landing just ahead!" the Obermun cried.

"Have we arrived at Klive so soon?"

"Oh, you could not come to Klive in this flier, Lady Marjorie. It is too noisy. It would upset the hounds. No, we will go from this point by balloon-car. Balloon-cars are virtually silent. And comparatively slow, so you will be able to see what is going on."

And in the luxurious cabin of a propeller-driven balloon-car, a car with windows at the sides and below and so overly garnished as to appear unintended for its function, they went forward to land silently upon a side lawn of Klive. They were greeted by Stavenger, the Obermun bon Damfels, and by Rowena, the Obermum bon Damfels, both dressed in black with small purple capes and veils. Mourning garb, obviously.

The visitors were offered wine. Rowena sipped. Stavenger took none. The Yrariers commented upon the fine weather. Marjorie murmured a few words of sympathy for their loss. Stavenger seemed not to hear what she said. Rowena, eyes deep-sunk in shadowed circles, seemed to be elsewhere, lost in some private grief too deep and remote to let her communicate with the outside world. Or perhaps verbal expressions of grief were not customary. Seeing the behavior of others around them, Marjorie gradually came to the conclusion that this interpretation was correct. Though the bon Damfels wore mourning, no one took any notice of it.

The Yrariers were introduced to other family members—two daughters, two sons, the names merely mumbled so that Marjorie was unsure of them. One of the sons gave her a long look, as though measuring her for a suit of clothing—or a shroud, Marjorie thought with a shiver. He was very pale and intense in his dark clothing, though no less handsome for that. It was a handsome family. The other bon Damfels children seemed remote and distracted, responding only to direct questions, and not always then.

Stella frankly flirted, in a gay, self-deprecating way. She had always found it useful in making friends, and it had never failed her until now. Only the one bon Damfels son returned her gambits with a few words and a half smile. All the others seemed frozen. Gradually the girl fell silent, confused, slightly angry.

A bell rang. All the bon Damfels but Rowena excused themselves and departed suddenly. One moment they were there, the next they were gone.

"They have gone to dress for the Hunt. If you will come with me," she invited in a near whisper, "we will watch from the balconies until the Hunt departs."

Tony and Marjorie went with her, casting one another questioning looks. Nothing here was predictable or familiar. No word, no attitude conveyed any emotion with which they could empathize. Rigo and Stella stalked along behind them, their dark, intense eyes eating up the landscape and spitting it out. There and there. So much for your gardens. So much for your hospitality. So much for your grief and your hunt which you will not share with us. Marjorie felt them simmering behind her, and her skin quivered. This was not diplomatic. This hostility was not the way things should go.

Still, they went on simmering as they were ensconced upon the balcony and provided with food and drink. Nothing was familiar, nothing resembled any such gathering at home. They looked down at the empty first surface for a time in silence, sipping, nibbling, trying not to seem ravenous, which they were, casting sidelong looks at Rowena's distracted face.

After a time, servant women in long white skirts came out onto the first surface, bearing trays of tiny, steaming glasses. The hunters began to trickle in. At first glance the hunters seemed to be dressed in familiar fashion, then one noticed the vast and padded trousers, like inflated jodhpurs, creating bowlegged, steatopygous curves, at first laughable, and then, when one saw the hunters' faces, not amusing at all. Each hunter took a pale, steaming glass and drank, one glass only, a swallow or two, no more. Few of them spoke and those few were among the younger ones. When the horn sounded, though it sounded softly, Marjorie almost leapt from her chair. The hunters turned toward the eastern gate, which opened slowly. The hounds entered and Marjorie could not keep from gasping. She turned toward Rowena and was surprised to see a look of hatred there, a look of baffled rage. Quickly, Marjorie looked away. It had not been an expression their hostess had meant anyone to see.

"My God," breathed Rigo in awe, all his animosity set aside in that moment of shock.

The hounds were the size of Terran horses, muscled like lions, with broad, triangular heads and lips curled back to display jagged ridges of bone or tooth. Herbivores, Rigo thought at first. And yet there were fangs at the front of those jaws. Omnivores? They had reticulated hides, a network of lighter color surrounding shapeless patches of darker skin. Either they had no hair or very short hair. They were silent. Their tongues dripped onto the path as they paced in pairs, split to go around the waiting riders, joined again in pairs, and proceeded toward another gate at the western side of the courtyard.

"Come," said Rowena in her expressionless voice. "We must go down the hall to see the Hunt depart."

They followed her wordlessly down a long corridor and onto another balcony which looked out over the garden beyond the wall— where jaw-dropping shock waited, and a blaze of fear which was like sudden fire. They stood swaying, clutching the railing before them, not believing what they saw. "Hippae." Marjorie identified them to herself, shuddering. Why had she supposed they would look like horses? How naive she had been! How stupid Sanctity had been. Hadn't anyone at Sanctity made any effort to— No. Of course they hadn't. Even if they had tried, there hadn't been time. Her thoughts trailed away into shivering depths of barely controlled terror.

"Hippae," thought Rigo, sweating, taking refuge in anger. Mark another one down against Sender O'Neil. That damned fool. And the Hierarch. Poor uncle. Poor dying old man, he simply hadn't known. Rigo held onto the railing with both hands, pulling himself together with all his force. Beside him he was conscious of Stella leaning forward, breathing heavily, quivering. From the corner of his eye he saw Marjorie put her hand over Tony's and squeeze it.

Below them the monsters pranced silently, twice the size of the hounds, their long necks arching in an almost horselike curve, those necks spined with arm-long scimitars of pointed, knife-edged bone, longest on the head and midway down the neck, shorter at the lower neck and shoulders. The eyes of the mounts were burning orbs of red. Their backs were armored with great calluses of hard and glistening hide.

Stavenger bon Danfels was preparing to mount, and Marjorie bit back an exclamation. The mount half crouched as it extended its left foreleg. Stavenger stepped up on the leg with his left foot, raising his left arm at the same time to throw a ring up and over the lowest of the jutting spines. With his left hand on the ring, close to the spine, he pulled and leapt simultaneously, right leg high to slide over the huge back. He settled just behind the monstrous shoulders, his hands parting widely to reveal thin straps which pulled the ring tight around the blade of bone. Stavenger turned his hands, wrapping the straps around his fingers, gripping them. "Reins," Marjorie thought fleetingly; then, "No, not reins," for the straps were obviously only something to hold on to, only a place to put one's hands. There was no way they could be used to direct the enormous mount or even to signal it. One could not take hold of the razorlike barb itself without cutting off ones fingers. One could not lean forward without skewering oneself. One had to brace oneself back, leaning back in an endless, spine-straining posture which must be agonizing to hold even for a few moments. Otherwise ... otherwise one would be spitted upon those spines.

Along the animal's mighty ribs were a series of deep pockmarks, into which Stavenger thrust the long pointed toes of his boots, bracing himself away from the danger before him. His belly was only inches from the razor edges. On his back, slung across his shoulder, he wore a case like a narrow, elongated quiver. As the mount turned, rearing, Stavenger's eyes slid across Marjorie's gaze with the slickness of ice. His face was not merely empty but stripped bare. There was nothing there. He made no effort to speak to the mount or guide it in any way. It went where it decided to go, taking him with it. Another of the Hippae approached a rider and was mounted in its turn.

Marjorie still held Tony's hand, turned him to face her, looked at him deeply, warningly. He was as pale as milk. Stella was sweating with a feverish excitement in her eyes. Marjorie was cold all over, and she shook herself, forcing herself to speak. She would not be silenced by these ... by these whatever they were.

"Excuse me," Marjorie said, loudly enough to break through their silence, through Rowena's abstracted fascination, "but do your ... your mounts have hooves? I cannot see from here."

"Three," murmured Rowena, so softly they could scarcely hear her. Then louder. "Yes. Three. Three sharp hooves on each foot. Or I should say, three toes, each with a triangular hoof. And two rudimentary thumbs, higher on the leg."

"And the hounds?"

"They, too. Except that their hooves are softer. More like pads. It makes them very sure-footed."

Almost all of the hunters were mounted.

"Come," Rowena said again in the same emotionless voice she had said everything else. "The transport will be waiting for you." She glided before them as if on wheels, her wide skirts floating above the polished floors like an inconsolable balloon, swollen and ready to burst with grief. She did not look at them, did not say their names. It was as if she had not really seen them, did not see them now. Her eyes were fixed upon some interior vision of intimate horror so vividly imagined that Marjorie could almost see it in her eyes. When they approached the car, Rowena turned away and floated back the way they had come.

Waiting near the car was Eric bon Haunser. "My brother has joined the Hunt," he explained. "Since I no longer ride, I have volunteered to go with you. Perhaps you will have questions I can answer." He moved somewhat awkwardly on his artifical legs, stopping at the door of the balloon-car to nod for Marjorie to enter first.

They rose to float silently over the Hunt, driven by silent propellers as they watched long miles flow by under the hooves of the mounts, longer and more tortuous miles run beneath the wider-ranging feet of the hounds. From the air the animals were only short, thick blotches superimposed on the texture of the grass, blotches which pulsated, becoming longer and shorter as legs extended or gathered for the next leap, mounts and hounds distinguishable from one another only by the presence of riders, the riders themselves reduced to mere excrescences, warts upon the pulsating lines. The hunters entered a copse, hidden from the air. After a time they emerged and ran off toward another copse. After a time, the Yrariers forgot what they were watching. They could as well have been observing ants. Or fish in a stream. Or water flowing, wind blowing. There was nothing individual in the movement of the beasts. Only the spots of red spoke of human involvement. Except for those dots of red, the animals might have been alone in their quest. Though occasionally the grass moved ahead of the mounts, the observers could not see whatever quarry the Hunt was chasing.

Marjorie tried to estimate how fast the animals below them were running. She thought it was not as fast as a horse would cover the same distance, though it might not be possible for horses to thrust through tall, thick grasses as the animals below were doing. She spent some time estimating whether horses could outrun the Hippae—deciding they might be able to do so on the flat, though not uphill—then wondered why she was thinking of horses at all.

At last they came to a final copse and hovered above it. Branches quivered. High upon the roof of the copse the fox crawled onto a twiggy platform, screaming defiance at the sky. Over the soft whir of the propellers, they heard him. All they really saw was an explosion of what might have been fur or scales or fangs, talons, a great shaking and scouring among the leaves, an impression of ferocity, of something huge and indomitable.

"Fox," Anthony muttered, his voice breaking. "Fox. That thing is the size of half a dozen tigers." His mother's hand silenced his words, though his mind went on nattering at him. Where it isn't toothy, it's bony. My God. Fox. Merciful Father, will they expect me to ride after that thing? I won't. Whatever they expect, I just won't!

Ride, Stella thought. I could ride the way they do. A horse is nothing to that. Nothing at all. I wonder if they'll let me . . .

Ride, thought Marjorie in a fever of abhorrence. "That isn't riding. What they are doing. Something within her writhed in disgust and horror; she did not know what the people below her were doing, but it was not riding, not horsemanship. Suppose they want us to join their Hunt? She thought. At least one of us. I suppose there are teachers. Will we have to do this to be respected by them?

Ride, thought Rigo. To ride something like that! They will not think me a man unless I do, and their tribal egotism will try to keep me out. How? We are being treated as mere tourists, not as residents. I won't have it! Damn Sanctity. Damn Uncle Carlos. Damn Sender O'Neil. Damn him and damn him."

"The whole of Grass is horse-mad," Sender O'Neil had said. "Horse-mad and class-conscious. The Hierarch, your uncle, suggested you for the mission. You and your family are the best candidates we have."

"The best candidates you have for what?" Rigo had asked. "And why the devil should we care?" The invocation of old Uncle Carlos was doing nothing to make him more polite, though it had made him slightly curious.

"The best candidate to be accepted by the aristocrats on Grass. As for why . . ." The man had licked his lips again, this time nervously. He had been about to say words which were not said, not by anyone in Sanctity. So far as Sanctity was concerned, the words were impossible to say. "The plague," he had whispered.

Roderigo had been silent. The acolyte had prepared him for this, at least. He was angry but not surprised.

Sender had shaken his head, waved his hands, palms out, warding away the anger he felt coming from Rigo. "All right. Sanctity doesn't admit the plague exists, but we have reason to keep silent. Even the Hierarch, your uncle, he agreed. Every society mankind has built will fall apart the minute we admit it and start talking about it."

"You can't be certain of that!"

"The machines say so. Every computer model they try says so. Because there's no hope. No cure. No hope for a cure. No means of prevention. We have the virus, but we haven't found any way to make our immune systems manufacture antibodies. We don't even know where it's coming from. We have nothing. The machines advise us that if we tell people . . . well, it will be the end."

"The end of Sanctity? Why should I care about that?"

"Not Sanctity, man! The end of civilization. The end of mankind. The mortality rate is one hundred percent! Your family will die. Mine. All of us. It isn't just Sanctity. It's the end of the human race. It's you as much as me!"

Rigo, shocked into awareness by the man's vehemence, asked, "What makes you think there's an answer on Grass?"

"Something. Maybe only rumor, only fairy tales. Maybe only wishful thinking. Maybe like the fabled cities of gold or the unicorn or the philosopher's stone . . ."

"But maybe?"

"Maybe something real. According to our temple on Semling, there is no plague at all on Grass."

"There's none here on Terra!"

"Oh, Lord, man if that were only true! There's none here that anyone is allowed to see. But I've seen it." The man wiped his face again, eyes brimming with sudden tears, and his jaw clenched as though he were holding down bile that threatened to flood his throat. "I've seen it. Men. Animals. It's everywhere. I'll show it to you, if you like."

Roderigo had already seen plague. He hadn't known it was on Terra or that it afflicted animals, but he, too, had seen it. He waved the offer aside, concentrating. "But there's none on Grass? Perhaps it's only hidden, as you do here."

"Our people don't think they could be hiding it. The Grassians seem to have no structure to hide it. Funny kind of place. But if there's none there . . ."

"What you're implying is that it's the *only* place where there is none. Are you saying there is plague everywhere else?"

Sender, pallid and sweating, nodded and then whispered, "We have at least one temple on virtually every occupied world. In the few places where there's no temple, there's at least a mission. We are responsible for hiding what's happening, so yes, we know where plague is. It is everywhere."

Rigo flushed with sudden fury. "Well then, for the sake of heaven, why aren't the scientists and researchers on the way there! Why come to me?"

"The aristocrats who run the place won't give permission for scientists and researchers to visit the planet. Oh, we could send our people into the port town, yes. Place is called Commoner Town. It's open to visitors. But there's no such thing as immigration. They'd get a visitor's permit, good until the next ship came through headed in the right direction. We've already done that a few times. Our people can't find out anything. Not there in the port. And do you think they can get anywhere else on Grass? Not on your life. Not on anyone's. Sanctity has no power on the planet."

Rigo stared, frankly unbelieving. "You really have no mission there?"

"The only contact Sanctity has with Grass is through the penitential encampment working on the Arbai ruins. Not all our acolytes work out. It won't do to send them home to teach other unwilling boys how to get out of their service. So we send them to Grass. Our encampment was already there when the Grassians arrived. The Green Brothers. So named because of the robes they wear. There must be over a thousand of them, but they have virtually no contact with the aristocrats. Over a hundred years ago the Hierarch ordered them to develop some interest they could use as common ground with the Grassians, but there really is no common ground."

"Trying to make your penitents into more of your damn missionaries," snarled Rigo.

O'Neil wiped his brow. "Oh, I won't deny that's what the man in charge of Acceptable Doctrine would like. His name's Jhamless Zoe, and he gets madder than a teased bull about our not converting the planet to Sanctity, by force if necessary. The Hierarch sends him word to calm down or come home, and it only makes him madder." O'Neil wiped his forehead where the sweat glistened.

"What did the brothers do to develop ties with the aristocrats?"

"They took up gardening." O'Neil laughed harshly. "Gardening! They've become specialists in that. Oh, they've become renowned for that. So well known even Jhamlees didn't dare put a stop to it. But that still doesn't give them any day-to-day contact with the rest of the planet, not enough to learn anything. And the damned aristos won't let us in!"

"Not even when you told them . . ."

"The Grassians aren't suffering. We've tried to describe to them what's happening, but they don't seem to care. They were separatists to begin with, more concerned with maintaining the privileges of their rank than with any human concerns. Lesser nobility. Or perhaps merely pretenders at nobility. European, mostly, and ridiculously proud of their noble blood, full of pretensions about it. That's why they've consistently refused permission for a temple or a mission. Ten generations on Grass has only made them more isolationist, more . . . more strange. It's like they've had iron walls built in their heads! They refuse to be studied. They refuse to be proselytized. They refuse to be visited! Except, maybe, by someone like you. . . .

"Sanctity has a navy." Rigo said it as fact. He disapproved of that fact, but it was true. Planetary governments were isolated and parochial and content to be so. Once the initial explosive overflow of humanity had taken place, Sanctity had done everything it could to stop further exploration. The faith had not wanted men to be so widespread they couldn't be evangelized and controlled. Discovery had stopped, along with science and art and invention. Though its military technology was centuries old, Sanctity maintained the only interstellar force.

Sender O'Neil sighed deeply. "It's been considered. If we take troopers in there, the reason couldn't be kept secret, not for long. All hell would break loose. We can't even consider it until we know for sure that there's something there. Please. Whatever you think of us, give us credit for some intelligence! We've computer-modeled everything. Our best people have done it over and over again. News of the plague *and* use of force would be equally disastrous! Have you heard of the Moldies?"

"Some kind of end-of-the-world sect, aren't they?"

"End of the universe, more likely. But yes, they fervently desire the end of the world, the human world. They call themselves the Martyrs of the Last Days. They believe the time has come to end all human life. They believe in an afterlife which will only commence when this one has ended, for everyone. We've recently learned that the Moldies are 'helping' the plague."

"My God!"

"Yes. Anyone's God!"

"How?"

"Carrying infected materials from one place to another. Like the ancient anarchists, destroying so that something better can come."

"What has this to do with—"

"It has this to do with. All Sanctity's resources are tied up in tracking and expunging the Moldies. They seem to be everywhere, to breed out of nothing. If they heard . . . if they knew there was a chance that Grass—"

"They'd go there?"

"They'd wreck whatever slim chance there may be. No, whatever we do, it must be covert, quiet, without drawing any notice. According to the computers, we've got five to seven years in which to act. After that, the plague may have gone so far that— Well. The Grassians have said they'll accept an ambassador."

"I see." And he had seen. The Grassians would consent to a delaying action. Enough to make Sanctity eschew any ideas of using force, but not enough to seriously inconvenience anyone on Grass.

"You say they ride?" Rigo had asked Sender O'Neil, trying to change the pictures of doom and destruction which had swarmed into his mind. "You say they ride? Did they take horses, hounds, and foxes with them when they settled there?"

"No. They found indigenous variants upon the theme." O'Neil had licked his pursy lips, liking this phrase and repeating it. "Indigenous variants."

Indigenous variants, Rigo thought now as he sat in a balloon-car poised above a copse of great trees on Grass and saw the thing called fox climb into view. He could not see it clearly. He did not glance at his family, though he felt the strain of their silence. He stared down, unconscious for the moment of the need to hide his feelings, and repeated O'Neil's phrase. "Indigenous variants." He said it aloud, not realizing he had spoken. When Eric bon Haunser looked at him inquiringly he blurted, without meaning to, "I'm afraid it is utterly unlike our foxes at home."

The huge, amorphous creature was pulled struggling from the crown of the copse while bon Haunser described what was probably taking place below the trees. He spoke openly, almost offhandedly, carefully ignoring their reaction to the sight of the thing.

When they had returned partway to Klive, Rigo recovered himself sufficiently to say, "You seem very objective about all this. Forgive me, but your brother seemed ... how can I describe it? Embarrassed? Defensive?"

"I don't ride any longer," said Eric, flushing. "My legs. A hunting accident. Those of us who don't ride—some of us at least—we become less enthusiastic." He said this diffidently, as though he were not quite sure of it, and he did not offer to explain what it was about the Hunt that made the current riders unwilling to talk about it. Each of the Yrariers had his or her own ideas about the matter, ideas which they incubated as they sailed silently over the prairies, in time each achieving an imperiled calm.

They arrived back at Klive before the riders did and were met, though scarcely welcomed, by Rowena. She escorted them to a large reception room overlooking the first surface, where she introduced them to the gaggle of pregnant women and children and older men who were eating, drinking, and playing games at scattered tables. She encouraged the Yrariers to tell the servants what they wanted to drink and serve themselves from the laden buffet, then she drifted away. Eric bon Haunser joined them. Very shortly thereafter a horn blew outside the western gate and the riders began to trickle in. Most went immediately to bathe and change their clothing, but a few came into the room, obviously famished.

Eric murmured, "They have drunk nothing for twelve hours before the Hunt except the palliative offered before the Hounds come in. Once the Hunt has begun, there is no opportunity to relieve oneself."

"Most uncomfortable," Marjorie mused, lost in recollection of the sharp implacable spines on the necks of the mounts. "Is it really worth it?"

He shook his head. "I am no philosopher, Lady Westriding. If you were to ask my brother, he would say yes. If you ask me, I may say yes or no. But then, he rides and I don't."

"I ride," said a voice from behind them. "But I say no."

Marjorie turned to confront the owner of the voice, tall, broad-shouldered, not greatly younger than herself, dressed in stained trousers and red coat, his hunting cap under his arm and a full glass held to his lips. She saw that those lips trembled, though so slightly she doubted anyone but herself would have noticed.

"Forgive me," he said. "I'm excessively thirsty." His lips tightened upon the rim of the glass, making it quiver. Something held him in the grip of emotion, slurring his words.

"I can imagine that you are thirsty," she said. "We met this morning, didn't we? You look quite different in your ... in your hunting clothes."

"I am Sylvan bon Damfels," he said with a slight bow. "We did meet, yes. I am the younger son of Stavenger and Rowena bon Damfels."

Stella was standing with Rigo across the room. She saw Sylvan talking to her mother; her expression changed, and she moved toward the two of them, her eyes fixed on Sylvan as she came. There were other bows, other murmurs of introduction. Eric bon Haunser stepped away, leaving Marjorie and the children with Sylvan.

"You say no," Marjorie prompted him. "No, that riding isn't worth it, even though you ride?"

"I do," he said, coloring along his cheekbones, his eyes flicking around the room to see who might be listening, the cords of his throat standing out as though he struggled to speak at all. "To you, madam, and to you, miss and sir, I say it. With the understanding that you will not quote me to any member of my family, or to any other of the bons." He panted.

"Certainly." Anthony was still very pale, as he had been since he saw the fox—or foxen, as most of the Grassians called the beast, meaning one or a dozen—but he had regained his poise. "If you wish it. You have our promise."

"I say it because you may be asked to ride. Invited, as it were. I had thought it impossible until I met your husband. Now I still consider it unlikely, but it could happen. If it does, I caution you, do not accept." He looked them each in the eye, fully, as though seeking their inmost parts, then bowed again and left them, rubbing his throat as though it hurt him.

"Honestly!" Stella bridled, tossing her head.

"Honestly, indeed," said Marjorie. "I think it would be wise as well as kind not to repeat what he said, Stel."

"Of all the snubs!"

"Not so intended, I think."

"Those mounts of theirs may scare you, and they may scare him, but they don't scare me! I could ride those things. I know I could."

Marjorie's soul quaked within her, and it was all she could do to keep her voice calm. "I know you could, Stella. I could, too. Given sufficient practice, I imagine any of us could. The question is, should we? Should any of us? I think we have one friend in this room, and I think that friend just told us no."

6

The Arbai ruin on Grass is, in most respects, like all Arbai ruins: enigmatic, recently abandoned—in terms of archaeologic time—and speaking of some mystery which man can feel without comprehending. Other cities of the Arbai, those found elsewhere, are populated by wind and dust and a scattering of Arbai bones. So few Arbai remains have been found in those other cities that man has questioned why, with such a meager population, the cities should have been so large. They are large in terms of size, of perimeter, if not in terms of height or mass. They sprawl. Their much-crafted streets curve and recurve; their carved housefronts arc gently in concurrence. No vehicles have ever been found in any of the cities. These people walked or ran about their mysterious business, whatever it may have been.

Each city has a library. Each has a mysterious structure in the town square which is identified variously as a sculpture or a religious icon. Outside each city are other enigmatic mechanisms which are thought to be garbage disposers or crematories. A few have suggested they might be transportation devices, no ships having ever been found. Some people think they may be all three. If they are furnaces, the bodies of the inhabitants of the cities could have been burned, which would explain the sparse scattering of remains. Equally well, the inhabitants might have moved on somewhere else. The diggers and theoreticians cannot agree upon either alternative, though they have argued learnedly for generations.

In the more representative Arbai cities only a few whole skeletons have been found, always in ones or twos behind closed doors, as though those Arbai who had stayed behind after the others had gone were too few to attend to the obsequies of departure. Not so upon Grass.

On Grass bodies lie by the hundreds in the houses, in the streets, in the library and the plaza. Everywhere the Green Brothers dig, they find mummified remains.

Most of the digging over the years has been done by strong young men who have had little interest in what they uncovered. Inevitably, however, there have been a few who found themselves fascinated and enthralled by the ancient walls, the ancient artifacts, the ancient bodies. Some few have willingly given their lives to this work, applying all their intelligence to it. Sometimes there have been two or three of these fanatics at a time.

But only one man is currently focusing his intelligence upon the Arbai. He, like others before him, has learned to hide his genuine interest from those in authority. Brother Mainoa, once a miserable young acolyte of Sanctity, long since exiled and grown to suck-toothed age, to the shaggy gray locks and the wrinkled eye-pockets of an elder though to none of the honors some find in that estate; Brother Mainoa, like his predecessors an amateur, a lover of his work, has found his heart's home amid these ancient stones. He has come to consider these trenchlike streets his own, these his dwellings and plazas, these his shops and libraries, though there is nothing in any of them that he can use or believes he will ever truly understand. Mainoa has uncovered almost half of the Arbai bodies himself. He has named them all. He lives out most of his life among them. They have become his friends, though not his only friends.

Of an evening, Brother Mainoa sometimes went away from the dig to a nearby copse where he could sit on a kneed-up root with his evening pipe, leaning against the trunk of the tree as he talked to the air. Tonight he reclined on his accustomed root with a sigh. His bones hurt. Not unusual. Most nights his bones hurt and some mornings, as well. Sleeping in barely heated quarters on a sack stuffed with grass didn't help much, though he'd been less achy since he'd fixed the roof. He took a deep puff of fragrant smoke, let it out slowly, then spoke, as though to himself.

"The purple grass, now, not that Cloak of Kings stuff but the lighter purple with the blue bloom on it, that goes well with the rose. Tests out a complete protein mixed about two to one, very sustaining. Flavor's nothing to proclaim at daily prayers, but it'll come, it'll come."

A sound as of some huge, interested purring came from the tree, high above the old man's head.

"Well, of course the yellowgrass is the old standby. Just before I left the Friary last time to come down here to the dig, Elder Brother Laeroa told me he'd improved on it. I don't know whether to believe that or not; it'd be hard to do. Yellowgrass is almost perfect as it is, just that there's so little of it. It wants the tall orange stem on the sun side of it and something lower, like little green or middle 'zure, on the shade side, the blessed angels know why, but that's the way it is. Elder Laeroa says he's tempted to plant it in stripes and see how it does, but that'd stick out like a sore thumb. . . ."

The purring again, with a note of interrogation.

"Of course they watch us," sighed Brother Mainoa. "Listen to the young Brothers, the cloud crawlers, the ones that wallow around up on that net among the towers. Listen to them tell it. What they see is eyes out there in the grass, staring at the Friary. Of course they watch us. That's what makes it so hard finding things out."

Nothing from above. Brother Mainoa risked a look straight up, seeing nothing but the pale sky through a thatch of twig and leaf, one star pricking out at the zenith, like a single sequin dropped from the skirt of a careless angel. A little to his left, so high that it caught the final rays of the sun with a silken glimmer, he could see a few strands of the net among the towers at the Friary itself, just over the horizon.

"Talking to yourself again, Brother?" said a reproving voice. Brother Mainoa started. The figure under the neighboring tree was half hidden in shadow. The voice was that of Elder Brother Noazee Fuasoi, deputy head of the office of Security and Acceptable Doctrine at the Friary, and what the blazing hell was he doing down here at the dig!

"Just muttering, Elder Brother," Mainoa murmured as he rose and stood respectfully, wondering if the man had followed him, and if so, how long he'd been standing there. "Muttering about the dig, trying to figure it out."

"Sounded like gardening to me, Brother."

"Well, yes. That, too. Trying out effects in my head, so to speak."

"Bad habit to get into, Brother Mainoa. Disruptive of the silence and demeanor of the order. Clinging to such bad habits is probably why you're still assigned to digging up ruins rather than to the more dignified duties your age would warrant. If you'd behaved properly, you'd have been assigned to a desk job back at the Friary a long time ago."

"Yes, Elder Brother," said Brother Mainoa obediently while thinking something not at all obedient about those who were assigned to desk jobs at the Friary. "I'll try to curb the habit."

"See that you do. I wouldn't want to call you up before Eldest Brother Jhamlees Zoe. Eldest Brother Jhamlees takes his Doctrine very seriously."

At least that was the truth. Jhamlees Zoe was too recently arrived to have calmed down yet. Still trying to find something on Grass to convert. Mainoa sighed. "Yes, Elder Brother."

"I came down here to tell you you're assigned to escort duty. We have a recalcitrant acolyte coming in from Sanctity. Brother Shoethai and I brought a car down from the Friary for you to use when you pick him up tomorrow morning."

Brother Mainoa bowed obediently and kept his mouth shut.

Elder Brother Fuasoi belched and rubbed his stomach reflectively. "Boy had less than a year to go and he went jerky. Lost his demeanor and had a fit in refectory, so I'm told. He traveled under his birth name. Rillibee Chime. Think up a Green Friar name for him."

"Yes, Elder Brother."

"The ship will be in early, so be ready. And no more talking to yourself." Brother Fuasoi rubbed at his belly again before he started off.

Brother Mainoa bowed humbly at Fuasoi's retreating back and hoped Fuasoi's belly would kill him soon. Shithead, he thought. All the men from Acceptable Doctrine were shitheads. And so was Elder Brother Jhamless Zoe, the mad proselytizer, cast away here on Grass with nobody to convert and going slowly crazy because of it. Nothing between their ears but excrement or they'd know what was really going on here on Grass. Anyone with any sense could see. . . .

The purr was back above, this time full of quiet amusement.

"You'll get me in big trouble," muttered Brother Mainoa. "Then what will you have to purr about?"

The hundred-square-mile area which the aristocrats called Commoner Town was divided into two parts by a precipitous, convoluted knob of stone which was called, half in jest, Grass's Only Mountain, or Gom. The mountain extended east and west in an uninterrupted wall, a sheer-faced outcropping that ran down on both sides to lose itself in the depths of the swamp forest, making an effective barricade between the permanent and transient. Craftsmen, farmers, merchants, and their families lived and worked north of the barrier in an area they called Commons, centered on the town. The area south of the wall, though largely sloping pastureland, contained the port and all its appurtenances.

Appurtenances included, adjacent to the port on the east, a district containing warehouses for the storage of goods being transhipped, hay barns for winter feed of Commons' livestock, various respectable shops and amusements run by local citizens, the Port Hotel, and the hospital. This area, including the port itself, was called the Commercial District.

Also included was an area on the west side of the port, where buildings blazoned with tawdry glitter stood along Portside Road, where the sensees stayed open around the clock and where visitors routinely stepped over bodies without worrying much about it. Not many of the bodies were dead; few of them were seriously wounded; some of them were still busily engaged. The crowded buildings breathed an indefinable stink made up of drugs, dirt, and various biological exudates. This disreputable area took its name from its road and was called simply Portside.

In addition to the Commercial District and Portside, the southern area contained about forty square miles of common hay meadow and grazing land, sloping on the east, south, and west from the high plateau of the port down to the swamp forest.

Connecting the port areas and Commons through a notch cut

through the wall of Gom was Grass Mountain Road, a well-traveled thoroughfare which ran along the east side of the peak past the order station and the tall, solid gates occasionally used to block all traffic. It was not unknown for freighter crews to emerge from Portside establishments in the waning hours of the night determined to seek the extraordinary pleasure that comes from disrupting the sleep of ordinary people. Under such conditions, the gates were shut. Usually, however, traffic moved along Grass Mountain Road between port and Commons with no hindrance.

The port was busy, far busier than the planetary population could have warranted on its own behalf. Grass lay at a topological crossroads, an accessible destination in qua-space that coincided with a planet in real-space, and this alone made it valuable. The aristocrats, isolated on their estancias and concerned with other matters, had never considered how advantageous Grass's location was. They would have been amazed to learn that the wealth of Grass was not, as they continued to believe, concentrated in the estancias, but was in fact held in off-planet banks by a sizable fraction of the people of the town. Few bons ever came to Commoner Town, and if they came at all, they came no farther than the merchants' offices. The residents of Commons who went to the estancias kept their mouths shut about town business. What the bons thought of as eternally true regarding their own social and economic superiority, Commons had long since discarded in favor of a more pragmatic view. Without the aristocrats becoming more than superficially aware of it, the Commercial District had gradually become a major transshipment point offering temporary lodging to sizable numbers of travelers.

While waiting for a connecting ship, transients staying at the Port Hotel often went into Commons in pursuit of local color. Sellers of grass cloth and grass pictures and cleverly woven multihued grass baskets shaped like fantastic birds or fish did a brisk business. The purchase of some such gimcrack was as close as any of the transients would come to seeing the reality of Grass. The aristocrats had forbidden aircar tours over the prairies. At one time the Port Hotel had offered tours into the edges of the swamp forest, but after a boatload of influential persons had failed to return, the tours had been discontinued. The only sightseeing was in Commons, which meant a constant easy flow of traffic along the road. Townees were not surprised to see new faces.

Thus, when Ducky Johns stopped early one morning at the Order Station with a beautiful girl in tow, the officer thought no more of it than that some off-worlder had escaped from the Port Hotel and fallen into questionable company. Not that Ducky Johns was a bad sort. She and Saint Teresa were the madams of the two largest sensee houses in Portside, and they often traveled into Commons with their housekeepers and cooks. Ducky was usually at the top of the list of contributors to any charitable cause, if Saint Teresa didn't have his name there first. Ducky's machines were well maintained and seldom damaged anyone other than superficially, and none of her girls or boys or genetically altered whatsits had ever tried to kill any of the customers.

"What's this, Ducky?" the officer, James Jellico, asked. He was a husky and muscular man of middle years, covered with the misleading layer of plushy flesh which had earned him his nickname. "Tell good old Jelly what you've got there."

"Damned if I know," replied Ducky, sketching helplessness with both shoulders, the flounces on her tent-dress quivering in response to the mountain of shivering flesh beneath. "I found it on my back porch, under the clothesline." Her flutelike voice made it a plaint, minor key. Her spangled eyebrows arched and the fringes of her tattooed eyelids drooped across her cheeks.

"You should've taken it back to the hotel," Jelly said, giving the girl a hard look, which she returned with a wide, innocent eye.

"I tried," Ducky said, sighing and pursing baby-lips, waving a baby-hand, the wrist braceleted with gems between tiny rolls of fat. "I'm not a fool, Jelly. I thought the same as you. Off a passenger ship, I thought, waiting around for another one. Wandered out of the Commercial District and got lost, I thought, just as you did. I asked it its name, but it didn't have a thing to say for itself."

"Mental, you think? Drugged up?"

"No sign of it."

"Maybe it's one of those, what you call 'em, de-personed things they sell on Vicious."

"I looked and it isn't. It's been used some, but it hasn't been tampered with, not the way they do there."

"So what did the hotel say?"

"The hotel picky-pecked at its little keyboards and winky-winked at its little screens and told me to take it away. Not theirs, they said. They didn't have any like this one, and if they did have, all theirs were accounted for."

"I be damned."

"Yes. Exactly what I said. Couldn't be a Commons townee, could it?"

"You know every one of 'em as well as I do, Ducky. You know every face and every figure and if any of 'em puts on five pounds or insults his sister-in-law, you'd know and so would I."

"Well, we both know what that leaves, Jelly. That leaves the estancias, that does. Lots of unfamiliar faces out there. But that's very puzzling indeed, isn't it, my dear? If it had come from there, we'd have seen it."

Aircars going between Commoner Town and the estancias were permitted to land only at the car terminal at the center of town or at the port. Any aircar landing at the port or in town would be observed. If this lovely creature with the strange eyes had turned up either place, surely somebody would have seen it.

"Off a ship?" hazarded Jellico.

"You know the silly regulations as well as I do, Jelly, dear. Passengers and crew off, fumigate at every port. How could this have lived on a ship while it was being de-bugged? No, it didn't come off an empty ship. And it didn't come from the hotel. And it doesn't belong to me or to Saint Teresa or to any of the other littly bit-players down in our place, no it doesn't. I'm afraid it's your problem, Jelly. Yours alone." Ducky Johns giggled, the ruffles on the tent-dress quivering, a fleshquake in paroxysm.

Jellico shook his head. "Not mine, Ducky, old girl. I'll get an image of her, then you take her back. You've got plenty of room in that place of yours. Put it in an empty room and feed it something. The stasis-tank is no place for that. Doesn't need freezing. Needs tending. Better with you."

"How trusting," she simpered.

"Oh, you won't sell her, Ducky. If she can't talk, she can't speak a consent waiver, and you know I'll be comin' down to look her over again next time I'm in Portside to check transience permits. And after I've had a chance to ask around. If this isn't the damnedest thing . . ."

He went on looking at the girl as he set up the imager, she returning his gaze with her head turned sideways so that he saw only one eye, an eye in which no intelligence showed at all. And yet, when he had finished recording the creature's image and Ducky held out her hand, the girl took it and smiled, turning the head upward and to one side again to cast a sidelong look.

Jelly shivered. There had been something strangely familiar about that look. Almost as strange as where the girl could have come from. Not through the swamp, that was certain. Not in an aircar. Not on a ship. Not from the hotel. And what did that leave?

"Damn all," whispered Jelly to himself, watching old Ducky loading the girl back into her three-wheeled runner before turning it back toward Portside. "Damn all."

The morning after the bon Damfels' Hunt, Marjorie was up before light. She had slept little, and that little restlessly. When she slept she had dreamed of Hippae, and her dreams had been threatening. She had risen in the night to walk about the winter quarters, going into the children's rooms, listening to them breathe. Anthony had been making little groaning sounds and shivering in his sleep, almost as El Dia Octavo had done that day she had seen the things on the ridge. Marjorie sat on the edge of his bed and ran her hands over his shoulders and chest, stroking him as she would have one of the horses, pulling the anxiety out of him until he lay motionless beneath her fingers. Dear Tony, little Tony, first born and much beloved. So like her that she could read every flicker of his expression, every line of his body. She yearned over him, wishing the disappointments away. They would come anyway. He was so like her that they must come, as day follows night.

In the neighboring room Stella slept soundly, rosy in the dim light, lips slightly parted. Each day made her resemblance to Rigo more pronounced—his passion, his pride, and a stunningly feminine version of his handsome face. Marjorie stood over her, not touching her. If Stella were touched she would come awake, full of questions, full of demands—questions Marjorie couldn't answer, demands she couldn't meet. Like Rigo, Marjorie thought to herself. Just like Rigo. And like Rigo, Stella demanded that the world understand her even while she overwhelmed any effort to be understood.

"I tried to know Rigo," Marjorie whispered to herself, an old litany, almost an apology, an excuse, something she said to herself again and again. Something she used to say to Father Sandoval before he had tried to mend what seemingly could not be mended by giving her penance after penance of obedience and submission until she had felt so trapped between them, she could not ask for forgiveness anymore. What she had told Father Sandoval was true, so far as it went. When she and Rigo had been newly married she had sometimes waited until Rigo was very tired or even asleep and then curled against him, pressed herself tight, wanting to feel him in his skin, feel all the muscles running there softly, getting to know the body of him as she did his face. He always responded, fiercely, passionately, hammering at her, until she was lost. There was no separate place she could stand to feel what he was like. If she stood apart from him, he accused her of being remote. If she came close, he swallowed her up.

"I tried to tell him," she whispered, still looking at the sleeping Stella. "I tried to tell him, just the way I've tried to tell you." And that, too, was true. She had tried to say, "Rigo, just hold me, gently. Let me learn the rhythm of your blood and your breath." Or, "Stella, be still a moment. Just talk to me. Let us know one another."

Marjorie remembered lying in the stable with her belly pressed close to a foal, quiet on the straw, the mare whickering above, soft nose pressing down on the foal and on the child-Marjorie both, until all three were same-scented, hay-scented, straw-smelling. Marjorie had felt the blood running in the foal's veins, felt the smooth pull of the muscles over the bone. Then later, when the foal grew and they raced together, she understood what it was that moved and the spirit that moved it. She had wanted to learn Rigo like that, but he wouldn't let her.

Stella was the same. Always passionate. Always in the depths or on the heights. Always give me, give me, give me, and never anything warm or gentle in return, never any simple affection. No hug. No little joke for the two of them to share. No peace. Not that Stella shared much with her father, either. No. If she was capable of affection at all, she had saved it all for her friend back home, the beatific Elaine.

Marjorie felt her own heart thudding away under her hand and smiled ruefully at herself. She was too old to feel this jealousy. It was not her heart that yearned toward Stella, it was her stomach, clenching now with an agony of helpless love which she could not show. Showing love to Stella was like showing meat to a half-wild dog. Stella would seize it and swallow it and gnaw its bones. Showing love to Stella was opening oneself up for attack.

"You don't really love me. When I was little, you promised me a trip to Westriding, and I didn't get to go!" This, the then sixteen-year-old Stella, rehearsing a grievance at least eight years old.

"You've been told a thousand times that Grandpa was ill, Stella. He was too sick to have company. He died not long after that."

"You promised and then you decided all by yourself we shouldn't go. You're always saying we'll do things and then we don't. Now you're dragging me off to this awful place, making me leave my friends without even asking me if I want to go! Why aren't we more like a family? I wish I were Elaine's sister. The Brouers don't act like you do."

"If she mentions the Brouers to me again," Marjorie had said to Rigo, "I will strangle her."

"They're friends," Rigo had replied, giving her a curious look. "They're best friends. Why should you resent that?"

"I don't resent that. I resent the Brouers being held up to me as a standard of perfection."

"All kids think some other family is perfect," he said.

"I never did."

"Yes, but," he had said, "you're strange."

"I'm strange," she told herself now, looking down at the sleeping girl, wondering what it was about the Brouers that had evoked Stella's admiration. What quality did the Brouer family have that attracted her? Family? What did Stella mean by family?

"I wish the Brouers were my family," Stella had said dozens of times, stubbornly, without explaining, knowing she was hurting, wanting to hurt. "They do things together. I wish I had a family like that."

"Well, we'll have a chance to be a family on Grass, Stella. There won't be anyone else around." Not that Stella ever wanted to do what anyone else did. Not that isolation would change her.

Stella had clenched her jaw at that, threatening angrily not to come to Grass at all. For weeks before they left, Marjorie had been sure that Stella would approach her with the suggestion that she stay behind with the Brouers.

"Mother, I want to stay here in Sanctity with the Brouers. They'd like to have me stay."

What would she have said? "Stella, that's fine. I don't want to go either. Neither does your father. I don't feel right about leaving my poor people in St. Magdalen's. Rigo doesn't want to leave his clubs and his committees and his nights on the town with Eugenie on his arm. We're going because we think we must, to save all of mankind. But there's no real reason you have to go. Stay here and die of the plague, Stella. You and Elaine and her whole perfect family. I don't care anymore."

And she had repented her anger, confessed her anger—though not mentioning several other sins which weighed even more heavily—received absolution for it, only to feel it again. And now they were on Grass, and Marjorie still felt anger, still repented, still confessed, still wondered what she would do with Stella, who was as sulky and rebellious and unloving here as she had been at home.

"Why, Father?" she had asked. "Why is she like this? Why is Rigo like this?"

"You know why anyone ... The church teaches ..." His gentle old voice had begun one of its learned and inflexible perorations.

She had interrupted. "Sin. Even original sin. I know what it teaches. It teaches that a sin committed by people thousands of years ago descends to me. Through my cells. Through my DNA. Mixed in there, somehow, along with my heart and my lungs and my brain, and infected my daughter. . . ."

He had cocked his head. "Marjorie, I've never thought that original sin is conveyed in the cells."

"Where else does it come from? What else is there? The soul comes with the body, doesn't it, Father? Sin comes with sex, doesn't it? It isn't just our souls in bed with each other, is it?"

Sanctity would say yes, the souls were in bed together. Sanctity said marriages lasted forever. Especially in heaven. Which wasn't what Old Catholics believed. Thank God. When she was dead at least that would be over.

She had wept then, feeling it was all her own fault, somehow. Father Sandoval had patted her shoulder, unable to offer comfort, unable or unwilling to make her feel less guilty. Nothing had done that, not even all the work at St. Magdalen's, which was supposed to be an expiation.

Marjorie left Stella's room, shutting the door quietly behind her, her mind moving in old, familiar patterns. Perhaps when Stella was older, middle-aged, they could be friends. Stella would marry someone. She would separate herself from them, by distance, by time. She would have children. In time, they might be friends.

The thought made her pale, gasp, made her bend over the sick pain that struck her. There might be no time for any of that. All the sulkiness, the lack of joy—there might be no time for it to work itself out. There might not be time for Stella. There was no proof they were protected here on Grass. There was only the assumption, the hope. And the children couldn't share even that. They couldn't be told the real reasons for the assignment. Too dangerous. So said Sanctity, and Marjorie concurred. Tony might forget himself. Stella might rebel. Either might say something undiplomatic to one of the bons and the fate of humanity could hang upon that saying. Assuming. Assuming there was any truth to the rumor. Assuming there was really no plague here on Grass.

She sat frozen then, waiting for the morning to come, using the rote of prayer to calm herself.

As soon as light showed clearly above the grasses, Marjorie went down to the cavern where the horses were stabled. She needed to feel them, smell them, be assured of their familiar reality, their uncomplicated loyalty and affection. They did not throw her love back in her face; they repaid a little attention a thousand times over. She went from stall to stall, petting and stroking, handing out bits of sweet cookie she had saved for them, stopping at last at Quixote's stall to peer in at him where he pawed the earth again and again, a nervous, begging gesture. She put her arms around him.

"My Quixote," she told him. "Good horse. Wonderful horse." She laid her face against his ebony muzzle, feeling the warm breath in her ear, for that instant forgetting Stella's sulks and Rigo's unfaithfulness and the Hippae and the hounds and the monsters that haunted her, the one called fox here, the one called plague elsewhere. "Let's go out, out into the meadows."

She did not bother to saddle him. This morning was not a time for schooling. This morning there would be only herself and Quixote, a togetherness more intimate than any other she knew. She wanted nothing between herself and his skin. She wanted to be able to reassure him with every muscle she had and take back his strength into herself.

She lay along his neck as they went down from the cavern, along the curving way which led to the arena. The path went down along a winding defile, then up, topping a rise.

As they approached the rise, the horse's skin quivered. He shook, silently, without even a whicker of protest, as though something deep within his great human-friend heart told him his only chance for continued life lay in making no sound. Only the breath came out of him like life leaving him. Marjorie felt it, as she always felt the least movement he made. She slid from his back in one fluid motion. Without going to the top of the rise, she knew what she would see there. Her stomach was in her throat, full of hot bile. She trembled as though half frozen. Still, one had to see. One had to know.

She pulled on the stallion's shoulder. He had been trained to lie down, and he did it now, almost gladly, as though his legs would barely hold him. She stroked him once, for his comfort—or her own—then crawled on shivering arms and legs away, up the rise a little to one side of the path so that she could look down through the fringing grasses without being seen.

And they were there. Three of them. Just as there had been three horses when she and Tony and Rigo had ridden here. Three Hippae doing dressage exercises, walking, trotting, cantering, changing feet to cross the arena on long diagonals. They did everything she had done with Octavo, did it casually, offhandedly, with a practiced ease, concluding with the three animals side by side, facing away from her, the saber tips of their neck barbs pointing at her like a glittering abatis, as threatening as drawn blades. Then they turned and looked up at the place where she was hidden, their dark eyes gleaming red in the light of dawn, soundless.

Amusement, she thought at first. A kind of mime. These Hippae had seen the humans and their horses and were amused at what these little off-world beasts had been doing with their human riders. She held the thought only fleetingly, only for a moment, trying to cling to it but unable to do so. They knew she was there. They knew she was watching. Perhaps they had timed this little exercise to coincide with her arrival. . . .

It wasn't amusement. Nothing in that red-eyed glare was amused.

She did not stay to confront what it really was. She fled from the ridge as one in fear for her life, down to where the stallion lay as though he had been felled, urged him onto his trembling legs, and then half lay on his back as they first staggered then ran away, back to Opal Hill, back to human country, to add another horror to those she already knew.

What she had seen in those red eyes was mockery—mockery and something deeper. Something abiding and unforgiving.

Malice.

James Jellico took himself home for lunch, as he often did, knowing his wife, Jandra, would be interested in the morning's happenings. Jellico's wife had no legs, and though she walked well enough on the elegant artificials he had obtained for her (a little bribery at the port, a little looking the other way when he was on customs duty), she said it pained her to use the legs. There were implants one could use for the pain, but Jandra, who often said she didn't like people fooling about with her head, preferred for the most part to wheel about the house in the half-person she had used since she was a child. About the house and the poultry yard as well. A third of the Jellys' income came from homely Terran geese and ducks along with Semling szizz birds and fat, delicious wingless things from the planet Shafne which Jandra called puggys.

He found his wife by the goose pen feeding greens to the geese, they gabbling and snatching grass fronds from one another and she humming to herself, as she did when content. "Ho, Jelly," she greeted him. "I've about decided to kill that one for dinner. She's so smug it serves her right."

The indicated goose succeeded in dragging the disputed shred of greens out of another's beak and swallowing it, at the same time tipping her head to one side to get a good one-eyed goose-look at Jelly. There was something in that cold, single-eyed stare, something in the line of beak and neck that shook him with a feeling which was at first déjà vu and then horrified recognition.

"That girl," he blurted. "She looked at me like that." Then he had to tell her all about the girl and Ducky Johns and how strange it all was. "And it looked at me like that, tipped its head like that, as though it could see me better out of one eye than out of both. Like an animal."

"Bird," corrected Jandra.

"Bird or animal," said Jelly patiently. "Any of 'em that don't have what-you-call-it. Binocular vision. They'll do that. Tip their heads to see you better."

"Why do you say 'it' when it was a girl, Jelly. Why don't you say 'she'?"

"Habit, I guess. With those from Portside, he's and she's would be wrong as often as they're right. They have he's that look like she's, and she's that look like he's, and it's that look like either. I just say 'it' about them all." He took the image file out of his pocket and put it in the imager, to show her.

Jandra shook her head, amazed at the ways of the world. She never tired hearing about them. Even simple things amazed her, though she was never shocked at the horrid ones. "I'll have to go down to Ducky's and see to this," she announced in a tone which allowed no contradiction. She peered at the image, looking at the creature's eyes. "It isn't right something human and helpless should be left down there. Was there something wrong with the girl's eyes?"

"Nothing I could see. Nothing wrong with any of it—her. Pretty, built nice, smooth hair and all. Just the face. Well, look at it."

"What do you mean about her face, Jelly?"

"Empty," he said after staring and thinking about it for a moment. "It looks just empty, that's all."

7

Some distance east of Opal Hill was a hidden cavern of the Hippae, one of many which could have been found on Grass if anyone had dared to look. Set deep into the hillside, its narrow openings shaded by great swaths of vermilion grasses which fell across the slender doors in gently moving curtains, the cavern was undergoing a periodic refurbishing. Arriving and departing at the northernmost slit were the creatures responsible, molelike migerers, diggers par excellence, scuttling now through the vermilion and the fuschia, out into the shorter, violet-colored grasses, their furry thigh-pockets full of loose earth recently scraped from the floor of the Hippae hall.

Inside that hall a shadowed emptiness was supported by pillars of rubbly stone, stones uncovered when the caverns were dug, each stone mortared into place with the adhesive which resulted from mixing migerer shit and earth. Marvelous creatures, the migerers—builders, almost engineers, certainly cave makers of no small talent who made similar, though smaller, caverns for themselves, each cavern linked to others by miles of winding tunnels.

In this great hall they blinked their squinty eyes, deep-pocketed in indigo fur, and chirped to one another in flute tones as they plodded across the cavern, scraping the high places into the low with urgent flat-edged claws, stamping the loose dirt down with the hard pads on their industrious hind feet.

A Hippae came into the cavern, striding on great tripartite hooves across the smoothed floor, quartering the cave again and again, nodding approval with his monstrous head, the teeth showing slightly where the lips drew back in a half snarl, the razorlike neck barbs making a dissonant clash as the beast tossed its head and bellowed at the ceiling.

The migerers affected not to notice, perhaps really did not notice. Nothing changed in their behavior. They still darted about under the very hooves of the prancing monster, scraping, packing, filling their furry pockets, and darting away into the grasses to dispose of this evidence of industry. Only when they were finished, when the floor was as smooth as their instinctive skills could make it, did they desist and fall to grooming round bellies and small tough feet, combing whiskers with curved ivory claws, blinking in the half light of the entrance slits. Then a whistle, a plaint on the wind as from some bird calling in mild distress, and they were gone, away, vanished in the grasses as though they had never been. In the cavern behind them the Hippae continued its slow parade, bellowing now and again to make the cavern ring, alone in majesty surveying and approving the work which had been done.

A second monster called in response, entering the cavern to begin a quartering of its own. Then came a third and fourth, then many, prancing in intricate patterns upon the cavern floor, interweaving and paralleling, twos and fours and sixes becoming twelves and eighteens, the files of them turning and braiding in complicated design, hooves falling as precisely as artisans' hammers into the tracks themselves had made.

Not far off, in Opal Hill village, Dulia Mechanic turned restlessly on her bed, half wakened by the subterranean thunder. "What, what's that?" she murmured, still mostly asleep.

"The Hippae are dancing," said her young husband Sebastian Mechanic, wide awake, for he had been listening to the rhythmic surge for an hour or more while she had breathed quietly beside him. "Dancing," he reasserted, not sure whether he believed it or not. Besides, he had something else on his mind.

"How do you know? Everyone says that, but how do you know?" she whined, still not awake.

"Someone saw them, I suppose," he said, wondering for the first time how that particular someone had seen what he claimed he had seen. Sebastian himself would rather face certain death than sneak around in the tall grasses, spying on Hippae. Without identifying the source, he murmured, "Someone, a long time ago," and went back to thinking what he had been thinking of for a long time now, about those at Opal Hill.

Out in the night, in the cavern where all the thunder came from, the Hippae moved their anfractuous quadrille along to its culmination.

Suddenly, without any sense of climax, it was over. The Hippae left the cavern as they had entered it, by ones and twos, leaving a pattern intricate and detailed as a tapestry trampled deep into the floor behind them. To them who made it, it had meaning, a meaning otherwise expressible only by a long sequence of twitches of hide and particular blinks of eye. The ancient Hippae language of gesture and quiver and almost undetectable movement was useless for this particular purpose, but the Hippae know another language as well. In the other language, learned long ago from another race, this design stamped deep into their cavern floor was their way of writing—and thereby giving notice of—a certain inexorable word.

In the stables at Opal Hill, the horses were awake, listening as they had listened many nights, most nights, since they had come to Grass. Millefiori whickered to the stallion, Don Quixote, and he in turn to Irish Lass next to him, the whispering rattle running down the length of the stalls and then back again, like a roll-taking. "Here," each seemed to say. "Still here. Nothing yet."

But there was something. Something they had begun to be more than remotely aware of. One of those shadows one shies at, one of those bridges one will not walk over. A thing like that, full of menace, which the riders usually do not understand. Most of them. The woman, she understood. She always understood. If there was a thing like that, she never insisted. Never. And in return, each gave her total trust. When she rode them at the high fence, the fence one could not see over, with no knowledge at all of what might be beyond, each one trusted that she would bring them safely down on the other side. They knew it as trust. She would not betray them, not one of them.

Not that they thought in words. They did not have the words. It was more an understanding of the way things were. The rewards, the threats. That thing out there on the ridge that day. This noise, moving in the night, this noise that tried to crawl into ears, into heads, to take over everything. These were threats.

But there was something else abroad in the night, and that ... that was something they could not identify as either a threat or a reward. It fought against the horrid noise; it kept the insinuating thoughts away. And yet, it came no closer, it offered no hay, it stroked no necks. It was simply there, like a breathing wall, a thing they did not understand at all.

So the whicker ran, left to right, then back again. "Here. Still here. All right. Still alive. Nothing. . . .

"Nothing yet."

Jandra Jellico did as she had threatened and went over to Portside in her half-person to visit with Ducky Johns. She'd met Ducky before and quite liked her, despite the business she was in, which Jandra didn't altogether approve of. Pleasure was pleasure, had been for ages, and people would seek it out. Some of the ways they sought it, though, in Jandra's opinion, were not quite tasteful.

Still, she made nothing of that as she sat in Ducky Johns' private parlor, sipping tea and staring at the girl who sat on the carpet, humming to herself. Itself. Whatever. When the girl got an itch, up came the skirt and the hand scratched, wherever the itch might be. No inhibitions at all, no more than a cat, licking itself where it needed it.

"My, my," Jandra said. "You can't keep her here, Ducky."

"Well, and who wanted to?" Ducky sulked, waving her tiny hands in circles to express innocent annoyance. "It was Jelly, your own Jelly, made me bring her back here. She's useless to me, dear. Can't sell her. Who'd want her? Needs to be trained before she's any use at all."

"Does she potty?" Jandra wanted to know.

"Except for eating, that's all she does, but potty she does. Like my wallo-pup, whines when she needs to go."

"Have you tried—"

"Haven't tried anything at all. No time. This business keeps me at it, day on day. No time for fooling with that!" The little hands waved again, then folded themselves into an obdurate lump buried deep in Ducky's lap. "Tell me you'll take her away, Jandra. Do say so. Anyone else, your Jelly would argue."

"Oh, I'll take her," Jandra agreed. "Or send for her, rather. But it's the strangest thing. The very strangest thing. Where'd she come from?"

"Wouldn't we like to know that, my dear? Wouldn't we all?"

Jandra sent for the girl that afternoon. Thereafter she spent a good part of several days teaching the girl to keep her skirts down and to eat with her fingers instead of burying her face in the food and to go potty by herself without whining. When she'd done that much, she called Kinny Few on the tell-me and invited her over, and the two of them sipped tea and nibbled at Kinny's seed cakes while they watched the girl playing with a ball on the floor.

"I thought you might know who she is," Jandra said. "Or who she was. Surely she hasn't always been like this."

Kinny thought hard about it. There was something in the tilt of the girl's head that reminded her of someone, but she couldn't say who. No one in Commons, that was certain. "She must have come in on a ship," she offered, having already been told that this was impossible. "Must have."

"I keep thinking so, too," Jandra agreed. "But Jelly says no. She was just there, on Ducky Johns' back porch, and that's it. Like she hatched there. No more memory than an egg."

"What are you going to do with her?" Kinny wanted to know.

Jandra shrugged. "See if I can find her a home, I guess. Pretty soon, too. Jelly's losing patience, having her around."

Actually, it was not Jelly's patience he was in danger of losing. Devotedly fond of Jandra though he was (and they two with an understanding about fidelity), the proximity of the girl's body, lovely and uninhibited as some half-tamed beast, was leading him to worrisome desires.

"A week," he told Jandra. "I'll give you a week." He thought he'd probably be able to control himself at least that long.

Rigo was determined to have a diplomatic reception. He was much encouraged in this by Eugenie, who was tired of the company of Opal Hill but who had no status which would allow her to go elsewhere. She could not even go to the Hunts. After the bon Damfels' Hunt the Yrariers had observed three other Hunts; twice as a family, once with Fathers Sandoval and James along as guests. It was quite enough, as Tony said, to know that they were all alike. They had declined to observe more, and by doing so had confirmed the bons' prejudice about them. By that time, however, Rigo had other things to think about. Some of the furnishings for the summer quarters had arrived along with Roald Few, who promised that everything would be completed in two weeks' time.

"Draperies, rugs, furnishings, image projectors for the walls—everything. Everything elegant and of the highest quality."

"Rigo wants to have a reception for the bons," Marjorie told him.

"Hmmph," snorted Persun Pollut.

"Now, Pers," chided Roald. "The ambassador doesn't know. During Hunt season, Lady Westriding, he's unlikely to get anybody but second leaders and lower. People who don't ride. Those who ride wouldn't even consider coming, don't you see?"

"We'd get Eric bon Haunser but not the Obermun?"

"That's right. You'd get nobody at all from the bon Damfels' except Figor. Obermum won't go anywhere Obermun doesn't. That isn't done. All the rest of the family rides, what's left of it."

Marjorie stared at him, evaluating the open countenance before her. The man seemed without guile, and thus far he had treated her fairly. "I need information," she said at last in a very quiet voice.

Roald dropped his own voice to a confidential level. "I am at your service, Lady Westriding."

"The bon Damfels were in mourning when we were there."

"Yes."

"They'd lost a daughter. In a hunting accident. Eric bon Haunser has lost his legs, also, so he said, in a hunting accident. When I looked about me after that first Hunt I saw more biotic appendages than I would have seen in a year at home. I would like to understand these accidents."

"Ah. Well." Roald shuffled his feet.

"There are various kinds of accidents," offered Persun in his soft, dry lecturer's voice. "There is falling off. There is getting oneself skewered. There is offending a hound. And there is vanishment." He said this last almost in a whisper, and Roald nodded agreement.

"So we understand, Lady. The servants at the estancias are kinfolk of ours. They see things; they overhear things; they tell us. We put two and two together to make forty-four, when we must."

"Falling off?" she asked. Riders fell off all the time. Rarely was it fatal.

"Followed by trampling. If a rider falls off, he or she is trampled into the grasses. Until nothing is left, you understand."

Marjorie nodded, feeling sick.

"If you've seen a Hunt, you've seen how a rider might get skewered. It doesn't happen often, surprisingly. The young ones ride simulators for days at a time, learning to stay out of the way of those horny blades. But still, once in a while someone faints or a mount stops too suddenly and the rider falls forward."

Marjorie wiped her mouth, tasting bile.

"Offending a hound usually results in the hunter having an arm or leg or hand or foot or two bitten off when he dismounts at the end of the Hunt."

"Offending . . . ?"

"Don't ask us, Lady," replied Persun. "There aren't any hounds in Commons. They can't get into town, and nobody with any sense goes far out into the grasses where hounds're likely to be. Close to the villages is fine, no hounds there, but farther out . . . those that go don't come back. We really don't know what would offend a hound. So far as we can tell, the bons don't know either."

"And vanishment?"

"Just that. Somebody starts out on the Hunt and doesn't come back. The mount disappears, too. Usually a young rider it happens to. Girls, usually. Rarely, a boy."

"Someone at the rear of the Hunt," she said in sudden comprehension. "So the others wouldn't notice?"

"Yes."

"What happened to the bon Damfels girl?"

"Same as happened to Janetta bon Maukerden last fall, her that Shevlok bon Damfels was so set on. Vanishment. The way I know is, my brother Canon is married to a woman who's got a cousin, Salla, and she's a maid at the bon Damfels. Practically raised Dimity from a baby. Last fall Dimity thought a hound was watching her, and she told Rowena. Next time out, same thing. Rowena and Stavenger had a set-to, and Rowena kept the girl from riding any more Hunts that season. This spring, Stavenger took a hand and made the girl go out again. First spring Hunt! Poof, she was gone."

"Dimity, did you say? How old was she?"

"Diamante bon Damfels. Stavenger and Rowena's youngest. Somewhere around seventeen in Terran terms."

"The bon Damfels had five children?"

"They had seven, Lady. They lost two others when they were young riders. Trampled, I think. I'm sorry not to remember their names. Now it's just Amethyste and Emeraude and Shevlok and Sylvan."

"Sylvan," she said, remembering him from the first Hunt. He had not been at any of the others they had witnessed. "But he wouldn't come to a reception, because he rides."

Roald nodded.

"There is the lapse," murmured Persun.

"I'd forgotten the lapse," said Roald in a tone of annoyance. "Here I am almost ten Grassian years old and I'd forgotten the lapse."

"Lapse?"

"Every spring there's a time when the mounts and the hounds disappear. Far's I know, no one knows where they go. Mating time, perhaps? Or whelping time. Or something of the kind. Sometimes people hear a great lot of baying and howling going on. Lasts a week or a little more."

"When?" she asked.

"When it happens. No exact time. Sometimes a little earlier in the year, sometimes a little later. But always in spring."

"But doesn't everyone on the planet know when it happens?"

"Everyone out here in the grasses, Lady. Tssh, in Commons we'd pay it no attention. Out here, though—yes. Everyone knows. If no way else, they go out to Hunt that day and no mounts or hounds show up. They know."

"So, if we sent an invitation, saying—oh, 'On the third night of the lapse you are invited to . . .'"

"It's never been done," muttered Persun.

"So, who's to say it shouldn't be?" Roald responded. "If your good husband is determined, my Lady, then it would be a thing to try. Otherwise, wait until summer when the hunting stops. Then you can have your reception among the summer balls."

Rigo did not want to wait until summer. "That's over a year and a half, Terran," he said. "We have to start getting some information from the bons, Marjorie. There's no time to wait. We'll get everything ready and send the invitation as soon as the place looks decent. Undoubtedly I'll hear from bon Haunser if we've overstepped some barrier of local custom."

The invitations were dispatched by tell-me to all estancias. Surprisingly, at least to Marjorie, acceptances were prompt and fairly widespread. She got a bad case of stage fright and went up into the summer rooms to reassure herself.

The chill rooms had been transformed. Though still cool, they glowed with color. From the greenhouse in the village—which had been half ruined until Rigo had ordered it rebuilt—had come great bouquets of off-world bloom. Terran lilies and Semling semeles combined with plumes of silver grass to make huge, fragrant mounds reflected endlessly in paired mirrors. Marjorie had provided holo-records of valued artworks the Yrariers had left behind, and duplicates of the originals glowed at her from the walls and from pedestals scattered among the costly furniture.

"This is a beautiful table," she said, running her fingers across satiny blue-shadowed wood.

"Thank you, Lady," said Persun. "My father made it."

"Where does he get wood, here on Grass?"

"Imports much of it. Much though they talk of tradition, now and then the bons want something imported and new. Things he makes for us, though, he cuts from the swamp forest. There are some lovely trees in there. There's this wood, the one we call blue treasure, and there's one that's pale green in one light and a deep violet in another. Clume wood, that is."

"I didn't know anyone could get into the swamp forest."

"Oh, we don't go in. There's a hundred miles of forest edge, and these are trees that grow at the edge. Even so, we don't take many. I'm using some native woods in the panels for your room." He had spent hours designing the panels for her study. He longed for her to praise them.

"Are you, now," she mused. Outside, on the balustraded terrace, a slender figure passed restlessly to and fro: Eugenie. Forlorn. Childlike. Head drooping like a wilted flower. Marjorie fingered her prayerbook and reminded herself of certain virtues. "Will you excuse me a moment, Persun?"

He bowed wordlessly, and she left him there while he tried to give the appearance of not staring after her.

"Eugenie," Marjorie greeted her with self-conscious kindness. "I've seen very little of you since we arrived." She had seen nothing of her at home, but this was a different world and all comparisons were odious.

The other woman flushed. Rigo had told her to stay away from the big house. "I shouldn't be here now. I thought I might catch a ride into town with the merchant, that's all."

"Something you need?"

Eugenie flushed again. "No. Nothing I need. I just thought I'd spend a day looking at the shops. Maybe stay at the Port Hotel overnight and see the entertainment. . . ."

"It must be dull for you here."

"It is bloody dull," the woman blurted, speaking before she thought. She flushed a deep, embarrassed red, and her eyes filled with tears.

This time Marjorie flushed. "That was tactless of me, Eugenie. Listen. I know you're not one for horses or things like that, but why don't you see if they have some kind of pets for sale in Commons?"

"Pets?"

"I don't know what they might have. Dogs, maybe. Or kittens. Birds of some kind, or something exotic. Little animals are very amusing. They take up a lot of time."

"Oh, I have so much of that," Eugenie cried, almost angrily.

"Rigo . . . well, Rigo's been very busy." Marjorie looked out across the balustrade of the terrace toward the multiple horizons of that part of the grass garden called the Fading Vista. Each ridge partly hid the one behind, each one was a paler color than the one before, until the horizon hill faded into the sky almost indistinguishably. She was amused to make a mental connection: In such fashion had her original animosity toward Eugenie faded, retreated, become merely a hazy tolerance almost indistinguishable from tentative acceptance. "We'll be having our first official party soon. Perhaps you'll meet some people. . . ." her voice faded away like the horizon line before her. Who could Eugenie meet, after all? The children despised her. The servants thought her a joke. No one among the bons would associate with her. Or would they?

"There are particular people I want you to meet," Marjorie said thoughtfully. "A man named Eric bon Haunser. And Shevlok, the eldest son of the bon Damfels."

"Trying to get rid of me?" Eugenie said with childish spite. "Introducing me to men."

"Trying to assure that you have some company," Marjorie said mildly. "Trying to assure that we all do. If some of the men find you fascinating, you and Stella and maybe me—though that wouldn't do to admit officially—perhaps they'll frequent the place. We're here to find something out, after all."

"Don't talk as though I knew anything about it. I don't. Rigo didn't tell me anything!"

"Oh, my dear," said Marjorie, more shocked than she could admit even to herself. "But he must have! Why would you have come, otherwise?"

To which Eugenie merely stared at her, eyes wide and wondering. This woman married to Roderigo Yrarier, this woman, his wife, mother of his children, this woman . . . She didn't know? "Because I love him," she said at last, almost whispering. "I thought you knew."

"Well so do I," Marjorie replied shortly, believing that she did. "But even so, I would not have come to Grass had I not known why."

Though Eugenie had not particularly appreciated Marjorie's advice about pets, she had heard it. Normally she would have ignored it as a matter of principle because it came from Rigo's wife and Rigo would be unlikely to appreciate his mistress taking his wife's advice about anything. As it was, however, Eugenie could not afford to ignore anything that would alleviate the blanketing boredom which afflicted her. At home there had been restaurants and parties and amusing places to go to. There had been shopping and clothes and hairdressers to talk with. There had been gossip and laughter. And running through all that, like a thread of gold through the floating chiffon of her life, there had been Rigo. Not that he'd been around a lot. He hadn't been. But for a long time he had been there, in the background, providing whatever she needed, making her feel treasured and important. Men such as he, Rigo had explained, with all his important work on committees and clubs and such, needed women such as she as a necessary relief from the tiresome but urgent works they were called upon to do. This made women such as she especially important. Eugenie thought of this often. Men had told her many sweet things about herself, but never before that she was important. It was the nicest compliment she had ever received.

And so she was here, and so was Rigo, and for all they saw of one another she might as well have stayed on Terra with some other protector—which she had, quite truthfully, considered. Had there been another man immediately available, she would probably have chosen to stay. Weighing the relative inconvenience, however, of finding a new man or submitting to packing and coldsleep, she had decided that finding the new man would be more trouble. Not so much finding him but learning about him. His little ways. His favorite foods and smells and colors and little magics in bed. All men believed they had their own magics in bed.

And then, too, she did love Rigo. When she had said that to Marjorie, it hadn't been a lie. Of all the men she had loved, she probably loved Rigo most. He had been most fun.

But Rigo was hardly fun at all in this place. When love wasn't fun, it was just boring and dull and achy. People had to have things that were fun for them. What Marjorie had said about pets was probably the best advice anyone was going to give her, even though it had come from Rigo's wife.

Eugenie begged a ride from Roald Few to Commoner Town, enjoying the trip because of all the sweet things he and the other men said to her. It was Roald himself who told her to look up Jandra Jellico. "If you're looking for something little and petful and fun to have, Jandra may have it or she'll know who has. She's got most everything in fur and feathers and pretty skin, Jandra does." He warned her, too, that Jandra would be in a half-person, as though Eugenie was the kind of person to make unkind remarks or stare.

And Jandra, after Eugenie had been with her for half an hour, knew everything about her just as Roald had. Knew and appreciated and felt a bit sorry for, while at the same time blessing her guardian spirits that Eugenie had come along just now to solve her dilemma.

"I've got just the thing for you," she said. "Something I got from Ducky Johns, down in Portside. Wasn't right Ducky should keep it down there among the sensees and the profligates, so I had her bring it here to me. I keep it in the spare bedroom."

She brought it out, the slender prettiness of it, the long-haired sweetness of it, the sidling, goose-eyed gaze of it, all done up in girl skin and girl smell and dressed in a pretty smock which it had learned to keep down. "I call her the Goosegirl," said Jandra, not saying why. Eugenie wasn't an awl-eyed one like Jandra's own dear Jelly, to see what others hadn't noticed, that almost mindless, birdish stare turned on each and every one as though to ask the world what there was to be afraid of out there, knowing already in its little bird mind that there was something.

"It's a girl," said Eugenie, uncomplaining, but definite. "Not an animal."

"Well there's one opinion and another about that," said Jandra, squeezing the end of her nose between her fingers as she did sometimes while puzzling out the ethics of a situation. "It doesn't know its name. It can't dress itself. It is potty trained, for which I'm more than grateful, so there's one small thing making it better than a puppy, which I haven't one of nor nobody else I know, so no matter. It'll sit brushing at its hair for the better part of a day, and it has a good appetite for most anything you'd eat yourself and I've halfway taught it to eat with a spoon. Sometimes it makes a noise as if it was about to say something. Not often, mind you, and it surprises itself when it does."

"You should say 'she,'" corrected Eugenie. The pretty thing was as female as she herself was, and very much of her own size.

"Well, there's one opinion and another about that, too. Still, I'd be inclined to agree with you, and I call her 'she' to myself, don't you know. It's a playful bit of a thing, too. Likes to roll a ball back and forth or play with a bobble on the end of a string."

"Like a kitten," purred Eugenie. "Do you suppose they'll let me keep her?"

Well, and if they wouldn't, it would be their problem, Jandra thought, not her own, which the Goosegirl had been up until now, her or it of the pretty hair and lovely little body and sweet face without two notions to jostle one another in her head. Last evening she'd seen Jelly looking at the girl in that certain way, and no time would be too quick to get rid of her, ethics or no. Still, if Eugenie had been someone else—Marjorie Westriding, say—Jandra would have felt uncomfortable giving her the Goosegirl as a pet. Someone like the Lady Westriding—Jandra had heard all about her from Roald Few, as had every other person with normal hearing—would dig and dig, puzzle and puzzle, making the poor creature's life a misery. And one couldn't give it to some man to use, though one would, rather than have Jelly doing the using.

Eugenie, though. Well, she wasn't a debauchee and she didn't look the type to go seeking causes or laying blame. She would not abuse the creature, nor wonder where the girl had come from or what brought her to Portside to be found under Ducky Johns' clothesline. She would see only a girl-sized walking doll, something with pretty hair to arrange, something to clothe and play with. As for Jandra Jellico, it looked the best thing she would be able to do for the Goosegirl and far better than she had recently feared.

One of Roald Few's workmen took Eugenie and her new pet back to Opal Hill, dropping them behind the Fading Vista from which

Eugenie was able to reach her own little house without being observed. Eugenie already had a dozen plans for Goosegirl. One of them had to do with teaching her to dance, but first and second on the list had to do with the sewing of astonishing gowns and the selection of a new and utterly elegant name.

Marjorie tapped at the door of Rigo's study and entered at the sound of his voice. "Am I too early?"

"Come on in," he said, his voice fuzzy with fatigue. "Asmir's not here yet, but I expect him momentarily." He stacked some papers together, thrust them into a lockbox, keyed the box to hold, and turned off his node. In the corner of the room the tell-me swam with wavering bands of color, silent. "You look as weary as I feel."

She laughed, unconvincingly. "I'm all right. Stella is on one of her usual tears. Some time ago I asked Persun to take her down to the village, thinking she could find someone there to share her time with. She's been there once or twice and refuses to go back. She says they're all provincials, ignorant as cabbages."

"Well, that's probably true."

"Even so—" she started to say, intending to make some comment about pride, realizing just in time that it would annoy Rigo, "Tony says not. He finds companionship there."

"Stella may find some kindred spirit at the reception."

Marjorie shook her head. "No one Stella's age is coming."

"We invited families."

"No one Stella's age is coming," she repeated. "It's almost as though they'd decided not to allow any . . . any fraternization."

He flushed angrily. "Damned hidebound . . ." His voice became a wordless snarl to which the knock at the door was a welcome interruption.

A servant announced the arrival of Asmir Tanlig, who had spent the time since his hiring inquiring here and there about illness on Grass. Who had died, and of what? Who was suffering, and from what? Who had gone to the doctors at Commons, and for what. Now he plumped his small square body down across from Roderigo and Marjorie, his round face puzzled, his mouth pursed, his precise little hands shuffling his papers, preparing to tell them what he had found.

"I'm not finding much, sir, madam, to tell you the truth. With the bons it's pregnancy and hunting accidents and liver renewals because of all the drinking they do." He wiped his lips on a clean handkerchief and lowered his already confidential voice as he leaned across Rigo's desk where the lamplight pooled in the dusk. "I've told my family in Commons to ask around, has anyone disappeared—"

"Vanished," murmured Marjorie. "We *know* they have."

"Yes, ma'am, except if you're talking about hunting, the vanished ones are mostly young. The ambassador told me . . ."

"I know," she murmured. "I just wanted to keep it in mind."

"As we shall," said Rigo. "What about the non-bons, Asmir?"

"Oh, it's everything. Accidents and allergies and in Portside there are always a few killings. Everyone accounted for, though; no disappearances except for those who've gone into the grass or the swamp forest."

"Ah?" asked Rigo.

"Of course that's always gone on," said the man, suddenly doubtful. "For as long as I can remember. People going into the swamp forest and not coming out. People getting lost in the grass."

"Who?" asked Marjorie. "Who, lately?"

"The last one was some big braggart of a fellow from off-planet." Asmir referred to his notes, written neatly in a tiny, meticulous hand on various scraps of paper, which he arranged and rearranged as they spoke. "Bontigor. Hundry Bontigor. Loud mouth, people said. Swagger. Full of dares and boasts. Someone dared him to go into the swamp forest, and he went. Didn't come out. He was only here on a weeklong permit, between ships. Nobody missed him much."

"Has there been a case in which someone disappeared and it was . . . merely *assumed* that the person had gone into the forest?" Marjorie ran pinching fingers up the bridge of her nose and across her forehead, trying to evict the headache that had settled there.

Asmir shuffled his notes once again. "Last ones, before Bontigor, were kids. Nobody saw them go in there, if that's what you mean. Time before that . . . well. Time before that was an old woman. Kind of gone, if you take my meaning. People couldn't find her, so they thought—"

"Ah," said Marjorie.

"Then there was that couple over at Maukerden village. And the carpenter from Smaerlok. And here's somebody from Laupmon—"

"Lost in the grasses?"

He nodded. "But that's always happened."

"How many?" asked Rigo. "How many do you have listed, within the past collect? No, that would have been winter. Say last fall. How many assumed lost in the swamp forest or the grass last fall?"

"Fifty," estimated Asmir. "Fifty or so."

"Not many," murmured Marjorie. "It could be what they think it is. Or it could be ... illness."

Rigo sighed. "Go on, Asmir. Keep gathering. Get everything you can about disappearances—who disappeared, how old they were, whether they seemed healthy before they went, things like that. Is Sebastian helping you?"

"Yes, sir. I gave you his information along with mine."

"Keep at it, then, both of you."

"If you could tell me—"

"I told you what I could when I hired you, Asmir."

"I thought ... I thought perhaps you didn't trust me then."

"I trusted you then and now." Rigo smiled, one of his rare and charming smiles. "I told you I'm taking a special census for Sanctity. It has to do with human mortality. I've told you quite lot about about Sanctity and how it tries to keep track of the human race, so you can understand why Sanctity would be concerned with what people die of. But the aristos won't allow Sanctity to have a mission on Grass, so Marjorie and I agreed to find out what we can. However, we're not going to offend the bons, so we'll do it quietly. All we want to know is if there is any unexplained mortality on Grass."

"If anybody mortals in the swamp forest, you'll never explain it," Asmir said firmly. "If they mortal in the grasses at night, it's probably foxen. You've seen foxen?"

Marjorie nodded. She had seen foxen. Not close enough to describe, but quite as close as she cared to come.

"You've seen more'n me, then," he said, lapsing into a less portentous style. "But I've seen pictures."

"I take it you don't go out into the grass?"

"Oh, sir, no! What kind of flick bird do you take me for? Oh, daytimes, yes, a little way, for a picnic or a romantic walk, say. Or to get away by yourself for a bit. But that's what village walls are for, and estancia walls too. To keep them out."

"Them?" queried Marjorie, gently.

He told the roll of them, words that clanged like the toll of a knell as his awestruck voice invoked incipient funerals out of each one: "Peepers. The thing that cries out in the deep night. The great grazers. Hounds. Hippae. Foxen. All them."

"And no one really goes far into the prairie?"

"People say the Green Brothers do. Or some of them. If so, they're the only ones that dare. And how they dare, I wouldn't know."

"The Green Brothers," mused Rigo. "Oh, yes. Sanctity's penitential monks. The ones digging up the Arbai city. Sender O'Neil mentioned the Green Brothers. How would we go about reaching them?"

Rillibee Chime, robed in unfamiliar green, his tear-streaked face unpowdered, crouched behind Brother Mainoa in a little aircar as it scuttled bouncily northward. "Can you tell me where we're going?" he asked, wondering whether he cared. He felt hag-ridden and nauseated, unsure even of his own identity, he who had always fought so hard to keep it.

"To the Arbai city I've been digging," said Brother Mainoa comfortably. "Some ways north of here. We'll stop there for a day or two, let you get to feeling better, then I'll take you on up to the Friary. I'm supposed to bring you directly there, but I'll tell 'em you were sick. Soon as you get to the Friary, either Jhamlees Zoe or the climbers'll be after you, and there's nothing I can do about that. So, best you be feeling well when we get there."

"Climbers?" Rillibee asked, wondering what on all this great, flat prairie there was to climb.

"You'll learn about them soon enough. Not much I could tell you. They started their nonsense long after I was young enough to take part in it. You'll feel better sooner if you lie down, you know. Lie down for a little bit and when we're out of this wind, I'll let the tell-me drive while I get you some broth."

Rillibee let his crouch sag into a slump, the slump into a prostrate misery full of gulpings and more silent tears. Ever since they had wakened him from coldsleep he'd had these nightmares, these horrid feelings, this insatiable hunger.

"What did you do to get sent to us?" Brother Mainoa asked. "Tear one of the angels off Sanctity and sell it to the Pope?"

Rillibee sniveled, finding this funny in a sodden way. "No," he managed. "Nothing quite that bad."

"What, then?"

"I asked questions out loud." He reflected. "Well, I screamed them, really. In refectory."

"What kinds of questions?"

"What good it would do to have us all listed in the machines when we were all dead. How reading our names in empty rooms gave us immortality. Whether the plague wasn't going to kill us all. That kind of questions." He sobbed again, remembering the horror and confusion and his own inability to control what he was doing.

Ah." Brother Mainoa struggled with the controls, grunting as he punched buttons that did not seem to want to stay punched. "Fouled up houndy uselessness," he muttered. "Damned shitty mechanics." At length the controls responded to being whacked with the palm of his hand and the car settled upon a level course. "Broth," he said calmly and comfortingly, smiling down at Rillibee. "So you asked about plague, did you?"

Rillibee didn't reply.

After a time the older man said, "We'll have to come up with a name for you."

"I've got a name." Even in the depths of his present depression he bridled at the thought that he could not keep his own name.

"Not a Friary name, you don't. Friary names have to be made up out of certain qualities." Brother Mainoa whacked the cooker with the flat of his hand, scowling at it. "Twelve consonant sounds and five vowels, each with its own holy attribute."

"That's nonsense," mumbled Rillibee, licking tears from the corner of his mouth. "You know that's nonsense. That's the kind of thing— That's what I was asking in refectory. Why so much nonsense?"

"Got too much for you?"

Rillibee nodded.

"Me, too," said Brother Mainoa. "Except I didn't ask questions. I tried to run away. You were probably a pledged acolyte too, weren't you? How long were you pledged for?"

"I wasn't really pledged. They took me, is all, when . . . well, when I didn't have anyplace else to go. They said twelve years and I could do what I wanted."

"Me, I was pledged for five years, but I couldn't get through them. Just couldn't. My folks pledged me from my fifteenth birthday. By age seventeen I was here on Grass, digging up Arbai bones, and I've been here since. Penitent as all get-out. Ah, well. Maybe if I'd been a little older." He took the steaming cup from the cooker. "Here, drink this. It really will help. Elder Brother Laeroa gave me some years ago when he fetched me from the port, though he was only young Brother Laeroa then, and I've given some to a dozen since then. It always seems to help. You'll be hungry all the time for a long time, then eventually it'll taper off. Don't know why. Just part of bein' on Grass. You can tell me about yourself, too. More I know about you, easier it'll be to help you out."

Rillibee sipped, not knowing what to say. "You want the story of my life?"

Mainoa thought about this for a time, his face adopting varying expressions of acceptance and rejection before it finally cleared. "Yes, I guess I do. Some people, I wouldn't, you know. But you, I think so."

"Why me?"

"Oh, one thing and another. The way you look. Your name. Now that's an unusual name for one of the Sanctified."

"I never was one of them. They just took me, I told you."

"Tell me more, boy. Tell me everything there is to know."

Rillibee sighed, wondering what there was to know, remembering, unable not to remember.

The house in Red Canyon had thick adobe walls, mud walls that stayed warm at night and cool in the day. The walls crumbled a little in the winter snow and when it rained, so that every summer Miriam and Joshua and Song and Rillibee had to spend most of a week putting more adobe on and smoothing it out and letting it dry. Inside the house the floors were tiled. One floor was red and the one in the next room was green, one was blue, the next one had patterns in the tiles. Song taught him to play hopscotch on the tiles in his bedroom, and there were dark and light ones in front of the fireplace, little ones, about two inches across, where Joshua and Miriam played checkers. The checkers were made out of clay, too, with leaves pressed into the tops so the pattern stayed after the leaves burned away. Miriam fired them in the same oven she fired the floor tile in, the funny old brick kiln out back, the one that pulled the fire in from the front.

There were three bedrooms, a little one each for Rillibee and Song-bird and a big one for Joshua and Miriam. Sometimes Rillibee called them Mom and Dad and sometimes he called them by their names. Miriam said it was all right, because sometimes he meant to talk to his Mom or his Dad and other times he just meant to talk to somebody named Miriam or Joshua.

The kitchen was a big room and the common room was bigger yet, with a painting of Miriam over the fireplace and two big, squashy couches. There were old, old Indian rugs on the floors and a table where they all ate supper. Mostly they ate breakfast in the kitchen.

Joshua's shop was off to one side, with a cellar partly under it and partly under Rillibee's room. Joshua used the cellar to store the wood he would turn into tables and chairs and cabinets after it had seasoned. There were power tools in the shop and Miriam's potter's wheel and a big door along the creek side that stood open all summer long.

The low, earthen bulk of the house and shop stretched along Red Creek beside monstrous old cottonwoods that dangled their leafy branches over it, green in summer, heartbreak gold in the fall. Miriam called it that. Heartbreak gold. So beautiful it made you catch your breath when the sun came through, like the touch of the hand of God. Miriam said a lot of things like that, old-fashioned kinds of things. Even her name was old-fashioned. A really antique name, from a long, long time before.

His father, too. Joshua. That was an antique name for you. Even the things Joshua and Miriam did were old-fashioned things, things nobody else did—woodworking, pottery, gardening, making things with their hands, growing things in the soil.

In between making stuff or growing stuff they were always taking Rillibee and Songbird out to show them something or other, a flower or a crawdad or a fish. There were lots of fish in the creek. There were deer in the canyon. There were sage chickens and wild turkey on the rimrock, way up there. "This is one of the few places on earth that man hasn't made garbage out of," Joshua said sometimes, pointing up the canyon. "Live in it. Watch out for it. Take care of it. Every springtime move out to the front edge of it and plant something that will live longer than you do."

Joshua and Miriam had been doing that for twenty years, ever since Joshua came back from Repentence, planting things every spring. Up the canyon along Red Creek the trees were old and big. Joshua's grandfather had planted those. Orchards stood below the house, apple and cherry and plum, trees four times as tall as Joshua, clouds of blossoms in the spring. Joshua's father had planted the fruit trees. Then came the groves Joshua had planted, young conifers, shorter and shorter ones as they reached the edge of the green belt Joshua and Miriam had made. Beyond the green was the gray, flat land: dry soil specked with knapweed and thistle and thorny brush, cut by the dusty knife edge of the road. Down that road was the town and the school, a Sanctity town and a Sanctity school. Rillibee's folks weren't Sanctified, but they sent Rillibee to school there anyhow. It was closest, and besides the things Joshua and Miriam taught him, he needed to learn the things a school could teach. School was only a mile away, easy to get to most of the year. Once in a while they'd be snowed in for a week or so, but that was rare. Sometimes Rillibee brought kids home from school with him, but that was rare, too. Mostly they thought he was strange.

Their parents all worked in comnet cubicles at their apartments, or they worked in one of the technical centers along the surface route. They went back and forth on covered walkways. If they needed to go very far, they had hovers. Joshua and Miriam had donkeys, for cries sake. Donkeys. It was enough to make Rillibee's schoolmates chop themselves into pieces laughing about the earthfreaks who ate food they grew themselves and wouldn't use dirty words and wore funny-looking clothes. Rillibee never heard the word earthfreak until he was in fourth category. Then he thought he'd never hear the end of it.

Rillibee minded more than Song did. She had a boyfriend who belonged to another earthfreak family over in Rattlesnake, and the two of them got along fine. Jason was his name. Another old-time name. Jason used some bad words, but never in front of Joshua. That's one thing Joshua was death on, bad words, and when he was around, Rillibee was careful not to say any.

"Why'd you call me Rillibee?" he complained to his mother after one particularly bad day at school when everyone was busy making fun of him for his name and his clothes and his folks. "Why Rillibee?"

"It's the sound the water makes running over stones," she said. "I heard it the night before you were born."

How could you yell at somebody over that? She just stood there, smiling at him, taking hot cookies out of the oven, piling them onto a plate for him, getting him a cup of the milk she'd put in the stream to cool. "Rillibee," she said, so that he heard the water sound in it. "Rillibee."

"The kids at school think it's funny," he muttered, mouth full.

"I suppose," she agreed. "They'd think Miriam is funny, too. What are they all called now? Brom. And Bolt. And Rym. And Jolt."

"Not Jolt."

"Oh. Excuse me. Not Jolt." She was laughing at him. "They all sound like laundry sonics."

He had to agree they did. Bolt sounded like something that would shake the donkey hair out of your socks. Jolt sounded even more so.

One day Joshua brought a parrot home. It was a small gray parrot with some green feathers on it.

"What on earth?" Miriam asked. "Joshua?"

"Those cabinets I built for the Brants, you know?"

"Of course I know."

"He really liked them. He gave me the bird as a bonus."

Miriam shook her head, annoyed. Rillibee knew she was thinking about the mess the bird would make. "Wanted to get rid of it, most likely."

Joshua put his hands in his pockets and stood there, looking at the bird where he'd set it on its perch at one side of the fire. "He said it was valuable."

Miriam was looking at the bird with her lips tight together as though she wanted to say something nasty.

"Shit," said the bird clearly. "Excrement." Then it shit on the floor.

Miriam laughed. She couldn't help herself. She was all bent over giggling.

Joshua was red in the face, mad, not able to say a thing.

"Well, he certainly talks," Miriam said.

"I'll take him back! Right after supper."

"Oh, for heaven's sake, Josh, leave him. We'll teach him some better language. You know, the bird doesn't know what he's saying. It isn't as though there's a brain there, telling him to talk dirty. He's just imitating sounds he hears."

"He didn't hear that!"

"Sounds he remembers."

So they'd kept the parrot. It never learned any nicer words about anything, though it didn't talk much; but every time Miriam got mad and acted like she'd like to say something but couldn't, darned if that bird didn't. Rillibee noticed it right away. Every time Miriam got really mad, here was the parrot saying "Shit" in this dreamy voice, or "Dammit" or once, "Fuckit." Joshua hadn't heard that one, 'or there'd probably have been a dead parrot.

Rillibee moved into the fifth category when he was eleven, becoming a five-cat before most of his age-mates. That hadn't made them any easier to get along with. His mentors were old lady Balman and old man Snithers. Balman taught programming and information. Snithers taught retrieval skills. The older kids in five called her Ballsy because, so they said, she had more than Sniffy did. Rillibee had no idea what that meant until he asked Joshua, and then he got about an hour's lecture on sexuality as metaphor in dominance. The truth of it was that Snithers was an old lady, all fussy and picky, while Balman had a fine the-hell-with-it attitude that all the kids liked, which was more or less what Joshua said only in different words.

There had been one particular day, an unremarkable day, with nothing much happening at school except that Wurn March told them goodbye because he was going to Sanctity for five years as a pledged acolyte. Wurn had looked confused about it. When they asked him if he wanted to go, he'd looked like he was about to cry.

Out in the corridor, Ballsy told Sniffy that Sanctity could have him and welcome, and then they both laughed and got red when they saw that Rillibee had heard them talking. He'd been on his way back from the toilets, and they sent him back to retrieval practice in a hurry. Rillibee agreed with Ballsy that nobody would miss Wurn March. Wurn had been in five for longer than he should have. He was larger than most of the boys, and louder, and he liked to hit smaller kids, and he always borrowed stuff and didn't give it back.

Other than that happening, it was just a day. It was the first day Rillibee had ever heard about pledged acolytes, but it was just a day.

When he got home, Miriam was in the kitchen, as usual at that time of afternoon. There were a lot of good smells in there with her, and Rillibee threw his arms around her, for once not caring what anybody else thought. She was his mom and if he wanted to hug her, so what.

So what happened was she gasped and pulled away. "Ouch," she said, smiling so he'd know it wasn't his fault. "I've got a sore place on my arm, Rilli. You kind of whacked it when you grabbed me."

He had been sorry, insisting on examining the sore place, which looked terrible, all gray and puffy. Joshua came in behind him and looked at it, too.

"Miriam, you'd better go to the Health Office about that. It looks infected."

"I thought it was getting better."

"Worse, if anything. You've probably got a splinter of something in there. Have it seen to." Then Joshua kissed her and the parrot said, "Oh, hell," which set everyone off, and that was all.

The next afternoon when Rillibee got home, Songbird was there but Miriam wasn't. Song was looking for the cake Miriam had baked the night before and hidden from them.

"Where's Mom?" he wanted to know.

"She went to the Health," his sister reminded him, burrowing in the cold cupboards.

He nodded, remembering. "When'll she be home?" He wanted to tell her about Wurn March and what the teacher said and ask her about pledged acolytes.

"When she's finished, dummo," Song said. "You ask the dumbest questions." She opened the side door and went outside to peer down the road.

Rillibee followed her. "You wanna hear a dumb question? When are you going to grow up? That's a dumb question, 'cause the answer is never."

"Brat," she said. "Dumb little brat. Still suck your thumb."

"Stop it," Joshua said, coming across the yard from his workshop. "The two of you! Song, there's no excuse for talking like that. I don't want to hear another word out of either of you. Song, go in and set the table. Rillibee, go pick up that junk you left scattered all over the common room last night. Put the rug back down, too. I'm going to start supper so your mother won't have to do it when she comes home."

There was quiet then, quiet for several hours. Rillibee remembered the quiet as a prelude to what happened later. Much later that quiet came to stand for tragedy, so that he would be uncomfortable with too much tranquility, too much silence. The evening sun slanting into the living room through the tall windows made pools of gold on Dad's wide-planked floor and on the castle Rillibee had built the night before. He destroyed it and all its battlements, picked up the pieces, packed up his warriors, and put the rug back down, taking time to comb out the fringes with his fingers so they laid straight, like soldiers. Above him, on the perch, the parrot shifted. Rillibee looked up at it, and it whispered, "Oh, damn. Damn. Oh, God. Oh, no." It sounded almost like Miriam's voice.

Time went on until the sunlight vanished and his stomach gave an unmistakable signal. He went to the kitchen to find his father and Song waiting and Mom not home.

"It's time to eat," he complained.

"So, we'll eat," his father said in a worried voice. "Your mom wouldn't want us to wait for her. She's been held up or something."

They were just sitting down at the table when the door-signal went. Somebody coming through the gate. Dad got up and went to the door, a smile on his face. Rillibee relaxed. She probably had stopped to buy groceries. Or sometimes she took a sample of her pottery to someone she thought might like to buy it. It was probably something like that that had kept her so long.

But the voice at the front door wasn't Mom's voice. Somebody loud, a man, demanding to know where she was.

"Miriam hasn't come home yet," Joshua said firmly. "We don't know." Then he exclaimed in anger as the man pushed past him and came on into the house. "What do you think you're doing?"

"Looking," the man said. He was a big man. Bigger than Dad.

Dressed in a white uniform with a mask thing around his neck and a green insignia on his shoulders. "Get on with your dinner, kids," he instructed them. "I'll only take a moment." And he went through into the kitchen, then back into the bedrooms. Rillibee heard the closet doors opening and closing, then the man went out the front door and around into the shop. They could hear him banging around out there. Rillibee put down his fork very carefully, looking at his dad, so pale all of a sudden.

When the man came out he stood in the yard for a while, looking around, then he came back to the front door and asked Dad to come out. He talked quietly out there, but Rillibee could hear words, single words, "authority" and "penalty" and "custody."

Rillibee fell silent.

Brother Mainoa waited awhile, then said, "They talk like that, don't they. People who get to tell other folks what to do. Full of powerful words, they are. Sometimes I think they have words where most of us have blood."

Rillibee didn't say anything.

"Hard for you to talk about?"

Rillibee nodded, gulping, unable to talk at all.

"That's all right. Wait until you feel better, then tell me."

They flew, the car bouncing a little on the sun-warmed air. After a time, Rillibee began to tell it again.

Then the big man was gone and Dad was in the common room, sitting down at the table once more, his face like a rock, all frozen and hard.

"Dad?"

"Don't, Rillibee. Don't ask me anything right now. The man was looking for your mother and she's not here. That's all I know right now."

"But who was he?"

"A man from Health."

"Oh, damn. Oh, God," the parrot said.

Joshua threw a soup spoon at the parrot. It made a splashy red place on the wall and fell on the floor. The parrot just looked at them, its black eyes swiveling back and forth as it whispered to itself.

The man didn't come back. Mom didn't come home. Dad paced

the room, stopping every now and then to punch up people on the comnet. People Mom knew. Her sister over in Rattlesnake. Her friends. People like that.

When bedtime came, Rillibee looked out of the window of his own room to see the hover parked out on the flat. The man was watching the house. After a long time, Rillibee got into bed, dark all around him, trying to see through it to the ceiling, to the walls, only a splinter of light under the door. Tears. Trying to be quiet so Song wouldn't hear him through the wall. Finally, sleep.

It had to have been sleep, because he woke up to a strange noise. Scratching, near his head. From under him, under his bed. Under the floor.

He thought about monsters first, not daring to move. Only after it had gone on for some time did he remember the cellar that Dad used to store wood in. A long time ago it had been a root cellar. Joshua had dug it bigger so it extended all the way to the shop. The entrance to it was out there in the shop, behind the woodstacks, but there was a hatch to it under Rillibee's bed, from long ago. Someone was in there, scratching.

He slipped out of the bed and went to tell Joshua. Then he kept still while Joshua moved the bed, a little at a time, almost silently, and heaved the doorway up and it was Mom down there, white and pale, with her face all streaked and her hair tangled and messy and her clothes dirty as though she'd been crawling, and she was saying, "Josh, oh, God, Josh, they were going to send me away, they were going to send me away, and I went out the window. I ran and ran. I crawled down the creek and came in through the little door behind the shop. Hide me, don't let them get me, Josh."

"Never, darling," he said. "Never."

Silence again.

Mainoa said, "Your father must have loved her a lot."

"I've never forgotten that," Rillibee said, his voice liquid and bubbling in his throat. "I think about it at night sometimes, when I'm trying to sleep. I hear their voices. I remember how confused I was. Why had someone wanted to get her? Why had the people wanted to send her away? What had she done? She and Joshua didn't tell me. They didn't tell Song. All they had said was to pretend she hadn't come home. Just pretend they hadn't seen her. . . ."

Mom went to bed in her own bed, with Dad. The next morning, real early, Rillibee had wakened to some unfamiliar sound, something happening on the road. He peeked out at the corner of the shade and saw the man getting out of the white hover, out beyond the baby trees. He woke Dad and Mom just in time. She barely had time to get back down in the wood cellar and have Rillibee's bed moved back on top of the hatch.

"Lie down there and look sleepy," Dad commanded on his way to answer the thunder at the door.

Rillibee put his head under the pillow and told himself he was dreaming. The man from Health stamped in and pulled the pillow off, but Rillibee managed to look confused and angry as though the man had wakened him.

After that, Mom slept in the cellar. Dad moved a cot down there and a special kind of toilet he put together in the shop, one that didn't need water. During the daytime, she came up whenever there was somebody there to watch for the man in the white hover, but if there was no one home, she had to hide.

Joshua bandaged the place on her arm. It was just a little place. About the size of a peach pit. By the end of the week, it had gotten quite a bit bigger, covering the whole elbow. It hurt her, too. Then it began to spread up and down her arm until the whole arm was raw and ugly, like meat. It hurt her to change the bandage, but if it wasn't changed, it started to smell. They changed the bandage every night. Song held the basin with warm water in it, to wash the raw place. Rillibee handed Dad the bandages. The parrot sat on its perch saying, "Oh, damn, damn. Oh, God," but none of them paid any attention.

The man came back. Once he brought two other men and they searched the house, but they didn't find the place under Rillibee's bed. By this time, Joshua had made the hatch almost invisible, fitting the wood together so you couldn't see where it joined.

Once in a while, she'd come up in the daytime, while Song and Rillibee were at school. At night, when she came up, she'd tell them what she'd done, where she'd walked. "The leaves are turning," she'd say. "Did you notice, Rillibee? Heartbreak gold. God, they're so beautiful." Then they talked about what they'd have for dinner the next night. She'd tell Joshua what to buy and how much. She'd tell Songbird how to cook it and Rillibee how to help. Then they'd talk awhile, maybe play a game, then change the bandage last thing and she'd go back down.

The bad night was when they were changing the bandage and some pieces came off. Mom made a noise, as though she was going to throw up, as though she was going to scream but couldn't get enough air.

"Out," Joshua said to both of them, pointing to the door, his face stretched into some horrible grin, like a pumpkin lantern, the sides of his mouth wide open and tight with all the teeth showing.

They ran into the kitchen. Song was crying and making a little grinding noise, trying to hold it in, and Rillibee was telling himself it was a dream, a bad dream, it wasn't really happening at all. He had seen the bones in Mom's hand, where the two fingers had come off, two round, white, slick things. The place wasn't bleeding, just kind of oozing, slow drops of grayish liquid pushing out from the flesh and running down to make a small stained place on the clean bandages that stank like nothing he could ever have imagined. The smell had settled in the back of his throat as though it would never leave.

After that, Dad wouldn't let either of them be in the room when he changed the bandage. After a while, he wouldn't let them be in the room with her at all. They could still hear her voice. For a while she sounded just like Mom. Once even they heard her laugh, a high, dreadful laugh. Then, after a while, there was no voice, just this high, whiny sound like a dog that'd been hit by a car, or a rabbit when a hawk takes it.

And the smell. Every night, rising at him out of the cellar below him. A terrible stink. Worse than any bathroom stink.

"Oh, oh, no," said the parrot. "Oh. God. No."

Dad changed rooms with Rillibee. Days went by and Rillibee never really saw her after that. He lay there in Dad's bed at night, trying to remember what she had looked like. He couldn't remember. He wanted to see the picture of her, the one over the fireplace.

In the living room, he turned on one lamp and looked up at the picture. She smiled down at him, out of the paint, her shiny hair falling over her forehead, her lips curved.

"Let me die," whispered the parrot. "Oh, please, please, let me die."

"Shut up," Rillibee screamed at it silently, the words pushing out of him like huge, burning pieces of vomit. "Shut up, shut up."

He told himself he wouldn't go in there anymore. He wouldn't listen to that bird anymore. He ate in the kitchen. He did his school-work. He didn't ask any questions. He didn't talk about Mom.

"That must have been hard," said Brother Mainoa. "Oh, that must have been hard."

"I couldn't stop thinking about her. I couldn't. Her face would come into my mind, but then it would turn gray at the edges, starting to curl, like a picture burning, and I couldn't see what she looked like, couldn't remember what she looked like. I stood it as long as I could, and then went into the living room once more to look at the painting of her.

"The parrot said, 'Kill me. Please, please, kill me.'"

It was the day after that, Rillibee's twelfth birthday, that he woke up knowing it had all been a dream. The sun poured through his window, heartbreak gold. He got up and dressed and plunged out into the living room. The parrot was walking up and down its perch saying, "Thank God. Thank God. Thank God."

Song was already there, sitting at the table. There was a package wrapped at his place. He sat down and grinned at it, turning it over and over, shaking it to guess what was inside.

"Happy birthday, Rillibee," Dad said from the kitchen door. "I'm making pancakes." His voice sounded funny, but the words were all right.

"Happy birthday, Rillibee," said Song. She sounded like a record-ing.

Dad came in with a pitcher of juice and leaned over the table to pour it.

There was a sore on the side of Dad's neck, toward the back. Little. The size of a peanut. Like the sore had been on Mom's arm. When Dad went back to the kitchen, Rillibee tried to tell Song, but Song just sat there, frozen, not saying anything at all. Then he noticed the bandage on her hand and wondered how long it had been there without his seeing it.

He got up without opening the package and went out of the house, through the orchard to the groves, and down through all of them, the trees getting tinier and tiner the farther he went, until he came to the place where there was nothing growing at all. . . .

"Did you ever see them again?" asked Brother Mainoa.

There was a long silence. Rillibee was staring out the window, mouth slightly open, tears washing his face. "I went crazy in school and started yelling something. That night when I got home, there was no one there. Just the man from Sanctity, who said to come along with him. I was going to be an acolyte, he said. They never said anything about Miriam or Joshua or Song. When I asked, they told me my people had died a long time ago, that I'd just forgotten. They never even asked if my family was Sanctity. We weren't. I'm still not."

Brother Mainoa sipped at his own broth, occasionally slapping at a control button that kept threatening to disengage itself. "Brother Lourai—how does that sound?"

"How should it sound?"

"Well, the *l* sound is for patience, and the *r* sound is for perseverance. I thought you could use a little of that."

"What does the *m* sound in Mainoa mean?" Rillibee asked tiredly. "And the *n*?"

"Resignation," murmured the other. "And reliability."

"Rebellion, did you say?"

"Shush, youngster. Lourai's a good name. You should hear some of the throat-stoppers Acceptable Doctrine comes up with from time to time. Fouyaisoa Sheefua. How would you like that? Foh-oo-yah-ee-soh-ah Shee-foo-ah. Or Thoirae Yoanee. You wouldn't want something like that hung on you. Lourai. That's good enough."

"What's acceptable doctrine?"

"Acceptable Doctrine?" Brother Mainoa asked. He took the empty cups away and put them down the recycler. "Well, if you'd been a little older before they dragged you off to Sanctity, you'd have learned what the Office of Security and Acceptable Doctrine is. That's the group of enlightened ones who tell us what we can believe and what we can't and make sure we do it. Here on Grass they're headed up by Elder Brother Jhamlees Zoe, with Elder Brother Noazee Fuasoi as his next man."

"Like the Hierophants," cried Rillibee. "God, I wish I could get away from that."

"You can. Just walk off the site into the grasses, any day. Put your shovel or your soil stabilizer down and go. Nobody'll come after you. I could've done that lots of times, but I always knew there'd be something interesting in the next shovelful, something intriguing behind the next bit of wall, so I don't. All in all, I'm glad to be here rather than there. Maybe you will be, too. Just bow your head and say, 'Yes, Elder Brother,' in a nice obedient tone, kind of sorrowful, and they'll let you alone."

"How can you do that?" Rillibee asked scornfully. "It's dishonest."

Brother Mainoa seated himself at the controls once more, scanning the dials and buttons with a skeptical eye. "Well, now, young Brother Lourai, I'll tell you. I'll deny having said it if you quote me, so don't try. The first thing you've got to do is tell yourself that the shitheads are wrong. Especially Jhamlees and Fuasoi. Not just a little bit wrong, but irremediably, absolutely, and endemically wrong. Nothing you can say or do will stop their being wrong. They're damned to eternal wrongness, and that's God's will. You follow me?"

Rillibee nodded, doubtfully. Whatever he might have expected, it had not been this.

"Then, you acknowledge that these wrongheaded fart-asses have been placed in authority over you through some cosmic miscalculation, and you reach the only possible conclusion."

"Which is?"

"Which is you bow your head and say 'Yes, Elder Brother,' in a nice humble tone, and you go right on believing what you have to believe. Anything else is like walking out into the grass when the grazers are coming by. You may be right, but you'll be flat right and there won't be enough left of you to scrape up."

"And that's what you do?"

"Umm. And you do it, too. Don't tell Elder Brother Jhamlees Zoe that your family wasn't Sanctified. You tell him that, he'll start working on your head, getting you to convert, get saved, get enrolled. Just nod politely and say, 'Yes, Elder Brother.' That way, likely, he'll leave you alone."

There was a long silence. Rillibee—Brother Lourai—rose from the padded floor and settled himself into the other seat. When Brother Mainoa showed no signs of breaking the quiet, he asked, "What's Arbai?"

"An Arbai, Brother, was the inhabitant of an Arbai city, dead some long while, now. An Arbai city is the only kind of ruins mankind's found on any world we've settled yet. The only intelligent race we've ever found."

"What were they like? Arbai?"

"Taller than us. About seven feet tall. Two-legged and two-armed, like us, but with a skin all covered over with little plates or scales.

We've found bodies pretty well mummified, so we know what they looked like. They were fascinating people. Like us, some ways. Spread all over a lot of worlds, like us. Had writing, like us, not that we can read it yet. Not like us at all, other ways. Didn't seem to have males and females like we do, at least there's no differences we've found yet."

"All gone, are they?"

"All gone. All died, everywhere, all sort of at once, like time had just up and ended for them. Except here on Grass. Here they all died from something tearing them apart."

"How do you know?"

"It's how we find 'em, Brother. An arm here, a leg there. A bone raggedy from teeth."

"What are you looking for?"

"Something to tell us why they died, mostly." Brother Mainoa looked at him curiously. "From what you say, you've seen plague, haven't you, Brother. You know it exists."

The other nodded. "They never told me so, but that's what killed my family. And the Hierarch died of it. Lots of the people at Sanctity have it. I may have it, without knowing it."

"Well, there's some of us think that's what killed the Arbai. Better tell you now, it's not Acceptable Doctrine; so don't go talking about it."

"Killed them," breathed Rillibee. "Going to kill us."

"Ah. Well, there is that. Maybe not, though. If we could find out something. . . ."

"Do you think we can find out anything about the plague?"

The other turned, the wrinkles around his eyes made deeper by the speculative squint with which the Brother was evaluating his new family member. "What I think," he purred, "is something you and I may talk about someday after you've been out in the grass." He pointed downward. There, spread across the short turf of the north, were the uncovered walls of the Arbai city and the complex network of ditches dug by the Brothers, some of them roofed with arched bundles of tall grasses. Mainoa pointed again, in the direction of their flight. Almost on the horizon, the ramified mass of the Friary bulked darkly against the pale sky. As they drew nearer, Rillibee/Lourai sucked in an astonished breath. Above the Friary floated a city of cobwebs, netted arches, and skeletal towers that moved in the light wind as though they were living things rooted in the soil far below. From some few of the lofty pinnacles flew the banners of Sanctity, complete with golden angels. On seeing these, Rillibee Chime gave one last, dwindling snarl.

"Home," said Brother Mainoa. "Not a bad place, really. Though the sky climbers will probably make paste of you for a few weeks. Heights frighten you, boy?"

"Falling frightens me. Heights don't."

"Well then, I'd say you'll survive it."

"What are sky crawlers?" Rillibee's stomach knotted at the picture this brought to mind.

"Boys no older than you, most of 'em. Most likely they won't harm you much. You'll get by; that is, you will if you can apply a few sensible restraints to your conduct."

"Yes, Brother," said Brother Lourai, his eyes cast humbly down. "I will try to restrain myself."

8

Before Rigo had a chance to meet the Green Brothers, a morning came when the tell-me shrilled news of the lapse. The bon Damfels had assembled for the Hunt, but no hounds or mounts had appeared. Salla, one of Roald Few's informants, had sent word to Commons and Roald had messaged Opal Hill.

Long-set plans moved into action. The embassy swarmed with cleaners and cooks, readying for the evening three days distant when the awaited reception would occur.

In the little house, Eugenie bit through a thread and bid her docile pet turn a quarter turn to the left. No one else at Opal Hill had seen Pet yet. And no one anywhere would have ever seen her like this.

At the bon Damfels', Stavenger ticked off the list of those who would attend. Shevlok, yes. Sylvan, yes. No one younger than Sylvan. None of the young cousins. Shevlok would be ordered to pay putative court to the *fragras* girl, Stella, and that would solve that problem.

In Commons the musicians went over their music and instruments, the wine merchant checked his stores, the extra cooks rolled their knives in their aprons. Aircars began to dart toward Opal Hill.

At bon Smaerlok's estancia, and at bon Tanlig's, at all the estancias, the grown women went through their ball gowns, deciding what to wear, while their daughters sulked. None of the young women were going, it had been decided. Too dangerous. Only older women, women with good sense, women with a number of liaisons behind them. Several of them had been picked to flirt with the Yrarier son, several good-looking, experienced ones. Whatever else might occur as the result of Sanctity's embassy reception on Grass, an inappropriate liaison with a young Yrarier was not going to be allowed. So said the elder bons.

And at Opal Hill Roderigo Yrarier went over the list of those who would attend, noting the absence of young people and simmering at the insult offered to his family and his name.

Obermun bon Haunser had remembered his promise to Marjorie when he had recommended Admit Maukerden as her "secretary." When she first got around to interviewing the tall, self-important individual, he told her that he knew every bon in every family and who the parents were and what the liaisons had been and who was in sympathy with and who out of sorts with whom. He expected, so he said, a private suite and a salary which made Rigo blink in surprise.

"I don't trust him," Marjorie told Rigo.

"Nor do I," Rigo confessed. "But hire him anyhow. Assign him something to do and let's see what he comes up with."

After a little thought, Marjorie asked Admit to compile a file on those who would attend the reception, giving family connections and such personal information as might be helpful to new acquaintances in conducting conversation. He spent a great deal of time at it for one who supposedly knew them all, presenting the final work with a flourish.

Marjorie thanked him with a smile which conveyed nothing but ignorance and appreciation. She and Rigo then gave the file to Persun Pollut.

"Oh, my lame left leg," Persun muttered. "That fool doesn't know a cousin from an aunt or a bon Maukerden from a bon Bindersen."

"Not accurate?" she queried sweetly.

"Except for the Obermums and Obermuns, there's hardly a thing here that's not plain wrong. He'd of done better guessing. If you'd done any introductions on the basis of this, the bons would have had your bones for supper."

"Which would indicate either monumental stupidity or purposeful misinformation." Rigo grinned through clenched teeth.

"He's intelligent enough in his own interest," Marjorie responded.

"Then he was instructed to be useless," Rigo said. "More than useless. Destructive. Which, I think, tells us all we need to know about him and a good bit more about them."

Thereafter, Marjorie pretended to consult Admit Maukerden from time to time and Rigo amused himself by giving the man false information about the purpose of the embassy, waiting to see which parts of it would come back to him, in whatever guise, via the bons.

Meantime, Persun corrected the file on the guests and went over it with Rigo's trusted assistant, Andrea Chapelside. It was Persun who set down accurate details about the bons. "This one is more important than he looks," he said. "This one is malicious and will misquote you."

And it was Persun, dressed in servant's livery, who was assigned to circulate among the guests to hear what he could hear. Admit Maukerden, splendidly costumed to fit his idea of his own importance, would be relegated to a post near the first surface from which he could announce the arrivals with a fine and completely spurious air of authority, separated by a thwarting distance from anything that might transpire in the rooms above him. Though Marjorie doubted that anything of consequence would happen, Rigo had faith that something of great importance would follow his enormous investment of time and attention.

The evening arrived. Aircars dropped swiftly to the gravel court to disgorge their bejeweled and ornamented riders, rising as swiftly to make room for those that followed. Marjorie and Stella, gowned as extravagantly as any of the bons—the dresses had been stitched by a whole family of Commons' seamsters nominated by Roald Few—

waited at the top of the stairs that the bons would have to ascend, Marjorie on Rigo's arm, Stella on Tony's.

Rigo had foreseen problems and had communicated them fully to the children. "They are not bringing anyone your age. They will not be so undiplomatic or ungracious as to exclude you from their attention, however. You may expect charm and flattery from some of them. Stella, some man or men. Tony, some woman or women. Be charming in return. Seem flattered. But do not be fooled! Do not lose your heads."

Seeing Tony pale and Stella flush angrily, Marjorie had nodded agreement and said soothing words. She had been warned by Persun Pollut as well, who had heard it from a villager who had heard it from a cousin at bon Maukerden's. "They want no real contact, Lady. They want no involvement. They have told off some of their family members to pay court to you and yours, but they will do it merely to keep you pleased with yourselves."

"Why?" she asked. "Why do they reject honesty?"

"Some of them would reject nothing. Some might say welcome if they thought about it. Eric bon Haunser, maybe. Figor bon Damfels, maybe. Some like that. But the Obermuns, the hunters, they say no. They say they came to Grass to get away from others, foreigners. They call you *fragras*. That is what they say, but I think what they feel is fear. And if you look for fear, look there, among the hunters."

Asked why the bons should feel fear, he didn't know. It was only a feeling he had, he said, and he couldn't say why.

"Why do they fear us?" she had asked Rigo.

"Fear us? Nonsense," he said angrily. "It is pure pride with them, pride in their fabulous ancestries—fabulous in every sense, for their nobility is more fable than reality. Sender O'Neil told me about their origins. The fool may not have had much right about Grass, but he did know where the bons came from. Their ancestors were minor nobility at best, and not much of that. They can't go on pretending to be important unless they've got something to be important about. When they came here, they brought along plenty of common folk to lord it over, you'll notice, and they've spent the generations since they arrived feeding one another puffery about their histories."

Marjorie, who had seen among the aristocrats certain twitches of skin, wrinklings around eyes, and pursings of lips, all unconscious, believed that Persun was right. What the bons felt was fear, though the bons might not understand what it was they feared.

Still, whether it was pride or fear that moved them made no difference in their behavior. They arrived as Persun had said they would, in order of their importance, a lot of small fry first: fourth and fifth leaders with their ladies, cousins, and aunts mincing up the stairs as though the treads were hot, old singletons like aged bulls, swinging their heads from side to side to feel their horns. As Admit Maukerden bellowed their names; Andrea, hidden in an alcove, looked each one up and recited the commentary into her whisperphone. *"This one is a Laupmon cousin, thirty-four Terran years. She is childless, and she still rides. The next one is an aunt of the Obermum. Fifty-two Terran years. No longer rides."*

Primed by Andrea's voice, which buzzed in their ears with an insect hum, the Yrariers responded appropriately to each of their guests with charm or pure formality or even frosty coolness to those so chilly they would resent anything else. "So glad you could come," they murmured, noting each detail of dress or feature and connecting it with the name humming in their ears so they would not forget to be wary of this one or that one as the evening wore on.

"Good evening. So very glad you could come."

On the balcony above the largest reception room, musicians played. A dozen villagers hastily trained and tricked out in livery circulated with glasses, putting on the fine air of pomp and disdain which Stella had suggested to them. "What you must convey," she had told them, giggling, "is that it is better to be a footman at Opal Hill than to be Obermun anywhere else."

"Stella!" Rigo had expostulated.

"It's all right, sir," Asmir Tanlig had said. "We understand the young lady right enough. She wants us proud enough to shame the bons."

And so they were to the last man, bowing like grandees as they offered their trays of glasses, their bits of tasty food, their sotto voce directions to the ladies' or the gentlemen's retiring room, along the balcony, near the musicians. The guests stood or sat or wandered, examining each bit of furniture, each set of drapes, some with a slightly discontented air. Little enough there for them to find fault with unless they found fault with themselves. Similar furnishings were found in every estancia. Similar images on the walls. Similar arrangements of flowers. Not so well done, perhaps, but similar. Too similar to cavil at, though one or two made the effort. "So ordinary," they said. "So everyday. One would think, coming from Sanctity . . ." As though they would not have belittled anything that had breathed of Sanctity.

"Good evening. How very glad we are to meet you."

Now the seconds and thirds were beginning to arrive. Eric bon Haunser with Semeles bon Haunser on his arm. "A *cousin*," said Andrea's voice. "*At one time said to have been Eric's lover. She will attempt to seduce Tony, or failing that, the ambassador.*"

Was there a quaver in Andrea's voice at the thought of anyone seducing the ambassador. Was it amusement, perhaps? Gray haired Andrea, who knew Rigo as though he were her own younger brother. Who knew all about Eugenie. Amused? Tony flushed as he bowed over the hand of Semeles bon Haunser. Stella snorted, and Marjorie bit back a cheerless giggle as she smiled and bowed in her turn as Figor took her hand.

"*Figor bon Damfels, younger brother of the Obermun. He has been instructed to flirt with Lady Westriding. Shevlok bon Damfels. He will pay court to Stella, though unwillingly, for he is still grieving over Janetta bon Maukerden. Sylvan bon Damfels. As usual, no one knows what he is up to.*"

Marjorie's placid voice adressed the bon Damfels' sons. "Good evening. How nice to see you both again."

"Good evening, Lady Westriding," said Sylvan, bowing. "It is kind of you to have planned this amusement for us. We have talked of little else for days." Smiling at Marjorie, at Stella, manfully clapping Tony on the shoulder, bowing slightly to Rigo. All this charm. In comparison, Shevlok was a poor player, able to muster only a muttered compliment, a sidelong glance, more cowed than seductive. Unconvincing, Marjorie thought. Damned loutish, Stella seethed. Unhappy Shevlok.

"Obermun Stavenger bon Damfels. Obermum Rowena bon Damfels."

Now the firsts were beginning to appear and Andrea's whisperphone was silent. The Yrariers already knew what was common knowledge about the Obermuns, the Obermums.

"Obermun Kahrl bon Bindersen. Obermum Lisian bon Bindersen. Obermun Dimoth bon Maukerden. Obermum Geraldria bon Maukerden."

"Good evening. We are honored to welcome you."

"Obermun Gustave bon Smaerlok. Obermum Berta bon Smaerlok. Obermun Jerril bon Haunser. Obermum Felitia bon Haunser."

"Good evening. Good evening."

"Obermun Lancel bon Laupmon."

"*Alone,*" whispered Andrea. "*Recently widowed.*"

Then, at last, one final man and an old, old woman in a mechanical chair. "Obermun Zoric bon Tanlig. Obermum Alideanne bon Tanlig."

"*She is the Obermun's mother and the eldest among the first leaders,*" whispered Andrea. "*She is always the last to arrive.*"

Now the Yrariers could follow the music and the smell of food, down a half flight from the long, chilly hall. Marjorie advanced into the ballroom, was swung into the dance by Rigo. Stella and Tony followed. They had practiced these antique steps under the watchful eye of a dancing master sent from Commons and they now swayed across the floor as though they had danced in this remarkably intimate fashion all their lives. The dance was called a valz. From here and there about the floor couples of the bons joined them on the floor, not so many as to look enthusiastic but not so few as to appear impolite.

"We are being put in our place," Marjorie said, smiling into Rigo's face.

"They can only do it if we appear to notice it." He smiled in return, flames of fury at the backs of his eyes.

They turned to other partners. Rigo allowed no opportunity for snubs. Though he was complimentary to all the bons, he asked no woman to dance who had not been ordered to approach him. Thanks to Persun, he knew who those were. As did Tony.

"Pretend it is an Olympic event," Marjorie had told her fretful son. "If you do it right, you will get a medal. Treat your partner as you would a willful horse, gently but firmly. It is only athletics, after all."

And so Tony danced and smiled and tried to flirt, though he had had sadly little practice at it. Stella was far better at it than he, anger only increasing her vivacity.

Marjorie drank fruit juice, provided discreetly by Asmir Tanlig, and chanted to herself as she sometimes did when duty bade her do things she did not want to do. "Bow, smile, be led into the dance. Smile, flirt, talk of nothing much. Flirt, charm, be led back to your chair. Charm, bow, begin again." The partners came and went, in relays. She began to long for a real drink, a real conversation.

"Will you dance with me, Lady Westriding?" Sylvan spoke, appearing from somewhere behind her.

She almost sighed with relief. Sylvan was not supposed to be one of those she had to be wary of. She went into his arms as to a refuge, not fleeing precisely, and yet not holding herself aloof. He led her gently, as though she were a hooded bird, accustoming her to his movements until they seemed to dance almost as one. She thought fleetingly of her advice to Tony, and was amused. Around them other couples circled, a little silence falling as bons whispered to one another. Sylvan was always interesting because he was not predictable. Look—Sylvan! Sylvan bon Damfels. . . .

Perhaps it was the quiet that drew Rigo's attention. He was on the balcony, standing at the entrance of the gentlemen's withdrawing room as he saw Marjorie circling in Sylvan's arms and felt his lip lift in a familiar snarl. She danced with the young bon Damfels as though he were an old and valued friend. Or a lover.

He struggled to control his face. He could not snarl or curse as he sometimes did when he saw her contented like this, moving in some exercise of horsemanship or dance or merely walking in the garden. There was an expression on her face at certain times, an expression of unconscious joy which came from a part of her he had always coveted, a separate being he never saw when he was with her. He had seen that being in the arena or the hunt, skimming the green pastures toward the high fences, all there between the posts and over the water, winging on danger and delight, a bird soaring with a singing face. He wanted to hold that bird.

He had wooed Marjorie and won Marjorie, but he had never gained possession of the thing he'd wanted. Seeking her soul, he had taken only her body, finding there a hollowness he had not expected, a vacant citadel he could storm again and again to no effect. In his bed she became someone else, someone dressed in childlike gowns, filmy white, sprigged with blossoms, her body fragile and boneless, her eyes focused far away on something he could not see. He had used every skill with her he knew, and some he invented for her alone, but she never came from Rigo's bed looking as she looked now, dancing with Sylvan bon Damfels, lost in movement and pleasure, eyes half closed, lips curved up in that gentle smile he had thought, once, would be his alone.

Andrea's voice in his ear, secret as a mole. "*Persun says your absence is being noted.*"

He smiled and went down from the balcony, looking for women's faces he could notice particularly, women's bodies he could admire with a significant glance, hinting something, promising nothing. It was all a game, a game.

And below him, Sylvan left Marjorie and turned to Stella with conscious gallantry. Marjorie took yet another glass of fruit juice from a tray offered by Asmir Tanlig and stood beside Geraldria bon Maukerden to join in witty admiration of the ladies' gowns, embroidered and beaded in fantastic designs. This, too, was a Grassian game, with its own language, its own etiquette. Persun had researched it and taught it to her.

Rigo swung past her in the dance, smiling like a mannequin at her over his partner's shoulder.

Beyond them, through the door to the terrace, Marjorie saw Eugenie. Had anyone been appointed to dance with Eugenie? What bon? Any bon at all? Perhaps she would have to beg Sylvan to dance with her husband's mistress. Though perhaps Shevlok would do so without prompting. He was near the door, looking out at Eugenie where she stood with someone.

With a girl? But there were no girls, no young women present. Except Stella, and Stella was dancing with Sylvan. Marjorie, possessed by a premonition of trouble, put down her glass.

Eugenie and her friend came through the terrace door, Eugenie clad all in rose, her gown fluttering behind her like sunset cloud, and the other one in a similar gown, violet as shadow, hair piled high, walking behind Eugenie with Eugenie's own half-gliding gait, head turned to one side so that she looked across the room with an odd, one-eyed glance, sidelong. . . .

A strange silence fell. Someone stopped talking and stared. Someone else's eyes followed the first stare. A couple stopped dancing. The music went on, but the people slowed, like moving toys that had run down, slowly, stopping.

Eugenie was halfway across the room, moving toward Marjorie. She would not go to Rigo, not publicly, she knew enough for that. She knew her public role was to be merely one of the group, a guest of the embassy, invited to participate in this gaiety. She smiled, holding out her hand as her companion passed the man near the door. . . .

And Shevlok screamed as though his heart had been torn out.

"Janetta!"

Eugenie glanced behind her uncertainly; then, seeing that her companion followed still, she came on again, her face collapsing in doubt.

"Janetta!" Now the woman beside Marjorie, Geraldria bon Maukerden, cried out that name.

And uproar. At Marjorie's side, Geraldria dropped her glass. It splattered into tinkling shards on the floor. The music faltered. Shevlok and Geraldria were both moving, like sleepwalkers, toward the girl, the strange girl.

Dimoth bon Maukerden was shouting, and Vince, his brother, and then others. The strange girl was surrounded, seized, though she did not react. She was passed from hand to hand, passive as a rag doll, looking toward Eugenie as though all her mind resided in the other woman, ending in Shevlok's arms.

"What have you done to her?" It was Sylvan, beside Marjorie, demanding. "What have you done?"

"To Eugenie?"

"To Janetta. To the girl."

"I never saw her before this moment!"

"That woman who has her. What did *she* do?" And when Marjorie shook her head helplessly, he went on, "Find out, quickly, or we will all be throwing dead bats at one another."

Marjorie had no time to ask him what he meant. And then Rigo was there, and were confronting Eugenie, who was crying and disclaiming any fault and making it hard for them by babbling but telling them nothing, nothing they could use against the mounting anger all around them.

"You filth, you *fragras*," trumpeted Gustave bon Smaerlok. "What have you done to Janetta?"

"Silence," bellowed Rigo, his voice shattering the other voices. "Silence!"

Then there was a little cup of quiet into which Eugenie's voice splashed like the thin cold juice of a bitter fruit. "I got her in Commoner Town," wailed Eugenie, "I got her from Jandra Jellico. All I did was make her a dress and fix her hair. She was just like this when I got her...."

Some few of the gathered aristocrats perceived that she was telling the truth, as much truth as she knew. Eugenie was as open as a child, weeping, not sure what it was she had done to make all this uproar. She had meant it as a surprise, bringing her pet to the ball. She had thought it would be fun.

"I told you we should stay far from this filth," trumpeted Gustave once again, red of face, spittle at the corners of his mouth.

Rigo was in front of him. This could not be allowed to pass. "Filth?" he snarled. "What kind of filth allows their daughters to fall into such a state, for others to find, for others to rescue and clothe and feed? Hah?"

"Rigo!" Marjorie called, moving between the two angry men. "Obermun bon Smaerlok, we do no good to call one another names. You are all very upset. So are we."

"Upset?" Dimoth cried. "My daughter!"

"Hear me!" Rigo thundered. "When did you see her last?"

There was silence, silence as each one contemplated an answer to that question. It had been— It had been last fall. Early last fall. She had disappeared last fall. No one wanted to say, to admit it had been that long ago.

"We heard of her disappearance," Marjorie said. "It happened long before we ever left to come here. Before you had even given permission for us to come."

The words hung there, unimpeachably true. Janetta had gone long before these people had come. Janetta, now standing at the middle of a small circle, dancing by herself, humming, lovely as a porcelain figure and as unpersonal. Nothing in her face or glance spoke of a person being there. In the circle around her was Shevlok bon Damfels, no longer clinging to her.

"It is not Janetta," he sobbed.

"Of course it is."

"Don't be silly, man."

"This is my daughter!"

"Not Janetta," he repeated. "No. No. This person is older."

"She would be," cried Geraldria. "She would be older, Shevlok."

"And not the same. Not the same."

Who could argue that? This creature was not the same as anyone. It turned to examine them with its odd, goose-eyed gaze, circling, as though to see if anyone had anything to interest it, some grain, perhaps, some bread. The moist, pink mouth opened. "Hnnngah," it cried, like a kitten. "Hnnngah."

Now there were quieter voices asking Eugenie again where she had found the girl, how long she had had the girl. Now there was movement among the bon Maukerdens, Obermun and Obermum, sisters and cousins, brothers and nephews.

Vince bon Maukerden, hotheaded, poised before Rigo. "No matter when she vanished. It was here she turned up, like that! How do we know it was not you who did it to her?"

"You," hissed Gustave from nearby, "who have not even the courage to ride with us. It is the kind of thing a *fragras* would do."

"For what reason?" asked Marjorie in a loud, mild tone. "It is simple enough to learn the truth. Ask the people in Commoner Town."

"Commoners!" sneered Gustave. "They have no honor. They would lie!"

And then movement of the crowd as they bore the strange girl away.

Some went then. Shevlok. The bon Maukerdens. Gustave and his Obermum. Others stayed. Of those who stayed, it was the bon Damfels who stayed longest, who went over and over the story Eugenie had to tell. Sylvan, particularly, who asked again and again, "Did she say anything, Madame Le Fevre? Ever? Any word? Are you sure?" To which Eugenie could only shake her head no, and no, and no. Pet had never said anything at all.

It was only later that Marjorie realized why Sylvan had been so intent. Dimity bon Damfels had vanished in the hunt as Janetta bon Maukerden had vanished. If Janetta had emerged in this fashion, might not Dimity still be found alive, somewhere, somehow?

Though there were no physicians among the bons, there were doctors in Commons. None of the aristos had ever lowered themselves to study the professions, but no such pride had prevented various commoners from flying off to Semling for a few years, returning with extensive educations. There were also no architects or engineers of any kind among the bons, but most kinds of technical expertise could be found in Commons. So it was from Commons that Lees Bergrem came to examine Janetta bon Maukerden—Dr. Lees Bergrem, head of the hospital.

A maidservant saw it all, heard it all, told a brother who told someone else who told Roald Few.

And Roald told Marjorie. "Dr. Bergrem put a thing on her head, to measure what was going on in her brain. And there was nothing, no more than a chicken."

"Will she be able to learn again?"

"Dr. Bergrem doesn't know, Lady. It seems so, for Miss Eugenie had taught her to dance, you know? Taught her to hum a song, too. It seems she will be able to learn. Dr. Bergrem wanted to take her back to the hospital, but Geraldria bon Maukerden wouldn't hear of it. Foolish, that woman. Dr. Bergrem studied on Semling, she did. And on Repentance, too. She's written books about her discoveries here on Grass. There's those who've been through here who say she knows more than many doctors, even those back on Terra."

Marjorie, ever mindful of her duty to learn everything possible about Grass, ordered copies of Dr. Bergrem's books to be facsimile transmitted from Semling Prime.

The tell-me hummed with the story. Janetta bon Maukerden, found alive. Of all those who had vanished over the years, she was the first to be found alive. First and only, and yet what hope this sparked among certain aristocratic parents and lovers and friends.

Rowena bon Damfels came to call, alone.

"You must not tell Stavenger I was here," she said, whispering, her face swollen with fear and grief. "He and Gustave have spent hours on the tell-me, bellowing to one another. He forbade me to come."

"I would have come to you," Marjorie cried. "You had only to ask."

"He would have seen you and driven you away. We are still in the lapse, and there is no Hunt. He would have seen you."

But it was really Eugenie that Rowena wanted to see, Eugenie she wanted to question, because she could not go to Commoner Town without Stavenger finding out. Marjorie stayed with them, and it was she who suggested, "Rowena, I will ask the man and the woman to come here. The man and woman who had her, in Commons. I will ask them to come here, since you say they cannot come to your estancia, and you can come here to talk to them yourself."

A fragile bond. A little trust. After Rowena left, Marjorie sighed, shook her head, sent for Persun Pollut.

"See if you can get the order officer and his wife to come out here tomorrow. The Jellicos. Tell them the Obermum wants to talk to them, privately. Secretly, Persun."

He laid fingers on his lips, over his eyes, noting that he said nothing, saw nothing, and then departed. He returned to say yes, they would come tomorrow, and Marjorie sent an enigmatic message on the tell-me which only Rowena would understand. While he was there, she asked Persun to explain something to her.

"At the reception, Sylvan said we would all be throwing dead bats at one another, Persun. What did he mean?"

"The Hippae do it," he said. "At least, so I hear. Sometimes on the hunt they do it. They kick dead bats at one another."

"Dead bats?"

"They are everywhere lady. Many dead bats."

It made no sense to Marjorie. She made a note in her book for later inquiry. There was no time now. "Rowena will talk to me," Marjorie said to Rigo. "I think we may find this has opened a door."

"Only while she's in this state. When she grows calm, she'll close us off again."

"You don't know that that's true."

"I believe it is," he said stiffly. He had been stiff with Marjorie ever since the reception, since he had seen her dancing with Sylvan with that look on her face. She recognized his stiffness as barely withheld anger, but she believed his discomfort had been caused by Eugenie. Long ago she had chosen not to notice how matters went between Rigo and Eugenie, so she did not seem to notice now. Because she made no response to his evident annoyance, he believed she did not care, that she was probably thinking of someone else. So he grew more angry and she more silent; so they danced, a blindfolded minuet.

Something in his manner, however, declared a decision had been made.

"Rigo, you're not—"

"Yes," he said firmly. "I have hired a riding master."

"Gustave was just being—"

"He was saying what all of them feel. That we are not worthy of their attention because we do not ride."

"It isn't riding," she said with loathing. "Whatever it is they do, it isn't riding. It's loathsome."

"Whatever it is they do," he growled, "I will do it as well as they do!"

"You won't expect me . . . or the children . . ."

"No," he blurted, shocked. "Of course not! What do you take me for?"

Indeed, what did she take him for? he asked himself. They were in this mess because of Eugenie, but Marjorie had not once reproached him for bringing Eugenie here, where Eugenie certainly did not belong. As a result he felt guilt toward Marjorie and chafed under the feeling. He felt he had ill-used her even though she showed no signs of caring, not now, not ever. She had never showed hostility toward him when he spent time with Eugenie, never showed anger that he was sharing another relationship. She never said anything bitter, never threatened anything. She was always there, unfailingly correct, concerned, always agreeable, acting appropriately under every circumstance, even those which he knew he had created especially to try her. He sometimes told himself he would give his soul if she would weep or scream or throw herself at him or away from him, but she did nothing of the kind.

He wondered if she confessed anger or jealousy to Father Sandoval. Did she tell him what she felt? Did she cry?

Long ago he had told himself that Marjorie would never love him as he had dreamed she would because she had given all her love to horses. He had even thought he hated Marjorie's riding because she gave the horses the thing she would not give him—her passion. Horses. Even more than motherhood, or her charities.

But now he wondered if that were true. Was it really horses who had taken her heart? Or had she merely been waiting for something else? Someone like Sylvan bon Damfels, perhaps?

What did she take him for?

He had to ask her. "Marjorie, did Sylvan bon Damfels say anything to you while you were dancing?"

"Say anything?" She turned an anxious glance upon him, still fretting over his intention to ride with the bons, not caring about anything else. "Sylvan? What kind of thing, Rigo? As I recall, he said conventional things. He complimented me and Stella on our gowns. He dances well. Since he wasn't one of the ones Pollut warned us about, I could relax enough to enjoy the dance. Why? What do you mean?"

"I wondered." He wondered what she was concealing.

"What has Sylvan to do with . . ."

What did Sylvan have to do with? With the way Rigo felt, seeing her. With the fact that Sylvan rode while he, Rigo, did not. He would not ask himself what the two things had to do with one another. He would not consider it. "Nothing. Nothing. I won't expect you and the children to ride in the aristos' hunt."

"But why must you!"

"Because they will not tell me anything until they trust me, and they will not trust me until I share their . . . their rituals!"

She was silent, grieving, not showing it on her face. There was malice here upon Grass, malice directed at them, at the foreigners. If Rigo rode, he would ride into that malice as into quicksand. "You won't change your mind." It was not a question but a statement, and he did not know how hopelessly she said it, all the love she thought she owed him hanging on the answer. "You won't change your mind, Rigo."

"No." In a tone that meant he would not discuss it. "No."

An awkward machine, the riding machine. Awkward and heavy, but little more ponderous than the riding master, Hector Paine, with his dour face and ominous expression and black garb, as though he were in mourning for all those he had taught how to die.

Rigo had picked an unused room in the winter quarter to use as a riding salon, and he came there with Stella, she very busy playing Daddy's little girl. There Rigo heard with disbelief that he would be expected to start his lessons at four hours per day. Stella did not seem to hear, did not seem to be paying attention. She was stroking the riding machine, humming to herself, not seeming to notice anything much.

The black-clad instructor was emphatic. "In the morning, an hour exercise, then an hour ride. Again later in the day. By the end of the week, perhaps we can manage three hours, then four. We work up to twelve hours at a time, every other day."

"My God, man!"

Stella felt the blunted barbs on the neck of the gleaming simulacrum, ran her finger around the loop of the reins where they hung on the lowest barb.

"Did you think it was easy, sir? Hunts often last for ten or eleven hours. Sometimes they go on longer."

"That leaves little time for anything else!"

"To those who Hunt, Your Excellency, there is nothing else. I thought you would have noticed that." There was nothing sneering in the man's voice, but Rigo gave him a sharp look. Stella had drifted away to a corner where she sat down behind some piled furniture, being inconspicuous, being unnoticed, eyes avid.

"You were available on short notice," Rigo snarled.

"I am available because Gustave bon Smaerlok told me to be available."

"He hopes to find me incapable, eh?"

"He would be gratified if you proved unable, I think. I speak only from impression, not from anything he has said."

"And have you agreed to report to him?"

"Only to tell him when I believe you are capable of riding in a Hunt. I will tell you this, Your Excellency. With the young ones, we begin before they are two years old—what would that be in your terms? Ten or eleven years of age? While they are still children we begin working every other day, every week, every period, throughout the seasons, perhaps for a year. A Grassian year. More than six of yours."

Rigo did not answer. For the first time he began to realize that he might not have long enough to ride to the hounds. Not if it took him as long as the children. . . .

Well, then he could not let it take as long. Focusing all his attention, he listened to what the riding master had to say.

In the corner, hidden behind the screen of displaced chairs and sofas, Stella listened too, focused no less intently on what the riding master had to say.

She had danced with Sylvan bon Damfels.

Only for a little time, enough time to know that everything she wanted was there, in his skin, behind those eyes, dwelling in that voice, in the touch of those hands.

When she came here she had thought she would never forget Elaine, never forget the friend she had left behind. Now there was no room, not even in memory, for anyone but Sylvan. When he had smiled at her on the dance floor, she had realized that she had been thinking of him since she had seen him first, at the bon Damfels Hunt. She had seen Sylvan then, in his riding clothes, seen him mount, seen him ride. On the dance floor, as her body moved with his, she had remembered each time she had seen him, each time he had spoken to her, her passionate heart demanding, as it always did, more. More. More of Sylvan bon Damfels. She would ride with Sylvan bon Damfels as she was dancing with Sylvan bon Damfels, as she could imagine—oh, imagine doing other things with Sylvan bon Damfels.

He had looked into her eyes.

He had told her she was lovely.

Behind the furniture she exulted, glad for the first time that she was here, on Grass. Ears pricked for every word the riding master was telling her father, she sucked in the information and remembered it all. She was determined that she, too, would learn. Quickly. More quickly than anyone had ever learned.

The same aircar which had brought the riding master to Opal Hill had also brought James and Jandra Jellico, who waited in Marjorie's study for Rowena's arrival.

Rowena, when she came at last, brought Sylvan with her.

"Tell us everything you can," Sylvan asked the Jellicos, his voice gentle. "I know neither of you did anything reprehensible, so just tell us everything you can."

Marjorie and Tony sat to one side, listening. No one suggested they should not be present. If they had, Marjorie had already decided she would listen outside the door.

There was so little to tell, and yet they spun it into an hour's telling, each little thing said ten times over.

"One thing you got to remember," Jelly told Sylvan. "Just because Ducky Johns' in the business she is, that's no reason to think she isn't honest. She's as honest as anybody. And I believe she found this Janetta right where she said she did, on her own back porch under her clothesline."

"But how?" cried Rowena, for perhaps the tenth time.

Jelly took a deep breath. He was tired of evasion, tired of euphemism, tired of bowing to the well-known eccentricity of the bons. He decided to tell the hard truth and see what this bon woman made of it. "Ma'am, last anybody saw of her, she was riding one of those beasts. Now anybody with any wits at all is going to suppose, wherever she ended up, that beast took her there or sent her there. And that's what I think."

So there it was. Oh, there it was, lying before them, the sound and look of it, a barbed and violent monster, a Hippae, drawn into it at last, told off by name, the aspect of the whole thing that none of the bons had mentioned, that none of the bons would speak of or allow others to talk of. The Hippae. The Hippae took the girl, or one of them did, everyone knew that. *They*, the Hippae, did something to her, did anyone doubt? *They* hid her. *They* kept her. Then she showed up again. Who knows why? Who knows how? Marjorie felt the questions bubbling and kept silent, kept her hand on Tony's as she felt him, too, quivering with questions unanswered, unasked. The bons had blamed the Yrariers rather than the Hippae. Even now, Rowena did not respond. Why?

The Jellicos made their farewells and went out. Rowena wept, clinging to Sylvan. He fixed Marjorie with a stern face, forbidding her to speak. She cast her eyes down, feeling his will upon her as though he had touched her with his hands.

"Mama, would you like to lie down for a moment?" he asked Rowena. She nodded, awash with tears.

"Tony, take her, will you?" asked Marjorie, wanting him to take the woman away, wanting to be left alone with Sylvan, in order to ask ...

"A moment," Rowena said.

Marjorie nodded.

"Lady Westriding ... Marjorie. A time may come when I can offer you help as you have offered me. If my life hangs on it, I will still help you." She laid her tear-wet hand on Marjorie's and went out with Tony, leaving her son behind.

"Don't," he said when they were alone, seeing the question in her face. "I don't know."

She could not hold the words in. "But you live here! You're familiar with the beasts."

"Shhh," he said, looking over his shoulder, running his finger inside a collar suddenly too tight. "Don't say beasts. Don't say animals. Don't say that. Not even to yourself. Don't think it." He gripped his throat as though something there was choking him.

"What do you say?"

"Hippae. Mounts," he gargled. "And not even *that* where they might hear. Nothing where they might hear." He gagged, begging for air.

She stared into his face, seeing the beads of sweat standing out upon his forehead, seeing him struggle to hold his face quiet. "What is it?"

The struggle grew more intense. He could not answer her.

"Shhh," she said, taking his hands into her own. "Don't talk. Just think. Is it something . . . is it something they do to you?"

A nod, the merest hint of a nod.

"Something they do . . . to your brain? To your mind?"

A flicker of eyelid, tiny. If she had not learned to read almost invisible twitches, she would not have seen it.

"Is it . . ." She thought coldly of what she had seen at the bon Damfels estancia. "Is it a kind of blanking out?"

He blinked, breathing deeply.

"A compulsion?"

He sighed, letting go. His head sagged.

"A compulsion to ride, but an inability to think about riding, an inability to talk about riding." She said it to herself, not to him, knowing it was true, and he looked at her out of shining eyes. Tears?

"Which," she continued, watching him closely, "must be more intense the more frequently you ride." She knew she was right. "You managed to speak to us once right after a Hunt. . . ."

"They had gone," he gargled, panting. "After a long Hunt, they go away. Today they are here, all around Opal Hill, nearby!"

"During the winter, the compulsion almost leaves you?" she asked. "And during the summer? But in spring and fall, you are possessed by it? Those of you who ride?"

He only looked at her, knowing she needed no confirmation.

"What do they do when winter ends? To bring you into line? Do they gather around your estancias? In their dozens? Their hundreds?" He did not deny it. "They gather and press upon you, insisting upon the Hunt. There must also be some pressure to make the children ride. Some compulsion there, as well?"

"Dimity," he said with a sigh.

"Your little sister."

"My little sister."

"Your father . . ."

"Has ridden for years, Master of the Hunt, for years, like Gustave. . . ."

"So," she said, thinking she must tell Rigo. Must somehow make him understand.

"I'll take Mama home," he whispered, his face clearing.

"How have you withstood them?" her voice was as low as his. "Why have they not bitten off your arm or leg? Isn't that what they do when one of you tries to stand fast?"

He did not answer. He did not need to answer. She could puzzle it out for herself. It was not that he withstood them while he was riding. If he had done so, he would have vanished or been punished for it. Oh, no, when he rode he was one of them, like all the rest. The secret was that he recovered quickly when the ride was over. Quickly enough to say some things, to hint some things.

"You warned us that time," she said, reaching out to him. "I know how hard for you it must have been."

He took her hand and laid it along his cheek. Only that. But it was thus that Rigo saw them.

Sylvan excused himself, bowed, and went away to find Rowena.

"A pleasant tête-à-tête." Rigo smiled fiercely.

She was too preoccupied to notice the quality of that smile.

"Rigo, you must not ride."

"Oh, and why is that?"

"Sylvan says—"

"Oh, I think it matters very little what Sylvan says."

She looked at him uncertainly. "It matters a great deal. Rigo, the Hippae are not merely animals. They . . . they do something to their riders. Something to their brains."

"Clever Sylvan to have thought up such a tale."

"Do you think he invented it? Don't be silly. It's obvious. It's been obvious to me since we saw the first Hunt, Rigo."

"Oh?"

"And since last night. For the love of God, Rigo. Didn't it strike you as odd that no one blamed the Hippae? Here's this girl who disappeared during a Hunt, and no one blames the Hippae she was riding on?"

"If you disappeared during a Hunt, my dear, and turned up later as a courtesan in some petty principality, should I blame your horse?" He gave her a wintry glance, then left her there, staring after him, trying desperately to figure out what had happened.

9

In the Friary of the Green Brothers, nights sat gently upon the sills.
The great, night-freezing cry which haunted the southern latitudes
was seldom heard here, though whole choruses of grublike peepers
filled the dark hours with dulcet sound. Days were spent in labor,
nights in sleep. Brothers, so it was said, had once spent their time
in study, but little study was needed here. All the questions had been
reduced to doctrine; all the doctrine had been simplified to catechism;
all the catechism had been learned long ago. Besides, what would
the penitents do with more knowledge? They had no use for it here.

The Friary sat upon shortgrass prairie, though there were tall grasses not far away. Every year in mid to late summer the Brothers went out to cut down quantities of strong, thick grass stems that grew to the height of seven or eight tall men. Other Brothers remained behind them at the Friary, digging deep and narrow trenches, in parallel pairs, outlining the new halls which would be needed during the Grassian year. Though penitents grew old and penitents died, the number of Brothers kept growing. Seemingly it was becoming a more frequent happening for acolytes of Sanctity to fly apart, like fragile wheels, spun too fast.

When the great grasses had been sawn through and tied in bundles, they were dragged back to the Friary and upended side by side in the waiting trenches. The top of each bundle was pulled over and tied partway down the bundle in the opposite ditch until the whole double line had been bowed into a vaulted hall which would be roofed with thatch, its openings walled with panels of woven grass. Within this lofty space the Brothers would build whatever kind of rooms were needed: a new chapel or kitchen or another set of cells.

So space was enclosed, said the historians of the order, long ago on another world by people who lived among tall grasses. The historians did not say what such people did in the winter. During winters on Grass, the Brothers retired below to a cramped underground monastery where they suffered through a lengthy season of sequestered and jam-packed irascibility. Winters drove more than a few of them past the pale of sanity. A sick wildness lurked among the brethren —skulking, endemic, more often erupting among the younger than among the aged. The old felt themselves past hope, but the young had hope continually frustrated and as continually strained against their frustration in strange and dangerous ways.

In the summer Friary, there was room enough for frustration to find an out. The narrow halls sprawled this way and that among the low grasses, some making vaulted cloisters around enclosed gardens, some with doors opening upon wide vegetable plots, some giving upon farmyards where chickens scratched or pigs grunted contentedly in their pens. If it had not been for the towers, the Friary could have been a tumulus left by a great tunneling mole, the round-topped halls dried to very much the color of the native soil.

But there were towers—towers everywhere. Demented with boredom, young Brothers had been erecting these grass-stalk steeples for decades. At first they were mere tapering masts, no taller than fifteen men, or twenty, topped by plumy seed-head finials. Later more elaborate three- and five-legged monstrosities had climbed into a cloud-streaked sky, almost beyond the sight or belief of those on the ground—always more towers, and more.

Over the wide courtyards lacy needles soared, their joints securely tied with tough ropes of wiregrass. Rearing upward at each juncture of the reed-vaulted halls, spidery pinnacles pierced the clouds. Filigree masts rose above the kitchens and gardens. Outside the precincts of the Friary, forests of spicules like those of some lacework sea urchin thrust into the Grassian sky in myriad gothic spires. From any place within or around the Friary, one could not look up without seeing them, fantastically high and ridiculously fragile, the steeples of the climbers.

Upon these structure young Brothers, shrunk by distance into the stature and compass of spiders, had crawled and swung among the clouds, trailing their slender ropes behind them, connecting all the towers with bridges which seemed no wider than a finger, scarcely stronger than a hair. Up ladders thin and wavery as web silk they climbed to the high platforms to keep watch. At first they had watched for hounds, or for grazers. Then they watched for golden angels like those on the towers of Sanctity, so said some of them, disillusioned with watching when no one ever saw anything interesting. Lately they had made a sport of seeing indescribable things, or so they said, and Elder Brother Laeroa had all he could do to keep them out of the hands of Doctrine. Jhamlees Zoe would have relished a good disciplinary session or even a trial for heresy. Those in the Office of Acceptable Doctrine were, after all, as bored as everyone else.

Over the decades the towers had been climbed by amateurs, then by enthusiasts, and finally by experts who had invented a cult with its own hierarchs and acolytes, its own rituals of baptism and burial, its own secrets shared among its own adherents. Each new acolyte was tested within days of his arrival to know whether he would be one of the climbers or not. When Brother Mainoa first warned Brother Lourai that the climbers would be after him, he spoke no more than the truth.

They did not wait long.

Brother Lourai, lately Rillibee Chime, sat in the refectory as generations had sat before him, the front of his robe rubbing another layer of gloss upon the table edge, waiting for the gong which would allow him to rise from the table, carry his plate to the service hatch, and then go out to the washing house for his evening duty. The voice which whispered at him came as a surprise, for it came from behind him. Nothing was there but a blank walled end of the hall without even a shelf on it.

"You, Lourai," it said. "Pay attention."

He looked up and around, doing it slowly so as not to attract attention. His nearest neighbors were some distance away, minor functionaries recently sent to beef up the Office of Acceptable Doctrine, or so Mainoa had said, and the least notice attracted from them, the better.

He saw nothing but the woven mats which made up the end wall of the hall. "You," came the voice again. "After duty tonight. Time for your initiation."

The sound that followed was suspiciously like a giggle, a nasty giggle, almost a snigger. Rillibee closed his eyes and prayed for help. All that came in answer was the sound of the old men shouting at one another far away on the dais. After a time, Rillibee opened his eyes and looked around him, wondering if he could find anything in the Great Refectory which would help him.

The refectory had four vaulted halls radiating like fingers from a central dome. Under the dome was the dais on which the Eldest Brothers sat: Jhamlees and Fuasoi and Laeroa, plus half a dozen others. Down the splayed halls, in long, single rows, stood the woven grass tables of the penitents, seated in order of seniority. The tables themselves were wonderful, or at least so Rillibee thought.

Strips of grass stem had been spiraled and woven into shapes representing twigs and leaves and blossoms. Tabletops curved down into serrated aprons and thence into legs bulging with rococo excess. At home, Rillibee's mother would have called it wicker, pointing out the similarities to the old brown rocking chair beside the fire. Here it was known only as grass weaving, but the grass had dozens of hues and a hundred tints.

Lifetimes of Brothers had fondled the braided arms of these chairs, rubbed the basketry seats smooth with their bottoms, shined the convoluted edges of these tables with their bellies and sleeves. Brother Rillibee/Lourai's place was at the far end of a row of tables so long that it dwindled almost to nothing as he looked along the tops toward the dome. It made eating a lonely business for the newest Brothers, however much it encouraged reflection.

And it made living a lonely business, too. The chairs to either side of him were empty. There was no one he could ask for help. Probably, no one who would help him if he did ask. And no time to ask, in any case, for the harsh clangor of the ending bell broke through all other sounds and stopped them. He rose to follow hundreds of other shuffling forms as they set their plates within the hatch and went out into the evening.

When he reached the open air, he turned aside from the court into an alleyway which led back beside the refectory to the washing house. There he stationed himself at one handle of the pump and waited for his coworker to arrive. This anonymous, middle-aged Brother sat down at his own handle and the two of them began the monotonous thrusting which would bring water from a hot spring far below. From the pump the water went into the hot kettles. When the kettles were full, the water went into the rinsing trough. By the time the rinsing trough was full, the kettles would be empty again.

"Damn fool thing," muttered Brother Lourai, thinking of solar batteries and wind-driven pumps, both of which were in use elsewhere at the Friary to pump bath water and fill the fish ponds and the large tank that provided drinking water.

"Hush," said the older man with a glare. Pumping was a penitential service. It wasn't supposed to be easy or make sense.

Rillibee hushed. No point in wanting it over sooner. Tonight, it would be better for it to last as long as possible. He spent the time thinking about the interview he'd had with Elder Brother Jhamlees the previous day.

"It says here, boy ..." the Elder Brother had announced, "it says here you flew apart in refectory and began making wild accusations."

Rillibee had started to retort, started to say something daring and angry, then had remembered Mainoa's advice. "Yes, Elder Brother," he had said.

"Only had two years to go," the Elder Brother went on. He was a man with a face like cork, evenly colored, evenly textured, as though he were wearing a mask. All his features were ordinary except his nose, so tiny a nose, like a slice off the end of a wine cork stuck on the middle of his face, the nostrils mere slits. Around that tiny nose the other features seemed disturbingly large. "Two years, and you had to go doubting. Well, we won't have any of that here, you know that."

"Yes, Elder Brother."

"Let's see what you remember of your catechism. Ah, well now, what is the purpose of mankind?"

"To populate the galaxy in God's time."

"Ah, well, what is women's duty?"

"To bear children for the population of the galaxy."

"Ah, well, how shall this population be accomplished?"

"By the resurrection of all those who have ever lived, to the time of our first parents."

"And how shall we be led?"

"By the resurrection of the Son of God and all the saints who shall again be saints, of the latter days, to guide us to perfect Sanctity, Unity, and Immortality."

"Hmm," said Elder Brother Jhamlees. "You know your doctrine well enough. What the hell happened to you?"

Mainoa's advice forgotten, Rillibee asked, "When we all get resurrected, Elder Brother, will the machines do it?"

"What do you mean, boy!"

"There won't be any people left. The plague will have killed us all. Will the machines do all the resurrecting?"

"That'll be ten stripes for impertinence," Elder Brother Jhamlees said. "And another ten for uttering falsehood. There is no plague, Brother Lourai. None."

"I saw my mother die of it," said Rillibee Chime. "And my father and my sister had it. I may have it. They say sometimes it doesn't come out for years. . . ."

"Out," the Elder Brother had blustered. "Out. Out." His face had turned pale as he bellowed, so pale that Brother Lourai wondered if the Elder Brother had ever met anyone who had actually seen the plague.

Brother Lourai had gone out. Ever since then, he'd been expecting someone to summon him to receive the twenty stripes Elder Brother Jhamlees had assigned him. No one had. The only summons had been the summons in refectory, the one he didn't want to answer. The one he was delaying now, pumping water while the dishes got washed.

Still, inevitably, the task was finished at last. The kettles were emptied into a ditch that led to the cesspool, the rinsing troughs emptied into a ditch leading to the gardens, the soapy steam vanished out the open door as Brothers scattered wordlessly. Rillibee's counterpart at the other end of the pump handle hitched up his robes and went out. After a long, silent moment, Rillibee did likewise.

He thought he might stay in the washing house and hide. He considered this for a time, quite seriously, knowing it for nonsense but unwilling to let the idea go entirely. Where would they be waiting for him? Outside the courtyard somewhere, perhaps in the alley which led to his dormitory?

"Come on," said an impatient voice. "Get it over."

It was too much trouble to answer the voice. It would be even more trouble to avoid it. Unwillingly, he shambled toward the summoner, through the gateway from the yard, into the alley, where three of them grabbed him and forced him through a door and down a hallway into an unfamiliar room. They wore only their tights and undershirts. Their faces were lit in the lantern light with shiny and unholy glee. There was no doubt at all that these were the climbers Mainoa had told him about. Not warned him. What good was it to warn someone about the inevitable? But one could be told. One could be given time to consider. Not that it had done Rillibee any good.

They pushed him toward a bench and he sat on it to hide the trembling of his legs. It wasn't fear. It was something else, something some of those confronting him might have understood if there had been time to talk. There was no time.

The foremost among those standing there—the group had grown to a dozen or so—struck a posture and announced, "Call me Highbones!" He was a lean, long-armed man with a taut-skinned boyish face, though the wrinkles around his eyes said he was no boy. A hank of dun hair fell over his forehead and was pushed back with a studied gesture. The color of the hair was ageless. His brows grew together over his nose. His eyes were so pale a blue as to be almost white. Everything about him was studied, his stance, his gesture, his manner, his voice. Created, made up, out of what?

Rillibee saw all this as he nodded an acknowledgment, just to let them know he had heard. No point in saying anything. Least said, the easiest denied, as the master of acolytes at Sanctity had been fond of telling them.

"As for you, having observed you carefully for several days, we can say without fear of contradiction that you're a root peeper." That snigger again, as though the insult meant something.

Rillibee nodded again.

"You're required to acknowledge, peeper. Say you're a peeper." The voice was like a chant, empty of any feeling. Like the mosquito voices at Sanctity.

"I'm a peeper," said Rillibee, without embarrassment or emotion.

"The point of all this is," Highbones went on, striking another pose, "that we climbers consider peepers to be the lowest possible form of life. Brother Shoethai, he's a peeper. Isn't that true, boys?"

There was a chorus of agreement. Yes. Grass peepers were beneath contempt.

Rillibee had seen Brother Shoethai, a misshapen creature of uncertain age, the butt of everyone's jokes—though covertly, for Brother Shoethai worked for the Office of Acceptable Doctrine. Highbones gave Rillibee little time to reflect on this.

"Of course, we realize that some are like old Shoethai, constitutionally incapable of climbing, and all of those will end up as peepers anyhow. Still, we'll give you a chance. Everyone gets a chance. That's only fair, wouldn't you agree?"

Unwisely, Rillibee risked a comment. "I'm willing to be a peeper."

There were yelps and halloos from those assembled, men who could have been Highbones' brothers or cousins, all as shiny-skinned and slender as he, all with that long-armed look, like ancient apes.

Highbones shook his head. "Oh, no, no you're not willing, peeper. No, you speak from ignorance. Perhaps even from congenital stupidity. Peepers get hung from the towers by their feet. Peepers get knocked about by this one and that one. Their lives are sheer misery, nothing but misery, nothing anyone would choose for himself. Far better to take the test and see how it all comes out, don't you think? And if you simply can't climb, well, then we'll consider mercy. But you have to try. Those are the rules." Highbones smiled. It was a kindly smile, a practiced smile; only the eyes betrayed the cruelty of it.

Rillibee, seeing those eyes, felt his stomach clench. They were like Wurn's eyes, long ago, big, angry Wurn, when he used to borrow Rillibee's school supplies, hoping Rillibee would say no so Wurn would have an excuse to hit. It had been only a matter of time until Wurn would kill someone. Only a matter of time until Highbones did, or had. Considering his age, he probably already had. He probably would again. He might tonight. Highbones wouldn't much care. He might not desire his victims dead, but he did not care so long as the process offered some amusement. Or perhaps not amusement. Perhaps something else.

Even now he was saying, "Peepers have such a horrible life, little man. Such a horror as you've never thought of. Ask old Shoethai, if you don't believe us!"

"Have you ever seen anyone dying of plague?" Rillibee asked, the words coming out without thought. He wished them back in the instant, but the group did not react as though they knew what he meant.

"Plague?" Highbones laughed. "No good trying to detour us, peeper. Tell your stories to somebody else but not to us. Time for you to climb."

"Climb where?" Rillibee asked. With difficulty he kept his voice reasonable and calm. This dozen and whatever others there were waiting elsewhere were a pack. Rillibee had seen packs when he was a child. Packs of coyotes. Packs of wild dogs. Joshua had explained about packs. Let one start baying, and all would follow. It had happened that way in Sanctity, too. Let one start panting and screeching and others would join in. They had done so when Rillibee started yelling. By the time they'd knocked him off the table and carried him away, twenty or thirty others were shouting as well. A pack. If one didn't want to deal with a pack, it was important to keep the leader from baying.

"Are you the only one with a name?" he asked of Highbones, attempting a diversion.

It worked, for a moment. Hardflight was introduced, and Topclinger. Mastmaster and Steeplehands. Roperunner and Long Bridge and Little Bridge. Rillibee distracted himself by memorizing their names, their faces. Lean faces, all atop slender forms, and most with those long arms and big hands. Light weight was obviously an advantage. Rillibee's hands were inside the sleeves of his robe, and he put his fingers around his arms, feeling the ropy muscle there. All those years of exercise at Sanctity. All those years climbing up and down the towers.

Topclinger was staring at Highbones, his face carefully blank, his eyes unreadable. Here was one who did not follow blindly, exclaiming and shouting. Here was one to whom appeals could be made, perhaps?

But there was no time to appeal to anyone.

"Time's passing," cried Highbones. "Light's going. Time to climb!"

Rillibee was surrounded by a whispering mob of them, hustled down one corridor and into a storage building, then up a flight of stairs and out a hatch onto the thatched roof of the hall. Beside him was the leg of a tower, a slender ladder running beside it to the first crossbrace. Above that were other legs, other ladders. The mists hung about the top of the towers, hiding them. Between the clouds and the earth speared the last rays of the setting sun, beginning the long dusk of Grass.

Topclinger whispered, "This one'll climb, this one will," gripping Rillibee's shoulder in his hard hand, squeezing it.

"Oh, I'll wager on that, Tops, I will," snarled Highbones.

Rillibee heard them through the muttering. All those years listening to the mosquito whines at Sanctity, picking meaningful language out of nonsense, let him understand what they said though they did not mean him to hear.

"Bet," responded Topclinger. "Bet one whole turn on kitchen duty."

"Done," said Highbones, giggling. "In my opinion he's a deader."

Rillibee felt the chill of that giggle run down his bones.

"Oh, God, oh," said the parrot in his mind.

"Shut up," he whispered to himself.

"Did you say something, peeper?"

Rillibee shook his head. Highbones was not the sort to leave the winning of his bet to chance. Highbones would try to make sure, up there somewhere.

But then, did it matter? Why not let him have his way?

"Let me die," begged the parrot.

The dozen surrounded Rillibee, all of them posturing now as though they were one creature, pointing upward toward the heights, toward the last of the sunlight.

"Will he climb?" they wanted to know, pressing closer to him as they explained the rules. They would give him three minutes' start and then come after him. If he could reach another ladder and get down without being caught, then he'd be a climber. If they caught him, he'd be a peeper, but they wouldn't beat him too badly if he gave them a good chase. If he fell off, he'd be a deader, depending on where he fell from. He might get away with no injury at all. But if he wouldn't climb, he would die right there on the thatch. They would rub his face in shit and keep hitting him in the stomach until he'd wished he'd died up there, rather than here. If he didn't climb, said Highbones, there were other pleasures some might find in Brother Lourai's anatomy before they killed him. Others agreed to this with wide, toothy grins and feverish eyes.

"Up," they chanted. "Up, Lourai. Got to be initiated. Got to climb!" The word "climb" was howled from half a hundred throats as others, drawn by the initial ruckus, ran to join the ten or twelve who had started the racket, clambering up the side of the hall on rope sashes dropped to them from those above, clustering upon the thatch. "Climb, Lourai! Climb," bellowed the Brothers of Sanctity, the Green

Brothers, with Green Brother names like Nuazoi and Flumzee and faces intent upon mayhem.

Bored, Brother Mainoa had said. Bored to insanity. And Brother Lourai would just have to learn to get along with them.

It wasn't their threats that moved Rillibee. He had considered death many times during recent years. He had seen no reason why he should go on living when Joshua and Songbird and Miriam had all died. Dying had not seemed a bad thing, though getting dead had seemed to be more difficult than he had liked. So now getting dead seemed the problem. If he gave himself to this pack, here and now, there would be pain first, and humiliation, neither of which he wanted. If he was to die, he wanted it to be in peace, and not at the hands of some long-armed barbarian like Highbones.

What really moved him to the first ladder, however, was the confounded noise they made, the derisive cacophony centered on him, the knowledge that they would give him no peace until he acted.

The ladder did not frighten him. All those years, up and down the towers of Sanctity, ten times taller than these. He knew enough not to look down. He knew enough to have a good hold before he shifted his weight. He went up the ladder, slowly at first, then faster, his eyes up, seeing something there that those assembled on the thatch evidently had not seen or had taken no notice of.

The mists were coming down. The fog was falling over the Friary. Even now, the tops of the towers were lost in it, the spidersilk bridges were striped with veils. Perhaps those down on the rooftop would not notice it in time, if he could get far enough ahead of them.

He came to the first crossbrace on the tower. Getting to the next ladder required that he move along a curved rod of grass as thick as his leg. Though this was rounded and the girders at Sanctity had been square, this was wider than the girders he had crossed in the drop shafts. Without stopping to think about it, Rillibee ran along the crossbrace and started up the second ladder, eyes examining the route above him. Where the ladders were. Where the bridges were. And where was the nearest cloud?

A howl from below greeted his run. Newcomers did not run across the braces! Though the allotted time had not elapsed, Highbones waited no longer. He started up the ladder even as some few below had the temerity to shout, "Time. Time. Unfair!"

Anger spurted in Rillibee Chime. Highbones had broken his own rules. What right had he to break his own rules?

Highbones did not acknowledge the shouts. After a moment, his followers started after him, Hardflight and Steeplehands in the lead with Long Bridge close behind. Topclinger did not follow. He stood aside, shouting, "You didn't give him his fair time, Bones. You didn't give him time." Rillibee heard it. He heard the shout of approval that greeted it, as well, a dozen voices perhaps. Topclinger had his admirers.

Rillibee also heard Highbones below him, heard the threats, the sniggers designed to make Rillibee nervous, to make him tremble. Instead, the sound only fed his anger, making him move more surely and swiftly upward. There were three more ladders between him and the cloud that was sinking toward him. He had already memorized the ladders and bridges above it. He had seen one thing that would be useful if he decided to try life and several things which would do if he decided to die. Now, spurred by his anger, possessed by a devil of contrariness, part fear, part hate, he lunged upward, hands and feet pulling and thrusting while the howl of the climbers rose from below as the time was up and all of them leapt for the towers.

"Comin' after you, peeper," cried Highbones exultantly from below. "Comin' after you."

Rillibee risked one quick glance. He was already a great height above the ground. The bottom of the ladder below him was swarming with climbers now, as were those to either side. He lunged upward. There were two more runs along crossbraces which grew more slender the higher he went, and finally the ladder which led upward into the mist.

His anger made him tense. The tension made him gasp for breath, made his arms ache. Not so hard a breath or so aching an arm as would make him fall. Not yet. But he knew that could happen eventually. In time. How much time? The wet of the fog lay on his cheeks, cooling them. He climbed.

Suddenly the mist wrapped him, sweeping across him like a fabric so that he was muffled in it, all at once draped in an impenetrable gauze. Those below him could no longer see him or be seen by him. He was alone in the cloud with only the trembling of the tower to tell them where he was moving, to tell him where they came after him. He climbed more slowly, looking to his side, peering through the growing dusk. The thing he had been looking for appeared at last as a shadow, an extrusion of the tower into space, ending out there, lost in the gray mist, only a few feet away.

Rillibee untied the knot of his rope sash, unwound it from his waist, tugged his robe off, rolled it up, and tied it in the end of the sash. Clad now only in slim trousers and sleeveless shirt, he crawled out onto the spur, the line draped around his neck, the tightly rolled robe dangling against his chest. The spur had obviously been left over from the time the tower had been constructed, a crane from which tackle had been suspended to raise materials from below. It was supported from below by a series of diagonal braces. Behind him the spidery legs of the tower vanished in the damp gray of the cloud. Just beyond the last brace he sat up and waited in a misty bubble where sound was muted.

Ten or twelve feet above the spur was a bridge, three ropes strung from this tower to another not far away, one rope to walk upon, two to hold onto, with slender lines woven between. Rillibee could not see it now, but he knew it was there. He had seen it from below and memorized its position. He hoped it was no farther above him than his rope sash could reach.

Balanced upon the spur, legs anchored in the angle of the brace below it, he swung his rolled robe, pendulum fashion, gaining length with each swing, finally throwing the robe up and over as it caught on the bridge above him. He had intended to tie the two ends of the belt together to make a loop and suspend himself under the bridge, lost in the mist where no one would think of looking for him. Now he tugged at the end of the rope, dismayed. It had caught on the bridge. Even as he jerked at it again and again he realized his scheme would not have worked. The rope bridge would have sagged under the weight of his body. Those who climbed these heights every evening would know that someone was out there in midspan. If they could not find that person on the bridge, they would look below it.

So. He took a deep breath and stayed as he was, squatted on the spur, the end of the rope still in his hand. Someone was grunting and mumbling below him on the tower, within a few arm's lengths. "Up here!" shouted Highbone's voice, cracking in hysterical delight. "He's up here." Other voices answered, not far below.

Rillibee waited. If they decided to climb out on the spur, he would jump. Getting dead from this height would be almost certain. He hoped he was over bare earth and not over a densely thatched roof which would break his fall. He kept his mind on this, scarcely breathing, still as a stone.

Someone climbed past him on the tower, then someone else. Sudden inspiration struck him, and he tugged at the rope, feeling the motion transmitted to the rope bridge above him.

"He's on the bridge," shrieked Highbones. "I can feel him. On the bridge!"

An answering bellow came out of the fog from the far tower where the bridge ended.

The rope in Rillibee's hands jiggled and danced, transmitting the motion of the bridge as the climbers moved out upon it. He left the rope hanging there, jiggling behind him, as he crawled back toward the tower, hand by hand, harkening to the sound of climbers-by, losing himself in the fog to descend as he had ascended, sometimes standing aside from the climbing shadows and shouting wraiths to let them go by, sometimes slipping down wet ladders, himself invisible in the mist, hidden by cloud, one with the sky. Above him was a discordancy of voices, directions and misdirections, shouts of "Here he is" mixed with cries of "Where is he?"

No one was guarding the bottom of the ladder he had climbed. The rooftop was empty. The fog had sunk almost to the level of the roof, and the door stood open with empty stairs below. From high above still came voices crying, "Here, here," and the ladder still trembled with the force of the bodies rushing to and fro. He went out silently, down the stairs and through the vacant hall, out into the alleyway and back to his cell in the new dormitory, which was still only partially finished and almost uninhabited. As he entered the dormitory, he heard a dwindling cry, as of someone falling forever from a high place.

Once inside his cell he crawled under his cot and lay there, almost without breathing, tight against the wall. Twice in the night his door opened and a light was thrust inside.

Before dawn he rose and climbed back onto the tower, moving through gray dusk to the bridge where his robe was caught, with the rope girdle still dangling below. A sleeve of the robe had come loose and wound itself around the foot rope of the bridge, only enough to prevent the bundle falling, not enough that anyone had noticed it. Rillibee retrieved his robe and put it on, then sat on a high crossbrace for a long time, looking out over the Friary and the surrounding prairie.

In his head the parrot said, "Let me die."

"I planned to," he replied. "This morning."

He put it off a little. He had planned to die this morning, but it was interesting upon the heights. The grass rippled below like an unending sea, stretching on every side to a limitless horizon. Things moved in the grass. Great beasts with barbed necks paraded on the ridge: Hippae. Torso-sized white crawlers struggled among the grass roots: peepers. Far to the south a line of great grazers moved slowly toward the east. He stared at them all, at the birds moving in clouds across the grasses, at the ripples here and there betokening mysterious movements by creatures he could not see. He wished there were trees. If there had only been trees. . . . Still, the warm light shone on him like a benison, like a promise of something good to come.

By the time the sun rose, he was hungry enough to climb down and go to breakfast.

He was interrupted twice while he ate.

Once by Highbones, who strolled down the long line of tables to hiss at him, "Nobody makes a fool out of me and gets away with it, Lourai. Watch your back, because I'm coming to get you."

Once by a man who called himself Ropeknots, accompanied by two others who seemed to be watching Ropeknots more than they watched Rillibee. Ropeknots had an angry, frustrated look as he said, "Topclinger got hisself killed last night, peeper. Some of us was his friends and we figure you must've knocked him off his perch tryin' to get down."

"I went up," Rillibee explained, not looking at Ropeknots—who was livid with resentment and obviously unable to listen—but at the other two. "I hid in the fog and then when everyone went past, I came down the same ladder again. I didn't knock anybody off anything, and by your own rules I'm not a peeper anymore."

The calmer two of the delegation exchanged glances. Ropeknots growled, "I was guarding the door. You didn't get past me. You killed Topclinger, then you got down somewhere else."

"I went down through the same door. There was no guard there," Rillibee said, tired of it all. "There was no one there at all."

"I was there," the other claimed with an ugly flush on his face and a sidelong glare at his companions. "Highbones told me to stay there and guard the door and I did."

He turned and went away, leaving Rillibee staring after. After a moment, his two companions followed him. Rillibee wondered if the lie had been as patent to them as it was to him. The man had been told to keep watch, but he had left his post. Afterward, he had denied it. The denial suited Highbones' purpose, too, for it served to throw suspicion for Topclinger's death upon Rillibee. If anyone had killed Topclinger, it had been Highbones himself.

So, a faithless guard and a treacherous pack leader. Fine enemies to have. Rillibee sighed, wishing he had thrown himself off the spur when he'd had the chance last night. Or jumped off at dawn, as he'd planned to do.

He was considering climbing back up the tower for that purpose when he was interrupted again. This time it was half a dozen young Brothers who rubbed his head and laughed and said he had done a good job of losing them and named him Willy Climb on the spot because he'd climbed better than any other peeper of their generation. They loved him because he had confounded Highbones, whom they disliked, and because he had amused them. He became one of them in that instant, a leader of them, with several promising to watch his back for him and protect him from Ropeknots because everyone knew he was a shit and from Highbones, too, who yelled at other people for breaking the rules but always broke them himself.

Their easy friendship was enough to make Rillibee stop thinking about dying for a while. In the company of these newfound companions he climbed to the heights each evening in the dusk hours to sit on a brace and chant his own name while the others played tag across the bridges. He was aware of no distractions except the great night moths that blundered into him with their squishy bodies and the peepers that raised their hymns from the grass roots. Each sundown he ceased being Brother Lourai and became Rillibee Chime once again. As night came down he sat in cloudy silence, remembering his people and his place, and chanted, over and over again, Rillibee Chime, Songbird Chime, Joshua Chime, Miriam Chime. When his friends called him Willy Climb, he answered to that name, too. He was Willy Climb among the pack and ruck, becoming, so he thought to himself, multiple. Rillibee, Lourai, Willy. As though he had been folded and trimmed, like paper dolls, a chain of him extending from the planet of his birth to these cloud-wrapped steeples, where he would die, pretty soon, when he grew bored and depressed once more.

In the offices of Jhamlees Zoe, head of the Office of Security and Acceptable Doctrine, the man responsible for the affairs of the Friary was undoing, for the third or fourth time, a packet which had arrived a considerable time ago. Inside was a wad of printing beginning, as did all communications from the Hierarch—or even putatively from the Hierarch—"Dear Brother in Sanctity." And so on and so on, wah, wah, wah. Pages of it, spewed out of a cleric-all, dull as porridge and meaningless as peeper song. The real meat was in the middle of this manuscript, two pages inserted there which were written in a familiar hand:

"My dear old friend Nods. By the time you read this, I will be the new Hierarch of Sanctity." Which was interesting. Cory had always said he would be Hierarch someday. When they had been in seminary together as boys, Cory had said it even then. Jhamlees Zoe nodded. It just went to prove how ruthless Cory really was.

He read further:

> The Hierarch past, one Carlos Yrarier, has for some esoteric reason picked his nephew Roderigo to go to Grass and find out whether there is plague or a cure for plague on your world. Pay attention, old friend. Though it is still policy to deny it, *there is plague here, as there is everywhere else*. If Yrarier finds no help upon Grass, we may have to depend upon the machines to resurrect us after the danger has passed. Some of us, at least. Thee and me, old friend. As you know, it has never been Sanctity's intention to resurrect many! Why bring all that fodder to life again when it did so little the first time around?

Jhamlees nodded once again. That was sound doctrine, though not doctrine ever shared with the masses. If the machines ever woke them into some new world, it would be a very selective waking. Jhamlees' cell-sample was in machine "A," along with a few hundred thousand others. The other billions could be roused if needed, but such need was doubtful.

The letter went on:

> However, since there is a chance you have no plague on your world, I plan to come to Grass with such personnel and so equipped as to do all that must be done in the shortest possible time to find a cure. But, we will do it quietly. *It is not our desire that either information about the plague or the cure, assuming we find one, be widely disseminated.* There are those among the Elders who see in this plague the Hand of God Almighty wiping out the heathen to leave worlds clean for Sanctity alone to populate. Hasten the day. While I am less inclined to see the Hand of God, I am no less willing to take advantage of the chance.

The information Sanctity initially received was that a

person or persons had arrived on Grass with the disease and departed without it. In the serene hope that this is true, I am coming to Grass very soon. Too precipitous a move would betray our purpose, therefore I must take more time than I like. Still, I should arrive not long after Yrarier himself, having first taken time to make ritual stops here and there—the putative reason for my journey. If necessary, some of these ceremonial visits may be cut short. At the first inkling that Yrarier has found something, even if only a hint, you are to send word in accordance with the itinerary enclosed.

Jhamlees unfolded the itinerary, then finished the letter.

Needless to say, we want no premature soundings of alarums. All is poised here as on the point of a needle, swinging wildly as a compass does when it finds no pole. As I write this the old Hierarch is dying of plague. Your old friend and cousin is not touched yet, and is determined to come to Grass in order that he may never be touched by any but the hands of friendship. Let me know what is happening!

It was signed by Cory Strange, Nods' oldest friend, a friend from the time he had been Nods Noddingale, which was many decades before he had become Jhamlees Zoe.

Well, Ambassador Yrarier had been on Grass only a short time. Jhamlees Zoe had heard nothing about plague yet. He thought it unlikely that he would hear anything about plague. Still, he would mention to his subordinate, Noazee Fuasoi, that he wanted to be informed of any unusual rumors. That should be vague enough.

So musing, Jhamlees Zoe wrapped the packet, the letter, and the itinerary once more and hid the resultant bundle in his files.

For a time, Rillibee spent his days in required prayer, in morning song and evening song, in special services now and again, with routine duties taking up all the time between. There was gardening to do in the sun-blessed springs and summers and falls, when crop succeeded crop endlessly under the light-handed benison of rain. Though the long, elliptical orbit of the planet brought it almost under the sun's eyelids during midsummer, this far north the heat was lessened to an almost tolerable level. There were pigs to care for and slaughter and chickens to feed and kill. There was food to put up for wintertime. They would keep him busy, they told him. Soon he would be assigned to his permanent job.

When that day came, Rillibee in his guise as Brother Lourai sneaked off to hide among the grasses with Brother Mainoa and talk about Rillibee's future. He had decided again, only that morning, not to die just yet, but that decision was not sufficient for the purposes of the Friary.

"They want to know what I want to do," Rillibee said in an aggrieved voice. "I have to tell them this afternoon."

"That's right," answered Brother Mainoa comfortably. "Now that you've settled down and it's known that the climbing apes aren't going to kill you—and that Brother Flumzee that calls himself High-bones has killed a few, though him and his friends always claim it was accidental—those set in authority over us have to decide what to do with you."

"I don't know why you think the climbers have given up wanting me dead," Rillibee objected. "Several of them are still set on killing me. Highbones wants me done with because he says I made a fool of him. He had some kind of bet that I'd end up splattered. Top-clinger's friends want him to pay up. He says his bet was with Top-clinger, and with him dead, there's no bet anymore, but they keep nagging at him, and that makes him hate me more. Ropeknots wants me out of the way because I've made him out to be a liar. The longer I stay clear of 'em, the worse they want me gone."

"Well, you should give them what they want, Brother. I always try to do that. When someone else wants something very badly, I always try to give them what they want. They want you gone, you should go. I think it's best if we can get you back to the dig with me, especially if we can do it before Elder Brother Jhamlees remembers those twenty stripes he promised you, which I heard about from someone I can't remember. However, if you say you *want* to come back to the dig with me, Elder Brother will send you anywhere on Grass except there." Brother Mainoa sucked at the grass stem he was chewing and considered the matter.

"What you should do, Lourai, is look depressed and ask them what there is for you to do. They'll mention half a dozen things, including the dig. They'll mention the gardens and the henhouses and the pig farm and carpentry shop and weaving shop and the dig. If they don't mention it, you do. Say, 'I saw the dig, too, when Brother Mainoa brought me in.' Get it into the conversation. Then, when they say 'dig,' you say, 'Dig, Elder Brother? I was there and I don't think I'd like that much.'"

"Why should I fool around with the Elder Brother? I thought you said Elder Laeroa was a sympathetic person."

"Oh, Elder Laeroa's good enough. He's interested in things, Laeroa is. In the dig. In the gardens. He's a good botanist, too. But it won't be Laeroa that assigns you to your job. That'll be assistant to the office of Sopor/ and Ignoble Doctrine, Elder Asshole Noazee Fuasoi. He hates people. His greatest joy comes from telling people to do things they don't like, so Asshole Fuasoi does all the assignments. Him and his assistant, Shoethai. Except Shoethai's so inconsequential, it's easy to forget him."

"How can you forget someone who looks like that?"

"His face is only a little lopsided."

"His face is a nightmare. And so is the rest of him. First time I saw him, I couldn't decide whether to throw up or kill him. He looks like a monster that someone tried to mash."

"I think someone did. His father, if one listens to rumor. When he saw what Shoethai looked like, he tried to kill him but didn't quite manage it. They took the man's cells out of the files and consigned him to absolute death. Then they brought Shoethai into Sanctity. He was raised there. Fuasoi got used to the way he looks, I suppose. Used to it enough to bring him here, anyhow. As for the other two Doctrine assistants, Yavi and Fumo, I've always thought they looked a little like peepers. Square and floppy and without much you could call a face." He chanted, "Jhamlees Zoe and Noazee Fuasoi, Yavi and Fumo and Shooothai," drawing the latter's name out into a chant. "Something strange about Fuasoi and Shoethai. Something weird!"

"And you want me to tell him . . ."

Brother Mainoa hummed. "Mind what I say. Just look depressed and tell him you don't think you'd like the dig much."

"Would I?"

"Would you what?"

"Would I like the dig much?"

"You'd like it better than staying here at the Friary for the next four or five Terran years, even though you've become quite a sky crawler in the last week or two. It may seem exciting right now, but it'll get boring if you live long enough. Once you've seen sky, you've seen sky, now, haven't you? Fog is fog and mist is mist and one moth is very like another. Eventually your bodyguards will get forgetful about watching out for you, and about that time Highbones or one of his cronies will knock you off a tower. Out at the dig, however, there's nobody trying to kill you and we're always finding new things. It's interesting. Here it's prayers five times a day and penitential walks between times. Here it's mind your Doctrine and keep your mouth shut, because if Fuasoi isn't listening, one of his little friends is. Yavi or Fumo or Shoethai, take your pick."

Brother Lourai grunted assent, got grudgingly to his feet, and went off toward the Friary. As he walked away, he managed to look adequately depressed without acting. Between his nighttime exaltations, he had begun to realize that though he might have found his real self again, he had found it in a foreign place that would be home for the rest of his life. Ever since they had taken him away from the canyon when he was twelve, he had hoped someday to go back home and see the trees. Sometimes he dreamed of trees. Now his hope of ever seeing a tree again was dying.

Brother Mainoa sighed, looking after the retreating figure. "He's homesick," he said to himself. "The way I was."

From the grasses came an interrogative purr, like a very soft growl.

Accustomed to this, Brother Mainoa did not even start. He shut his eyes and concentrated. How did one explain homesickness? Longing, he thought, for a place one knows very well. A place one needs to be happy. He thought the words, then tried to come up with a few pictures. Coming home in the lamplit evening. Opening a familiar door. The feel of arms around him. . . .

Tears were running down his cheeks and he pushed them away, half angrily. As often happened, the feelings he was trying to transmit had been picked up and amplified back at him. "Damn all you creatures," he said.

The growl became sorrowful.

"Last time I saw you, you were down near the dig. What are you doing up here, anyhow?"

Into his mind came a picture of a copse near the dig. At the center of it was a blankness. Amorphous blobs in shades of amethyst and pink prowled around the blankness, howling.

"You missed me?"

A purr.

"I'm coming back in a day or two. I'm just trying to get Brother Lourai to come with me, if they'll let him. A new man without all the sense knocked out of him is better for me than one of the old ones that's all soft and mushy like a sponge. 'Yes, Brother. No, Brother.' Agreein' with everything I say and then runnin' off to report me to Doctrine the minute they can. And don't you let Brother Lourai see you until I say so. You'd scare him out of a year's growth. He isn't even grown up yet. Poor lad. He's all adrift. He was to have gone home this year, but he fell apart too soon."

The picture of the opening door, the feel of arms. Brother Mainoa nodded as he tamped his pipe with a horny finger. "That's right." He shook the bag he kept his tobacco in, dried grass he called tobacco still, after all these years. He sighed.

"I've about run out of that scarlet grass that smokes so well. There's that other one somebody mentioned to me. . . ."

There was silence, no purr, nothing except a feeling of quiet breathing. Slowly, carefully, an image began to form in Brother Mainoa's mind. It was of the buildings at Opal Hill. Brother Mainoa knew them well. He had helped design the gardens there.

"Opal Hill," he said, showing that he understood.

. The picture expanded, grew more ramified. There was a woman, a man, two younger people. Not Grassians, from the way they were dressed. And horses! God in heaven, what were they doing with horses?

"That's horses," he breathed. "From Terra. Lord, I haven't seen a horse since I was five or six years old." He fell silent, aware of the pressure in his brain, the demand.

"Tell me," the pictures in his brain were asking. "Tell me about the people at Opal Hill."

Brother Mainoa shook his head. "I can't. I don't know anything. I haven't even heard anything."

A picture of a horse, strangely dwarfed against its human rider, a sense of interrogation.

"Horses are Terran animals. Men ride on them. They are one of the dozen or so truly domesticated animals, as contented in association with man as they would be in the wild. . . ."

Doubt.

"No, truly." Wondering if it was, truly.

Brother Mainoa received a strong feeling of dissatisfaction. His questioner wanted more information than this.

"I'll try to find out," said Brother Mainoa. "There must be someone I can ask. . . ."

The presence was abruptly gone. Brother Mainoa knew that if he looked into the grasses, he would see nothing. He had looked many times and had always seen just that: nothing. Whatever it was that spoke to him (and Mainoa had his own suspicions about the identity of the conversationalist), it wasn't eager to be seen.

A hail came from the pathway, Brother Lourai's voice. "Main—oh-ah." Brother Mainoa got up and started in the direction of the voice, plodding down the trail toward the Friary with no sign of either haste or interest. Brother Lourai was hurrying toward him, panting.

"Elder Brother Laeroa wants you."

"What have I done now?"

"Nothing. Nothing different, I mean. Elder Brother Laeroa caught me just as I was going into Elder Brother Fuasoi's office. It's the people from Opal Hill. They want an escorted tour of the Arbai ruins. Elder Brother Laeroa says since you'll have to go back to be tour guide, you can take me with you and just keep me there."

Interesting. Particularly so inasmuch as Mainoa's questioner had just been asking about Opal Hill. "Hum. Did you tell the Elder Asshole you didn't think you'd like the dig much?"

Brother Lourai nodded, half hiding a grin. "I thought I'd better since I was in his office. He just glared at Laeroa and told me I have to go there and be your assistant. It will teach me humility, he says."

"Well," Brother Mainoa said with a sigh. "It will teach you something—and me too, no doubt—but I doubt humility will be it."

10

When Rillibee and Brother Mainoa arrived at the dig, Mainoa lectured upon what was known about the Arbai while the two of them walked through the topless tunnels that had once been streets. To either side the fronts of houses were charmingly carved with stylized vines and fruits and humorous figures of the Arbai themselves, frolicking among the vines.

"These pictures aren't of them when they were here on Grass, then," Rillibee remarked. "There aren't any vines like that out here."

Mainoa shook his head. "No vines like that out here on the prairie, no. But there are vines with leaves and fruit like that in the swamp forest, twining around the trees, making hammocks and bridges for the birds. Almost everything that's carved on these walls and doors can be found somewhere here on Grass. There's Hippae and hounds and peepers and foxen. There's flick birds and different kinds of trees, carved so detailed you can tell what kind of trees they are, too."

"Where are the trees?" Brother Lourai wanted to know.

"In the swamp forest, boy. And in copses, here and there. I'll show you a little copse not half a mile from here."

"Trees," breathed Brother Lourai.

"There's thousands of pictures of the Arbai themselves on these walls, doing one thing and another," Brother Mainoa went on. "Happy things on the fronts of the houses, ritual things on the doors. We think. At least, on the housefronts they seem to be smiling and on the doors they're not."

"That's a smile?" Brother Lourai said doubtfully, staring at a representation of one toothy face.

"Well, given the kind of fangs they've got, we think so. What the researchers did was, they searched the archives for pictures of all kinds of animals in situations where one could postulate contentment or joy. Then they compared facial expressions. The high mucky-mucks say those are smiles. But the expressions carved on the doors aren't. Those carved on doors are serious creatures doing serious things."

Brother Lourai examined an uninjured portion of door. The faces did seem very solemn. Even he could see that. The carving was of a procession of Arbai, bordered as always by the stylized vines. "But there aren't any labels. No words."

"Lots of words in the books, we think, but none that we've ever found connected to a carving, no."

Brother Lourai sighed. It would have been pleasant to study the language of these Arbai, see what they had to think about things, see if it was the same as humans thought about things. There was a noise in the sky, away to the southwest, and his head came up—sniffing as though to smell out the sound the way Joshua always did when he heard something in the woods, like a bear, like a deer—peering into the clouds. "I hear an aircar."

"Them from Opal Hill, I guess," said Brother Mainoa. "I wonder what they wanted to see this place for."

Marjorie, aloft in the car, was wondering the same thing. It was Rigo who had wanted to meet the Green Brothers, Rigo who had felt they might have useful information. Now, however, Rigo had no time to follow up any such idea. These days Rigo had time for nothing but riding.

Marjorie had volunteered to find out if the Brothers knew anything useful, but it was the invaluable Persun Pollut who suggested that if she wanted information she should stay away from the Friary.

"They've got a kind of committee there," he had said, "an office. Acceptable Doctrine, it's called. Everyone on the committee is mostly concerned about what people believe. They're running things, too; don't let them tell you they aren't. Truth doesn't enter in. If they've decided something is doctrine, they'll ignore all evidence to the contrary and lie to your face. You don't want to run afoul of those types, do you? Not if you have questions to ask. No. Better for you to meet some of the more sensible ones. I've met Brother Mainoa, now, when he's come into the port for one thing and another. He's just as down-to-earth as any one of us commons. If there's any health problems among the Brothers, he'll tell you."

"How do I meet Brother Mainoa without involving the—the committee?" Marjorie asked.

"You might just ask to tour the Arbai ruin," Persun suggested. "He's usually there, and nine chances out of ten they'd send Brother Mainoa to guide you in any case. Mostly because the rest of them don't want to be bothered."

"I might ask to see the ruins at that," she admitted, deciding after a moment's consideration that it made good sense to do so, as well as offering a chance at amusement. There had been little amusement for any of them thus far on Grass.

Hungry for some family affection and fun, she packed an enormous lunch and asked the children if they would like to see the ruins. Tony said yes. Stella said no, she was tired, though what she had to be tired of, Marjorie couldn't imagine. Though she believed she was aware of every emotion the girl felt, Marjorie had no notion that Stella spent each night riding endlessly across the simulated prairies of Grass, creeping down the stairs to ride the Hippae machine every night while the rest of the family was asleep, retreating to her bedroom only when dawn came. Stella had told no less than the truth when she said she was tired. Only the resilience of youth helped her give the appearance of normalcy.

So Tony and Marjorie had determined to make a party of it. At the last minute, however, Father Sandoval had asked if he and Father James could go along, and so there were four of them in the over-ornamented aircar piloted by Tony with reasonable proficiency, considering he had flown the thing only a dozen times. As they approached the ruin, a misty rain began to fall, fading all the colors of the landscape into indistinct grays. When they landed they were met by two of the green-clad Brothers, an old fat one with interested eyes and a young skinny one with a tight cap of brown, curly hair, and a sad, drawn expression. When the old one saw Father Sandoval, he blinked as though he recognized ... what? A colleague? An age-mate? Someone who might be expected to be sympathetic? Or antagonistic?

"Religious?" asked Brother Mainoa. "Are you, sir, a religious?" He reached a hand toward the priest's collar, turning it into a palm-up gesture of supplication. "You and the other gentleman?"

Father bent his thin shoulders and cocked his head, nodding, as though to ask why this minion of Sanctity should care, perhaps slightly offended.

"We are Old Catholics," Father acknowledged. "This is Father James. I am Father Sandoval."

"Look at them, Brother Lourai!" demanded Brother Mainoa. "Old Catholics. Now there are ones who chose their life. Not like us." He winked at the older priest, cocking his head to a similar angle. "Brother Lourai and I, we were given, Father. Given to celibacy. Given to silence. Given to boredom. We had nothing at all to say about it. And when we couldn't tolerate what we were given to, why, then we were sent here, for punishment."

"I had heard something of that," admitted Father Sandoval, not unsympathetically. "His Excellency the ambassador told me something of the kind."

"I ask you to keep it in mind, Father. As we progress. With your tour...." He bobbed his head, chuckled, then turned and led them away. The rain had stopped. All around them the velvet turf was jeweled with droplets. Mainoa's feet made dark tracks across the gemmed surface.

Father Sandoval looked questioningly at Marjorie. She shrugged. Who knew what the old man meant? He seemed to be amused by the idea of digging up an Arbai city as punishment, though she might have misunderstood. Only Father Sandoval had been introduced by name, but perhaps it didn't matter. Perhaps the guides already knew who she was, who Tony was. As for them, the old one was Mainoa, no doubt, and he had called the other one Brother Lourai. Enough to begin with. She gestured the priest forward and followed him, Tony trailing behind her, his head swiveling as he tried to see everything at once.

The ruin was set in an area of violet grass, like soft fur upon the soil. Dug into this were sprawling trenches reached by a flight of stairs made out of ebon stems, the stout bundles staked into position, their tops flat, their stems rubbing together beneath the weight of feet to make a sound like a reprimand.

"Take off your shoes," they seemed to say. "This is death's ground. Show respect."

It was as though the visitors heard the words. Almost, Tony knelt to take off his shoes, feeling his knees bend, coming to himself with a start, shamefaced. Father Sandoval crossed himself with an expression of alert surprise and anger. Father James reached out as though to catch himself from falling. Marjorie looked bemused, wondering. She had heard voices!

Brother Mainoa looked at them and chuckled. "You heard that? I hear it, too, and so does Brother Lourai here. Elder Brother Fuasoi doesn't hear it, or says he doesn't. You're angry, Father? Thinking somebody's playing tricks? I cut those grass bundles myself, Father Sandoval. No trickery to it. I just walked out into the prairie until I found a stand of grass thick enough, then I cut them and bundled them and put them down there with strips across the top to hold them flat. And I hear voices when people step on them, and you hear things when you step on them, but others don't. Keep that in mind, Fathers, ma'am, young sir."

The shallow flight of stairs led to a street paved in stone. Where had the builders found stone among these interminable prairies? And yet stone it was, glistening in the fall of light rain, still polished after buried centuries. The stone was interrupted at intervals by curbs and pediments surrounding open spaces in the pavé.

"There were trees here." Brother Mainoa gestured upward. They looked up, feeling the shadow of moving branches, hearing the rustle of leaves. Marjorie's eyes widened. There were no trees. Only the empty plots. And yet she had seen, heard the sounds of foliage, the movement of leaves. . . .

"What kind?" she asked. "Of trees, what kind?"

The young, skinny brother answered, eagerly telling her what Mainoa had told him. "A tree found only in the swamp forest, ma'am. Some of the wood was still here when the town was uncovered. Preserved, it was. They examined the remains, and they weren't a kind of tree that grows out here. A fruit tree, they think it was."

Fronting on the narrow street were carved housefronts and wooden doors, the doors carved, so Brother Mainoa instructed them, with scenes of religious life among the Arbai.

"Religious?" Father Sandoval asked. He was too well schooled to sneer, but his doubt was manifest.

Brother Mainoa shrugged. They were scenes definitely mysterious, possibly mystical. What were they doing in those carvings? How could one be sure? What meant these figures offering tiny boxes or cubes to one another, these figures in procession? What meant these kneeling creatures, seeming to watch a grass peeper with expressions of awe upon their faces? The unknown artist had carved the peeper as though it was almost spherical and bracketed it with two hounds, noses pointed upward, surrounding the design with vines and leaves as all the designs were surrounded with vines and leaves. Personally, Brother Mainoa thought the carvings were religious. He smiled at Father Sandoval, daring him to disagree.

Father Sandoval smiled in return, keeping his opinion to himself. Father James looked from face to face, fretfully.

On another door two Hippae were back to back, kicking clods of earth at one another. Or perhaps at the strange structure between them. Was it a sculpture? Or a machine? Beside them the Arbai stood, solemnly watching. What did it mean? And how could one tell what details might have been lost when the doors were broken?

For they were broken. Splintered. Fragmented and crushed inward upon their hinges. Inside the excavated rooms—simple rooms, floored in the same stone as the streets, walled with what Brother Mainoa said was polymerized earth, with wide windows which had once looked out onto the prairies—inside those rooms were bones, hides, scales, mummified forms of people who had lived here once. Arbai. Near enough human-shaped to evoke human responses when humans saw their agony.

There were mouths open as though screaming. Empty eye sockets gazing upon horror. Here an arm and there the body, the remaining three-fingered, double-thumbed hand reaching toward the detached limb as though to reclaim it, possess it, at least to die whole—a denial of whatever horrible thing was happening.

Young ones, or at least small ones, torn in half, with adults clutching what remained to their breasts. Elsewhere, time had disintegrated the bodies and there were only piles of bones and piles of the glossy scales which had covered their hides. Everywhere the same, down every street, in every house.

Marjorie shut her eyes, hearing voices the next street over. A slippery language, full of sibilants, but punctuated with very human-sounding laughter.

"Are there other friars here?" she asked. "Digging? Working?"

"None today." Brother Mainoa smiled, regarding her curiously. "What you hear is what you hear? The sounds of this city, perhaps? Or is it only the wind? How many times I have asked myself that question. 'Mainoa,' I say. 'Is it only the wind?' Or is it the sound of these people, Lady Westriding?"

So he had already known her name.

Tony said, "I get the feeling that this place is . . . well, intentionally strange. For this world, I mean."

Brother Mainoa gave him an approving look. "So I have felt, young sir. Intentionally made, by these poor creatures, a little like their own home place, perhaps?"

"There are many strange things about Grass," Marjorie agreed, looking away from a screaming face. "Dr. Bergrem, in the town, has written about some things that make the planet unique. There is something our cells use, some long name I forget, which exists in a unique form here on Grass. She's been studying it."

"On any other world, the doctor would be renowned," Brother Mainoa said. "Her reputation is greater than the people here know."

"She could probably explain these sounds," Marjorie remarked, fighting down an overwhelming terror and despair, trying to convince herself she did not hear murmured conversation in wholly unhuman voices, musical voices with a burbling, liquid sound. "Have you asked her?"

"I have reported the effects," Brother Mainoa said. "I think the authorities believe I imagine them. So far no one has come to see whether I imagine them or not."

Father Sandoval, seeing Marjorie's distress, decided to warn her off. "Such places as this occasion superstitious awe in the unwary. We must be alert to protect ourselves from such, Marjorie. These were merely creatures, now extinct. There must have been some central business or supply area. These houses seem almost rural. They lack an urban feeling."

"So it is with all Arbai cities or towns," said Brother Mainoa. "Though we diggers know they traveled through space—perhaps in ships as we do, though we have found none, or by some other means—we know also they chose not to live in great aggregations as we humans often do. We have found no town capable of holding more than a few thousand or so of them. On most worlds there are several towns of that size, but never many."

"And here?" Marjorie asked.

"This is the only one we have found on Grass."

Father Sandoval frowned. "It is not a subject I know much about. Is it known where their home world was?"

Brother Mainoa shook his head. "Some think Repentance because there are several such cities on Repentance. I have not heard that anyone knows for sure."

"Somewhere there could be Arbai still living, then?" Father James mused, kicking at a bit of protruding stone.

The Brother shrugged. "Some believe these dead towns were only outposts, that their cities will yet be found elsewhere. I don't know. You asked about a business or market section in this town. What we assume is the market section is down this street to the left. At least, the structures there do not seem to be dwellings."

"Shops?" Father Sandoval asked. "Storerooms?"

Mainoa shrugged. "There is an open space, a plaza. With three-sided structures that could have been booths for a market. There is a building full of jars of many sizes and shapes. A building full of baskets. A central dais in the plaza, surmounted with something that could be a machine, a sculpture, a place for posting notices. Perhaps it was an altar, or a place for a herald to stand, or a place to sit while watching the stars. Or even a stage for acrobatic display. Who knows? Who can say? One building is full of their books, books which look very much as our own did, a century or so ago, before we had scanners and decks and screens."

"Bound volumes?" Marjorie asked.

"Yes. I have a team of penitents taking images of each page. I should say I have them intermittently. When there is nothing better for them to do. Though I am here much of the time, I have a crew at work only now and again. Copying the books is dull work, and lonely, but necessary. Eventually, a full set of copies will be available at Sanctity and at some major schools, like the University at Semling Prime."

"But no translation." Marjorie stared through an open door at the carnage within, willing it to be otherwise.

"None. Line after line, page after page, signs made of curving lines, intertwined. If there were something we could call a church, we could look for a repeated sequence and hope it meant 'God.' If there were a throne, we could look for the word 'King.' If there were words on the door carvings, we could feed the context into our computers, which might make sense of them. If there were even pictures in the books . . . I will show you some of the books before you leave."

"Artifacts?" asked Father James.

"Baskets. Plates. Bowls. We do not think they wore fabric, but there are belts, or more properly, sashes. Woven strips of grass fiber about six inches wide and a couple of yards long. Nicely colored, beautifully patterned. The result is much like linen, the experts tell me. The Arbai have few artifacts. It is as though they chose very carefully each thing they used. Chose each one for line or color, what we would call beauty, though many of them—the pots, particularly—do not seem beautiful to us. Perhaps I should say, 'to me.' You may find them lovely. Each thing is handmade, but without inscriptions, nothing we might translate as 'Made by John Brown.' We will see the artifacts later, Lady Westriding. We have found nothing made by machines and nothing we are sure is a machine. There are the things called the crematoria and the thing in the center of the town. Perhaps they are machines. Perhaps not. And yet, the Arbai traveled. They must have had machines. They must have had ships, and yet we have never found any."

"Are the towns everywhere like this?" Tony ran his hands along the carving, cupping the time-worn line of an alien face.

"Where there is earth, they built of earth, polymerizing the walls, making vaults or thatching the roofs. Where there are forests, they built of wood. Where there is sufficient stone, they built of stone. Here on Grass the stone comes from a quarry not far distant. The grasses have covered it, but the signs of Arbai work are there, nonetheless. Each city is different, depending upon the materials. On one planet they built high among the trees."

"Where is that?"

He looked at her as though he had forgotten who she was, trying to remember something, his face intent upon some interior search. "I . . . I can't remember. But I know they did. . . ."

"How many of their cities have you seen?" Marjorie asked.

Brother Mainoa chuckled, himself once more. "This one, lady. Only this one. But I have seen pictures of them all. Copies of reports are shared among those of us sentenced to this duty. In case something found in one place casts light on something found elsewhere. Vain hope. And yet we go on hoping."

"All like this. And all the inhabitants died," Tony said.

"Perhaps. Or went elsewhere."

They walked through what might have been a marketplace, or a meeting ground, or even a playground. At the center was the dais Brother Mainoa had described. Upon it an enigmatic strip of material curled and returned upon itself, making a twisted loop through which a tall man might walk. Tony struck it with a knuckle, hearing it ring in response. Metal. And yet it didn't look like metal. Along the edges were scalloped and indented designs, as though the molten stuff had been imprinted by mysterious fingers. The same designs decorated the edges of the dais. In the open space small flags marked the places bodies had been found, slaughtered in the open, bodies now moved under cover for later study. One flag lay within the looped structure, several others lay beside the dais, as though a gathering had been interrupted there. "What killed these people?" Tony asked.

"Foxen, some say. I think not."

"Why do you think not?" Father James was curious, brought out of his usual reticence by the strangeness of this place.

Brother Mainoa looked around him, ignoring the presence of Brother Lourai, but looking for anyone else who might be within earshot. There were no diggers on duty today, but Brothers did drop in from time to time on one errand or another, to make a delivery of foodstuff, to pick up the most recent copies of Arbai books. Some of them were undoubtedly spies for Doctrine.

When he had satisifed himself that no one was listening, Mainoa said, "We Green Brothers have been here for many years, young sir. Many years. Many Grass years. Wintered here, packed up in winter quarters like so many pickles in a jar. We've spent every spring and summer and fall among the grasses. In all that time, not one of us has ever been attacked by the foxen." His tone carried more than conviction. It carried certainty.

"Ah," said Marjorie. "So."

The Brother nodded, looking long into her eyes. "Yes, Lady Westriding. So."

"You mean the Hippae?" Tony asked, apalled. "Surely not!"

"Tony!" Marjorie said emphatically. "Let him say."

"I have nothing to say." Brother Mainoa shook his head. "Nothing at all. I would not offend unwilling ears, young sir."

"Offend my willing ones," cried Marjorie.

He gave Tony a look which said volumes before turning to Marjorie. The boy flushed.

"To you, madam, then I say this. Look at these poor creatures dead all these centuries. Observe their wounds. Then look among the aristocrats at those who no longer hunt. Look at their artificial hands and arms and legs. And tell me, then, whether that which did the one thing has not also done the other."

"But the Hippae are herbivores," Tony protested still, thinking of his father. "Behemoths. Why would they—"

"Who knows what the Hippae do, or are?" offered Brother Mainoa. "They stay far from us, except to watch us. And when they watch us—"

"We see contempt," breathed Marjorie so quietly that Tony was not sure he had heard her correctly. "We see malice."

"Malice," agreed Brother Mainoa. "Oh, at the very least, malice."

"Oh, come, come," said Father Sandoval doubtfully, almost angrily. "Malice, Marjorie?"

"I have seen it," she said, putting her arm around Tony's slender shoulders. "I have seen it, Father. There was no mistake." She confronted his scolding look with a fierce one of her own. Father Sandoval had always maintained the spiritual supremacy of man. He did not like discussion of other intelligence.

"Malice? In an animal?" asked Father James.

"Why do you say 'animal'?" asked Brother Mainoa. "Why do you say that, Father?"

"Why . . . why, because that is what they are."

"How do you know?"

Father James did not reply. Instead he reached out to help Father Sandoval, who was angrily wiping his brow and looking around him for a place to sit down.

"Over here, Fathers." Brother Lourai beckoned. "We have made our home in this house of the Arbai. I have something here for us to drink."

They sat, grateful for the refreshment and the chairs, somewhat disconcerted at the proportions of them. The Arbai had been a long-thighed race. Their chairs did not fit man. At least not these men. They perched, as on stools.

Father James returned to their conversation. "You asked why I thought the Hippae are animals? Well, I have seen them. They show no signs of being more than animals, do they?"

"What kind of sign would you accept?" Brother Mainoa asked. "Tool-making? Burial of the dead? Verbal communication?"

"I don't know. I haven't thought about it. Since we've been here, I've heard no one suggest that the Hippae or the hounds or . . . or any other animal on Grass was any more than just that."

Brother Mainoa shrugged. "Think about it, Father. Ma'am. I do. It's an interesting exercise, leading to much fascinating conjecture."

They shared lunch together, the Brothers' rations plus the plenty that Marjorie had packed. Then they walked again, down other streets, into other rooms. They saw artifacts. They saw books, endless books, pages covered with curvilinear lines. They came back past the thing on the dais that might be a machine but was definitely represented on at least one door carving, and they went on to see other things that might or might not be machines.

The light began to slant across the trenches, throwing them into shadow. Marjorie shivered as she asked, "Brother, would you come to Opal Hill to meet my husband? He is Roderigo Yrarier, ambassador from Sanctity to this place."

Brother Lourai looked up, suddenly attentive. "But I have met him!" he exclaimed. "He came to Sanctity. The Hierarch was his uncle. We spoke about the plague. The Hierarch said he must go—come here, that is—because of the horses!"

Tony turned, mouth open, not sure what he had heard.

Brother Mainoa faced Marjorie, reached out to her. "My young colleague has been indiscreet. Acceptable Doctrine denies that plague exists."

"Mother?"

"Wait, Tony." She brought herself under control. So. He had found out. Better he than Stella. She turned to the nearest of them, Rillibee. "Brother, what do you know about the plague?"

Rillibee shivered, unable to answer. "Let me die," the parrot cried from the top of a ruined wall, fluttering its gray wings.

"The boy saw his family die of it," Mainoa said hastily. "Don't ask him. Instead, think on this. Elsewhere, something killed the Arbai slowly. I know that here something killed them quickly. I know that men are dying, everywhere, and that no cure exists. So much I know. That, and the fact that Sanctity denies it all."

Her jaw dropped. Was he saying that the current plague had happened before? "What do you know about it here, on Grass?"

"We at the Friary seem to have escaped it, thus far. What else is there to know?"

"How many have died of it here on Grass?"

He shrugged. "Who can count deaths that may be hidden? Sanctity says there is no plague. Not now. Since they deny plague exists, they do not tell us if anyone dies of it. And, since there is none now,

Sanctity finds it expedient to deny that there could ever have been plagues in the past. Acceptable Doctrine is that the Arbai died of ennui. Or of some environmentally related cause. But not of plague. 'Not only are there no devils now, there never were,' says Doctrine. Still, those of us who came from outside know that plague did exist, once. And devils, too."

"You think that devils exist?" she asked with a sidelong look at Father Sandoval, whose mouth was pursed in distaste at this subject. "Have existed always, perhaps? Waiting for intelligent creatures to reach the stars? Waiting to strike them down, for hubris, perhaps?"

"Perhaps."

"You have not answered. Will you come see my husband?"

He cocked his head again, staring over her shoulder at something only he could see. "If you send a car for me, ma'am, I'll come, of course, since it would be discourteous to do otherwise. You might want to consult me about the gardens at Opal Hill. I helped plant them, after all. It would be an understandable request. If you ask my superiors to send me for any reason, likely they won't."

She was silent for a moment, thinking. "Are you very loyal to your superiors, Brother Mainoa?"

Rillibee/Lourai snorted, a tiny snort. Brother Mainoa gave him a reproving glance.

"I was given to Sanctity, ma'am. I had no say in the matter. Brother Lourai, here, he was given, too. And then, when we didn't like it, we were brought here. We had no say in that, either. I don't recollect ever being asked if I was loyal."

Father Sandoval cleared his throat and said firmly, "Thank you for your time, Brothers."

"And yours, Father."

"I'll send a car," Marjorie promised. "Within the next few days. Will you be here?"

"Now that we're here, we'll stay until someone makes us go back, Lady Westriding."

"How is it, Brother, that you knew who I was, though we had not met before?"

"Ah. A friend of mine has been interested in Opal Hill. Your name came up." He smiled vaguely. "During our discussion."

The Brothers watched the aircar leave and then returned to their quarters, where Brother Mainoa took out his journal from a hidey-hole and wrote his comments upon the happenings of the day.

"Do you always do that?" asked Rillibee/Lourai.

"Always," the older man sighed. "If I die, Lourai, look in these pages for anything I know or suspect."

"If you die." The other smiled.

Mainoa did not return the smile. "If I die. And if I die, Lourai, hide this book. They will kill you, too, if they find it in your possession.

Tony heard the word "plague" as he would have heard a thunderclap. The word began to resonate in his mind, causing other ideas to reverberate with them. Plague. One had heard of it, of course. One whispered about it. Sanctity denied there was any. For the first time he wondered why Sanctity had to continually deny something that did not exist. Why had his father gone to Sanctity and met with the Hierarch about plague?

Plague. He had seen no signs of it here. No one even talked of it, here. Tony spent a good deal of time with Sebastian Mechanic down at the village, learning the local way of things, meeting the people, getting to know them, but no one had mentioned plague. Illness, yes. The people had illnesses. Things went wrong with old bones and joints. Hearts wore out. There was very little lung trouble, though. The air breathed cleanly and caused no problems here. There were few if any infectious diseases. They had been wiped out in this small population, and the quarantine officers at the port kept Commons clean.

But plague?

"Mother," he asked softly, thinking of people he had left behind, of one person he had left behind, "is there plague at home?"

She turned a horrified look upon him, prepared to lie as she had told herself she must. "Yes," she confessed to his open, waiting face, feeling the words leave her in an involuntary exhalation. "Yes, there is plague at home. And on every other inhabited world as well."

"Here?"

"Except here. Maybe. We think. We have been told."

"You're here to find out?"

She nodded.

"You didn't tell us?"

"Stella . . ." Marjorie murmured. "You know Stella."

"But me, Mother. Me?"

"It was thought you were too young. That you might forget yourself."

"A secret? Why?"

"Because . . ." said Father Sandoval, leaning forward to grip the young man's arm, "because of the Moldies, the nihilists. If they learned of it, they would try to bring the plague here. And because the Grassians do not care if all the other worlds die. They do not wish to be disturbed."

"But . . . but that's inhuman!"

"It is not fair to say they do not care," Marjorie murmured again. "Let us say rather that they do not perceive. Various efforts to make them perceive have resulted in nothing but their annoyance. Father Sandoval is right, they do not wish to be disturbed; but there is more to it than that. Something psychological. I should say, pathological. Something that prevents their seeing or attending. So we are here under false pretenses, Tony, as ambassador and family. What we are really here for is to find out whether there is plague here. If there is not, we must somehow get permission for people to come here and find why not."

"What have you found?"

"Very little. There does not seem to be plague here, but we are not certain. Asmir Tanlig is finding out from the villagers and from servants in the estancias whether there are any unexplained deaths or illnesses. Sebastian Mechanic knows many of the port workers, and he is trying to find out the same information from them. The two men don't know why they are asking the questions. They've been told that we're making a health survey for Sanctity. We need information from the bons, as well, but we seem unable to establish any contact with them beyond the purely formal. We have been trying to make friends."

"That's why the reception was held."

"Yes."

"Eugenie's showing up with that girl didn't help things, did it."

"No, Tony. It didn't."

"Eugenie hasn't the brains of a root peeper." He said it hopelessly, waving his fingers, as though to wave Eugenie away. Neither he nor Stella could understand their father's fondness for Eugenie. "No brains at all."

"Unfortunately, that's probably close to the truth." She caught Father James' eyes upon her and flushed. Rigo's nephew probably had family loyalties to Rigo. She should not have criticized Rigo before him. She should not do it before Tony, either, except that Tony already knew . . . so much.

"I wondered what could be important enough to get you to come,"

Tony said, shaking his head. "Leaving your work at Breedertown that way. But surely they can't be depending only on us. What is Sanctity doing?"

"According to Rigo, everything they can. They can't get any animal, including man, to create an antibody to the virus. They can kill the virus, but not in a living creature. Eventually, if we find there is no plague here, we will ship some tissue samples from here back to Sanctity."

"Tissue samples? Will the bons let you do that?"

"They have no physicians among themselves, Tony. If they are injured, they must call upon doctors from Commons. I think we can buy whatever samples will be needed."

"But so far, Sanctity has found nothing."

"Nothing. No tissue they have tested makes antibodies to the virus."

The four of them were huddled together like conspirators. "Tony, you mustn't—"

"Mustn't tell Stella. I know. She would blurt it out, just to prove we can't tell her what to do."

Father Sandoval nodded in agreement. "I think that's probably true." He had known Stella since she was a child. She confessed a fair number of sins—usually, with maximum drama, not the ones she was most guilty of. Anger, mostly. Anger at Marjorie for not having provided that indefinable something Stella had always wanted. After long thought and meditation, Father Sandoval had decided it was perhaps the same thing Rigo wanted—the thing called intimacy. Though neither of them would set themselves aside long enough to work for it. They wanted family, but they wanted it on command, like water from a spout, ready when they turned it on, absent otherwise. "Help me now, give me now, comfort me now. Then, when you've done it, get out of my way!"

Father Sandoval sighed again, wishing his years had given him better insight into Stella, and into her father. Stella, of course, would eventually marry and could then be instructed to be obedient to her husband as she was now instructed to be obedient to her parents. But what could one do with Rigo? Both he and Stella were too impatient to woo. They would storm or nothing. Overwhelm, or nothing. They would not beg. They would take by right. Even things they should not take at all.

Unaware of Father Sandoval's concern, Stella, meantime, was upon the simulacrum in the sixth hour of her current ride: eyes glazed, back braced, beyond hunger or thirst in a trance of her own evoking.

Her father had finished his own session on the machine hours ago. Hector Paine was gone. No one else would come into the winter quarters. She had set the timing mechanism for seven hours, two hours longer than she had ever ridden before, and had vaulted aboard. There was no way to stop the machine once she had started, no way to get off the mount save by falling.

On the screens around her the grasses whipped past. Devices at her side mimicked the blows of the blades, striking her hat, her coat. The machine rocked and twisted, always slightly off rhythm so that she could not relax. The body stayed alert, but the brain eventually gave up thinking and retreated into some never-never land beyond exhaustion. Stella was there now, dreaming of Sylvan bon Damfels.

During the reception at Opal Hill, she had watched him as he danced with Marjorie, watched, devoured, swallowed him whole. When she had danced with him, she had absorbed him through her skin, taken his image into herself so that he dwelt there, a paradigm of the real and genuine man. And since that time she had undressed him and possessed him and done with him all those things she had not yet done with others, not through any sense of morality but because she had not yet found one she thought worthy of herself. Now she had. Sylvan was worthy. Sylvan was noble. Sylvan was one to whom she might be mated. No! The one to whom she would be mated. In just a little time. In the time it would take for her to ride, as he rode, so that she might ride by his side.

She ignored what he had said to Marjorie about riding, ignored his advice to the Yrariers. It did not fit her picture of him, so she struck it from his image as she built him anew, according to her own needs—the gospel of St. Sylvan, according to Stella, his creator.

The machine galloped on, its springs and levers walloping and sliding, the sound of hooves thundering softly from its speakers, the pictured stems of grass fleeing everlastingly on either side, the blades lashing at her with softly sounded strokes.

In some remote part of her mind she told Elaine Brouer all about Sylvan, about their meeting, the way their eyes had met. "He loved me in that moment. In that very moment, he loved me as he had never loved anyone before."

Sylvan was saying much the same thing to himself as he walked a winding path deep in the famed grass gardens of Klive. "I loved her in that moment. I loved her the moment I saw her. The moment I took her into my arms. As I have never loved before."

He was not speaking of Stella. He was speaking of Marjorie.

11

"Bless me, Father, for I have sinned." Marjorie was kneeling in the confessional at the side of the chapel, the evening light falling upon her face. The chapel was dusk dim, the light near the altar making a watchful eye in the shadow. "I have resented my daughter. And my husband. . . ."

She was alone in the chapel except for Father James. Rigo was closeted in the winter quarters with Hector Paine. Stella and Tony and Father Sandoval had ridden the mares down to the village to visit Sebastian Mechanic and his wife, Dulia, who was, said Sebastian, the best cook on any six planets. Since the reception, Eugenie had scarcely put her nose outside her house and was there now. As Marjorie had come through the gardens to the chapel she had heard Eugenie singing, a slightly drunken lament with no particular burden of woe. The blues, Marjorie recalled having read somewhere, needed no proximate motivation. Any common grief would do. The ancient song, though not particularly melodic, had entered Marjorie's ear and now turned there, playing itself over persistently, hating to see the evening sun go down.

"I have lost patience with Stella," she said. Father James needed no explanation for this. He knew them all far too well to need explanation. "I have had angry words with Rigo. . . ." Words about the Hunt, words about his risking his neck and more than his neck. "I have doubted God. . . ."

Father James woke up at this. "How have you doubted?"

If God were good, Rigo and I would be in love, and Rigo would not treat me as he does, she thought. If God were good, Father Sandoval would not treat me as a mere adjunct to my husband, sentencing me to obedience every time I am unhappy. I haven't done anything wrong, but I'm the one who is being punished and it isn't fair. She longed for justice. She bit her lip and said none of this, but instead dragged false scent across the trial. "If God is truly powerful, he would not let this plague go on."

There was silence in the confessional, silence lasting long enough for Marjorie to wonder whether Father James might not really have fallen asleep. Not that she blamed him. Their sins were all boring enough, repetitive enough. They had enough capital sins roiling around to condemn them all. Pride, that was Rigo's bent. Sloth, Eugenie's trademark. Envy, that was for Stella. And she, Marjorie, boiling with uncharitable anger toward them all. Herself, who had always tried so hard not to be guilty of anything!

"Marjorie." Father James recalled her to herself. "I cut my hand upon a grass blade a few days ago, a bad cut. It hurt a great deal. Grass cuts do not seem to heal easily, either."

"That's true," she murmured, familiar with the experience but wondering what he was getting at.

"It came to me suddenly as I was standing there bleeding all over the ground that I could see the cut there between my fingers but I could not heal it. I could observe it, but I couldn't do anything about it even though I greatly desired to do so. I could not command the cells at the edges of the wound to close. I was not, am not privy to their operations. I am too gross to enter my own cells and observe their function. Nor can you do so, nor any of us.

"But suppose, just suppose, that you could create ... oh, a virus that sees and reproduces and thinks! Suppose you could send it into your body, commanding it to multiply and find whatever disease or evil there may be and destroy it. Suppose you could send these creatures to the site of the wound with an order to stitch it up and repair it. You would not be able to see them with your naked eye. You would be unable to know how many of them there were in the fight. You would not know where each one of them was or what it was doing, what agonies of effort each was expending or whether some gave up the battle out of fatigue or despair. All you would know is that you had created a tribe of warriors and sent it into battle. Until you healed or died, you would not know whether that battle was won."

"I don't understand, Father."

"I wonder sometimes if this is what God has done with us."

Marjorie groped for his meaning. "Wouldn't that limit God's omnipotence?"

"Perhaps not. It might be an expression of that omnipotence. In the microcosm, perhaps He needs—or chooses—to create help. Perhaps He has created help. Perhaps he creates in us the biological equivalent of microscopes and antibiotics."

"You are saying God cannot intervene in this plague?"

The invisible person beyond the grating sighed. "I am saying that perhaps God has already done his intervening by creating us. Perhaps He intends us to do what we keep praying He will do. Having designed us for a particular task, he has sent us into battle. We do not particularly enjoy the battle, so we keep begging him to let us off. He pays no attention because He does not keep track of us individually. He does not know where in the body we are or how many of us there are. He does not check to see whether we despair or persevere. Only if the body of the universe is healed will he know whether we have done what we were sent to do!" The young priest coughed. After a moment, Marjorie realized he was laughing. Was it at her, or at himself? "Do you know of the uncertainty principle, Marjorie?"

"I am educated," she snorted, very much annoyed with him.

"Then you know that with very small things, we cannot both know where they are and what they are doing. The act of observing them always changes what they are doing. Perhaps God does not look at us individually because to do so would interrupt our work, interfere with our free will. . . ."

"Is this doctrine, Father?" she asked doubtfully, annoyed, wondering what had come over him.

Another sigh. "No, Marjorie. It is the maundering of a homesick priest. Of course it isn't doctrine. You know your way around the catechism better than that." He rubbed his head, thankful for the seal of the confessional. Even though Marjorie needed to take herself far less seriously, Father Sandoval would not appreciate what he had just said. . . .

"If the plague kills us all, it will be because of our sins," she said stubbornly. "Not because we didn't fight it well enough. And our souls are immortal."

"So Sanctity says. So the Moldies say," he murmured. "They say we must all be killed off so our souls can live, in the New Creation."

"I don't mean we're excused from fighting the plague," she objected. "But it's our sins that brought it on us."

"Our sins? Yours and mine, Marjorie?

"Original sin," she muttered. "Because of the sin of our first parents." First parents very much like Rigo and Stella, passionately acting out whatever moved them, without thought. Even laughing, perhaps, as they tore the world apart. Never sober and reverent as they ought to be. Never peaceful. She sighed.

"Original sin?" the young priest asked, curious. At one time he had believed it without question, but he wasn't sure anymore. There were some other catechetical things he wasn't sure of, either. His doubt about doctrine should signal some crisis of faith, he thought, but his faith was as strong as it had ever been, even though his acceptance of details was wavering. "So you believe in original sin?"

"Father! It's doctrine!"

"How about collective guilt? Do you believe in that?"

"What do you mean?"

"Are the bons guilty, collectively, for what happened to Janetta bon Maukerden?"

"Is that a doctrinal question?" she asked doubtfully.

"How about the Sanctified?" he asked. "Are they collectively guilty of condemning their boy children to prison? Young Rillibee, for example. Was he sent into servitude because of collective guilt, or because of original sin?"

"I'm an Old Catholic. I don't have to decide where Sanctity went wrong, so long as I know it did!"

He kept himself from laughing. Oh, if only Marjorie had more humor. If Rigo had more patience. If Stella had more perception. If Tony had more confidence. And if Eugenie had more intelligence. Never mind their sins, just give them more of what they needed.

He sighed, rubbing the sides of his forehead to make the sullen ache go away, then gave her both absolution and a reasonable penance. She was to accept that Rigo would ride to hounds and she was to try not to judge him harshly. Father Sandoval had been sentencing Marjorie to affectionate support for years. Father James thought affectionate support was probably a bit much. Marjorie, repentant but weary, ready to grit her teeth over yet another session of affectionate support, was surprised enough by the penance to accept it. She wouldn't judge Rigo, but she needn't support him, either. It was not until later, as evening drew on, that she remembered what Father James had said about thinking viruses and guilt and sin. Once she began considering the questions he had asked, she could not get them out of her mind.

In the chapel, meantime, Father James knelt to beg forgiveness for himself. It had been wicked of him to challenge Marjorie's faith when what he was really wanting was to shore up his own. He was not at all sure that being nonjudgmental about Rigo was a good thing for Marjorie to do. If what the bons were doing was sinful, then Rigo had no business doing it at all. Rigo had convinced himself he was joining the bons in their obsession out of a sense of duty. Father James thought ego was the more likely reason, and Father Sandoval was too set in his ways to offer anything but clichés. Father James wished for Brother Mainoa to talk with. Or the younger one, Lourai. He had a feeling they shared a good many things besides their age.

In the night, a rhythmic thunder.

Marjorie woke and went walking through the halls of the residence, encountering Persun Pollut, himself stalking nervously from place to place, pulling his long ears, twisting his beard into tails.

"What is it?" she whispered. "I've heard it before, but never so close as this."

"The Hippae, they say," he murmured in return. "In the village, that's what they say. Often in the spring they hear this sound, many times during the lapse. It woke me, so I came up here to the big house see that all of you were all right."

She laid a hand on his arm, feeling the shivering of his skin beneath the fabric. "We're fine. What are they doing, the Hippae?"

He shook his head. "I don't think anyone knows. Dancing, they say. Sebastian says he knows where. Someone told him where, but he doesn't like to talk about it."

"Ah." They stood together, looking out the tall windows across the terrace, feeling the beat of the thunder through the soles of their feet. A mystery. As all of Grass was a mystery. And she, Marjorie, was doing nothing about it.

She was still thinking of viruses, considering what a thinking virus might do, one whom God did not observe or command but merely allowed to do what it was created for.

"Ask Sebastian to come see me, will you, Persun?"

"Tomorrow," he promised. "When it gets light."

Far across the grasses, beyond the port and Commons, beyond the swamp forest, the same sound beat upon the ears of all those at Klive. The bon Damfels family was wakeful, listening. Some were more than merely wakeful.

In a long, dilapidated hallway in the far reaches of the vast structure, Stavenger bon Damfels dragged his struggling Obermum down a long, dusty hallway. One of his hands was twisted into Rowena's hair, the other held her by the collar of her gown, half throttling her. Blood from her forehead dripped onto the floor.

"Stavenger." She choked, clinging to his legs. "Listen to me, Stavenger."

He seemed not to hear her, not to care whether she spoke. His eyes were red and his mouth was drawn into a lipless line. He moved like an automaton, one leg lurched forward, then the other drawn up to it, heaving at her with both hands as though he lifted a heavy sack.

"Stavenger! Oh, by all that's holy, Stavenger! I did it for Dimity!"

Behind the struggling pair, hiding themselves around corners and behind half-open doors, Amethyste and Emeraude followed and cowered. Since they had seen Stavenger strike Rowena down in the gardens—he either not noticing his daughters behind a screening fountain of grass or not caring if they saw—they had followed him and their mother. The corridor they had come to was ancient, littered, untended and untenanted. The five-story wing that held it had not been used for at least a generation. Above them, the ceiling sagged in wide, shallow bubbles, stained with water which had leaked through the rotted thatch and permeated the three floors above. The portraits on the walls were corrupted with mold, and the stairs they had climbed were punky with rot.

"He doesn't know what he's doing," Amy whispered, tears running down her face and into the corners of her mouth. She licked them away and said again, "He's gone crazy. He doesn't know!"

"He does," Emmy contradicted, pointing to the light she carried. "There haven't been any lights in this old place since before we were born, but there's everlights all along the hall. He got them out of the garage, just like I got this one. He put them here before. He planned it."

Amy, looking at the dim lanterns set here and there on rickety tables or hung on doorknobs, nodded unwillingly. "Why! Why is he doing this to her?"

"Shhh," her sister cautioned, pulling them both back into the shadow. Stavenger had stopped at the end of the corridor to thrust Rowena through an open door, pulling it closed behind her and locking it. The key ground in the lock with a rusty finality. He thrust it into his pocket and then stood there, as though listening.

"Rowena." A voice like metal—harsh and hideous.

No sound from beyond the door.

"You'll never go there again! Never to Opal Hill again! Never consort with *fragras* again! Never betray me again!"

Silence.

He turned and took up the nearest lamp, then came down the corridor toward them, gathering up the everlights as he came. Slowly he plodded, his face expressionless, passing the door behind which his daughters trembled, leaving the place in darkness, going away as though forever.

They waited, listening for the sound that came at last, the heavy thunder of the door closing, two stories below.

Behind the locked door at the end of the corridor rose the sound of a woman's howling, an interminable, grief-driven wail of pain and betrayal.

With trembling fingers, Emeraude turned on the everlight she carried and the two of them ran to the door, stumbling over warped floorboards, kicking up small, choking clouds of dust.

The door was heavy and thick, made of wood from a swamp-forest tree and hung by great metal hinges in a solid frame. Only a few doors at the estancia were this heavy, this immovable. The main door of the house. The door of Stavenger's private office. The treasury door. What had this room once been, to have needed all this weight of wood?

They knocked, called, knocked again. The howl went on and on.

"Find Sylvan!" Emeraude urged her sister in a frantic whisper. "He's the only one who can help, Amy."

Amethyste turned haunted eyes on her sister, babbling, "I thought I'd ask Shevlok—"

Emmy shook her, demanding her attention. "Shevlok's useless. He's done nothing but drink since Janetta showed up at that party. He isn't even conscious most of the time."

"If the lapse would get over—"

"If the lapse would get over, he'd go hunting all day and be drunk all night. Find Sylvan!"

"Emmy . . ."

"I know! You're scared to death of Papa. Well, so am I. He's like . . . he's like one of the Hippae, all shining eyes and sharp blades so you can't come near him. I keep thinking he will knock me down and trample me to death if I open my mouth. But I'm not going to leave Mama bleeding in there, penned up like that with no food and no water. I won't let her die like that, but you know Papa will if we let him."

"Why did Papa—"

"You know perfectly well why. Mama went to Opal Hill, she talked to the people who found Janetta. She's got the idea that . . . that . . ." Emeraude struggled for words, choking on them, eyes bulging as she tried to say what she was not permitted to say.

"Never mind," her sister said, shaking her. "I know. I'll find Sylvan. You stay here and tell him what happened, in case I don't have a chance to explain."

"Take the light. I'll wait here."

Amy sped down the stairs, shuddering away from the banister, which creaked and sagged outward beneath her hand. This ruin was connected to the main house by the old servants' quarters and the aircar garage. The connecting door was locked, had been locked by their father when they had followed him here, he with that wild, mad look in his eyes, dragging Rowena as though she had been a sack of grain. He had locked the door again when he went out, but there was a broken window nearby which gave onto a long drying yard and the summer kitchens. The girls had come through that. It was almost midnight. The servants would long ago have gone to bed. Even if one or two of them lingered in the kitchens, their sympathies would be with Rowena more than with Stavenger.

A Stavenger who was at this moment in the main hallway screaming unintelligibly at Figor, ranting and threatening so that the whole household had wakened to hear him. Figor, wisely, was saying nothing while allowing the storm to pass. Other family members, wakened by the uproar, stayed out of the way. The great building hummed with murmuring voices, clattered with doors opening and closing, and was yet quiet, silent except for the bellowing voice.

Amy ignored the noise. At this hour, Sylvan would be in his room, or in the library, or in the gymnasium, two floors below. The library was closest, and she found him there in a secluded corner, eyes fixed on a book, fingers in his ears. She knelt beside him and pulled the fingers away.

"Sylvan, Papa has beaten Mama and locked her in the old wing. Emmy's waiting there. Mama's got no food, no water, Sylvan. Emmy and I think he means to leave her there. . . ."

She was talking to the chair. Sylvan was up and gone.

In the first light of morning Sebastian Mechanic came to the estancia, where he found Marjorie having a very early breakfast. In answer to her request, he pointed a direction, though unwillingly, suggesting to her that going out into the grasses alone was not a good idea. He did not like the look of her. Her eyes were haunted and she was too thin. Some deep tiredness seemed to oppress her. Despite her appearance of weariness, perhaps illness, she was sensible enough to agree with him that it would be foolish to go into the grasses. She told him she had simply been curious, then asked after his wife and family and made small talk with disarming patience and charm.

When he, assured that she had been merely inquisitive, had gone back to his work, Marjorie went out to the stables and saddled Don Quixote. It was not part of her intention to tell anyone where she was going, though she did leave a message with one of the grooms.

"If I'm not back by dark," she said, "but not before then, tell my husband or son I'd like him to come look for me in the aircar. I'm carrying a beacon, so I should be easy to find." The personal beacon was strapped to her leg under her trousers. Any sharp blow would set it off. If she were thrown from a horse, for example. Or if she struck it sharply with her fist. She was carrying a trip recorder of the type used by cartographers, which would serve as a direction finder. She had a laser knife with her as well, to clear her way through tall grass if that became necessary. She showed both of these to the stableman, telling him what they were for. She wanted everything about her journey to speak of purpose. She wanted no one to suppose that she had planned not to come back. It was a risk, that's all. Still, if something happened to her, it would solve Rigo's problem. And Stella's. And her own. Resolutely, she did not think of Tony.

Quixote pawed the soil, flickers of movement running up his twitching hide from fetlocks to withers and down again. Not nerves, not precisely. Something more than that. It was a kind of agitation Marjorie was unfamiliar with, and she stood for a long time stroking his legs, talking to him, trying to imagine what had brought him to this state. He leaned into her, as though for support, yet when she mounted him he trotted out into the grasses as though for a ride on any ordinary day. He meant by this that he trusted her. Though he might die of it, he trusted her. He could not quite keep the nervous quiver from his skin, however, and the message eventually reached her after they had traversed some little distance. She flushed, ashamed to be using him in this fashion when his own nature spoke so strongly against it. She stroked him, expressing her own trust. "Father James says God has made viruses of us, Quixote, but I suppose one virus may still love another, or have another kind of virus as a friend. I won't put you into a trap, my friend. I won't let you get close enough for that." And myself? she thought. Shall I put myself in danger?

Suicide was forbidden, but much glory was given to martyrs. If she killed herself, would God even notice? According to what Father James had said, God probably did not know which of His viruses were involved in doing His work. To God, she had no name. No individuality. If she killed herself, would He even know? Did it matter if He knew? When He had created her, had He also created a mechanism for saving her soul? Did viruses even have them?

Still, there had been all those years of being taught it was wrong to take one's own life. She would not feel right about getting herself purposely killed off. She could take a calculated risk, however. If she died, it would be accidentally, and Don Quixote would survive. Fleet as the wind, Quixote. Without her on his back he could outrun the devil himself. So she told herself before she stopped thinking about it, devoting most of her energy to not thinking of it. She could not help wondering about Rigo's reaction if she didn't return. "That silly fool," he would say. "That silly woman who never loved me as she ought."

She did love him. Or, she wanted to love him. Wanted to love him and wanted to love Stella with a desire that poured out hurtfully until she was exhausted from the flow of it. At home, she had known about Eugenie, and the one before Eugenie, but they had not been nearby. At home, Stella had had distractions and friends. Here, both Stella and Eugenie beat at her like huge trapped birds, pecking at her. Their frustrations hammered at her. She had not expected to feel weak, to be sleepless, to feel the threat of death always at her back. Each day on Grass had taken a little more of her strength, a little more of her purpose. Lately she had felt no hope, she who had always lived from disappointment to disappointment on a childlike, hopeful optimism which she could now barely remember.

She rode past the little arena where the horses were exercised, a place that lay just outside the grass gardens of Opal Hill, though it seemed remote because of the topography. Now, for the first time, Marjorie was leaving the close confines of that area which those who defined such things considered to be the estancia. The gardens were behind her. The prospects that the gardens overlooked were behind her. She was entering upon the wild grasses, the surface of the planet, the part into which men and their works and their creatures were not allowed to intrude. She rode, eyes forward, not thinking about anything very much except that she was unhappy enough that if the Hippae were to be found, out here in the grass, perhaps she would learn something useful about them or they would kill her, and she did not at that moment much care which.

The howl, when it came, made Don Quixote tremble, ears up, stopping dead still. Marjorie sat, scarcely breathing, aware that the howl had come from behind her. In that instant she remembered Janetta bon Maukerden and realized that the Hippae, if they found her, might do less—or more—than kill her. She had considered that they might kill her and had accepted that. She had not considered the range of alternatives which might result from her behavior, and she was abruptly both shamed and terrified.

They had been following a kind of trail, a winding path of short grasses among the taller ones. She urged Don Quixote off this easy way and into the taller grass, dismounting to tug stems into line to hide the way she had come.

"They'll smell you," she told herself, trying to quell her alarm by moving slowly and deliberately. The wind was blowing toward her from the direction the howl had come. That one would not smell her. Some other one might. It would be wise to return. Overwhelmed with the stupidity of what she had been doing, she told herself that returning would be the best possible thing to do.

She opened the trip recorder, watching it as she guided the stallion in a shallow turn which ended with him headed back toward the embassy, still hidden in tall grass, now traveling toward whatever it was she had heard. He went only a little way, then stopped. Something howled again, quite close, between them and the embassy.

The horse turned and walked quietly on his own trail. When Marjorie attempted to guide him, he ignored her. After one brief spasm of panic, she sat quietly, letting him alone. So. So, he knew something she didn't. Smelled something she couldn't. Felt something she couldn't. She sat still, not bothering him, trying to say an act of contrition, unable to remember phrases she had known since childhood. The words didn't fit, anyhow. How could she be heartily sorry for having öffended God when, for all she knew, she was doing exactly what God intended!

The stallion moved up and down hills, along the sides of ridges, always walking, not hurrying, ears alert, as though someone were whispering his name. When he slowed at last, it seemed to be in response to other sounds, ahead of them. When he stopped, he went down on his side all at once, without the signal. She drew her leg from beneath his upcurved body and stood up, staring at him. He flattened himself, ears still alert, watching her.

"All right," she whispered. "So now what?"

He made no sound, but his skin quivered, flicked, as though stung by flies. Danger. All around them.

Marjorie felt it, could see it on the horse's skin, could smell it. The trip recorder said that they had come in the general direction Sebastian had indicated. A repetitive sound, not loud but persistent, made Don Quixote move his head about, seeking its source. It was not the violent thunder of the previous night, but rather an organized series of moans and cries, rhythmic both in occurrence and volume. Quixote's nostrils dilated, his skin jerked as though from a terrible itch. The wind had gusted toward them, bringing the sound clearly and a smell . . . a smell of something totally strange. Not a stink. Not a perfume. Neither attractive nor repellent. Marjorie got out her laser knife and cut armfuls of grass, laying these across Don Quixote's body, hiding him, perhaps hiding his smell. Then she fell to her belly and crawled through the taller grasses toward the sounds the wind brought, down from a low ridge to the south. As she crested the ridge, she lay quiet, peering through the grass stems.

Toward the smell the wind brought. She breathed it in, lungs full.

The sky dilated and she fell simultaneously upward toward it and downward, crushing herself.

Under her chin her arm flattened, becoming no thicker than a sheet of paper.

Something stepped painlessly on her head, smashing it.

Her body vanished. She tried to move a finger and could not.

Hounds. A shallow, grassy bowl of hounds, seated hounds, crouched hounds, gray and algae green and muddy violet, heads back and lips drawn to reveal lengthy fangs and a double row of teeth down each side of the massive jaws from which the grunting, rhythmic chorus came. Their hides danced, plunged, were jabbed at erratically from within, as though they had swallowed living things which fought to gain release. Blank, white orbs of eyes stared at the sky. The open, falling sky.

The smell. The shallow bowl of earth was full of the smell. She lay at the edge of that bowl. Her tongue lolled on her lower teeth, dripping.

There, across the bowl, an abrupt, vertical wall, the wall pierced with tall, evenly spaced openings through which the morning light intruded to reveal a cavern beyond. Hippae moved there, one or two, in a pattern, weaving, prancing, feet high, heads back, barbs clashing.

Among the crouching hounds, heaps of pearly spheres the size of her head. Migerers there, moving the spheres, shifting them so that all lay in the sun evenly, turning them over, holding them up in horny forepaws and listening to them. What were they then? Eggs?

There, also, in the bowl outside the cavern, some dozens of the sluglike peepers, only the rippling movement of their hides betraying that they were living things.

The smell seemed to press her down. She was two-dimensional, a limp cloth lying flat behind the grasses, a cloth with eyes.

The hounds were large, very large. As large as draft horses, though not so long in the leg. The peepers were huge ones, twice the usual size. Within the cavern, a myriad of tattered shapes danced on the air, dark batlike creatures with a fringe of fangs. One of them landed on the back of a hound's neck, fastening itself there. After a time it detached and began its jerking, erratic flight once more.

One of the hounds began to pant, then to howl. The howling faded into a whining cry, then the panting began once more. On the sunlit soil, the peepers drew themselves into spherical masses, all wrinkles smoothed away. So familiar. She had seen it before. Somewhere. Somewhen.

Gradually, all sound ended. The creatures seemed frozen in their immobility. The violent motion inside the hides of the hounds ceased. There was quiet, long quiet.

A Hippae emerged from the cavern, pacing slowly, feet raised high at every step, nostrils flared, lips opening to emit breathy barks, warning sounds. After a time, the other Hippae came out to confront the first, neck swollen, jaw pulled back against the arching neck, eyes rolling wildly as it joined in the brusque, hostile sounds.

They backed away from one another, turning their heads, bowing their necks, the wicked neck barbs bristling to one side like a fan of sabers as they moved back, back, the distance widening between them. Then they charged one another, each array of barbs passing through the other, to gouge long wounds along the other's ribs and flanks. Long streaks of blood appeared on their sides, and they pawed the ground with razorlike hooves, hammering at it before they turned to charge again. Again the flashing barbs and the streaks of blood. Marjorie cowered, mentally, as they thrust at one another, rearing high, hooves flashing.

Until, at last, one of the Hippae fell to his knees and was slow to rise to all four feet again.

The other animal backed away to the front of the cave and rummaged there. It turned its back on its enemy, kicked backward, sending black missiles flying. What was it kicking at its defeated opponent? Black things. Powdery black things that broke when they landed. Like puffballs, bursting into clouds of black dust when they struck. Kicking dead bats at one another. The thing Sylvan had said. . . .

Silent. A game. The game. In silence.

The victorious Hippae tossed its head, sought with its teeth for new missiles from around the entrances to the cavern, laid them out in the open, then turned to kick back once more. One of the missiles struck the head of the kneeling beast, covering it in black dust. The defeated one bowed low, struggled to its feet, and departed, walking up the bank of the hollow and away.

It had had the pace and finish of ritual. A ritual battle. Now over.

And then sound. The wind was blowing from behind her. One of the swollen peepers ripped open. Protruding from the torn skin of the peeper was the triangular, fanged head of a hound. The peeper skin ripped further. Two hound forelegs emerged, and then, very gradually, the entire beast.

It looked small and ridiculously fragile as it staggered to its feet and stumbled through one of the vertical openings into the cavern, carefully avoiding the heaped eggs. Marjorie heard the sound of lapping from within. After a long pause, the creature emerged once more with dripping jaws, already more sure upon its feet, already sleek, its body distended with moisture. The Hippae stood upon the edge of the hollow, whistling. The young hound climbed to meet it, nibbling, as it went, at the low, blue grasses which grew there. Even as Marjorie watched, the beast seemed to enlarge in size, gaining both stature and bulk. After a time it went away, slowly though purposefully. The wind was blowing harder.

Another ripping sound drew her eyes across the hollow. As a hound had emerged from the torn skin of a peeper, so now a Hippae was emerging from the torn skin of a hound. Metamorphosis. Through the sundered skin of one of the huge hounds a row of barbs protruded, tiny blades which slit the skin, allowing the Hippae head to emerge. The process stopped when the head was out, its eyes closed and unseeing. All was silent.

What was she doing? The wind was strong now, blowing the smell away. What was she doing? Lying there? Flat? Only her eyes had dimension. Only her eyes.

They hurt. She blinked, noticing that they were dry, aching. She hadn't blinked. Not for a long, long time. The skin on the back of her neck itched, as though something were watching her. She turned, trying to see through the curtaining grasses. Something was out there. She couldn't see it or hear it, but she knew it was there. She wriggled back down the slope, stumbled through the grasses to find Quixote where he lay as she had left him but with his head up, ears erect and swiveling, nostrils twitching. The sun was falling toward the horizon. Tall grasses feathered the hollows with long, ominous shadows. She urged him up and mounted, letting him have his head, trusting in his ability to bring them both home if they were ever to come there again.

The stallion moved by a route more direct than the one they had taken in the morning, though still moving as though someone called his name. He was as aware as she that darkness was not far off, more aware than she of the threat abroad in the grasses. Quixote could smell what she could not, Hippae, many of them, not far away but upwind from them. They had been coming closer for the past hour, moving this way and that, as though searching. Quixote leaned into his stride, eating the prairie with his feet, returning to Opal Hill in a long curve which took him as far from the approaching Hippae as he could get, gradually lengthening the distance between them. Out there, somewhere, something approved of him. Something told him he was a good horse.

They arrived at the stables just at dusk. The stableman she had entrusted with her message was waiting for her, his eyes on the horizon as though to judge whether she had returned by sundown or not. "Message, Lady," he told her eagerly. "Your son's been looking for you. A message came for you, private. From bon Damfels' place, he thinks."

She stood beside the horse, trembling, unable to speak.

"Lady? Are you all right?"

"Just . . . just tired," she mumbled. She felt dizzy, unfocused, unsure what had happened to her. It was like a dream. Had she really gone out alone? Into the grasses alone? She looked into the horse's eyes, finding there an unhorselike awareness which for some unaccountable reason did not surprise her. "Good Quixote," she said, running her hands down his neck. "Good horse."

She left him with a final pat and went up the path as quickly as she could, still stumbling. Tony was watching for her from the terrace. "Where've you been? You tell me not to go out there alone and then you go off for a whole day. Honestly, mother! You look awful!"

Carefully, she decided not to respond to this. No matter how she looked, she felt . . . better. More purposeful. For the first time since her arrival in this place, purposeful. "The stableman said something about a message?"

"From Sylvan, I think. He's the only one who calls you 'The honorable lady, Marjorie Westriding.' It's keyed for you. I couldn't read the thing."

"What on earth?"

"What on Grass, more likely. Come on."

"Where's your father?"

"Still on that damned machine." There was a catch in his voice, as though either grief or anger lurked just below the surface.

"Tony. There's nothing you can do about it."

"I keep feeling I ought to—"

"Nonsense. He ought to stop this nonsense. If you took part in it, too, everything would be worse than it already is."

"Well, there's no way to interrupt him, and he's got another hour or two."

She sat down at the tell-me, letting the identity beam flick across her eyes. The message began on the screen: PRIVATE. FOR THE INTENDED RECIPIENT ONLY.

"Tony, turn your back."

"Mother!"

"Turn. If he's said something embarrassingly personal, I don't want you seeing it," she said, wondering as she said it why she should think Sylvan would be that personal.

She pressed the release and saw the message in its entirety. PLEASE HELP. NEED TRANSPORT FOR SELF, MOTHER, TWO OTHER WOMEN TO COMMONER TOWN. CAN YOU BRING AIRCAR QUIETLY TO BON DAMFELS VILLAGE? SIGNAL PRIVATE.

"Turn around, Tony. It's all right."

The boy read, stared, read once more. "What's going on?"

"Evidently Sylvan needs to get Rowena away from Klive but can't do it on his own. He has to do it secretly. The implication of that is that he has to keep it from someone, probably Stavenger."

"Do you think Stavenger bon Damfels found out that Rowena came here to ask about Janetta?"

"Possibly. Or maybe she's had a fight with Stavenger and is afraid. Or you make up some other story. Your plot is as likely to be true as mine is."

"I'm pretty good with the aircar by now."

"So's Persun Pollut. I need you to stay here and explain to your father if he asks where I am, which he probably won't." The bitterness in her voice was clear to the boy.

He flushed, wanting to help her but not knowing how. "Why don't you let me take them. Or send Persun alone."

"I've got to talk to Sylvan. I saw something today. . . ." She described the cavern and its occupants in a rapid, excited whisper while he stared, asking no questions. "Metamorphosis, Tony! Like butterfly from caterpillar. The eggs must be Hippae eggs. They hatch into peepers. I didn't see that, but it's the only thing that makes sense. The peepers metamorphose into hounds, and the hounds into Hippae. A three-stage metamorphosis. I don't think the Grassians even know," she concluded. "No one's said a word about the peepers metamorphosing into hounds and the hounds into mounts. Not even Persun."

"How could they live here for generations and not know?"

She started to tell him the truth, started to say, "Because the

Hippae kill anybody who spies on them." She knew it for truth, knew she had escaped only by chance. Or, remembering the way Don Quixote had moved, as though guided, for some other reason. She did not want to admit her own foolhardiness. "The taboos would prevent their finding out, Tony. They've got taboos against scarring the grasses by driving vehicles. They have no friendly mounts, like horses, so if they wanted to explore, they'd be limited to walking. There may be a taboo against that, as well. Something deep, psychological. Not merely custom. They may think it is only custom, but it's more than that. They may think they are free to do what they like, but they aren't."

"You mean they think they decided not to scar the grasses, but really—"

"Really, they had no choice. That's what I mean, yes. I think the Hippae have been directing them for . . . for God knows how long. I have a hunch that anyone who goes out on foot into the grasses to explore ends up dead. I had feelings when I was out there today . . . Don Quixote had feelings. He was terribly frightened, moving as though he were walking on eggshells. Besides, Asmir gave us quite a list of disappearances."

"And you were out there alone!" He shook his head. "Mother, damn it. What were you thinking of?" Then, looking into her shamed face, "For the love of God, Mother!"

"Tony, I made a mistake. You're not to say anything to your father that you know anything about the plague or that I was out riding today. In his present state of mind, he might blow up and start bellowing. I can't take much more of that. And then, too, Stella would be sure to find out."

"I know."

"If he wants to know where I am, tell him I've helped take Rowena to Commons. Don't mention Sylvan unless it comes up. Rigo's become very strange about Sylvan. I don't know why."

Tony saw that his mother did not, in fact, know why, though Tony himself had a very good idea what was disturbing Rigo Yrarier. While Marjorie had been dancing with Sylvan at the reception, Tony had been up on the balcony near his father and had seen his father's face.

It was full dark when Persun Pollut dropped the Opal Hill aircar at the edge of the bon Damfels village as silently as a fallen leaf.

Sylvan was waiting with Rowena and two commoner women. Rowena's face was bandaged, one arm was bound up. The two women half-carried her aboard. Marjorie wasted no time with questions or comments but told Persun to ascend immediately and get them to town as quickly as possible. Rowena bon Damfels obviously needed medical care.

"I cannot thank you enough, Lady Westriding," Sylvan said in an oddly formal tone much at variance with his disheveled look. "There was no way I could get one of our aircars away from the estancia without causing great difficulty. I apologize for my appearance. It was necessary to break down a few doors this evening, and I haven't had a chance to change since."

"Your father locked her up?"

"Among other barbarities, yes. I doubt that he even remembers he did so. The Hunt is set very deep into my father, with all its little ways."

"Where are you taking her, Sylvan?"

"I don't think father will suspect she's left the place. If he misses her and remembers what he did, he'll probably think she escaped and went out into the grasses. He may look for her, but I doubt it. Meantime, these women have relatives in Commoner Town who will keep her hidden, keep her safe."

"Are your sisters safe?"

"For the moment. Since both have lovers, I have urged them both to get pregnant as quickly as possible. Pregnant women are not expected to ride." His voice was flat, without feeling. "If there were any way to manage it, I would take them to Commoner Town as well. They would not be content to stay in hiding, however, and I'm afraid hiding is the only way they could avoid being brought back."

"They are welcome at Opal Hill, Sylvan."

"That would mean the end of Opal Hill, Marjorie." He reached out to her, touched her arm, for the moment moved from his own troubles by her concern. "You were only allowed there as a feint, a distraction, to keep Sanctity from doing something intrusive. Our ... our masters do not want you on Grass. They do not want any outsiders on Grass."

"They allow Commons! They allow the port!"

"They can't get at Commons or the port. That may be all that has kept the town safe thus far. I don't know. I don't know what to do. All of us bons are so ... so hypnotized. A few of the younger ones, like me, a few who haven't hunted for a few years, we can talk about things; but even with us, when we start to get close to—" He choked. When he was able to, he said, "It's better in Commoner Town. Whenever I've been there, I've been struck with how clear everything is. I can think anything I please and nothing binds on me. I can talk about anything there."

"Are you going to stay in town?"

"I can't. Father might suspect about mother if I did. He might come after her. He might start something between the estancias and the town. That could only mean ... well, loss of life. Tragedy." He fell broodingly silent, his eyes on his mother's bandaged face. "Why did you and your family really come here?"

"I think Sanctity told you about the ... the disease."

"Your plague, yes," he said impatiently. "We know about that." His face betrayed that he did not think it terribly important. Marjorie stared at him, wondering what he had been told, what he was being allowed to believe.

"It isn't 'our' plague, Sylvan, any more than it is your plague. It is a human plague. If it goes on for a few more decades, there will be no more human life."

He stared at her, unable to believe what she was telling him. "You're exaggerating."

She shook her head. "I'm not. Only another lifetime, Sylvan, and you here on Grass may be all the human life left in the universe. We'll be like the Arbai. Gone."

"But we here ... we haven't heard. . . ."

"There doesn't seem to be any plague here. Or there's something that stops it. You wouldn't let us send in any scientists or researchers, but you did say you'd allow an embassy. Those idiots at Sanctity thought you would accept us because of the horses, so we came, Rigo and I, to find out what we could and to talk sense to you, if you'd allow it."

"We wouldn't allow it. I should have known. That's why the Hunt masters picked those who came to your reception so carefully. No one among them who could be swayed. All old riders. Except me. And they don't know about me."

"Swamp forest coming up below," called Persun. "Where do you want me to land?"

Marjorie looked at Sylvan, and he at the two women. They conferred quietly, then asked that the car set down at the port.

Sylvan agreed. "The hospital is at the Port Hotel. Besides, we're less likely to be noticed there at this time of night."

They dropped quietly, allowed the women to depart, then took off again for Klive.

As they approached the estancia, Marjorie leaned forward to put her hand on Sylvan's arm. "Sylvan. Before you go, I have to tell you something. I came just to tell you."

She poured the story of her day's discovery at him, watching him twitch with discomfort and run his finger around his collar. She wondered whether this was something he was allowed to believe or whether counterbeliefs had been given him.

"Peeper to hound," he choked at last. "Hound to mount. That's interesting. It could explain why they hate the foxen so much. Foxen eat peepers."

"How do you know?"

"When I was a rebellious child, I found out I could stay away from the Hippae if I made my mind a blank. A little talent I have, or had then, that no one else seems to have. I used to sneak off into the grasses sometimes for hours at a time. Not very far, you understand, just farther than anyone else dared to go. If I was near a copse, I'd find a tree and climb it, then lie there with a glass and spy on all that went on. I've seen the foxen eat peepers. Peepers are easy to catch. They're nothing but a gut with some flesh around it and rudimentary legs along the sides. I'd like to see how they change."

"If you can get to Opal Hill before the lapse is over, I can show you where the cavern is."

"Getting to Opal Hill," he said, choking on his words, "would be the least of it, Marjorie. Going out into the grass would be worse. Much worse. I'm not a child anymore. I'm not as good at it as I once was. If there were any Hippae within miles of me, I'm not sure I'd be allowed to return."

The aircar dropped once more. Sylvan took her hand and pressed it, then thanked Persun Pollut as he left, disappearing into the dark.

The car returned to Opal Hill and landed in the gravel court, where Marjorie bid Persun good night and set out for the side door which was closest to her own quarters. As she approached, she heard the thunder begin once more, off in the grasses, a sound the more ominous for having no cause, no reason attributable to it. It threatened without leaving any possibility of reply.

Rigo's voice, coming demandingly from behind her, startled her into a tiny scream, abruptly choked off. "May I ask where you have been?"

"I went with Persun Pollut to take Rowena bon Damfels to Commons, Rigo, where she could get medical care. Her son and two serving women were with her. We dropped him back at the bon Damfels village and came straight home."

Looking into her wide eyes, innocent of any attempt to deceive him, he tried to sneer, tried to say something cutting, but could not quite. "Rowena?"

"Stavenger had beaten her—badly, I'm afraid."

"For what?" he asked in astonishment. To beat a woman had always been, in Rigo's philosophy, to abandon honor.

"For coming here to ask about Janetta," she said. "Rowena and Sylvan came here to ask about Janetta. They hoped ... hope that Dimity may turn up alive. Dimity. Rowena's youngest daughter. Sylvan's sister. The girl who disappeared. That's why they were here."

"I didn't see *Rowena* here," he said, his emphasis reminding her that he had seen Sylvan.

"When they were here, Rowena started sobbing. She left the room for a few moments. Tony took her to my room."

"Leaving you with her son. And what did you two talk about?" He felt his habitual anger surging just below the surface. What had they talked about, Sylvan and Marjorie? What had she shared with him that she would not share with her husband!

She sighed, wearily rubbing at her eyes, which infuriated him further. "I tried to tell you before, Rigo, but you don't want to hear about the Hippae. You didn't want to listen."

He stared at her for a long, cold moment, trying not to say what, eventually, he could not keep himself from saying. "No. I do not want to hear any of Sylvan's fairy tales about the Hippae."

She swallowed painfully, trying not to let the frustration show on her face. "Are you interested in hearing what Brother Mainoa of the Green Brothers may have to tell you about the same subject?"

He wanted more than anything else to hurt her enough that she would cry. He had seldom seen her cry.

"Brother Mainoa?" he sneered. "Are you having an affair with him, too?"

She stared at him in disbelief, noting his heightened color, his fiery eyes, like Stella's eyes. He was saying the kinds of things Stella liked to say, wanting to hurt, not minding that he knew they were not true.

Before he had spoken, she had almost cried, out of weariness if for no other reason, but his words burned all that away. Flames came up around her, red and hot and crackling. It was an unfamiliar feeling, an anger so intense that there was no guilt in it at all. The words came out of her like projectiles, fired without thought, without needing to think.

"Brother Mainoa is about the age of my father," she said in a clear, cold voice which she could scarcely hear over the flame noises in her head. "An old man, rather unsteady on his feet. He has been here for many, many years. He may have some clue which would be valuable to us in the task we were sent here to do. But do not trouble yourself about Brother Mainoa. . . .

"Perhaps when you have ridden to the Hunt and proven your manhood as you so constantly need to do—and if you return— perhaps then we can discuss what we are here for."

He tried to interrupt her, but she held up her hand, forbidding him, her face like fiery ice. "In the meantime you may be assured that I have never had an 'affair' with anyone. Until now, Rigo, I had left the breaking of our vows to you."

He had never heard her speak in that way. He had never known she could. Tonight he had wanted only to crush her self-control, believing it stood as a barrier between them. He had wanted their growing coldness to be burned away by anger so she would come to him, as she always did, apologizing, asking his forgiveness. . . .

Instead he had provoked an anger he could neither calm nor encompass. She turned and went away from him and he saw her go as though she were leaving him forever.

It was not only at Opal Hill and at Klive that matters boiled and suppurated on that night of the lapse. Far from either place, in the kitchen court of Stane, the estancia of the bon Maukerden's, a door opened upon the night to spill slanted light onto the court, throwing a sharp wedge of brilliance into which the Obermum Geraldria stepped to make a stump of shadow. She was a stocky pillar of a woman, her hair tumbled around her heaving shoulders as she wept hopelessly into the towel she held to her face. After a time she lifted reddened eyes to stand peering into the night, unable to see anything both because of the darkness and of the tears that filled her eyes and dripped unregarded from her heavy jaws. At the far end of the kitchen court was a gate opening on the path to Maukerden village. She walked heavily to the gate, opened it, then beckoned toward the open door.

Two figures emerged, so slowly as to seem reluctant. One was Geraldria's serving maid, Clima. The other was the Goosegirl, Janetta bon

Maukerden, swaying beneath a voluminous cloak as though to the sound of music she alone could hear, her face utterly tranquil in the yellow light. Clima wept, Geraldria wept, but the Goosegirl showed no sign that she saw or cared that either of the women grieved.

The Obermum held the gate open as Clima approached. "Take her to the village, Clima. As soon as you can, take her to Commoner Town. See if Doctor Bergrem . . . see if Lees Bergrem can help her. I should have let her go before. I thought she'd learn to recognize us." Geraldria pressed the sodden towel to her face once more, muffling the sounds she could not seem to keep from making. When the spasm had passed, she fished in a pocket for the credit voucher she had put there earlier. "This will get you whatever you need. If you need more than this one, let me know. Tell Doctor Bergrem . . . tell the doctor to send her away from Grass if that will help."

Clima pocketed the card. "The doctor could maybe come here, mistress. Maybe they'd come here." She caught at the Goosegirl's arm to keep her from dancing away, tugging her through the gate and onto the path.

"The doctor said she needed her machines, the things she has at the hospital. Besides, the Obermun won't. Won't have it. Won't have her."

"Not her fault . . ." Words muffled by tears.

Geraldria cried, "Dimoth says yes. He says it was Janetta's fault. He says it wouldn't have happened otherwise. Vince agrees with him."

Clima spoke indignantly. "That's not true! Not my Janetta."

"Shhh. Take her." Darkness fell onto the path as she shut the gate, peering over it at the two of them outside. "Take her away, Clima. I cannot bear it any longer. Not with the Obermun saying the things he says." She fled toward the house, shutting the door behind her.

Clima took the girl by the hand and urged her down the path, the light of the torch making a puddle before them on a route as well known to Clima as the rooms in her own house. She had gone only far enough to be hidden from the house by the grasses when someone stepped out of them behind her and pulled a sack over her head and down her body, knocking her down in the process and leaving her to writhe helplessly for the moment, her hands frantically seeking the rope her assailant had knotted at her ankles. She had been too surprised to shout.

She wriggled herself upright and fumbled at the rope, wrenching at the knot with hasty fingers. She heard the sound of an aircar taking off from the grasses to one side of the path, where no aircar was supposed to be. The knot came loose at last and she stripped the sack off, turning her torch around her in bright searching spokes.

She called, went scrambling among the grasses, even brought back several men from the village to help her look, but the girl was gone.

Suddenly, the lapse was over. The Hunt began again. For Rigo, riding the simulacrum took every moment of his waking time. For Stella, though they did not know it, it continued to take every hour that the rest of them slept. Superbly conditioned by their previous horsemanship, both Rigo and Stella took less time than the bons might have expected. The day soon came that Rigo announced he would attend the Hunt at the bon Damfels estancia, two days hence.

"I expect you all to be there," he said grimly to his family. "You, Marjorie. Tony. Stella."

Marjorie did not reply. Tony nodded. Only Stella burbled with excitement. "Of course, Daddy. We wouldn't miss it for anything."

"I've ordered a balloon-car so that you can follow the Hunt."

"That's very thoughtful of you," said Marjorie. "I'm sure we will all enjoy that very much."

Stella cast a sidelong look, disturbed by her mother's voice. The words, the phrasing—all had been as usual, and yet there had been something chill and uncaring in that voice. She shivered and looked away, deciding it would not be a good time to twit her mother about the Hunt. Besides, there was too much to do. Stella was determined to ride when her father rode, but obtaining the proper garb had not been easy. She had forged orders over the name of Hector Paine and sent them to Commons, intercepting the deliveries when they arrived. She now had everything she needed, the padded trousers, the special boots, narrowed at the toe to catch between the ribs of the mount. Her own coat and hunt tie would serve, her own gloves and hat. All of them were ready to be hidden in the aircar and transported to the bon Damfels estancia. This would be one of the last Hunts at Klive. Within a few days, the Hunt would move to the bon Laupmons'.

Since the lapse was over, Marjorie judged that the cavern of the Hippae would no longer be guarded. Very early the following morning, while all the family still slept, she took the trip recorder from the previous journey and rode Quixote across the long loops they had made on the previous trip. She found the ridge, the shallow declivity, and the cavern. There was no smell except the smell of the grasses. There was no sound. Perhaps the thunder had been their mating

frenzy, if Hippae had mates. Or, perhaps the frenzy was merely reproductive frenzy, like the mindless thrashing of fish.

In the shallow hollow, nothing remained except pieces of dry and
brittle shell. The eggs had hatched. The cavern was empty except for
piles of powdery clots near the entrance. She looked at these, rec-
ognizing them at last as dead bats, those same flitterers she had seen
before in the cavern. These were what the conquering Hippae had
kicked at the defeated one. She stepped over the dusty bodies as
she walked into the cavern, noting its similarity to the one at Opal
Hill. Both had the same rubble pillars, the same tall openings, the
same spring at one side.

There was one notable difference. The earthen floor of this cavern
was incised with a pattern, a pattern cut by the hooves of the mounts,
an interlaced pattern as complex as those she remembered seeing
as a child, carved on prehistoric Celtic monuments. Moved by an
inexplicable impulse, Marjorie drew out the trip recorder and walked
the design from one end to the other, every curl and weave of it,
seeing the pattern emerge on the tiny screen in its entirety. It would
do no good to ask Rigo what he thought it might mean. Perhaps,
however, she could ask Brother Mainoa when she saw him again.
When she had looked at everything, recorded everything, she returned
to Opal Hill without incident, feeling, so she told herself, a certain
viral satisfaction.

The day of Rigo's first Hunt arrived inevitably, and Marjorie steeled
herself to observe the Hunt. She wore one of her Grassian outfits, a
flowing, many-layered gown, the skirts of each loose dress slightly
shorter than the one beneath to reveal the silky layers of the gowns
below, the outer coat a stiff brocade ending at the knees and elbows
so that the extravagantly ruffled hems and sleeves of the undergowns
could show. It was similar to the dresses she had seen on pregnant
women or on matrons who no longer rode. She let her hair fall into
a silken bundle down her back rather than drawing it up in its customary high, golden crown. At her dressing table, she used a good
deal of unaccustomed makeup, particularly about the eyes. She did
not try to explain to herself why she did this, but when she went
down the hall toward the graveled court where Rigo waited, she
looked like a woman going to meet a lover—or to meet other women
who might wonder if her husband loved her. Rigo saw her and quivered. She did not look like Marjorie. She was a stranger. He chewed
his lips, shifting from foot to foot, caught between a desire to reach
out to her and a determination to take no notice.

Persun brought the aircar around. Tony came breathlessly from the house, adjusting his clothing, then Stella ran out in a gown similar to her mother's, though not as complexly layered. She had seen what Marjorie planned to wear and had dressed herself accordingly. The individual layers were loose and easy to remove. It suited her to have something that would come off quickly. She would not have a lot of time in which to change.

There was mercifully little conversation as they went. Marjorie sat next to Persun as he drove, and the two of them conducted a stilted practice conversation in Grassan. "Where is the Master of the Hunt?" "The Master of the Hunt is riding down the path." "Have the hunters killed a fox?" "Yes, the hunters have killed a fox today."

"It sounds like toads gulping," said Stella, with a sniff. "Why would anyone invent such an ugly language?"

Marjorie did not answer. In her mind she was so far from the present location that she did not even hear. There was a fog around her, penetrable only by an act of will. She had separated herself from them. "What is the Obermum serving for lunch?" she asked in a schoolgirl voice.

"The Obermum is serving roast goose," came the reply.

Someone's goose, Persun thought to himself, seeing the expression on all their faces. Oh, yes, we are serving someone's goose.

At Klive, Amethyste and Emeraude were playing hostess, both blank-faced and quiet, both dressed very much as Marjorie was. "The Obermum sends her regrets that she cannot greet you. Obermum asks to be remembered to you. Won't you join us in the hall?"

Somehow Marjorie and Tony went in one direction while Rigo and Stella went in another. Marjorie did not miss Stella immediately. She found herself drinking something hot and fragrant and smiling politely at one bon and another, all of them shifting to get a view of the first surface. There the riders were assembling, faces bland and blind in the expression Marjorie had grown to expect among hunters. Sylvan came into the room, not dressed for the hunt.

"Not hunting today, sir?" asked Tony in his most innocent voice, busy putting two and two together but not sure how he felt about the resultant sum.

"A bit of indigestion," Sylvan responded. "Shevlok and Father will have to carry the burden today."

"Your sisters aren't hunting either," murmured Marjorie.

"They have told father they are pregnant," he murmured in return, almost in a whisper. "I think in Emeraude's case it may be true. One does not expect women of their age to be able to Hunt as often as the men. Father realizes that."

"Has he—"

"No. No, he does not seem to miss . . . he does not seem to miss the Obermum. He does not seem to know she is gone."

"Have you heard from her?"

"She is recovering." He turned and stared out the arched opening to the velvet turf, jaw dropping, eyes wide in shock. "By all the hounds, Marjorie. Is that Rigo?"

"Rigo. Yes. He feels he must," she said.

"I warned you all!" His voice rasped in his throat. "God. I warned him."

Marjorie nodded, fighting to maintain her mood of cool withdrawal. "Rigo does not listen to warnings. I do not know what Rigo listens to." She took a cup of steaming tea from the tray offered by one of the servants and attempted to change the subject. "Have you seen Stella?"

Sylvan looked around the room, shaking his head. The room was crowded, and he walked away from Marjorie, searching the corners.

"If you're looking for the girl," muttered Emeraude, "she went back out to the car."

Sylvan conveyed this to Marjorie, who assumed that Stella had forgotten something and had gone to retrieve it. The bell rang. The servants in their hooped skirts skimmed into the house. The gate of the hounds opened. The hounds came through, two on two, gazing at the riders with their red eyes.

Marjorie took a deep breath. Rigo was standing at the extreme left of the group. When the riders turned to follow the hounds out the Hunt Gate, he was behind them all.

Except for one final rider, late, who came running from around the corner of the house onto the first surface, head tilted away from the observers, following Rigo out through the Hunt Gate at the tail end of the procession.

A girl, Marjorie thought, wondering why Stella had not returned. A girl.

Something in the walk, the stance. A certain familiarity about the clothing, the cut of the coat. . . .

Surely, oh, surely not.

"Wasn't that your daughter?" asked Emeraude with a strange, wild look at Marjorie. "Wasn't that your daughter?"

They heard the thunder of departing feet from outside the gate.

When Sylvan got to the gate at a dead run, there was no one left. All the riders had mounted and gone.

Stella had assumed that Sylvan would be among the riders. Despite what she had been told of the Hunt and had seen for herself, she had also assumed that she would find a way to bring her own mount near his. All such assumptions were forgotten the moment she vaulted onto the back of the mount that came forward for her. Before arriving at the bon Damfels', she had worried that a mount might not be available, might not, as it were, be expecting her. Everything she had been told during her observation of the Hunt, however, indicated that there were always exactly as many mounts as needed for the hunters who assembled. If someone decided at the last minute not to ride, no mount showed up outside the gate. Since it was part of her plan to come into the garden late, after the hounds had gone through, there was no opportunity for anyone to intercept her. She came to the gate as her father was mounting, and then felt, rather than saw, a mount appear before her, extending its massive leg. She went through the movements she had rehearsed so many times on the machine that they had become automatic.

Until that moment everything had happened too quickly to think about, to consider, to change her mind. Then all at once the barbs were there, only inches from her breast, gleaming like razors. As she stared at them, half hypnotized and beginning to feel fear for the first time, the mount turned its head and drew back its lips in a kind of smile, a smile like enough to human for her to know that it held something like amusement, something like contempt, something, peculiarly, like encouragement. Then it lunged off after the others and she gasped, putting all her concentration into keeping herself braced away from the bony blades.

They had gone some distance before she thought to look for Sylvan. From behind, all the riders looked alike. She could not tell if he was there or not. The rider directly ahead of her was her father. She knew his coat, cut unlike the coats of the other hunters.

After a time she thought to look for Sylvan. All the riders looked alike. Except for her father. His coat was different from the others. . . .

After a time she looked for Sylvan. Her father was riding ahead of her. . . .

Her father was riding just ahead . . . ahead. . . .

It was a good day for the Hunt. Though summer was over, the

pastures were still green from recent rains. The farmers had taken down some of the worst of the wire fences, and those that were left were clearly visible. Ahead, crossing the silver-beige stubble of an oat field, she could see the foxhounds, running hard, before the pack lost itself behind the slope to her left. The light wind brought the yelp and clamor of the dogs and the sound of the Huntsman's horn. Dark figures fringed the top of the hill, followers, hands shielding their eyes from the sun. One among them waved his hat and pointed the way the fox had gone. She reined her horse to the left, down along a spinney and around once more, up and over the crest of the hill, the short way around. From the top of the hill she could see the fox fleeing across the pasture below, nose low, bushy tail straight behind as it darted under a fence, then atop a long log and into Fuller's Copse. She urged her mount over the fence toward the copse, taking the jump cleanly, joining some hunters already there, hearing the thud of hooves as others arrived. The Master gestured for them to circle the copse, and she turned to one side, positioning herself near a ditch where the fox might flee.

She could hear the hounds in the copse. The Huntsman was in there with them; his voice rose, calling individual hounds by name, urging them on. "Bounder, get out of there. Dapple, up, up girl. . . ."

Then there was a shout and they were away again, the horn, and the hounds giving voice. . . .

Sylvan.

Someone was supposed to be riding with them today. A guest? Someone not a member of this Hunt.

Sylvan. Here he was. Beside her, turning in the saddle to look adoringly at her. She felt her face flame and drew herself up proudly.

Some of the riders had fallen back. They had been at it all the morning, and it was noon now, with the sun overhead and hot on her hat. The fox had taken refuge in Brent's Wood, and the Huntsman and whippers-in were among the trees. The Master, too, which was strange. Standing on his horse like some circus acrobat, standing and throwing things.

And then . . . a surge of feeling. A jolt of pure pleasure that streaked up from her groin. An orgasm of sheer delight which seemed to go on and on and on.

Sylvan felt it, too. They all felt it. Every face showed it. Every body lashed with it, heads jerking, jaws lax.

Then at last the Huntsman was sounding the kill. There was the Huntsman with the fox's mask, and the horses turning for home. Now the sun was behind her. A long ride home. Even if they went the short way, along Magna Spinney and onto the gravel road past the Old Farm, it was still a long way home.

She was desperately tired when they returned. Her father came over to her and took her arm, roughly, too roughly, and they walked through the gate with the others.

"What in God's name were you doing here?" he demanded, his mouth almost at her ear. "Stella, you little fool!"

She gaped at him. "Riding," she said, wondering why he asked. "Why, Daddy, I was riding."

She followed her father's gaze, up to the terrace. Mother stood there, a glass in her hand, very pale, very beautiful. Sylvan was beside her. He had his arm around Marjorie, pointing down at them. How could he be there, not even in Hunt dress, when he had been riding just moments ago?

Stella felt her face growing red. Sylvan hadn't really been on the Hunt. He couldn't have been. Her father walked away from her, up the flight of shallow stairs. Mother was clutching the balustrade with both hands, tightly, her knuckles white. Sylvan was holding her up, snapping his fingers at a nearby servant. Then Father was there, shouldering him aside.

"Marjorie!"

His wife looked blindly at him, as though she did not know who he was. "Stella," she said, pointing. "Her face . . ."

Rigo turned to look back at his daughter where she stood at the foot of the stairs, turned just too late to see what Marjorie had seen, the same chill, senseless gaze that the Goosegirl had worn when she had appeared among them at Opal Hill.

As for Stella, she tottered upon her feet, trembling between fury and shock with the realization that Sylvan hadn't really been there to see her riding and that she could remember almost nothing about the day at all. She remembered horses and hounds and a fox, but they were real horses, real dogs from some other time, years ago. She remembered that jet of feeling which had filled her and the memory made her flush, but she did not know why she had felt it. Staring up at Sylvan's concerned face, at her father's furious one, at her mother's anxious one, she had the fleeting realization that there were things happening all around her, hideous, important things, and that she had not paid attention to what was going on.

12

Shoethai, assistant in the Office of Acceptable Doctrine, sat in the dining room of the port facility waiting for a ship to unload. Elder Brother Noazee Fuasoi had explained that the ship carried a very important cargo, and he had sent Shoethai to receive it.

Shoethai's automatic response had been unvoiced. "Why me?" Even now he studiously avoided looking at himself in the window, where his reflected image was superimposed over the ship in question like a hovering and misshapen ghost. The face was sufficiently grotesque to have made several staff people at the port pretend they hadn't seen him, including two of the waiters in this dining room.

Shoethai was so accustomed to his appearance and to the way people reacted to it that he no longer showed his hurt and outrage, though the emotions seethed below the surface, more malevolently violent with every passing day. Elder Fuasoi could have sent someone else. Yavi, or Fumo. Either of them. They didn't look like much but they didn't look like monsters, either. The question was eternal. "Why me?"

Back in Sanctity, very occasionally some well-meaning idiot had tried to comfort Shoethai by saying something like, "Still, you're glad to be alive, aren't you? You'd rather be alive than dead, wouldn't you?" Which just went to show how stupid and unfeeling they were, mouthing clichés at him that way. No, he would not rather be alive. Yes, he would rather be dead, except he was afraid of dying. Best yet would be if he'd never lived at all, if they'd let his father kill him when he tried to. Father, at least, had cared about him and wanted what was best for him. What was best was never to have been born or, if that wasn't possible, never to have lived past a few weeks when he was still too little to know anything. What would have been absolute best was never to have looked at this face, conscious that it was his own.

Still, the Elder Brother hadn't sent Fumo or Yavi. The Elder Brother had sent Shoethai, and that meant something. It meant that Fumo or Yavi weren't supposed to know about this shipment. If Fumo and Yavi weren't supposed to know, then Elder Brother Jhamlees Zoe didn't know, and Sanctity didn't know either. And that meant it was something that only Shoethai and Fuasoi knew about, only those two.

"Do you know what Moldies are?" the Elder Brother had asked him one day, out of nothing, while Shoethai was cleaning the Elder Brother's office.

"It's martyrs of something," Shoethai had said.

"Martyrs of the Last Days," the Elder Brother had said. "A group of men who are dedicated to hastening the end. Have you ever read the *Book of Ends*?"

Shoethai merely stood there, mouth open, shaking his head. Of course he hadn't read any Moldy books. You could get yourself terminated by Sanctity for reading Moldy books.

The Elder Brother had read his mind. "I know. It's among the forbidden volumes. Still, I think you'd be interested in reading it, Shoethai. I'll grant a dispensation for you. Take the book with you when you leave, but don't let anyone else see it. Particularly, don't let Jhamlees Zoe see it."

It wasn't even a reader. It was an old-style book, with pages. Elder Fuasoi laid it out on the desk and just left it there, an old brown thing with the words *Book of Ends* in gold across the front. Shoethai had hidden the book in the deep pocket of his robe, had read it only when he was alone—which was most of the time. By now he had it almost memorized and frequently quoted sections of it to himself.

"Garbed in light, we will dwell in the house of light," he recited to himself now as he sucked his tea through the gaps in his teeth. After the end of mankind would come the New Creation. In the New Creation he would no longer wear this face and this body. In the New Creation he would no longer be deformed. He would dart like a spear, clothed only in radiance, beautiful as an angel. Elder Fuasoi had taken particular notice of this, reading the proper section from the book and pointing to the illustrations, but Shoethai had believed it from the moment he read it for himself. It was as though it had been written just for him. Fair was fair. If people didn't have a fair try in this life, they would in the next one.

"Let the changes come," he whispered, inhaling another sip of tea. "Let the New Creation manifest itself." The manager of the dining room had brought the tea after a furious whispering match with his two waiters. Shoethai prayed silently that the waiters would be among the first to be cleansed away, most painfully. Of course it would be painful. Elder Fuasoi had already told him that. Elder Fuasoi had seen the plague. Elder Fuasoi had actually spent almost a year in a plague camp. Elder Fuasoi was a Moldy. He said nobody could see the plague and be anything else.

Once Elder Fuasoi confessed that he was actually a Moldy, Shoethai had become a willing and dedicated convert even though they were the only Moldies on Grass and Jhamlees Zoe would have them both killed if he found out. Doing what the Moldies needed doing didn't need more than two. Two, Elder Fuasoi had told him, would be more than enough.

"Bless me, O Creator," Shoethai mused silently as he stared through his own image at the scurrying figures around the ship, "for I will cleanse thy house of ugliness." Ugliness itself was a sin against Creation. The Elder Brother had even hinted that the Creator had given Shoethai this face in order to make explicit to Shoethai a certain knowledge, the knowledge of the absolute depravity and unworthiness of man, printing that message on Shoethai's flesh for everyone to see. Elder Fuasoi said that what Shoethai appeared to be on the outside, all mankind actually was on the inside. What Shoethai looked like, mankind actually was. Misshapen. Deformed. A freak of Creation. Intelligence should not exist in such stinking, fallible flesh. Flesh was all right for animals, but not for intelligent beings, and mankind was an experiment that hadn't worked out. For the few who helped clean up the mess, there would be divine rewards. And for the others there would be a final end which would leave the universe cleansed and purified and ready to start over.

Below him, he saw ground vehicles moving from the ship toward the port building. The shipment would be in one of them. Brother Shoethai decided to stay where he was for a time. Let the crowd clear away before he went down to the cargo office. There was no hurry. Once Elder Fuasoi had the shipment and distributed it, everyone on the planet would die, but it would take some time. The virus didn't work for a long time, sometimes. There was no hurry. An hour more or less would make little difference. Shoethai giggled as he sipped at his tea. Then, seeing what the giggle did to his reflection in the window, he stopped and turned slightly away so that he would not be able to see himself anymore.

In his office at the Friary, Elder Brother Noazee Fuasoi leaned on his desk, choking down the pain from his belly. The second stomach and gut transplant hadn't worked any better than the first one, even though the office had scoured the penitents for as close a tissue match as possible. That was the best the doctors could do here on Grass, and even then they'd objected that the donor hadn't made a free gift of his body prior to getting fatally wounded in the head by (so Elder Fuasoi had informed them) an unfortunate fall from the towers. There were no facilities for cloning body systems on Grass, and while Elder Brother Noazee Fuasoi of Sanctity had sufficient clout to go back to Sanctity and wait while they cloned a gut for him, Jorny Shales the Moldy hadn't wanted to take the time.

"One would think . . ." he snarled to himself in a litany that was repeated every time his gut pained him, "one would think the Creator could grant surcease to those of us doing His work."

"Pardon, Your Emminence?" said Yavi Foosh from his own desk by the window. "Pardon?"

"Nothing," snarled the Elder. "I've got a pain, that's all. Probably something I ate."

Though it wasn't anything he had eaten. It was flesh, that was all. Fallible flesh. Full of stinks and pains and rot. Full of weakness and foolish, ugly appetites and dirty excretions. There would be no flesh in the next creation, not for those who had cleaned up this one. Elder Fuasoi gripped the edge of the desk and sweated, thinking of other times and places as he waited for the cramp to pass.

He had never really been aware of pain until the camp. His name had been Jorny then, a boy of fifteen dragged into the camp with his uncle Shales. One day he had been living with Uncle Shales in the fishing town, going to school, fishing off the pier, going out in the boat when the weather was right, writing love notes to Gerandra Andraws, cute little Gerry with the perky little bottom, wondering if he was old enough to really do something about her. The next day he had been there in the camp, crowded with fifteen other men and boys in one room with no school, no girls, no fishing, and no Uncle Shales.

The people in the camp either had the disease or were close family members of people with the disease. Uncle Shales was dying, they told him. Jorny had to stay in the camp until they found out whether he was going to die, too.

He wanted to see Uncle Shales, but they wouldn't let him. He sneaked around until he found what building Uncle was in and where his bed was, and then he got up close to the wall, around back. Uncle Shales would open the window a little bit and they'd talk, at night. Uncle Shales told Jorny not to be afraid. Everything that happened, happened for the best, he said. Jorny sat crouched under the window, tears running down his face, trying to keep Uncle from hearing him cry. Then one night Uncle didn't answer him and the window wasn't open, so Jorny waited until everyone was asleep and sneaked in. He couldn't find Uncle Shales. In the bed where Uncle had been was only this thing, this kind of monster, partly bandages, with one eye peering out and a round, raw hole where its mouth ought to be, leaking all over the place and stinking.

Later, when he asked, they told him Uncle had died. He thought they'd let him go then, but they didn't. They kept looking all over him for sores, like the sores most of the people in the camp had.

Then one day there was a Moldy preaching in the camp. Preaching how it was near the end of the time for man. How it was time for man to depart, for he was only rotten flesh and decaying bone. How it was time to leave the universe clean for the next generation. How those who died now would rise again in the New Creation, clad in light, beautiful as the dawn.

Jorny knew then what had happened to Uncle Shales. He had shed his flesh so he could come back, dressed all in light, like an angel.

Jorny cried, the first time he'd let himself cry out loud, right there in the dusty street of the camp, half-hidden behind one of the scruffy trees. He had waited until the Moldy was finished and had gone up to him and said who he was and that his uncle had died and he wanted to get out of the camp. The man had patted him on the shoulder and said he could get him out, that Jorny could become a Moldy right then, without even having a toothbrush. He got in a truck with the man and they looked him all over to see if he had any sores on him, and when they saw he didn't they hid him under some stuff while they smuggled him out to a place where there were lots of people and other kids and nobody had sores on them anywhere. Not that they'd really had to smuggle him. The camp commander had been paid off, the Moldy said. Paid off to let the Moldy preach and bring comfort to the dying.

That night Jorny slept. Whenever he thought about Uncle, he made himself stop thinking. At first he thought maybe he should have gone home to say goodbye to the people he'd known, but then after a while he figured most of them were dead and it didn't matter. They were all dead and ready to be reborn. The Moldies pointed out people who were already transformed. Before the sun went down, sometimes you could see them, slanting down from the clouds, golden beams of fiery light. Later on, Jorny figured out that was just stories, just sunlight, but it didn't matter. Later on he realized who that monster on the corner bed had been, too, but by that time he had it all figured out.

When he was seventeen, the Moldies had sent him to Sanctity as an acolyte with instructions to study and work and rise in the hierarchy. He had become a member of the Office of Acceptable Doctrine. It was the Moldies, paying people off, that got Sanctity to send him to Grass. It was time for Grass to join the other homes of man, the Moldies said. Time for Grass to be cleansed.

And now he was here, ready to spread the plague which had killed everything he had cared about. If Uncle Shales had deserved the plague, then there were none who did not deserve it. If Uncle Shales had died, then everybody ought to die.

He opened his eyes, surprised to find them wet, feeling the cramping in his belly wane to its usual dull, wallowing ache. Standing across the desk from him was his superior in Sanctity, Elder Brother Jhamlees Zoe.

"You don't look well, Fuasoi."

"No, Elder Brother. A bit of pain is all."

"Have you seen the doctors in the town recently?"

"Not for several weeks, Elder Brother."

"What have they said is wrong?"

"The systems transplant isn't doing as well as they'd like."

"Perhaps it's time to ship you back to Sanctity."

"Oh, no, Elder Brother. Much too much work here."

Elder Brother Jhamlees fretted, moving his hands, scratching his infinitesimal nose, rising on his toes, then down again. "Fuasoi . . ."

"Yes, Elder Brother?"

"You haven't heard of there being any . . . sickness around, have you?"

Fuasoi stared at him in disbelief. Sickness? Was the man crazy? Of course there was sickness around. "What does the Elder Brother refer to?"

"Oh, any serious sickness. Any, ah . . . well. Um. Any, ah . . . plague?"

"Sanctity teaches us that there is no plague," said Brother Fuasoi firmly. "Surely the Elder Brother is not questioning Sanctity's teaching?"

"Not at all. I was thinking more of . . . something contagious, you know, that might threaten the Friary. Still, good to know there's nothing. Nothing. Take care of yourself, Fuasoi. Let me know if you'd like to go back. . . ." And he was out the door, hurrying away down the corridor.

Well, well, thought Fuasoi. I wonder what occasioned that?

"Shoethai's here," said Yavi, interrupting his thoughts. "I can hear him coming down the hall." He got up and went to the door, opening it slightly and turning to peer inquiringly back at his superior.

"Let him come in," Fuasoi said, nodding. The pain in his belly had passed. The other pain, the one that brought him awake in the night, sweating and weeping, that one would pass when everything was all over. He patted his forehead with a throwaway and stared at the door. "I want to speak to him privately."

Yavi shrugged and went out, passing Shoethai in the door.

"Your Emminence." Shoethai fell to his knees.

"Get up," Fuasoi directed impatiently. "Did you get it?"

Shoethai nodded wearily, rising to put the small package on the desk. "Once I found somebody to look for it. Mostly they try to pretend I'm not there."

The Elder gestured with his fingers to give the package to him. When he had it, he opened it carefully, revealing a fist-sized packet within.

"Is that it?" Shoethai begged, wanting to be reassured once more.

"That's it." His superior smiled, content at last that the work could go forward and his own pain would end. "Plague virus. Packed especially for Grass."

Brothers Mainoa and Lourai arrived at Opal Hill just in time to interrupt an altercation. When Persun Pollut announced the arrival of an aircar bearing the Green Brothers, Marjorie was for the moment shocked into inaction. She had forgotten they were coming. After the momentary pause, however, she went out to bring them in, hoping their arrival would put an end, however temporary, to the discord between Rigo and Stella.

Ignoring the arrival of the two strangers, Rigo went on shouting at Stella, furious that she had not told him she intended to ride, furious at her for having ridden at all without his permission. Though Tony and Marjorie were angry too, angry with both the riders for risking their lives, they felt the conflict had gone on long enough. Marjorie intruded upon the sounds of battle by introducing the brothers to her husband and daughter.

As Rigo turned and offered his hand to Brother Mainoa, his face still suffused with anger, he suddenly remembered his words to Marjorie about this man. The Brother was shortsighted and elderly, rotund and half bald. Rigo was instantly aware that he had made himself ridiculous by his accusations then and that he was not improving matters by his manner now. All he could bring himself to do was to make brusque apologies and go off with Stella still frothing after him like a small, mad animal determined to bite, leaving Marjorie and Tony to make amends.

Mainoa waved her apologies away. "All families have their upsets, Lady Westriding. I understand your husband and daughter rode to hounds yesterday."

"How did you know?"

"That information spread across Grass within moments of their leaving Klive," the friar replied. "A servant called a friend on the tell-me. The friend called someone else, who called three others. One of the Brothers came to tell Brother Lourai and me, bringing the news down into the Arbai street we are currently unearthing. Oh yes, Lady Westriding, everyone knows."

"The two of them have been been fighting over it," she confessed unnecessarily. "Tony and I are afraid for them."

"As you might well be," the Brother agreed.

Since Stella had left them, Rillibee had stood looking after her, an expression of wonder on his face. Now he sat down abruptly. "She's determined to go on?" he asked.

"Rigo is determined to go on. Stella is no less determined, though not for Rigo's reasons. My husband thinks she should not. The reasons he gives her for not riding are the same reasons I give him for not riding. He says in his case it is different." She sighed, throwing up her hands.

"It's all become rather nasty and boring," said Tony, trying to make light of what had been a very hostile encounter. "Everyone telling each other the same things, and no one listening."

"I'm told that Rowena, Obermum bon Damfels, is at Commons," Brother Mainoa remarked. "I hear that Obermun bon Damfels does not seem to know she is gone."

"You hear everything," Marjorie said ruefully. "Have you heard what any of it means?"

"As you do, Lady Westriding. As you do."

"Call me Marjorie, Brother. Please. Father James wants to see you while you are here. He particularly asked to be included."

Brother Mainoa nodded, smiling. He had wanted very much to talk with either of the Fathers.

When the time came, he spoke to the young priest, quiet young Father James—Rigo's nephew, Marjorie informed them—and also to Father Sandoval, and to Tony and Marjorie as well. Their luncheon was served on the terrace in the mild airs of spring. Neither Rigo nor Stella joined them. Neither Rigo nor Stella could be found.

"I wanted particularly to speak with you Fathers," Brother Mainoa confided in his comfortable voice, "because I have a philosophical matter which I am seeking advice upon."

"Ah?" Father Sandoval acknowledged in a patronizing tone. "You wish an answer from a religious point of view?"

"I do," said the Brother. "It pertains to creatures which are not human. You may regard the question as hypothetical but nonetheless important."

Father Sandoval cocked his head. "You mean in a doctrinal sense?"

"Precisely. A matter of no practical relevance whatsoever, but important in a doctrinal sense. To ask my question, I must ask you first to suppose that the foxen here on Grass are sentient beings and that they are troubled by matters of conscience."

Tony laughed. Marjorie smiled. Father Sandoval seemed only slightly amused. "I can accept that as a ground for ethical argument."

Brother Mainoa nodded, gratified. "It is a question of original sin."

"Original sin?" Father James looked as though he was genuinely amused. "Among the foxen?" He looked at Marjorie with a smile, as though reminded of their recent conversation on the same subject. She looked down at her plate. She was still troubled by the things he had said, and was not sure it was a laughing matter.

Brother Mainoa saw this interchange but pretended not to notice. "Remember that you agreed to accept that they are thinking beings, Fathers. Accept it. Regard them as fully sentient. As much as you yourself may be. Now, having done so—do not laugh, sir," this to Tony—"we are supposing that the idea of original sin oppresses the foxen. They are carnivores. Their bodies require meat. So, they eat meat. They eat the peepers, the larvae of the Hippae."

"You know!" exclaimed Marjorie. "You know what the peepers really are."

"I do, madam. Not many know, but I do. And let us suppose the foxen do, as well. They eat them."

"And the foxen consider this sinful?" Tony asked.

"Well, young sir, it is an interesting point. If these were men, you yourself would consider it sinful. If a man or woman kills an unborn child, your faith and Sanctity both consider it murder, do they not? The larvae of the Hippae are not thinking beings. They are as near mindless as makes no matter. However, when they grow great and fat and unable to move, they make their first metamorphosis and emerge as hounds."

"Ah." Father Sandoval had already heard of this from Marjorie and he now saw where Mainoa was leading.

"The hounds, some say, are thinking beings. Certainly they are capable of some thought. I believe they are self-aware. Whether they are or not, they undergo a further metamophosis and become something else. . . ."

"Mounts." Marjorie nodded. "I have seen them."

"Of course. And as Lady Westriding knows in her heart, as we all know in our hearts, the Hippae are thinking beings. You and I have discussed this before, have we not? So, when foxen eat the peepers, they are killing the young of a thinking race."

"But if they know this, why—"

"What else can they eat? The mounts? The Hippae themselves? There are a few other creatures, all of them too fleet or too small to be of any use. The grazers are too huge. No, the foxen eat the peepers because they are available and abundant. There are many more peepers than the world could hold if all of them went through metamorphosis, and history upon Terra tells us what horrors follow upon religious mandates of unlimited reproduction. That is not the point, however. The point is that foxen eat and relish peepers, but let us suppose that in recent years, since being exposed to the thoughts of man, the foxen have acquired pudency. They have learned to feel guilt."

"They had no guilt until man came?"

"Let us suppose not. Let us suppose that they had reason, but no sense of shame. They have acquired it from men."

"They must have acquired it from the commoners, then," said Tony. "I've seen little enough among the bons."

Brother Mainoa laughed. "From the commoners. Surely. Let us say they have learned it from the commoners."

"Those of our faith," said Marjorie with a frown, "seem to agree that the original sin of humankind was ah . . . an amatory one."

"And the foxen, who have learned of this doctrine from someone, heaven knows who, wonder if it is not as valid to have one that was and is gustatory. Let us suppose they have come to me with this matter. 'Brother Mainoa,' they have said, 'we wish to know if we are guilty of original sin.'

"Well, I have told them I do not understand the doctrine of original sin, that it is not a doctrine Sanctity has ever concerned itself about. 'I know someone who knows, however,' I have told them. 'Father Sandoval, being an Old Catholic, should know all about it,' and so they want to discuss the matter."

"Discuss the matter?"

"Well, in a manner of speaking. Let us postulate that they have found some way to communicate."

Father Sandoval's brow creased and he sat back in his chair, fingertips of his hands pressed together to make a cage, staring at it for a time as though it held his thoughts captive. "I would tell them," he said after a considerable pause, "that their sense of guilt does not arise from original sin at all. It is not their first parents who have committed the sin, *if* it is a sin, but they themselves."

"Does this make a difference?"

"Oh, yes. A sin that they themselves have committed, if it is a sin, can be remedied by their own penitence and forgiven by God. If they are penitent. If they believe in God."

If God believes in them, amended Marjorie, silently. If God did not know the names of his human viruses, would he care about foxen?

Brother Mainoa shifted the utensils before him, frowning in concentration. "But suppose it had been a sin of their . . . their ancestors."

"It is not simply a matter of who committed the sin, whether the creatures themselves or their ancestors or their associates with or without their connivance or acquiescence. We would have to ask how God sees it. In order to have been the equivalent of original sin, then it would be necessary to determine whether the foxen had ever existed in a state of divine grace. Was there a time when they were sinless? Did they fall from grace as our religion teaches us that our first parents fell?"

Brother Mainoa nodded. "Let us suppose they did not. Let us suppose things have always been this way, so far back as anyone can remember."

"No legend of a former time. No scripture?"

"None."

Father Sandoval grimaced, drawing his upper lip back and ticking his thumbnail against his teeth. "Then it is possible that there is no sin."

"Not even if, in this latter day, these reasoning beings are beset by conscience over something they have always done?"

Father Sandoval shrugged and smiled, raising his hands as though to heaven. "Brother, let us suppose that we think they may be guilty of original sin. First we must establish whether their salvation is possible—that is, whether any divine mechanism exists to remove their sense of sin by forgiving them. They cannot be truly penitent for something they did not do, and therefore penitence is useless to them. They must rely upon a supernatural force to redeem them from a sin committed long ago or by someone else. Among Old Catholics, that redemption was offered by our Savior. We are granted immortality through Him. Among you Sanctified, redemption is offered by your organization. You are granted immortality through it."

"The Sanctified believe in the same Savior," Brother Mainoa remarked. "They once called themselves His saints."

"Well, perhaps. If so, it is no longer any significant part of Sanctity's belief, but I will not argue that point with you. This is no time to discuss the types of immortality and what our expectations may be. My church teaches that those pious men and women who lived prior to the human life and sacrifice of the Savior were redeemed by that sacrifice despite the fact that they lived and died long before it was made. So, I suppose, might these foxen have been saved by that same sacrifice despite the fact that they lived and died in another world. I would not say, here and now, that this is impossible. However, it is a question for the full authority of the church to decide. No mere priest should attempt to answer such a question."

"Ah." Brother Mainoa grinned widely, shaking his head to indicate amazed amusement. "It is an interesting point, is it not. It is with such conjecture I while away the time while I am digging and cataloguing."

Seeing the slightly angry expression on Father Sandoval's face, Marjorie turned to the younger Brother in an effort to change the direction of their conversation. "And you, Brother Lourai. Do you also consider such philosophical and ethical points?"

Rillibee Chime looked up from his salad, peering deeply into Father Sandoval's eyes, seeming to see more there than the old priest was comfortable with.

"No," he said. "My people sinned against no one, and I have never had any chance to be guilty. I think of other things. I think of trees. I remember my parents and how they died. I think of the name they gave me. I wonder why I am here."

"Is that all?" She smiled.

"No," he replied, surprising both her and himself. "I wonder what your daughter's name means, and whether I will see her again."

"Well," said Mainoa, lifting his brows and patting his younger colleague on the arm. "He's young yet. I thought of such things too, long ago."

A brooding silence fell. Marjorie persisted in moving the conversation away from these troublesome areas. "Brother Mainoa, do you know of an animal here on Grass which looks something like a bat?" She described the creature she had seen in the caverns, dwelling upon its most noteworthy feature, the fringing teeth.

"Not only know it," the friar answered, "but been bitten by it. Most people have, at least once. It's a bloodsucker. It comes out of the dusk and hits you right here—" he clamped a work-roughened hand on the back of his neck, just at the base of his skull, "and tries to sink those teeth into you. Since our headbones get in the way, they don't do much damage to humans. Evidently the Grassian animals have a notch in the skull right there. Miserable-looking things, aren't they?"

Marjorie nodded.

"Where did you see them?"

She explained, telling the story of the cavern once more. Rillibee and Father James were interested, even though Brother Mainoa was quite unsurprised.

"Then you undoubtedly saw dead ones, also. Their bodies lie around the Hippae caverns like leaves on a forest floor in a Terran fall. I do know about them. I'm among the few who've sneaked up on a cavern and gotten away afterward." He gave her a look which told her that he guessed more of her reasons for going into the grasses than she wanted him to.

"Gotten away?" she repeated faintly.

"I would say it's a rare thing to get away, Lady Westriding. If you'd been smelled or spotted, they'd have had you." He had fallen into his colloquial, avuncular manner.

"I was riding. On a horse."

"Still, I find it amazing. Well, if your horse got you out of there quickly, you may have outrun 'em. Or maybe the wind was just right and you simply weren't noticed. Or maybe the smell of the horse confused them just long enough. You took your life between your teeth, Lady." He gave her a concentrated, percipient look. "I'd suggest you not do it again. Certainly not during the lapse."

"I . . . I had already decided that." She cast her eyes down, embarrassed at Tony's scowl of agreement. Could the man read her mind?

"They don't like to be spied upon?" Tony asked.

"They won't tolerate it. That's why so little's known about 'em. That's why so few people that wander off into the grasses ever come home. I can tell you, though. Hippae lay eggs sometime during the winter or early spring. I've seen the eggs in the backs of caverns in late spring and I know they weren't there in the fall. When the sun gets enough warmth in it, the migerers move the eggs into the sun and shift 'em around until the heat hatches 'em. About the same time, some of the peepers and some of the hounds, those that are grown enough, come back to the caverns and change themselves into something new. The Hippae guard 'em while they're doing it. That's why the lapse."

"The bons don't know," Marjorie said, a statement rather than a question.

"Right, they don't know. Don't know, won't be told, don't want to hear. Taboo for 'em."

"I do have something you may not know," she said, getting up to fetch the trip recorder and punching up the pattern she had walked over in the cavern. "I have been told that the thunderous noise we sometimes hear is Hippae, dancing. Well, this seems to be what the dancing produces."

Brother Mainoa stared at it, at first in confusion, then in disbelief.

Marjorie smiled. Good. For all his knowing looks, he wasn't omniscient, then.

It was Rillibee who said, almost casually, "It looks like the words in the Arbai books, doesn't it, Brother?"

"The spherical peepers!" Marjorie exclaimed, remembering suddenly where she had seen the rotund peepers and heraldric hounds, carved on the housefronts of the Arbai city. The twining design did look like the words in the Arbai books—or like the vines carved on the housefronts. She mentioned this, occasioning a deep and thoughtful silence from everyone.

Though the conversation later turned to other things, including whether there was or was not unexplained death upon Grass (for Marjorie and Tony remained aware of their duty) the pattern on Marjorie's recorder was in all their minds. Brother Mainoa, particularly, wanted very much to show it to a friend—so he said as he departed—and Marjorie let him borrow the recorder, believing he meant some friend among the Green Brothers.

It was only after he was gone that she began to wonder how it was that Brother Mainoa had seen the caverns of the Hippae and had escaped to tell them about it.

When Rigo left for the Hunt on the following day, the last Hunt to be held at Klive, Stella, who had been thinking much of Sylvan, demanded to go with him.

"You said you wouldn't risk the children," Marjorie reminded him. "Rigo, you promised." She would not cry. She would not shout. She would merely remind him. Still, the tears hung unshed in her eyes.

He had forgotten he had wanted tears, and tears over the children would never have satisfied him in any case. "I wouldn't have," he explained in his most reasonable voice. "I would never have ordered any of you to ride. But she wants to. That's a different matter."

"She could die, Rigo."

"Any of us could die," he said calmly, gesturing to convey a hostile universe which plotted death against them all. "But Stella won't.

According to Stavenger bon Damfels, she rode brilliantly." He said the word as though it had been an accolade. "Stavenger urged me to bring her again."

"Stavenger," Marjorie said quietly, the name seething on her tongue. "The man who beat Rowena half to death and attempted to starve her. The man who hasn't figured out yet that she is gone. That Stavenger. Why would you risk Stella's life on Stavenger's say-so?"

"Oh, Mother," Stella said in a voice very much like her father's in its obdurate reasonableness. "Stop it! I'm going, and that's that."

Marjorie stood on the terrace steps and watched them go, staring into the sky until the car became merely a dot and vanished. As she was about to go in, Persun Pollut came up behind her.

"Lady . . ."

"Yes, Persun."

"You have had a message on the tell-me. Sylvan bon Damfels asks if you will be attending the Hunt. I told him you would not. He says he wishes to visit you here, this afternoon."

"He may have word of Rowena," Marjorie said sadly, still staring at the empty sky where they had gone. "Bring him to my study when he arrives."

When he came, he did have some word of Rowena. As Marjorie commiserated and exclaimed, he told her that the wounds to Rowena's flesh were healing. The wounds to her mind were more troublesome. Finding Dimity had become an obsession with her. She could not admit that the girl was gone forever, or if not, that finding her might be more heartbreaking than considering her dead.

None of which was what Sylvan had really come to say. He soon left the subject of Rowena and Dimity, which he found painful, and began to talk of something else. It had been so long since Marjorie had been the object of anyone's overt romantic intentions that he had managed to get out most of what he had planned to say, however allusively and poetically, before she realized the tenor of his words.

"Sylvan," she begged, suddenly terrified. "Don't."

"I must," he whispered. "I love you. I've loved you since the moment I saw you. The moment I first took you into my arms on the dance floor. You must have known. You must have felt—"

She shook her head, forbidding him to say anything more. "If you say anything else, Sylvan, I will have to forbid you this house. I am not free to listen to you. I have a family."

"So? What difference does that make?"

"To you, none perhaps. To me, all the difference."

"Is it your religion? Those priest persons you have with you? Do they guard you for Rigo?"

"Father Sandoval? Father James? Of course not, Sylvan. They help me guard myself!" She turned away from him, exasperated. "How can I explain to you? You have none of the same ideas. And you are so young. It would be a sin!"

"Because I am young?"

"No. Not for that reason. But because I am married to someone else, it would be a sin."

He looked puzzled. "Not on Grass."

"Have you no sacrament of marriage upon Grass?"

He shrugged. "It is not marriages the bons need but children. Proper children, of course, though the fiction will often do as well as the fact. There's many a bon with commoner blood, though the Obermuns would deny it. Well, look at it yourself! Why should Rowena have a lonely bed all spring and all fall while Stavenger hunts, or recovers from hunting, or sweats thinking of hunting again? I have no doubt Shevlok is Stavenger's son, but I have some doubts about myself."

"Have you no sins upon Grass? Nothing that you feel is wrong to do?"

He stared at her, as though trying to see past her surface to the mystery she confronted him with. "It would be wrong to kill another bon, I suppose. Or to force a woman if she weren't willing, or hurt a child. Or to take something from some other estancia. But no one would see it as wrong for us to be lovers."

She regarded him almost with fear. His eyes glowed with fervor, his hands reached out to her. Her fleeting desire to take those hands filled her with panic. So she had once longed to take Rigo's hands. How could she convince someone who had so little in common with her when her own self was conspiring against her? "You say you love me, Sylvan."

"I do."

"And by this you mean more, I presume, than mere lust. You are not telling me only that you want my body." She flushed, saying this, a thing she had never said, not even to Rigo. It was only possible to say it if she walked away from him, to the window where she stood looking out.

"Of course not," he blurted, stung.

She spoke to the garden. "Then, if you love me, you will say nothing further about it. You must accept what I tell you. I am married to

Rigo. It does not matter if that marriage is happy or unhappy. It doesn't matter that you and I might be happier together than either of us might be with others. None of that matters, and you must not speak of it! My marriage is a fact in my religion, and that fact can't be changed. I will be your friend. I cannot be your lover. If you want religious explanations, ask Father Sandoval to explain it. If I were even to converse with you about it, it would be an occasion of sin."

"What can I do?" he begged. "What can I do?"

"Nothing. Go home. Forget you came here. Forget you said anything, as I will try to do."

He rose, unwillingly, reluctantly, far more stirred to passion by her refusal than he would have been by her consent. He could not let her go. "I will be your friend," he cried. "And you must be mine. This business of the plague, we must not forget that. You need me to help you with that!"

She turned back to him, her arms crossed protectively across her breasts. "Yes, we need you, Sylvan. If you will. But not if you talk about this other thing." Her throat was dry. She longed to comfort him, he seemed so distraught, but she did not dare touch him or even smile at him.

"Very well, then. I will not talk about this other thing." He made a wide, two-handed gesture, as though casting everything away, though he gave up nothing. If talking of love was not the way to Marjorie's affection, he would try to find some other way. He would not give up courting her. He did not understand Marjorie's religion, but he would learn about it. Obviously it tolerated many things it did not allow. Otherwise that proud, harsh man, her husband, would not be able to keep his mistress almost upon his wife's doorstep!

He stayed, for a time, sitting a good distance from her, discussing the things she needed to know. He promised to do everything he could to find out whether there was any unusual disease upon Grass. He let nothing happen to disturb her again, controlling their conversation with a courtly charm, seeing her gradually relax, lower her defenses, become the woman he had danced with. When he left her, he felt his eyes grow wet, wondering what she thought of him, amazed that it mattered to him that much. He was no youngster to worry what a woman thought! And yet ... and yet he did.

She, looking after him, was more stirred than she had been in years, wishing with all her heart that he had never come, that he had never spoken, or that she had met him before she had met Roderigo Yrarier.

It was an evil thought. She went to the chapel and prayed. Over the years, prayer had comforted her. It did not do so now, though she knelt for most of an hour, seeking peace. The light over the altar glowed red. Once she had thought of it as a holy eye, seeing her, but she did not think it saw her now. She had been God's child once. Now she was only a thinking virus, a thing beset by longings with no appeasement allowed. "How long has it been since I laughed at something?" she asked herself. "How long since we have had any fun at all, as a family?" She could remember both, and it had been long, too long ago, when Stella was still a child, before Rigo had Eugenie.

She went outside. The afternoon had grown chill. From the northeast came the muted roar of an aircar. She hurried toward the graveled court where it would land, stood there shivering and looking up. She needed Rigo, needed Stella, needed family, needed to belong to someone, be held by someone. She would make them offer her something, make them show some affection. She would beg it, demand it!

The car came slowly closer, from a speck to a ball, from a ball to an ornament, one of the ornaments her family had used to hang upon trees at Christmas time, bulging with rococo extravagance.

It landed. The door opened and the servant who had piloted it got out and went away, without looking at her. Rigo came out, facing the car, turning slowly until he saw her. He did not move then, just stood there, his face still and empty. There was an endless moment during which nothing moved at all, a moment in which a first dreadful suspicion hardened into certainty.

"Stella!" she cried, her voice shrilling into the wind.

Rigo made a hopeless gesture but said nothing. He did not move toward her. She knew he was too ashamed to do so, that he knew there was nothing he could ever say which would help at all.

"Brother Mainoa," she insisted, pounding her fist on the kitchen table where she found Father James and her son having an evening snack together. "Brother Mainoa knows something! He's been out in the grass. He's seen. Things. If the Hippae have taken Stella, he's the only one who can possibly help us."

"Where is your husband?" the priest asked. "Marjorie, where is Uncle Rigo?"

"I don't know," she said, turning wild eyes upon him. "He came into the house."

"What exactly did he say?"

"That she was gone. Vanished. She never returned. Like Janetta.

Like the bon Damfels girl. Gone." She gulped for air, as though she could not possibly get enough into her lungs. "He won't be any use. He's like them. Like Stavenger and like the Obermun bon Haunser. I've been thinking who to ask. Not any of the bons. They don't do anything about it when their own children get carried off; they wouldn't do anything for mine. Not anyone from Commons. They don't know anything about it. Not villagers. They're frightened to death of the grass. I wish you could have seen Sebastian Mechanic's face when he was telling me about the thundering in the night. But someone told *him*! Who do you suppose? I asked. He says Brother Mainoa. It always comes back to Brother Mainoa!"

"Do you want to go there now, Marjorie?"

"Now. Yes."

"Have you checked to be sure he's there?"

"No." She sobbed helplessly. "He has to be there."

The priest nodded at Tony, then toward the tell-me link in the corner of the kitchen, before rising to fold Marjorie in his arms. He was no taller than she, and slighter, but he gave her enough support that he could urge her into a chair and make her sit there until she grew quieter. Tony muttered in the corner once, then again before snapping off the link and turning back to them.

"He's there. Him and the other one. I told him what happened. He says he'd come to you but he doesn't have a car. You can come to him, or I'll go get him and bring him here."

"I'll go." She jumped up, staring wildly around herself. "I was wicked, Father James. I resented her. God has taken her away because of—"

"Marjorie!" he shouted, shaking her. "Stop that! Is God so unjust that he would punish your daughter because of something you did? You won't help Stella by having fits of guilt. Stop it."

She gulped again, visibly taking hold of herself. "Yes. Oh, yes, of course. I'm sorry. You're right. Tony, grab whatever food you can put together in five minutes. You and Father James will be hungry. I must get my coat."

She ran out and they heard her footsteps clattering along the hallway, stumbling at first, then slowing into a firm, rapid walk as she took better control of herself. She returned in moments and did not break down again during the flight.

In the Arbai city, Brother Lourai took them to the home he and Mainoa occupied, one of the excavated houses made weathertight, with a stove in one corner and a few pieces of furniture that fit human bodies. Brother Lourai conducted them there through a downpour of rain, and Brother Mainoa refused to let Marjorie talk until she had shed her wet cloak and was settled with a steaming cup before her. Then, unable to contain herself a moment longer, she poured out the story of Stella's disappearance.

"Why did you come to me?" he asked.

"You know why," she answered, like a challenge. "You may have fooled everyone else with that business about theoretical discussions and postulating what the foxen think, but I think that was real, at least partly. I think you know things the rest of us don't know. About the Hippae, maybe. About the foxen. About what goes on out there in the grasses."

"You want to find your daughter."

"Of course I want to find my daughter."

"Even if she is like the other girl. Janetta bon Maukerden. Even if your daughter is like that?"

"Damn it," Tony interjected angrily. "Did you have to bring that up?"

Brother Mainoa gave him a long, measuring look. "Of course I did, young man. I don't know where your sister is. I know the Hippae took her. I wasn't at your reception, but I've heard about Janetta bon Maukerden showing up. I've talked with Jandra Jellico on the tell-me. I've heard what happens when the Hippae take young women, and you've seen it for yourself. Before we all risk our lives on something hideously dangerous, it's best to know that we really want to, wouldn't you say?"

"Hush, Tony," said Father James to the angry boy. "The man is right."

Rillibee/Lourai got up from his place by the wall and refilled their teacups. "They had Janetta for a long time. They've only had Stella since today." He sounded more concerned than Marjorie had expected, in the light of Brother Mainoa's comments.

Brother Mainoa nodded. "My colleague is right. There is hope that if we find Stella—assuming that is soon—she might not be . . . very different than she was when she vanished."

"It wouldn't matter," Father James said tiredly. "Even if we knew she would be like that other girl, if we have any chance of success we must still try to find her. Not if it means certain destruction, however. I will not allow that, Marjorie, so set the idea aside. We must have some hope of succeeding."

"You've been out there, haven't you?" Marjorie demanded of Brother Mainoa once more. "You've seen things and the Hippae haven't killed you."

"I had protection," Brother Mainoa said. "Protection to go alone into the grass and look at things. I have no idea whether *we* can obtain protection to go into the grasses and look for someone. It might be better to let me try it alone."

She shook her head. No. Not alone. She herself had to go. "Now, at once!"

"No. Not at once," he cut her off. "Soon, but not at once. Since we returned from Opal Hill, Brother Lourai and I have been trying to make sense of that design you showed us. Many volumes of Arbai books have already been filed with the tell-me computers at Commons. They have a link with the network on Semling. Brother Lourai and I have been feeding in the designs carved on the doors and the houses. Within hours we may have some . . . some indication that there are correlations."

"Is that more important than Stella's life?" Marjorie was incredulous.

"It could be the key to Stella's life," he said patiently. "If the design in the Hippae cavern has meaning, if it seems they comprehend that meaning, perhaps it gives us a way to reach them. Wait here. It may be only an hour or two."

It was less than an hour before the report came, peeping out of the tell-me into a portable link-reader that Brother Lourai had ready. When all the information had been recorded, Brother Mainoa pocketed the device and got hurriedly to his feet, summoning the others with a gesture. "I've skimmed over it. We won't take time to study it now. Remember that we can see nothing helpful from the air. We must go on foot. And we must start from where Stella started. The bon Damfels estancia." He turned toward the door, leaving his other papers on the table behind him.

"Not on foot," Marjorie contradicted him as she put her still-damp cloak around her. "No, Brother Mainoa. We can do better than that. We'll go on horseback."

Rigo had gone first into the house for a drink. After a few glasses of the excellent brandy Roald Few had provided, Rigo had gone to look for his family, not finding Marjorie or Tony or even Father James when he went down to the priests' house. Father Sandoval told him they had gone.

"To the Arbai dig, I think I heard Father James say. Marjorie thinks there may be some help there."

"Help for what?" Rigo snarled, angered that he had not been asked to go along.

"To find Stella," the old priest said. "For what other reason?"

"Does she think I have no interest in that?" Rigo demanded. "Doesn't she think I care?"

Father Sandoval struggled to find something that would calm Rigo's anger. "I haven't talked to Marjorie, Rigo. I know only what Father James told me."

Rigo snarled again wordlessly and left the old priest while he, Rigo, wandered aimlessly in the garden, cursing to himself. When his feet brought him to Eugenie's house, he went in, telling himself he would stay only for a short time. He wanted to be in his own room when Marjorie returned. Still, Marjorie had gone some distance, so there was no hurry. He began to unburden himself to Eugenie, telling her many things to which she murmured sympathetically without paying any attention at all.

She poured him another drink, and then several more. Rigo grew at first angrier, then sad and maudlin. He wept, and she comforted him. They found their way into the summer bedroom. Neither of them heard the aircar return in the middle hours of the night.

Father James, who had done some show riding in his youth, saddled Millefiori, the most spirited of the mares, while Marjorie, who had already saddled Don Quixote for herself and El Dia Octavo for Tony, urged Brothers Mainoa and Lourai to help her with Her Majesty and Blue Star. These two were graceful and elegant mares with habits of calm good sense. "You'll ride these two, Brothers. All you need to do is sit on top and relax. The horses will do the rest."

Brothers Mainoa and Lourai looked at one another in embarrassed surmise. Rillibee had ridden something a few times in his childhood, ridden at a slow walk, with someone leading the horse or donkey or whatever it had been. Brother Mainoa could not remember ever having touched a riding animal of any kind before. Marjorie had no time to reassure them. She was busy at the top of a short stepladder, putting a saddle on the great draft horse, Irish Lass.

"Who's going to ride that?" Rillibee/Lourai asked.

"Irish Lass will carry most of our supplies. And Stella can ride her, when we find Stella."

When we find her, Father James thought quietly to himself. If. If we find her. He had not gone back to the house he shared with Father Sandoval. He had not told the older priest he was going on this wild venture. It would be easier to ask forgiveness later than to seek permission now, permission which he would not receive.

"I have to go out into the grass for a while before we leave," Brother Mainoa said. "Something I need to do if we want to get where we're going."

Marjorie stared at him, eager to be off and yet aware of what dangers lay out there. "Is it necessary?"

"If we're going to get to bon Damfels in one piece, yes."

She gestured, biting her lip. "Hurry. If you can." Then she stood looking after him into the darkness, wondering what he was up to.

Tony came into the stables with a pile of things which he set down on the floor, announcing, "These have to be sorted out. There's food and some equipment. I have to make another trip."

"Father James?" Marjorie indicated the pile. "Is there anything that we need that Tony hasn't found?" She leaned wearily against the flank of the huge horse, asking Tony, "Did you tell your father where we're going?"

"I didn't find Father," Tony reported. "I went through the house."

"Leave him a message on the tell-me," Marjorie said, relieved that Rigo was not shouting at them, telling them they could not go. He was probably with Eugenie, but it wouldn't be appropriate for Tony to seek him there. "Leave him a note, Tony. Tell him we've gone looking for Stella, that we've taken the horses."

"I did," the boy replied. "I already did that."

"Water bottles," said the priest. "First aid supplies."

"I'll get them."

The boy turned and left, the priest following him, calling, "Dry clothes in something waterproof."

"Do you have everything you need?" Marjorie asked Brother Lourai.

He shrugged, elaborately, as though to ask who knew what was needed. "We each brought a change of clothes and boots. Brother Mainoa raided our dry stores to bring what food he could. We could use something to cook in or heat water in."

"There." She pointed at a miniature cooker in the pile. "And over there are the saddlebags. Before we came to Grass, Rigo and I thought we might be taking extended rides. We brought camping gear, as we would have done for endurance rides at home."

"Home. Where was your home?"

"Lesser Britain. And then, later, Old Spain. After Rigo and I were married."

"Old Spain?" Rillibee asked.

"The southwestern province of Western Europe."

"Are there many Old Catholics there?"

"Many. More than anywhere else. Sanctity has not had good luck with converts in Spain."

"Where I lived, only a long time before, there were Old Catholics."

"Where was that?"

"In New Spain, the Middle American Provinces. Joshua, my father, said our province was once called Mexico."

"Your father was Old Catholic? But you are one of the Sanctified."

He shook his head no. "I am whatever Joshua was. But I don't know what he was. He wasn't Old Catholic, I know that." He leaned against the horse she had told him to ride, imitating her stance, stroking the animal as she did hers, feeling the stiff, glossy hair slide beneath his fingers. "He loved trees. Miriam loved trees, too." Tears came and he blinked them away. He had seen no trees on this place, except for the small copse near the dig. There had been no trees at Sanctity. Sometimes he thought if he could only see trees, then he would not feel so alone.

Tony and Father James returned with more supplies. Brother Mainoa, looking pensive, came in to help them sort the supplies into the saddlebags, including the two hamper-sized containers that Irish Lass was to carry. When they were done, they stood looking at one another as though reluctant to take the next, inevitable step. It was Brother Mainoa who broke the silence.

"I'll lead if I may, Lady Westriding. For a little while. After that, it shouldn't be necessary. If you'll tell me how to steer?"

Marjorie explained the use of reins and legs and rode out beside him to make sure he understood. Within moments they had left the garden trail and were pushing through tall grass, each barely able to see the nearest rider. Then, almost before they had had a chance to be annoyed by the lash of the thick growth, they came through the tough stems into lower grass and turned purposefully toward the northeast. They rode silently except for Brother Mainoa's occasional querulous, "Tell me again what I do to get farther right?" And then, after he had been told two or three times, he did not ask again. They rode for some time in silence except for the soft plop of hooves and the rustle of the grass.

Marjorie, riding alongside Brother Mainoa, thought she heard him speak and leaned closer to whisper, "What was that, Brother?" She heard the same sound again. A snore. He was riding asleep while Blue Star went placidly along the sides of starlit hills and down winding shadowed vales as though she were on her way home, her ears forward as if hearing someone there calling her name.

Rigo woke with gritty eyes and a sour taste in his mouth. For a moment he did not remember where he was; then, seeing the flash of a flick bird across the tall windows and hearing a grass peeper call repeatedly from the grass garden, he remembered Grass. It was the soft, rose-colored curtains blowing in the morning wind that told him he was in Eugenie's room rather than in his own bedroom adjoining Marjorie's. The bed beside him was empty.

Eugenie came in like the head of a small tray-bearing comet, billowing hair and silken draperies in a turbulent tail behind her. "The girl doesn't get here until later, Rigo, so I made you coffee my own self." She plumped his pillow, sat beside him on the bed, and leaned prettily forward to pour. The cups were pink, curved like the petals of a flower. The cream was steaming.

"Where did you get cream?" he asked. "I haven't had cream since we've been here."

"Never you mind." She pouted, flushing with pleasure at his pleasure. "I have my ways."

"No, really, Eugenie. Where did you get it?"

"Sebastian brings it to me. His wife has a cow."

"He never said a word to me about—"

"You didn't ask, that's all." She stirred his cup and handed it to him. "You flirted with him."

She didn't deny it, merely smiled through her lashes at him, sipping at her own cup.

He started to say something about flirting, about Stella's flirting, and the memory came back. The cup dropped from his hand and rolled across the thick carpet and he struggled to get out of the clinging sheets.

"Rigo!" It was a protest.

"I forgot about Stella," he cried. "I forgot!"

"You didn't forget," she told him. "You told me, last night."

"Oh, damn you, Eugenie. That's not what I meant." He went away from her, into the bathroom. She heard water running as she sat staring into her cup, not drinking anymore. If he only hadn't remembered. For a little while.

He went straight to the kitchen, then to Marjorie's room, and then Tony's. Only after finding all three places empty did he think of the tell-me. There he found a message, brief but complete: Tony and his mother had gone. They had taken the horses. They had gone to find Stella. Rigo howled, half in anger, half in pain, making the crystal ornaments complain in icy voices. Where would Marjorie have gone? Tony hadn't said, but there was only one logical starting point for a search. Bon Damfels' place.

He flushed, remembering how he had left bon Damfels' place the day before, begging, pleading with them to help him find his daughter, while Stavenger, at first frostily cold and then heated with anger, had accused him of undisciplined, un-Huntly behavior; while Stavenger and Dimoth and Gustave told him to go home and mourn Stella in private and quit shouting about her; while bon Haunser and bon Damfels aunts and cousins pointed derisive fingers at him. Despite all that, the people of Klive were not at a Hunt today, and he would return to Klive.

In the garage, he found both aircars partially disassembled, with Sebastian hovering over a case of new parts.

"What in the name of God . . . ?"

"Your driver said the stabilizer was malfunctioning yesterday," Sebastian said, startled. "We've had trouble with both of them, and since there is no Hunt today . . ."

Rigo bit back a roar of outrage. "Is there any other vehicle here? Or in the village?"

"No, sir. I can have this one reassembled in an hour or two. If you must travel before then, perhaps someone from Commons . . ."

Persun Pollut called his father, but Hime Pollut was out of his shop. No one knew when he would return. Roald Few was not available. Three other persons who Persun called were at the port—a long-awaited shipment had come in. Persun made exaggerated swoops with his eyebrows, indicating annoyance.

As for Rigo, while hours passed, he seethed, barely able to contain his frustration at Marjorie's passing slowly, slowly away to someplace where he might never find her.

13

When Marjorie and the others arrived at Klive, Marjorie rode directly to the Kennel Gate. It was the closest place she knew to the first surface, one of the two familiar approaches to the mansion. Above the first surface was the terrace, and fronting on the terrace were the reception rooms. She was halfway across the terrace before someone saw her and moved swiftly to intercept her. Sylvan.

"Marjorie!" His voice was a muffled shout of dismay. "What are you doing here?"

"I've come to find out what I can about Stella." She confronted him, arms folded, half angry, half pleading.

He took her arm, pulled her away from the windows. "You Yrariers do believe in courting danger. For the love of whatever you hold dear, Marjorie, come away from the doors. Let's go down into the garden." He turned away, still pulling at her, and she followed him, somewhat unwillingly and too late. The stentorian bellow startled them both. Stavenger had come out the doors and stood towering at the top of the steps, face purple with fury.

"What are you doing here? *Fragras!* I'm speaking to you!"

His fists were clenched as though he intended to strike her. Her own frustration and fury rose to meet his, all in a moment. She drew herself up, one hand forward, the index finger pointing him out.

"You," she screamed. "You unholy monster!" Her voice hung on the air like a smell.

He shuddered and drew back, more surprised by her attack than he would have been by any other tactic. He was not accustomed to either defiance or reproach, and he had been so far from sensible thought that it took him time to puzzle out that he had intended to attack her.

"You despoiler of children!" she cried. "You barbarian! Where was it you saw my daughter last?" She moved up toward him, waving the finger as though it had a cutting edge, like a sword.

"I never saw her," he snarled. "I didn't look."

"How can a Master not observe his Hunt?" she cried. "Are you so enslaved to your mounts that you're insensible?"

His face became even darker, his neck swelled, his eyes bulged as he howled inarticulately and came toward her like a juggernaut. Sylvan caught her from behind and dragged her away.

"Move!" he hissed at her, a long, frightened exhalation. "He'll kill you if he gets the chance!"

He pulled her down the steps, away down the Hounds' Way and through the Kennel Gate, then shut the heavy gate behind her. Through it she could still hear Stavenger's wordless bellows of fury.

Sylvan leaned against the gate, his face pale. "I knew you'd want to know. I found out for you. I asked Shevlok and some of the others. They don't notice much during a Hunt, quite frankly, but it was Darenfeld's Coppice, the same as Dimity, the same as Janetta. That's the last place anyone saw her."

"Show me!" she demanded, leaping up into Don Quixote's saddle. "Now!"

"Marjorie—"

"Now! You can ride Irish Lass. She's smaller than those monstrosities you're used to riding." Then, seeing him looking vacantly at the big horse, "Put your left foot in the stirrup, that metal thing there. Grasp the saddle and pull yourself up; she's not going to put her leg out for you. Now, take the reins, as I have mine. Don't bother doing anything with them. She'll follow us. Now, show me where!"

He gestured off to the left and they all rode in that direction, gaining only a little distance before they heard the gate bang open and looked back to see Stavenger howling after them. The riders looked resolutely forward as they entered the taller grasses which soon hid them from view.

Sylvan sat very quietly on the horse, occasionally reaching forward with his feet as though to find the toe spaces he was accustomed to on his Hippae mounts.

"Sit up," Marjorie instructed him tersely. "She has no barbs to skewer you with. Lean forward. Pet her. She likes it."

He did so, slowly, almost fearfully, relaxing gradually.

"A different kind of beast, eh?" queried Brother Mainoa. "Though I am very sore from this unaccustomed position, I am not afraid."

"No," Sylvan agreed abstractedly. "No. But then, one really isn't afraid while on the Hunt, either." He stared around himself, as though seeking landmarks. "There." He pointed ahead of them, a little to the right. "That's the Ocean Garden. Normally we'd ride on the other side, but we can get where we're going around this way." He gestured, showing Marjorie the way, and she rode ahead, letting him call directions to her as they went.

"Why was your father in a rage?" Tony asked.

"Because of *your* father. When they returned last night, from the Hunt, Roderigo demanded that they help him search for your sister. It isn't done. When someone vanishes, everyone pretends not to notice. No one searches. No one demands help from others. Father —my father—couldn't keep his temper. He's been wild, ever since yesterday. Seeing you set him off, and then when your mother accused him . . ." Sylvan's eyes opened widely, and he stroked his throat. "How can I . . . ?"

"No Hippae around," murmured Brother Mainoa. "Not just now. I think our . . . well, our guides have frightened them off. Or perhaps they have gone for reinforcements."

"Guides?"

"Do not speak of it. Perhaps we will, in time, but now is not the time. We do not want to think cheese with hunger all around us."

Sylvan went back to massaging his throat and staring incredulously about himself. Only after they had gone some miles through the grasses did he settle down, though he still managed to disconcert Marjorie from time to time by standing upright on Irish Lass's back. "I have to get up here to see," he explained, waving toward a distance the others could not perceive. "There, off there, is the ridge that leads to the copse."

They turned in the indicated direction and moved on, gaining a lower limb of the ridge and following it as it wound its lengthy way onto the height. From there they could look down into a valley dotted with copses. Sylvan pointed to the largest of them. "Darenfeld's," he said.

"Why Darenfeld?" asked Rillibee/Lourai. "There are no bons by that name."

"There were," Sylvan replied. "There were eleven families originally. The Darenfeld estancia and all the family perished in a grass fire several generations ago. Others had been burned out before."

"A grass fire?" Marjorie wondered. "We've seen no fires since we've been here."

"You haven't been here in summer." He gazed out toward the horizon. "There is almost no rain in the summer, but there is lightning. The fires come like great waves, eating the grass, sending smoke boiling up into the clouds. Sometimes there are fires in the spring, but they are small ones because the grass is still fresh and full of moisture—"

"And a summer fire burned the Darenfeld estancia?"

"It was before they had grass gardens," Brother Mainoa remarked. "We at the Friary have designed the gardens to stop the flames. There are areas and aisles of low turfs which smolder but do not burn. They break the fire so that it goes around rather than through. We have done the same thing at the Friary, to protect it, and at Opal Hill and the other estancias. The great gardens of Klive were not planted merely for their beauty."

"True." Sylvan nodded. "None of the bons would have gone to the trouble merely for beauty."

Marjorie urged Don Quixote toward the copse below them. It loomed dark and mysterious among the soft-hued grasses, the more so the closer they came. Small pools sucked at the horses' feet. Great trunks went up into gloomy shade, gnarled roots kneed up to brace their monstrous bulk, their lower branches as huge as ordinary trees.

Rillibee leaned toward the copse as though toward a lover.

"Now what?" asked Tony.

"The hunt came here and left here. We should find a path trampled into the grasses where many Hippae went. Then we should find another, where one Hippae went."

"If it went," said Brother Mainoa. "Though this is called a copse, it is in fact a small forest. What would you say, Sylvan? Half a mile or more through?"

Sylvan shook his head. "Estimating distances is not something we do much of, I'm afraid. On the Hunt, it doesn't matter. We measure Hunts in hours, not in miles or kilometers or stadia, as they do on Repentance."

"From the ridge it looked to be half a mile," Father James agreed. "Enough territory in here to hide any number of Hippae."

"If we do not find a trail leading out," said Marjorie wildly, "then we will search within, among the trees." She appealed to each of them in turn, seeking agreement. Brother Mainoa sat very still upon his horse. His expression was alert, as though he heard something she could not hear. "Brother Mainoa?" she asked. "Brother?"

His eyebrows went up, and he smiled at her. "Of course. Of course. Let us first look for a trail."

The way the Hunt had come was easy to find. The way the Hunt had gone was equally easy. Crushed grasses testified to the fact that more than one Hunt had come this way recently. Some stems were completely dried, others were newly broken and still leaking moisture. Brother Mainoa rode down this broad trail and then pulled Blue Star to a halt as he pointed off to the left. All of them could see the narrow trail which wound into the grass. Father James picked a stem of broken grass and handed it to Marjorie. It was still moist.

"So," she said. "So."

"If a Hippae has her," Tony said in a carefully emotionless voice, "how are we to get her?"

"Hide," she said. "Wait until it leaves her alone. Steal her back."

"I wish we had weapons," Father James said.

"So do I," she admitted. "But we don't."

He shook his head, only slightly. "Let us hope we find only one of the beasts opposing us."

Rigo boiled the morning away, waiting while Sebastian reassembled the aircar, a longer process than had been anticipated. The new parts, though appropriately numbered, were not a precise fit. Sebastian took them to his own shop in the village, as he put it, "to shave them down a bit."

By midafternoon the first car had been put together and tested. Driven by Sebastian, with Persun Pollut along for whatever assistance he might offer, Rigo set out for Klive. The trip took slightly more than an hour, across the southern tip of the swamp forest with the clutter of Commons off to their left. They landed in the gravel court beyond the first surface and crossed that surface on their way to the terrace of Klive.

"Your Excellency," a little voice cried from behind the balustrade. "Your Excellency!"

Rigo turned, surprised to see one of the bon Damfels daughters beckoning to him. He moved toward her, impatiently, wanting to go on into Klive to see whether Marjorie was there.

"They've gone," the girl said. "Roderigo Yrarier, your wife and son and the Green Brothers, they've gone."

"Gone where?" he blurted. "Where?"

She shook her head, tears suddenly starting down her cheeks. "You mustn't go up there. Father, the Obermun, is in a rage. He will kill you. He has half killed Emmy already. Your wife came to ask where your daughter had been lost. Sylvan told her. He found out from Shevlok, and he told your wife. Sylvan went with them. Father had been screaming since then. Emmy tried to calm him and he beat her—"

A bellow from the house above them sent the girl fleeing along the side of the house. Rigo stopped, put one foot on the step before him, and felt himself pulled firmly away. Sebastian had one arm and Persun the other, and they seemed determined to drag him away from Klive, by brute force if necessary.

"Don't go up there, sir. He will not listen to reason. Listen to him. He sounds like a bull!"

"Listen to Pollut, sir. He will not give you any help, not now. You must wait. Wait until he is calmer. Wait until you can speak with someone else."

"At the Hunt," Sebastian suggested. "Tomorrow. At the bon Laupmon Hunt." They dragged Rigo away, he resisting them but not protesting, as though some part of him realized the sense of what they said even though his body was unwilling to agree.

The horses followed the trail in single file, their riders at first alert for any sound, then gradually, as mile succeeded mile, growing slack and distracted. Mainoa and Lourai were preoccupied with pain, aching joints and throbbing buttocks. Marjorie was thinking of Rigo, and

Sylvan of Marjorie. Father James was praying that he had not done the wrong thing, and Tony was thinking of a girl he had not seen for a very long time. The slap of the grass blades on their bodies had become hypnotic. Even Marjorie, usually alert to the nuances of horse behavior, did not notice that the horses were acting very much as Don Quixote had acted when she had ridden him away from the Hippae cavern. Ears alertly forward, they moved as though they were headed home. As though someone spoke to them. The riders did not comment upon this. With the sun on their backs, they rode, unspeaking, the only noise the sound of the horses' hooves.

The world spun the sun to the center of the sky and then downward once more. The light was on their faces. They had stopped once or twice to drink and relieve themselves, but the trail winding enigmatically ahead of them had enticed them to keep the stops brief. The first howl came from behind them, far off to the right.

Marjorie stiffened. She had heard the sound before, and it meant terror.

"Hippae," said Sylvan in a hopeless voice. "Do they know we are here?"

"Not yet," said Brother Mainoa.

"How do you know?" Marjorie demanded.

"You came to me for help, Lady Westriding, and I'm giving you help. How or why isn't something we can talk of yet. I tell you truthfully that the Hippae do not yet know we are here. They will know, shortly, but not yet. I would suggest we move more rapidly."

Tony sat up, kneeing El Dia Octavo into a canter. He rattled away down the narrow trail, the others following. Brothers Mainoa and Lourai were hanging onto their saddles, grunting with effort. "Push down with your feet," Marjorie cried. "Sit straight. It's no more difficult than a rocking chair."

Brother Mainoa pushed down with his feet and continued to hang on. After a time the rocking motion became predictable and his body adapted to it. Rillibee/Lourai was quicker. He found the motion exhilarating. Grass heads slapped him in the face and he grinned widely, seeds in his teeth.

More howls from behind them, to both right and left.

"Do you know where we're going?" Marjorie demanded over her shoulder.

"Swamp forest," Mainoa said, grunting. "Just ahead."

He had no sooner said it than they came through the last of the tall grasses to see the forest at a considerable distance ahead and below them, stretching to the limits of sight in either direction. The trail they had been following ran toward the forest like an arrow flight, one aimed at a rocky knob which raised itself above the level of the distant trees. The bowl of grasses before them came only slightly above the horses' bellies.

"Can the horses run faster?" Mainoa called plaintively. "If they can, we should."

Don Quixote and El Dia Octavo had made the same decision—or had been informed of it—at the same moment. They waited for no signal from their riders but sped down the slope, tails streaming behind them, ears flattened. The mares plunged after them, Irish Lass thundering away at the rear. For Mainoa it was as though he rode a nightmare. Though he knew he would fall, he did not. Though he knew he could not stay on, he did. The horse beneath him seemed determined to keep him in the saddle, and through all his panic he perceived that fact even as he heard the howls rising from the height they had just left. He could not risk looking back to see how close the Hippae were.

Sylvan could. Over the drumming of the hooves he heard the wild screaming from the ridge. He spun half around on the broad back, holding tight to one of the vast panniers Irish Lass carried. A dozen enormous beasts pranced upon the height. Around their feet a great pack of hounds leapt and yammered. As though in response to some signal that Sylvan had not seen, the whole Hunt of them plunged down the slope after the fleeing horses. Not silently, as when they hunted foxen, but clamoring as with one shrill ear-shattering voice.

He turned. The other horses were ahead of him, far ahead of him. This great beast was not as fleet as the others. He lay forward on her neck and whispered to her. "Do the best you can, my lady. I think otherwise, both you and I will be meat for them." He turned to watch the pursuit. One huge violet-mottled Hippae led the charge, mouth wide, nostrils flared. It seemed to stumble in the grass, then again. It fell, eyes rolled back. A ripple in the grass fled to one side.

Behind the fallen monster the others slowed, prancing uncertainly. "Go," called Sylvan to his mount. "Go, lady. As best you can."

Irish Lass heard him and went. The distance between her and the other horses had grown. She did her best to decrease it, but it became wider yet.

Again the Hippae howled pursuit. Again the foremost among them tripped and fell. Again a ripple in the grass fled away, out of their path.

El Dia Octavo had reached the forest. Don Quixote was just behind him. Millefiori was next. Then Blue Star and Her Majesty. The riders had dismounted and were waiting for Sylvan.

Beside Sylvan a hound ran even with Irish Lass, its head darting through the grasses, teeth bared to strike at the running legs of the horse. Beyond the hound the grass quivered and something made of shining barbs snatched the hound away. Sylvan had not seen what it was, but he heard the hound screaming. Seemingly, so did the rest of the pack. The sound of their howling fell farther behind him. The great horse grunted beneath him. Her hide was wet and sleek. Foam flew from her mouth. "Good Lass," he whispered. "Good Lass."

And then, at last, he was there among the others. He turned once more to see the grass behind him alive with ripples. Something was moving there. Something the Hippae-hound pack was aware of, for it stood away, circling, screaming defiance but coming no nearer.

Irish Lass stood with her head dragging. "Ah, Lass, Lass," Marjorie was saying. "Poor girl. You're not built for it, are you Lass, but so brave! Such a wonderful girl." She led the mare in a tight circle as she talked. Gradually, Lass's head came up.

"Where now?" asked Tony. "We don't dare ride in there." He gestured toward the trees, where water glimmered among the dark foliage.

"Yes," said Brother Mainoa. "In there. Following me."

"Have you been in there before?"

"No."

"Well, then . . ."

"I haven't been out in the grasses on a horse before either. But we are here. The immediate threat is past. We were guided. Protected."

"By?"

"I won't tell you until your knowing can't endanger us. Those things"—he thrust a hand in the direction of the Hippae—"can read *your* thoughts. We have to get into the forest. The barrier between us and them is more pretense than real. If we stay here too long, the Hippae may realize that."

Tony looked at his mother, as though for permission. Father James was already mounting once more. With a sigh, Brother Mainoa heaved himself up, struggling to get his leg across the horse. Brother Lourai helped him. Sylvan was still atop Irish Lass.

"Go," Marjorie said.

Blue Star moved into the shallow water, picking her way among towering trunks and through thickets of reedlike growths. The others followed. The mare took a winding path, turning abruptly to take new directions. "Follow her closely," Brother Mainoa called hoarsely. "She is avoiding dangerous places." So they went, a slow, splashing game of follow the leader, with Blue Star following who-knew-what.

When they had come into the swamp far enough that they could no longer see the prairies, Blue Star stopped her twisting path and led them straight along a shallow channel between two impenetrable walls of trees. This watery aisle seemed to go on for miles. At last a gap appeared in the endless line, and the mare struggled up a shallow bank and onto solid ground.

"An island?" Marjorie asked.

"Safety," Brother Mainoa said, sighing and half sliding, half falling off his horse and lying where he fell.

"How? Safety?"

"The Hippae will not come in here. Nor the hounds." He spoke from the ground, staring up through the trees to far-off glimmers of sunlight, like spangles. Like gems. His eyes would not stay open.

"One did," she contradicted. "We saw the trail."

"Only as far as the swamp," he acknowledged. "And then, I think, perhaps it went along the side. . . ." His mouth fell open and a little sound came out. A snore.

"He's old," Rillibee said to them defiantly, as though they had accused the old man of some impropriety. "He falls asleep like that a lot."

Sylvan had dismounted. "What do I do for her?" He asked Marjorie as he stroked the mare.

"Rub her down with something," Marjorie said. "A clump of grass, a fistful of leaves, anything. If we're going to stay here awhile, take the saddle off."

"We can't go on until he wakes up," said Tony, indicating the supine form of Brother Mainoa.

"We can't go on until the horses rest a little anyhow," Marjorie sighed. "They had quite a workout. About a day and a half a night of steady walking plus a mad run. Don't let her have much water," she cautioned Sylvan. "Walk her until she's cool, then let her have water."

"Otherwise what?" Sylvan asked. "Would it kill her?"

"It could make her sick," Tony answered him, looking up as Mainoa had done before he fell asleep. Sun spangles, very high. Something else up there, too. Something high that blocked the sun. Tony pointed. "What's up there?"

Sylvan turned to look. "Where?"

"Right up in the top of this tree, running over to that other one . . ."

"This island is quite sizable," said Father James, rejoining the group from among the trees. "There's a grassy clearing through these trees. Enough pasture there for the horses to have a good feed."

Rillibee/Lourai pulled the saddles from Blue Star and Her Majesty and stacked them against the root buttresses of a tree. "The sun is low. It'll be dark before long. Too dark to ride."

"How long will Brother Mainoa sleep?"

Lourai shrugged. "As long as he needs to. He's been up since the middle of the night, on a horse most of that time. I told you, he's an old man."

Marjorie nodded. "All right, then. If he rests, we will all rest. Tony?"

The boy pointed upward. "We were just trying to figure out—"

"Figure out whether there's any firewood, while it's still light. Sylvan, please help him. We need enough wood to last all night. Father, if you'll find the clearest water possible and fill this bucket—"

"What about me?" Brother Lourai asked.

"You and I will be chief cooks," she said, burrowing in the capacious baskets Irish Lass had carried. "When we have eaten we will talk about what we do next."

Tony and Sylvan wandered toward the nearest thicket, Tony taking out his laser knife. When he used it to cut an armload of dried brush, Sylvan exclaimed, "What's that?"

Tony gave it to him, explaining.

"Is this something new?" Sylvan asked.

"Of course not. They've been around forever."

"I've never seen one before," Sylvan marveled. "I wonder why."

"Probably because they wouldn't let you," Tony said. "It would make a handy weapon."

"It would, wouldn't it?" Sylvan said, turning the device over and over in his hand. He sighed, gave it back to Tony, and turned his attention to carrying wood. Still, he thought of the knife with wonder. Why hadn't he known about such things?

Brother Mainoa awoke about the time the food was ready, quite willing to interrupt his rest to join them for supper. When they had eaten, when the utensils were cleaned and put back in the panniers, they sat around the fire, waiting.

Marjorie said, "Well, Brother Mainoa. So, we are here."

He nodded.

"Are we any closer to Stella than when we set out?"

"The trail led along the swamp-forest," he said. "Outside it, un-fortunately. We could not have stayed there."

"Tomorrow?"

"Perhaps. If the Hippae have gone. Tonight we would be unable to see anything."

She sighed.

Tony said, "Mother, it's just as well. The horses couldn't have gone much farther."

Marjorie was still looking at Brother Mainoa. "You know some-thing," she said. "You obviously know much more than you have told us."

He shrugged. "What I know, or think I know, is not something I can share with you, yet. Perhaps tomorrow."

"Will you decide?" she asked with a percipient glare.

"No," he admitted. "No, the decision won't be mine."

"What does it—they—want? To look us over?"

He nodded.

Tony asked, "What are the two of you talking about?"

"Yes, Marjorie. What are you—?" Sylvan asked.

Father James gave Marjorie a percipient glance and said, "Let it alone, Sylvan, Tony. For now. Perhaps Brother Mainoa has already presumed upon his acquaintance with . . . well, the powers that be."

Mainoa smiled. "A way of saying it, Father. If you can bear it, Lady Westriding, I would suggest that we rest. Sleep, if possible. We are quite safe here."

Safety was not what Marjorie wanted. If she had been in danger of her life, at least she would have felt she was doing something. To sleep in safety meant that she was slacking while Stella was in danger, but there was no argument she could make. It was already too dark to find a trail. She rose from her place beside the fire and made her way among the trees to the grassy area where the horses grazed. There she sought the comfort from them which she did not receive from those in her company. It was only when she leaned against Quixote's side that she realized how desperately tired she was.

Behind her the others made their beds near the fire. Tony put his mother's bed to one side, screened from the others by low brush, where she would have some privacy. When she returned, he pointed it out to her, and she went to it, grateful for his help. Silence came then, broken by Mainoa's low, purring snores, the cries of peepers distant upon the prairie, and the cries of other less familiar things in the swamp around them.

Marjorie had thought she would lie sleepless. Instead, sleep came upon her like a black tide, inexorably. She went down into it, dreamless and quiet. Time passed, with her unconscious of it. The hand that was laid upon her arm did not wake her until it shook her slightly.

"Ma'am," said Rillibee Chime. "I'm hearing something.

She sat up. "What time is it?"

"Midnight, more or less. Listen, Lady. It's sounds that woke me. People, maybe?"

She held her breath. After a moment she heard it—them—the sounds of voices, wafted to them on a light wind which had come up while she slept. A conversation. No words she could understand, but unmistakably the sound of people talking.

"Where?" she breathed.

He put his hand on her cheek and pushed so that her head turned. As she faced in another direction, she heard them more clearly. "Light," she whispered.

He already had it in his hand, a torch which shed a dim circle before their feet. He handed her another, and they walked among the trees, through the meadow where the horses grazed with a sound of steady munching, beyond the meadow into the trees once more. Rillibee pointed up. It was true. The sounds came from above them.

She was no longer sure they were people. The sound was too sibilant for human people. And yet . . .

"Like the sounds in the Arbai village," she said.

He nodded, peering above him. "I'm going up," he said.

She caught at him. "You won't be able to see!"

He shook his head. "I'll feel, then. Don't wait for me. Go back to the others."

"You'll fall!"

He laughed. "Me? Oh, Lady, at the Friary they call me Willy Climb. I have the fingers of a tree frog and the toes of a lizard. I have stickum on my knees and the hooves of a mountain goat. I can no more fall than an ape can fall when it creeps among the vines. Go back to the others, Lady," and he was away, his torch slung about his neck, the light dwindling up the great trunk of the tree as he swarmed up it like a monkey.

When the circle of light had dwindled to nothing, she went back the way she had come, certain now that she would not sleep again. Yet when she lay down upon her bed she found sleep waiting for her. She had time only to wonder briefly what Brother Lourai would find among the branches before she was deeply asleep once more.

At the Friary, Elder Brother Fuasoi was sitting late at his desk, angrily turning the pages of a book. Yavi Foosh sat disconsolately on a chair nearby, yawning, trying to keep from nodding off.

"No sign of Mainoa or Lourai, then?" Fuasoi asked for perhaps the tenth time.

"No, Elder Brother."

"And they didn't mention to anyone where they were going?"

"There wasn't anybody there to mention to, Elder Brother. Mainoa and Lourai were all alone at the ruins. The library crew had changed shifts three days ago. Shoethai and me didn't take the replacement men back until this evening. When we got there, Shoethai and me went to tell Mainoa, but he was gone. Him and Lourai. We looked all through the ruins, Elder Brother." He sighed, much put upon. He had told the story four times.

"And you found this book where?"

"Shoethai found it, Elder Brother. On Brother Mainoa's worktable. He thought—since they were gone—there might be something written down somewhere. The book was the only writing Shoethai found. He brought it straight here to you."

Fuasoi glared at the book, obviously a new one, with only a few pages written in. Oh, indeed there was something written down. All in Brother Mainoa's own hand. Conjecture about the plague. Wonderment that it hadn't infected Grass. Conjecture about the Moldies, and whether there might not be some on Grass. And if so, what they might be up to. Interest in the people at Opal Hill, and what they were doing, which was working to thwart the work of the Moldies. Working for Sanctity to stop the plague. To find whatever had kept Grass free of it up until now.

He swore, slamming the book shut. Mere chance had kept Grass free of the plague until now! Mere chance. The virus hadn't come here until now because . . . because it was remote. Because it simply hadn't, yet. There couldn't be anything on Grass that stopped it.

But . . . but if there were, no one could be allowed to learn of it. If they learned of it, they might stop the plague elsewhere. Mainoa and those from Opal Hill would have to be stopped.

"Elder Brother?" Yavi murmured.

"Yes," he snarled.

"Could I be excused now? I've been here for a very long time."

"Go," he growled. "Go, for God's sake, and send Shoethai here."

"Shoethai, Elder Brother?" Shoethai had been dismissed an hour ago.

"Are you deaf! I said Shoethai." Not that Shoethai would be of any help, but at least he would listen to Fuasoi talk.

Shoethai surprised his fellow Moldy by having an idea.

"You should send Highbones after them," the misshapen Brother suggested. "Highbones and Ropeknots and Steeplehands and the two Bridges."

"Who the devil are you talking about?" Fuasoi blurted.

Shoethai flushed. "The climbers. Those are some of the names they call themselves. Highbones is Brother Flumzee."

"Why should I send climbers?"

"Because they hate Brother Lourai. Because he climbed better than any of them. Because some of the younger brothers called him Willy Climb."

"Willy Climb?"

"That's the name they gave him. It's a better name than Highbones, even. When they made him climb the towers and he outclimbed them all. He got up and got down again without being caught. But Highbones had a bet he would die upon the towers, so Highbones hates him."

"It would depend, wouldn't it?"

"On what, Elder Brother?"

"On where Mainoa is."

Shoethai shrugged, his gargoyle face twisting into a hideous grin. "Doesn't matter so long as he's with Brother Lourai. If he's at Commons, Highbones would kill him there. If he's at one of the estancias, Highbones would kill him. If he's out in the grasses . . ."

Highbones had been one of Shoethai's most diligent persecutors. Shoethai loved the idea of Highbones out in the grasses, where the Hippae were, and the hounds.

Elder Brother Fuasoi put the book in the drawer of his desk as he mumbled to himself. "If Mainoa is out in the grasses, we needn't worry about him. No, no. The first thing to do is find out where he went. And the most likely place is Opal Hill. I'll try that first."

Elder Brother Fuasoi reached Persun Pollut. Persun Pollut, with a caution which was natural to him, said that he believed Brothers Mainoa and Lourai might have gone away with Lady Westriding and some other persons but he did not know where.

Shoethai mumbled, "The daughter of that house vanished during the Hunt yesterday. Everyone is talking about it. She vanished somewhere near the bon Damfels estancia. Perhaps they went there."

Elder Brother Fuasoi regarded his assistant with unusual interest as he keyed the tell-me once more. Who would have thought that Shoethai had any interest in Grassian gossip? At Klive he reached a subordinate family member who verified that "some people from Opal Hill" had come to Klive and had gone again. "Out in the grasses," the voice said with a breathless hint of laughter, as though hysteria waited backstage for its entrance cue. "Out in the grasses, to Darenfeld's Coppice."

"If they went in the grasses," Shoethai mumbled, "there will be a trail." He sighed with pleasure. "Send Highbones and the others to follow them."

"On foot?"

"No, no," Shoethai amended thoughtfully. "In an aircar. To find the trail in an aircar." He thought about aircars. It would be easy to fix an aircar so that it would fly quite a long way and then fall. "I'll get one ready for them."

"Who did you say?"

"Brother Flumzee. Brother Niayop. Brother Sushlee. Brothers Thissayim and Lillamool. Highbones, Steeplehands, Ropeknots, Long Bridge, and Little Bridge."

Bones, Ropes, Steep, Long, and Little—who had tortured Shoethai too many times to be forgiven. Who didn't need to wait for the plague because they hadn't deserved the New Creation anyhow.

"Have they hurt you?" Elder Brother asked, suddenly aware of the flame burning at the back of Shoethai's one good eye.

Shoethai frowned and picked at a scab on his cheek, licking the blood from his finger with every evidence of relish. "Oh, no, Elder Brother. It's just that they're always bragging about who they'll do in next." He said nothing more about the aircar. Maybe it would be better not to let Elder Brother know he was going to fix it. That way, when Bones and the others didn't come back, nobody would know it was Shoethai's doing.

Yavi Foosh had left Elder Brother Fuasoi's office only to report directly to that of Elder Brother Jhamlees Zoe, where he waited for half an hour to see his superior.

"What's Fuasoi up to now?" Jhamlees wanted to know.

"Shoethai found a book Brother Mainoa had been writing, and he brought it back to Fuasoi. And now Fuasoi's all in a uproar about it."

"What's in the book?"

"I don't know, Elder Brother. Shoethai found it, and he wouldn't let me see it."

"He should have brought it to me!"

"Sure he should, Elder Brother, but he didn't. I even told him he should bring it to you. But Elder Fuasoi's his bosom friend, so that's where he took it."

"I think I'll walk on down there and see what's going on." Elder Brother Jhamlees rose from his chair and strode down the hall. Yavi Foosh stayed a sensible distance behind. He didn't want to be identified as Jhamlees' man, the way Shoethai was identified as Fuasoi's man. Once that happened, people didn't let you alone.

The door to the office was open. The room itself was empty. Jhamlees stared at the emptiness a moment, then went in and pulled out the drawer in the desk. "This it?" he asked, waving the book as he beckoned Yavi closer.

Yavi nodded. "That looks like it."

"You won't say anything about this?"

Yavi shook his head. Of course he wouldn't say anything about it. Jhamlees Zoe could take all the books in the world, and Yavi wouldn't say a word.

Rillibee moved upward along the trunk of a giant tree, his feet finding a path in the twine of a woody vine, in the ascent of a forking branch. Branch led to branch, vine to vine, a barkway opened before him. He fumbled with the light, trading it from hand to hand as he climbed, once or twice holding it in his mouth when he needed both hands for holding on. As he came up into the first levels of foliage, however, he began to see the forest around him. The leaves glowed, some of them, or creatures upon them glowed in soft fluorescence: green puddles swam at the base of branches, yellow lines delineated twigs, blue dots gleamed from indigo masses. Branches cut darkly across these shining nebulae, these glowing galaxies, and he climbed on structures of solid shadow among moving effulgences.

A small wind came through the trees, bearing a cloud of winged pink blossoms. When the wind died, they perched all together, turning a sapling into flame. Larger wings the color and scent of melons beat slowly from trunk to trunk, the creatures at rest assuming the shape of cups in which golden light pulsed to attract other fliers, darts of violet and a blue so pale it was almost white.

"Joshua," Rillibee whispered. "You'd have loved this. Miriam, you ... you'd have loved this."

"Heaven," said the parrot from the top of a tree. "Died and gone to heaven."

Leaves brushed his face, exuding resinous sweetness. A hard knob of fruit knocked against his arm. He picked it, smelled of it, bit into it. Crisp, sweet-sour, the juice ran into his mouth and was followed by a tingling, almost as though the fruits themselves were effervescent.

The sounds he had heard on the ground were all around him in the trees. Voices. One laughing. One speaking, as though telling a long story to an eager audience, interrupting itself with little side chains of sound. "You're not going to believe this, but ...." "So then, what do you think happened?" If Rillibee closed his eyes, he could see the speaker, cheerfully telling a tale, leaning across a tavern table.

He moved slowly through the branches. The sound faded behind him. He turned and moved toward it once more, caressing the branches with his fingers, loving them with his feet. The voices were off there somewhere among the glowing trees. He would find them eventually.

There was something else to find as well. The girl. Stella. He had set her name beside the other names in his litany. She was to belong to him, to Rillibee Chime. Though her family was wealthy and important, still she would belong to him. Though she herself would disdain him, still ...

"Heaven," whispered the parrot above him.

So he climbed in the night hours. At dawn he found the voices when the sun slanted into their city through leaves of heartbreak gold.

Marjorie woke to birdsong and the music of water. It took her a few moments to remember where she was and a little longer to remember the interruption in the night. When she did, she looked about for Brother Lourai, not finding him but meeting Mainoa's eyes.

"He hasn't come back," the old man said.

"You knew he'd gone off...."

"I knew he woke you and you both went off. But you came back."

"He went up there." She gestured at the high spangle of sun among the boughs. "He told me they call him Willy Climb and that he'd be all right."

Mainoa nodded. "Yes. He *will* be all right. He's like you. When things get very difficult, he thinks of dying from time to time, but he's too curious about what may happen next."

She flushed, wondering how he knew so much about her. It was true. She was curious about what would happen next. As though something awaited her, personally. Some opportunity. . . .

Father James returned from the nearest pool with a full bucket of water, looking alert and rested. "I haven't slept that well in weeks," he said. "I had the oddest dreams."

"Yes," said Brother Mainoa again. "I think we all did. Something here invaded our dreams."

Marjorie stood up and looked about her, suddenly concerned.

"No, no." The old man rose in slow motion, grasping knobby excrescences on the nearest tree to lift himself up. "Nothing inimical, Marjorie. They, too, are curious."

"They?"

"Those I think we will meet today, later. After Brother Lourai returns."

"Hasn't he some other name?" Tony asked.

"Brother Lourai? Oh, yes. As a boy he was Rillibee. Rillibee Chime. You think he doesn't look like a brother?"

"Tony is thinking that he doesn't look like the Sanctified we know," Marjorie offered. "His eyes are too big. His face too lean and intelligent. His mouth too sensitive. I always think of the Sanctified as thick, enthusiastic people with simple thoughts and a great need for answers. Old Catholics are supposed to be slender and ascetic-looking, with huge, philosophical eyes. These are stereotypes, and I'm sometimes ashamed of my thoughts, but they persist, even when I look into a mirror. You don't look like a Sanctified either, Brother. But I suppose you've used the name Mainoa for too long to give it up." She turned away in order not to see Father James' amused and evaluating gaze.

"Far too long," Mainoa said in agreement, laughing. "But do use Rillibee's own name. It means much to him. He will appreciate that."

"We'll go out and try to pick up the trail today," Marjorie said.

Mainoa amended her statement. "It may not be possible to do so for a day or two."

She turned on him, exasperated and frustrated, ready to scream at the delay. Father James laid a hand on her arm.

"Patience, Marjorie. Don't be obsessive. Let it go a little."

"I know, Father. But I keep thinking what may be happening to her."

Father James had been thinking of that, too. His mind dwelt all too frequently on certain monstrousnesses he had heard of in the confessional, on certain perversions and horrors he had read of that he could never have imagined for himself. Why these memories were associated in his mind with the Hippae he did not know, but they were. He set the evil thoughts aside. "We will find her, Marjorie. Trust Brother Mainoa."

She desisted, willing herself to trust Brother Mainoa, since there was no one else to trust.

They ate cold rations. They washed themselves in a placid pond, one of those which encircled the island. Marjorie and Tony examined the horses, looking closely at their hooves, their legs. Despite the wild run of yesterday, the animals seemed to be uninjured. Though she did her best to remain calm, Marjorie felt herself ready to explode from impatience before they heard the call from above.

Rillibee swarmed down a great vine-draped tree like an ape. "I got turned around," he said. "The trees look different in the light, and it took me a while to find my way back."

"Did you find them?" she asked. "The voices?"

"I found their city," Rillibee answered. "You have to come see it."

"We have to go the other way"—she pointed—"to find the trail . . ."

"Up," he insisted. "I think we should."

"Up," agreed Brother Mainoa. "If we can."

"One of the things that took me so long was finding a trail the horses can follow," Rillibee said. "That way." He pointed deeper into the swamp. "Then we'll climb."

"Why?" Marjorie cried. "Stella isn't in there. . . ."

"The trail is out there among the grasses, Marjorie," Brother Mainoa said. "But that's not necessarily the way. While you were still asleep, Tony and I went to the edge of the forest. The Hippae are still there. There is no way we can go out that way just now."

"But why?" she gestured upward, fighting tears. "I don't want to go sightseeing, for the love of God."

"Perhaps it is for the love of God we should go," Father James said. "Do you know what's up there, Brother Mainoa?"

"I suspect," he replied. "I suspect what is up there. I have suspected since the report came from Semling."

"What is it?"

"I think it is the last Arbai city," he said. "The very last."

He would tell them nothing more. He said he didn't know. When they asked Rillibee, he said only that they would see for themselves. He led them as they rode across shallow pools, down aisles of trees. Sometimes he stopped and simply looked at the trees while they waited. Once he dismounted and put his hands on a tree, leaning against it as though it had been a friend. Sylvan started to say something during one of these pauses, but Brother Mainoa laid a hand on his shoulder to silence him. They crossed small islands, coming at last to a very large one with a hill at its center.

On a flat pedestal of stone stood a twisted monument much like that in the plaza of the Arbai city.

"Arbai?" Marjorie whispered, staring at it, unbelieving. Despite what Brother Mainoa had said, she had not let herself believe him.

Rillibee pointed upward along a flank of the hill where a trail wound toward a precipitous cliff edge.

"That's how I came down," he said. "Leave the horses. They'll be all right here."

They dismounted, trying to do it quietly so they would not interrupt the voices above them. People were talking. Singing. Telling stories to the accompaniment of muted laughter. Rillibee led them up the trail. At the cliff edge a bridge led between fantastically carved posts across a gulf of air into the trees—a bridge made of grass and vines and splits of wood, intricate and closely woven as an ornamental basket. The railings were laced into designs of leaves and fruit. The floor was plaited in swirls of color, solid as pavement. Two hundred feet in the air they walked behind Rillibee into the shadow of the trees.

There were dwellings—gazebos and cupolas, tented roofs and conical spires, woven walls and latticed windows—hung like fruit in the branches of the trees, opening upon wickerwork alleys and suspended lattice streets. Aloft were sun-dappled pergolas, shaded kiosks, intricate cages, all joined to those below by spider stairs. Lacework houses hung in the high branches like oriole's nests.

There were inhabitants calling from windows, talking from rooms above and below, conversing as they moved along the roadways, their voices growing louder as they came near, dwindling away as they passed. Shadowy forms met along the railings. A group leapt from a doorway into the play of light from the applauding leaves. They were graceful, only slightly reptilian. Their eyes lit with laughter, their hands extended to one another as though to say, "Welcome."

But there was no one there. No one at all.

A pair of lovers leaned on the railing of the bridge, arms entwined. Rillibee walked through them, his face spattered with their faces, his body with their bodies, and they reassembled behind him, still staring into one another's glowing eyes.

"Ghosts," breathed Tony. "Mother . . ."

"No," she said, tears on her cheeks at the sight of the lovers. "Holos, Tony. They left them here. The projectors must be somewhere in the trees."

"They gave them to one another," Mainoa said. "Toward the end. When there were fewer and fewer of them. To keep the last survivors company."

"How do you know?"

"I was told," he said. "Just now. And it fits in with other things I have learned since we had lunch together that day at Opal Hill."

"The language . . ." Marjorie turned to him, eyes wide.

"The language, yes."

"I was so eager to get away, to find Stella, I never thought to ask—"

"The great machines at Semling have chewed on the problem, chewed and swallowed and spat it out again. The machines can translate the books of the Arbai. Some. Oh, half, let us say. Half they can read. The other half they can guess at. The clue was there in the vines on the doors. Where we had never thought to look."

"And the carved doors themselves?"

"They can read those as well."

"What do they say?"

Brother Mainoa shook his head, trying to laugh, the laugh becoming a cough which bent him double. "They say the Arbai died as they lived, true to their philosophy."

"Here?"

"There on the plain they died quickly. Here in the trees they died slowly. Their philosophy prevented their killing any intelligent thing. In their city on the plain, the Hippae had slaughtered their kinfolk. Those who lived in this summer city among the trees could not go back to live there safely. They did not wish to die. So they lived out one last summer here, and when winter came they slowly died here, knowing that in all the universe they were the last of their people."

"How long ago?"

"Centuries. Grassian centuries."

She looked around her at the woven buildings and shook her head.

"Not possible. These structures would not last. The trees would grow; eventually they would die and fall. These woven roadways would rot away."

"Not if they were renewed, hour by hour, day by day. Not if they were mended."

"By whom?"

"Yes, Marjorie, by whom? We all wonder, don't we. Yes. I think we will meet them very soon."

Rillibee led them along the woven streets. Before them the way widened, expanding into a broad platform with rococo railings and spiraled pillars supporting a wide witch's hat of a roof.

The town square, Marjorie thought. The village green. The meeting hall, open to the air, to the wind and the sound of birds. All around it shadowy figures walked and danced and saluted one another, shadows so thickly cast that for a moment the humans thought the mighty figure padding toward them from across the platform was another shadow. When they saw that it was not, they drew together, Tony reaching for the knife he carried.

"No," said Brother Mainoa, putting his hand on the boy's arm. "No." He walked forward to see what he had so often longed to see with his eyes instead of his mind. "No. He won't hurt us."

They saw an expanse of trembling skin over eyes they could not quite see. Fangs, or something like fangs, in a gleam of blued ivory. Flaring wings of hair, doubly flaring violet auroras, like spurts of cold lightning.

Brother Mainoa murmured, head down, as though he addressed a hierarch, "We are honored."

The being crouched. It gave the impression of nodding. Paws curled—no—hands curled upon the braided walkway. Hands which seemed for an instant to have three fingers and opposed, furry thumbs. Behind maned shoulders lay an armored expanse of mottled hide and callused plates, seen only for an instant, or perhaps not seen at all. It was an impression only, gone too quickly to define. They could not describe it except to say it was not like anything else, not like any earth creature, not like any Grassian creature except itself. The proportions were wrong. The legs were not the usual thing one thought of as legs.

Brother Mainoa confronted this mirage with an expression of awed interest, blinking rapidly, as they all were, trying to clear their vision. "Perceiving you for the first time has made me wonder what evolutionary tangle led to the development of this ferocious aspect," he murmured, eyes down.

Great orbs may have widened. Perhaps a long, curved talon extruded from a half-furred, half-scaled finger and pointed toward Brother Mainoa's throat.

Brother smiled as though at a joke. "I cannot believe you mean that. You don't need any of it against me. You don't need much of it against mankind unless they choose to use heavy weaponry against you, and if they did, all your armor wouldn't help much. Men are expert killers, if nothing else."

Eyes narrowed, possibly, and Brother Mainoa seized his head in both hands. The others fell to their knees, holding their heads, except for Sylvan, who started forward, anger and fear combining to make him reckless.

"Whoa. Whoa." Mainoa drew himself erect, gasping. "I wish they wouldn't do that." Now he knew what evolutionary tangle had led to this armour. There had been an enemy once, a huge, inexorable creature. Brother Mainoa had received an excellent picture of it rampaging about, devouring both Hippae and hounds. His head ached from the assault.

"Extinct?" he asked, receiving a feeling of agreement. "Did you kill them?"

They received an impression of perplexity, then sureness. No. The Arbai had killed them. The armored monsters had not been intelligent things. They had been only walking appetites. The Arbai had done away with them to protect the Hippae. Since that time, there had been many, many Hippae.

Brother Mainoa sat down on the walkway, suddenly lost in weariness. "This being is my friend," he said to the other humans. "He and I have been talking for some time." Now that he had almost seen the creature, he felt weak with anxiety over all the times he had talked with it, unseen. If he had seen, would he have said—? No. If he had seen, he could not have said anything. One could talk to gods and angels only so long as they did not look like gods and angels, he thought. In order to approach them, we must think of them as like ourselves, and one could not think of the foxen as like oneself. . . .

"Foxen," Tony breathed. He was still on his knees with the others.

"Foxen," Mainoa agreed. "He or they managed to keep the Hippae at bay long enough for us to get here. He and a few of his friends wanted us to come here, where they could get a good look at us."

"Does he know where Stella . . ." Marjorie pleaded.

She had the impression of a vast head turned in her direction.

She shuddered as she said, "I see. Of course. Yes."

Sylvan said, "Marjorie?"

"I can hear him," she cried. "Sylvan, I can hear him. Can't you?"

He shook his head, casting a suspicious glance at the place he thought the foxen was. "No. I hear nothing."

"You have been a hunter too long," Mainoa said. "You have been deafened by the Hippae."

"Is he speaking?" asked Sylvan.

Rillibee nodded. "It's somewhat like speech. Pictures. Some words." He rose to his feet, utterly immune to further wonder. The trees were wonder enough for one man. He needed nothing else. He did not want to talk to foxen. He, like Marjorie, wanted to find Stella.

"What does he say about your daughter?" Sylvan asked.

"That others of his kind are looking for her," Marjorie replied. "That they will tell us when they find her."

"There are many things they want to tell us, to ask us," Brother Mainoa said wearily, longing for and yet dreading that converse. "Many things."

"I'll go back down and unsaddle the horses," said Rillibee. If they weren't going to hunt for Stella, then he wanted to be by himself, to cling to the trunk of a huge tree and let the feel and smell of it sink into him. In the darkness, they had looked like the spirits of trees. In the light, they looked like themselves. Joshua would have given his soul for trees like these. On all of Terra there were no trees like these. Trees, all around him, like a blessing. He turned to go back the way they had come.

Sylvan followed him. "I'll help you," he said. "I'm no good here."

Ungraciously, Rillibee nodded. The others did not even see them go.

In his suite high in the bon Damfels estancia, Shevlok bon Damfels reclined on a window seat and sipped at a half-empty glass of wine. Dawn stood at the edge of the world. Through the open window he could see the huddled houses of the village, tied to the sky by the smoke rising from their chimneys. Dead calm. The morning had not yet been broken by sound. Even the peepers were silent at this hour.

A case of bottles stood open beside him, half of them empty. On the tumbled bed the Goosegirl slept. She had not left the bed for days. She had slept sometimes. Sometimes she had lain unmoving beneath him while he stroked her, whispered to her, made love to her. Her body had reacted to his manipulations. Her skin had flushed, her nipples had hardened, her crotch had grown moist and welcoming. Beyond that, she had given no evidence that she felt anything at all. Her eyes had stayed open, fixed somewhere in the middle distance, watching something Shevlok could not see.

Once, only once in the midst of his lovemaking, he thought he had seen a spark in her eye, the tiniest spark, as though some notion had fled across her mind too swiftly to be caught. Now she slept while Shevlok drank. He had been drinking since he had first brought her there.

She was to have been his Obermum. She was to have ruled the family with him, when Stavenger died. She was fitting. More than that, he had loved her passionately. Janetta had been everything he had wanted.

But the thing on the bed was not Janetta, not anymore.

He was trying to decide whether he should keep her or not.

Someone rapped at the door, and then, without waiting for an invitation, came in.

"You did do it!" It was Amethyste, peering across the dim room at the girl sprawled on the bed. "Shevlok, what were you thinking of?"

"Thought she'd know me," Shevlok mumbled, the words sounding sticky and ill-defined coming from lips numbed by the wine. "She didn't. Didn't know me."

"How long has she—"

He shook his head. "Awhile."

"What are you going to do with her?"

"Dunno."

"Everyone says someone took her. From her mother's servant. You did that?"

Shevlok gestured, hand tipping one way then the other, conveying that yes, he had, probably.

"Then you'd better give her back. Take her back to bon Maukerden village. Send word so they'll be looking for her."

"Better dead," Shevlok said with surprising clarity. "She'd be better dead."

"No," Amy cried. "No, Shevlok! Suppose it was Dimity. Pretend it's Dimity."

"Better dead," Shevlok persisted. "If it was Dimity, she'd be better dead."

"How can you say that!"

He rose, took his sister's arm roughly, and dragged her to the bed. "Look at her, Amy! Look at her." He stripped the blanket away to show the girl who lay there naked, face up. With a hard thumb he pulled back the girl's eyelid. "Janetta's eyes were like water over stones. They sparkled with sun. Look at this one! This one's eyes are like the pools that collect in the cellars in spring when the snow melts. No sun in them. Nothing normal swims there. Nothing good lives there."

Amy jerked her arm away. "I don't understand what you're saying."

"When I look in these eyes, all I see is dark going down and down into bottomless muck where there's something squirming that's maimed and horrid. She's been short-circuited. They've done something inside her. She can't feel anything anymore. She doesn't know anyone anymore."

"Give her back, Shevlok. I know there's nothing there anymore—"

"Oh, there's still something there. Something dreadful and perverse. Something they could use. . . ." He gasped with sudden pain. "Damn them."

His sister laughed bitterly, rubbing her bruised arm. "Damn *them*, Shevlok? Damn *them*? You're one of them. You agreed. You all went along. You and Father and Uncle Figor all knew what the Hippae did to girls, but you still made me ride, me and Emmy and Dimity."

He shook his head like a baffled bull. "I didn't know what the Hippae did."

"My God, Shevlok, what did you think happened when girls disappeared? When they vanished? What did you think!"

"I never thought they did that," he insisted. "Never thought they did that."

"You never thought!" she shrieked at him. "Right! You never thought. It wasn't you, so you never thought. Oh, damn you, Shevlok. Don't go blaming the Hippae for getting her like that. You did it. You and Father and Figor and all you damn riders . . ."

"Not . . . not my fault."

"If this hadn't happened, you'd have married Janetta and had children and made them go hunting, too," she accused him. "You'd have seen your daughters vanish and your sons get their arms bitten off, but you wouldn't have stopped!"

"I don't know. I might have. I don't know."

"Are you going to bon Laupmon's to the Hunt today?"

He shrugged. "Probably."

"You see! You know what happens, but you'll still go. And some bon Laupmon girl or some bon Haunser girl will disappear, but that won't matter because you're not in love with them." She wiped her face with her fingers, then pointed to the sleeping girl. "What will happen to her?"

"I've got a woman from the village to come feed her, wash her, play with her, like a kitten."

"If you're going to Hunt, and Father goes . . ."

He shook himself, looking at her for the first time, trying to smile. He was fond of her, and of Emeraude. He kept trying to remember that. He was fond of her and Emeraude and Sylvan, and of his mother. "I heard about Emmy. You want an aircar, don't you. To take Emmy in to Commons. Is she bad?"

"She's as bad as Father could do before we pulled him off her. She won't die, if that's what you mean. Not if I can get her away from here. Her, and me."

"Take her, then."

"Father told the servants not to obey me. He didn't tell them not to obey you."

"I'll tell old Murfon. After Father's gone to bon Laupmon's, Murfon will take you. I'll tell him to pick you up from the village. Don't let anyone see you."

"Shall I take her, too?" Amy gestured toward the sprawled girl on the disordered bed.

Shevlok staggered to his feet and went to look down at the sleeping figure. He sobbed once, a sound that held more anger than grief. "You might as well. If you leave her here, I'll kill her."

14

Rigo asked Sebastian Mechanic to accompany him to the bon Laupmons' place. He asked Persun Pollut and Asmir to come along as well, spending a few futile moments wishing the men were bigger, wishing they had weapons, wishing they were not commoners but bons so they would be taken seriously. Well, what use to wish? They were commoners and there were no weapons on Grass, none he had seen. None except the harpoons of the hunters, and the ungainly length of those instruments made them useless for protection. He felt very much alone and was foolishly ashamed of himself for feeling so.

He dressed with meticulous care, hating the froggy spread of the trousers, the effete look of the long pointed toes on his boots. Finally he took his hat and gloves from his villager-turned-valet and examined himself in the glass. At least from the waist up he looked like a proper gentleman. As though that made any difference. As though anything would make any difference!

He would not apologize for taking Persun and Sebastian and Asmir along. It was certainly not improper to take servants to the Hunt. Others did. When a bon Haunser returned from a bon Damfels Hunt and went into the bon Damfels' guest quarters, it was his own servants who had prepared a room for him, his own servants who had kept the bath hot and laid out fresh clothing. When Rigo had ridden for the first time, he hadn't known. No one had told him. He and Stella had had to return all the way to Opal Hill before they could bathe.

When he had ridden the second time he had brought a man along but there had been no question of bathing. Stella had vanished, and that is all he had been able to think of. Now, for the first time, he wondered what would have happened if Stella hadn't vanished. He, Rigo, had taken a man along. He had forgotten to provide anyone for Stella. It was an uncomfortable thought, and he pushed it aside.

"Rigo?" A soft voice from the door.

He turned his self-hatred on her. "Eugenie! What are you doing here?" Ridiculously, for a moment he had thought it was Marjorie.

"I thought you might need some help. With Marjorie gone—"

"I have a valet, Eugenie." Behind him the man prudently left the room. "Marjorie doesn't dress me."

She fluttered her hands and changed the subject. "Have you had any news about Stella?"

"I haven't heard anything about any of them. And you don't belong here in my bedroom. You know that."

"I know." A tear crept down her cheek. "I don't feel like I belong anyplace."

"Go to Commons," he told her. "Take a room at the Port Hotel. Amuse yourself. For God's sake, Eugenie, I don't have time for you now."

She caught her breath. Her face went white and she turned away. Something in that turn, the curve of the neck. Like Marjorie. Now he had insulted them both! God, what kind of man was he?

Full of angry self-loathing, he went out to the gravel court where the aircar waited, then stood about impatiently while Sebastian arranged for the other car to take Eugenie to Commons if she wanted to go. Women. Damned women. With no other driver available, Asmir would have to stay to take Eugenie into town.

"Grass can be very boring for women," Persun Pollut remarked. "My mother has often mentioned that." Persun stood with his hands linked behind him, his long, lugubrious face turned toward the garden.

"From what you have said, your mother keeps very busy," Rigo commented, his voice still full of edgy hostility.

"Oh, I don't mean life is boring in Commons, Your Excellency. I mean out here. Out here can be death for women. From boredom. From the Hunt. From so many things...."

Rigo did not want to think about women. He did not understand women, obviously. He was no good with women. Marjorie. No good with her. Who would have expected her to take the initiative this way, go running off to involve Green Brothers, dragging Tony and Father Sandoval along. She had never been like that. On Terra she'd contented herself with being mother or horsewoman. There'd been that little charitable thing that took too much of her time, Lady Bountiful carrying cast-off clothing to the illegals. But then, what had she had to do with herself otherwise? She wasn't like Eugenie, to spend half a day at the loveliness shops. Or like Espinoza's wife, that time, getting hauled in by the population police because she'd been mixed up in illicit abortions to save some ignorant little cunts from getting executed. Poor 'Spino hadn't been able to face his friends. No, whatever Marjorie had done on Terra, she'd kept it insignificant, she hadn't encroached on Rigo's responsibilities....

There was some kind of mental trap there. He avoided it by returning to his earlier thoughts about weapons. Why were there no weapons on Grass? Surely the order officers at Commons must have some kind of tanglefoots or freeze batons. Such items were ubiquitous wherever there were ports and taverns and the need to knock down unruly men. Why didn't the people at the estancias have them? Characteristically, preferring actual ignorance to the appearance of it, he did not ask Persun, who could have told him.

He got into the car at Sebastian's summons. They flew in silence. The bon Laupmon estancia was about an hour distant, farther east than the bon Damfels' place. Rigo was considering how he might approach Obermun Lancel bon Laupmon. What he might say to Eric bon Haunser, or Obermun Jerril bon Haunser. Both of them had been helpful and diplomatic when the Yrariers had arrived upon Grass. Still, they were hunters, and hunters did not seem to act logically.

There was no point in talking to Gerold bon Laupmon, Lancel's brother. According to Persun, the man's comprehension was exceedingly limited. Lancel was a widower. There was a son, Taronce, related somehow to the bon Damfels, but Rigo had not met him. Perhaps there had been other children. Perhaps they had vanished, and bon Laupmon had ignored that fact, just as Stavenger had. As he continued to do.

Rigo ground his teeth. There had been a time on Terra when children had been sacrificed. To Moloch. To Poseidon. Even to God. There had been dangerous rites on Terra long ago. Maenads had run wild upon mountaintops, tearing youths apart with their teeth. Secret societies had demanded blood and silence. And yet, he could not recall a time in Terran history that men had lost their children and pretended not to notice. Never. Now, nowhere else. Only here, on Grass.

He shuddered, then drew in a deep breath, confused. Why was he going to this Hunt? Was he really going to ride? Again? Knowing what he knew now?

Why was he going?

To demand help in finding Stella, of course.

From whom? He went over the roll of all the bons he had met, listing them by families, ticking them off, going back to see if he had forgotten any.

"Pollut," he said at last in a shamed voice. "Will any of them help me find my daughter?"

Persun Pollut gave him a long look. Around the eyes His Excellency looked rather like an old bit of carving, badly abused, chipped, and abraded. For a moment Persun considered equivocation, then discarded the idea. He owed it to Lady Westriding to tell the truth.

"No," he said finally. "None of them will."

"Marjorie warned me," Rigo said in a whisper.

Despite the whisper, Persun heard him. "Many of us tried to warn you, sir. Lady Westriding has a clear eye. She was not taken in by these Hippae."

"You believe it's true that they do things to people's minds. . . ."

With some effort Persun kept any taint of sneer from his voice as he asked, "Has the ambassador any other explanation?"

"Landing!" said Sebastian. "There's a considerable crowd on the court, sir. Almost as though they were waiting for us."

Rigo looked down with a sense of forboding. Many pale faces looked up. And there were already Hippae down there! It was indeed as though they had been waiting. He thought of telling Sebastian to go back, return home. But that would seem such arrant cowardice! Death before dishonor, he sneered at himself. Of course.

"Set it down," he said.

When he opened the car door, Obermun Jerril bon Haunser was poised outside, his face empty of any emotion.

"Your Excellency," he said. "I have the honor of conveying to you the challenge of Obermun Stavenger bon Damfels. He wishes me to say that the whore, your wife, has taken away his son, Sylvan. And that you will answer for it or be trampled to death." He gestured backward, toward the wall of the estancia, where a dozen Hippae stood, shifting from foot to foot, clashing the barbs on their necks despite the empty-faced men and women on their backs.

Rigo felt molten iron rise into his face. That Jerril bon Haunser had said no more than he, Rigo, had implied toward Marjorie only redoubled his fury. "How dare you?" he snarled. "How dares any of you?" He raised his voice to a shout. "A mother goes to look for her daughter, and you call her a whore? It is your wives who have made themselves whores. Your wives and your daughters! Who have whored themselves to them!" He thrust a rigid finger at the rank of Hippae along the wall. "Your wives and daughters have spread their legs for lovers who are not even human!"

There was no quiver of movement among the mounted men. Obermun bon Haunser's face did not change. He might as well have been deaf and blind. He seemed not to have heard Rigo's contemptuous insult. He bowed, twisted his lips into a vacant smile, and gestured toward an approaching Hippae. "Your mount," he said.

Rigo felt Persun seize his arm. "Let us leave, Your Excellency. We can!"

Rigo shook off Persun's hand. "I will not run," he snarled through a red curtain of rage. "Not from them, not from any of them."

"Then for God's sake take this," and Persun thrust something into Rigo's jacket pocket from behind. "A laser knife, Your Excellency. One of my carving tools. The Lady Marjorie will not forgive me if I let you die."

Rigo heard him at some level, though his anger would not let him respond. He dropped out of the car and stood waiting for the Hippae. It grinned at him, showing its teeth, eyes gleaming. There was no mistaking the impudence, the malice, the arrogance in those eyes. With a surge of panic Rigo realized that Stavenger bon Damfels had not issued the challenge. The challenge had come from the Hippae! It was they who had arranged and directed this confrontation, they who had choreographed this movement of men and beasts. Jerril bon Haunser did only their will, not his own.

Rigo cast a quick glance upward, toward the estancia. There were people gathered on the terraces, watching, mouths open in astonishment or wonder or fear. So this was not a familiar sight. How had the beasts managed it? How had they winkled their riders out of the estancia? How had they assembled these hunters?

There was no time to consider hows or whys. The Hippae before him thrust out a mottled blue leg, muscled like a monument. Rigo fumbled for his rein ring, found it in his pocket, tossed it clumsily over the bottom barb, and felt it tighten as he leapt upward. His toes found the stirrup holes. He braced himself just in time as the beast reared high. He was staring at the sky, suspended only by the tightened reins and his toes, leg and back muscles locked rigid to hold him in place. The Hippae walked on its hind legs, stalking, laughing an almost human laughter, seeming to move as easily in that position as it did on four legs. After what seemed an eternity, it dropped forward once more.

Another beast loomed beside him, a great green Hippae, lining up beside the blue as for a parade. Stavenger sat upon the green, face forward and empty as a hatched egg, only the shell which had once housed him remaining. The green Hippae clashed its barbs and Stavenger shouted. There were no words, only meaningless rage. His mouth opened. His face reddened. He howled. Then his mouth closed and he sat there once more, unmoved.

The blue beast clashed its barbs and Rigo felt himself shouting. He bit down on the shout, closed it off, swallowed it. Fury rose up in him and forced the Hippae out of his mind. The beasts danced, side by side, like a pair in a quadrille. They galloped, trotted, changed legs, did it once again. The horseman in Rigo grew even more wrathful. They had learned this from Don Quixote and El Dia Octavo. This was mockery. This was humiliation. He twisted his left hand tightly in both reins to free his right hand, then felt in his pocket for the laser knife. A simple, ordinary tool, one that Persun used to carve bits of wood and grass stem, one he had probably used on the panels in Marjorie's study. A simple tool.

And yet . . . it could be a weapon. He stared at the neck barbs clashing before him. They looked like horn. Or like teeth. If they were indeed like teeth or horn, the beast might not feel it if they were cut. The knife had a blade of variable power and length. At higher power the blade could take off these barbs at flesh level. As the Hippae danced, Rigo reached one hand forward, thumbed the knife on, and touched the top of the second barb. The knife cut a notch into it, like a heated blade into wax. The Hippae didn't react. Rigo cast a quick look around. No one had seen him. No one was looking. This prancing dance was not for the benefit of the zombies along the wall, not for Jerril or Eric or even Stavenger. This was for the Hippae themselves. They were the only ones enjoying it, and they were so arrogantly intent upon displaying their power that they had not bothered to keep watch upon the riders. Rigo cut away the sharp edges of the first barb, narrowing it to make a place he could grip, then slipped the knife back into his pocket and waited to see what would happen next.

Next was a challenge. Bellowing at one another. Turning their backs on one another and using both front and rear feet to kick clods at one another. Clods? Something black and powdery that they took some trouble to find. Black dust powdered down upon him. Then the Hippae faced one another again and rose on their back hooves. Clashing barbs, hissing through teeth they separated, dancing backward until a considerable distance had opened between them. A hundred yards. Two hundred. Rigo risked a look at the assembly on the walls, at the mounted men. Nothing. No cries, no excitement. Only this deadly calm. He gritted his teeth and hung on. At last, the green beast lowered his head and charged. Rigo's mount did the same.

The opposing mount was coming up on his right, neck arched down and turned so that the barbs jutted wickedly outward. Rigo's mount had taken the same position. They were like two warhorses, thundering toward one another. Neither of the beasts could see where he was going. Each threatened the other. Stavenger sat like a dummy, unseeing. At the last possible moment, Rigo jerked the toe of his right boot out of the stirrup hole and stood on his left toe, right leg high and bent back, holding himself high by locking his left hand tightly around the blunted barb.

The barbs of Stavenger's beast meshed with those of Rigo's mount, passed through and raked the place where Rigo's booted leg had been, missing the blue Hippae skin by the thickness of a finger. Still holding himself high, Rigo could see Stavenger's right boot in tatters. Blood blew from the man's leg, long ragged lines trailing into the dust. The animals had no intention of hurting one another. The barbs were aimed at their rider's legs.

Rigo settled upon the creature's shoulders, and as they moved apart he took out the knife and cut the four barbs immediately in front of him, striking them to make them fall to one side. Though there were longer barbs on the neck, the amputation made him safe from being skewered, at least. The Hippae had turned and were readying themselves for another charge. They had to aim themselves like missiles; once their heads were down, they could not see where they were going. Some instinct or long practice let them know precisely where their opponent was, however. They passed this time on the left, the barbs meshing like gears, screaming as they plunged past one another, and once again Rigo moved his leg and balanced high on the opposite side of his mount, glued there by equal parts rage and fear.

This time Stavenger's left boot was in tatters, his left leg streaming blood. There was still no expression in his face. The Hippae would keep it up even if Stavenger fell, even if he died. The Hippae would keep it up until Rigo was dead. There was no point in trying to kill Stavenger. It would be like killing a flea on the neck of an attacking dog. No. To stop the battle, the Hippae themselves would have to be stopped.

The next charge was to the right again. Rigo wound the reins around his left arm, grasped the smoothed barb in his left hand, withdrew his right leg, threw himself across his mount as the other went by, and struck at its rear legs with the knife extended to its full length. The blade hummed and sliced, through the flesh as it had through wood.

The green beast screamed, tried to walk on a leg half cut through, and crashed to the ground. Rigo's mount pranced and howled and lashed back at him with barbs that were no longer there. Rigo reached low along one side and cut a back leg from beneath it, rolling away as the beast fell.

Noise. Two beasts screaming. He staggered to his feet, eyes fixed on them. They were trying to crawl toward him, trying to get up on three legs. He turned the knife to its maximum length and moved forward, slashing once, then again, cleaving the two skulls down through those clamping jaws, to leave the truncated, cauterized necks to lash themselves into quiet.

A great noise was coming from somewhere else. He turned just in time to see the Hippae who had been ranked along the wall charging at him, hooves high, jaws extended. There was no way to avoid them. He threw himself behind the bodies of the dying Hippae and cut at the legs and teeth that sought him from above. Blood rained down on him, blinding him.

Something struck him on the head. He slumped, stunned. There was sound, roaring, screaming, voices howling, Hippae shrieking as they backed off. Blackness came up around him, sucking at him.

Persun Pollut's voice said, "Up, up, sir. Get in. Oh, get in, we can't hold them off for long."

Then vibration, the sound dwindling, and at last the blackness took him entirely.

It was Figor bon Damfels who reached Stavenger first, after waiting a considerable time for the Hippae to finish their slaughter and go away. Roderigo Yrarier's servants had driven the Hippae off with the aircar, had leapt out and rescued him. Figor was astonished at this. None of the bon Damfels servants or the bon Laupmon servants had made any move to protect their masters. The twelve riders had borne the full brunt of the Hippae fury. All twelve had died, most of them bon Laupmons, fourteen deaths including Stavenger bon Damfels and Obermun bon Haunser. Stavenger showed no wounds, though he was pale and cold. His boots were in tatters. Figor unbuckled the strap that held the boots high and drew them off. Stavenger's feet came with them. Only a thin strip of leather on the inside had kept the boots together. They had filled with blood and overflowed. Stavenger had bled to death, without moving.

Four Hippae were dead also, the two who had taken part in the joust and two others, their legs lopped off as though by some great cleaver. It was this death of Hippae that the others had sought to avenge.

The death of Hippae, though perhaps Yrarier's escape had infuriated them more. They had danced and howled and leaped, trying to get their teeth into the ascending car. While all of it had been going on, Figor had not had time for much thinking, not time, nor ability. There was nothing in anyone's mind then but red rage and a furious astonishment. After the Hippae had gone away, however, room for some thought had opened up. Thought and reflection on what eyes had seen even while minds had been unable to comprehend.

"Figor," his cousin, Taronce bon Laupmon, said. "I found this where the *fragras* was."

Figor took it. Some kind of tool. It had a thumb switch and he clicked it on. The blade quivered, humming with deadly force, and he clicked it off again. He whispered, shocked, "By our ancestors! Taronce!"

"It must be what he used on the mounts," cousin Taronce whispered, rubbing at his shoulder where his prosthesis joined his body. "Cut their legs out from under them. Chopped their heads in two. The way they chop at us. They way they chopped at me." He looked around, guiltily. "Put it away before someone sees it."

"What does Obermun bon Laupmon say? Lancel?"

"He's dead. Gerold is alive. He wasn't one of the mounted ones."

"How did this all ..." He gestured around him. "When I got here, it was already started."

"The Hippae were waiting this morning, waiting on the gravel court. They took people, that's all. They took Stavenger as soon as he arrived, and bon Haunser, as well."

"No one bothered me."

"No one else was bothered. Just twelve riders, and Stavenger, and Jerril bon Haunser. And now they're all dead."

"Plus four mounts," whispered Figor. "I've got the thing put away. I won't let them know we have it."

"You'd use it, wouldn't you?"

"Would you?"

"I think so. I think I'd use it. It's so neat. So little. You could keep it in your pocket. They wouldn't know you had it. Then, if one of them came at you ..."

"If Yrarier had this thing, they're probably easy to get. In Commons, maybe."

"Why didn't we know? Before?"

"They didn't let us know before. Or maybe we haven't wanted to know, before."

When Persun and Sebastian Mechanic reached Opal Hill they left Rigo in the aircar while they called Persun's father on the tell-me and told him they wanted to evacuate the estancia. Rigo was unconscious. There was nothing they could do for him; he needed to go to the hospital in Commons at once, but there was this other very important consideration.

"Evacuate the village?" Hime Pollut asked. "You're joking, Pers."

"Father, listen. Rigo Yrarier killed at least two Hippae. I don't know how many men died in the ruckus we left behind us, but some must have. I'm remembering the stories of Darenfeld estancia. How it was burned after somebody wounded a Hippae. How all the people in the village died. The people at Opal Hill village, the servants here in the big house, they're our people, Father. Commons people."

"How many at Opal Hill?"

"A hundred and a bit. If you can get Roald Few to send out some trucks . . ."

"Will the people be ready?"

"Sebastian is on his way to the village now. If you can get the trucks we use when we go into winter quarters, they can bring the livestock in. They'll need their animals. . . ."

A long silence. "Can you bring the foreigners from the estancia?"

"His Excellency, yes. His secretary and her sister. The old priest. That's all."

"Where's the wife? The children? The other priest? Yrarier's fancy woman?"

"Asmir Tanlig took Eugenie to Commons this morning. None of the others are here, but I don't have time to explain about them now." He left the tell-me and ran through the dwelling, stopping all the servants he met. They were all from the village. Some he sent to find Father Sandoval and Andrea Chapelside and her sister, telling them he could allow only an hour for packing. Waiting even that long might endanger Rigo's life, but he could not simply gather up the women and fly away, leaving all their belongings behind. They would need things. Women always needed things.

Marjorie. She, too, would need things. He gathered three of the maids together and told them to pack Marjorie's things. "Her clothes," he said. "Her personal things."

And Stella's? Would Stella ever be found? What did Stella value?

"How long, Persun? What shall we pack?"

"Never mind," he said in frustration. "Take a few sensible clothes for Marjorie and Stella, their jewelry and treasures, and leave it at that."

And perhaps it was all mere supposition, mere paranoia. Perhaps the Hippae would do nothing to Opal Hill at all. Perhaps the village would be safe.

And perhaps not. In panic he went back to the tell-me.

"Roald Few has borrowed four cargo trucks from the port," his father said. "They're on their way. He agrees on the importance of saving the livestock."

Well then, it was not merely his own fear. Or, if it was, he had been successful in spreading it about. He scurried through the place to Marjorie's study, intent upon saving anything there that she might

:ver want again. He came face to face with the panels he had carved for her, a lady moving among the trees of a copse, sometimes clearly seen, sometimes hidden, her lovely face always slightly turned away. Like a dream, just out of reach. There were birds in the trees. He reached out to touch one of them, stroke one of them, wondering foolishly if there were time to cut the panels out and save them. He broke away with an exclamation. No time.

When he had gathered together what he could, he picked up Sebastian and those who were ready and drove the aircar directly to the hospital near the Port Hotel. The doctors carried Rigo away; Andrea, her sister, and Father Sandoval went to the port hotel.

Asmir was there. "Where's Eugenie?" Persun asked.

"I don't know. Wasn't she with you?" Asmir asked in return.

"This morning she wanted to come in to Commons."

"She told me she'd changed her mind. I just came to pick up some supplies."

Persun counted his passengers on his fingers and ran to ask them where Eugenie was. No one knew. He flew back to Opal Hill, anxious to use all the daylit hours. In the village the trucks were loading: people, livestock, necessary equipment. Another truck landed as he stood there. Sebastian was driving it.

"I can't find Eugenie," Persun yelled at him.

"His Excellency's woman? Isn't she in Commons? Didn't she go in with Asmir?"

"She didn't, Sebastian. She changed her mind."

"Ask Linea, over there. She took care of Eugenie."

Persun chased the indicated woman and asked. Linea didn't know. She hadn't seen Eugenie since early this morning. She thought Eugenie must be in her own house, or perhaps in the garden.

Persun ran back up the trail to the estancia, to Eugenie's house, cursing under his breath. She wasn't there. Soft pink curtains blew in the spring wind. The house smelled of flowers Persun Pollut had never seen. The woman wasn't there. He went out into the grass garden and searched for her, down this path and that, the mild spring airs moving above him and around him, the perfumes of the fragrant grasses like a drug in his nostrils.

He called, "Eugenie?" It did not seem a dignified thing to do, to walk about the gardens calling her by her first name, but he knew no other name to call her. It was what everyone called her. "Eugenie!"

From the village the trucks rose with a roar of engines. He went there once more, plodding. A few remaining people. A few remaining pigs, chickens, a lonely cow lowing at the sky. The sun, down in the west, burning its hot eye into his own.

"Are they coming back?" he asked. "The trucks?"

"You don't think we planned to stay here with everyone gone, did you?" an old woman snapped at him. "What happened? No one seems to know, except that the Hippae are coming to slaughter us all in our beds."

Persun didn't answer. He was already on his way back to the house to try one last time. He went through the big house, room by room. She wasn't there. To her own house again. She wasn't there.

He did not think to go to the chapel. Why would he? The people of Commons had scant use for chapels. Some of them claimed religions, but they were not of edificial kinds.

He went out to the car, offered the old woman a seat in it, loaded her crate of chickens aboard, and took off once more, flying low as he cross-hatched the grass gardens, looking for Eugenie. Once at commons, he searched for her again, thinking perhaps she had been in one of the trucks.

Darkness came. "I have to go back," he cried to Sebastian, who had just returned from a final trip. "She has to be still out there."

"I'll go with you," the other said. "I've got everyone unloaded. They're all getting settled down in winter quarters."

"Have you heard any news of His Excellency?"

Sebastian shook his head. "No one's had time to ask. How was he hurt?"

"His legs were trampled. And he was struck on the head. He was breathing well, but he didn't move his legs at all. I think he may be paralyzed."

"They can fix that kind of injury."

"Some kinds they can fix." They lofted the car once more and headed it away from Commons toward Opal Hill. They had not gone far before they saw the fire, wings and curtains of fire, sweeping across the grasses and towering above the estancia.

"Ah, well then," murmured Persun. "So I was not a hysteric after all. Father said I might be."

"Are you glad of that?" Sebastian asked curiously, turning the car in a long curve so that he could look down on the blaze. "Or would you rather have been called a hysteric and Opal Hill still be whole? I saw the panels you carved in the lady's study. They were the best things I have seen in a long time. No, the best I have ever seen."

"I still have my hands," Persun said, looking at them, turning them over, thinking what might have happened to them if he hadn't been skittish as any old woman. "I can carve more." If Marjorie was safe, he could carve more. If they were for her.

"I thought the gardens were supposed to stop the fires."

"They do. Unless the fires are set and dragged through the gardens and carried into the buildings. As these were, Sebastian. As these were." He peered down at the ruin, biting back an exclamation. "Look! Sebastian. Look at the trail!"

Away from Opal Hill, toward the swamp forest, straight as an arrow, a trail trampled into the grasses as though ten thousand Hippae had marched there in files. The two looked at one another in horrified surmise.

"Do you suppose she's down there?" Sebastian whispered.

Persun nodded. "Yes. She is. Was. Somewhere."

"Shall we—"

"No. See there, in the flames. Hippae. There must be hundreds of them. Some dancing near the flames. Some going down that great trail. How many of them did it take to make that trail? And hounds, too. Every hound on Grass must be down there, all moving toward Commons. No. No, we can't go down. We'll come back tomorrow. When the fire burns out, we'll look. Maybe she got into the winter quarters. I hope she doesn't burn."

Eugenie didn't burn. The hounds that had swept through the place ahead of the flames had seen to that.

Commons was in a considerable uproar, busy with speculation and rumor. The housing of a hundred or so people was no great thing. The winter quarters were large enough to hold the entire population of Commons plus those of the villages, and only the very young among them found these underground halls and rooms at all new and frightening. The caverns had been here when men first came, but they had been enlarged and fitted out for human occupancy, and everyone over one Grassian year of age knew them well. The evacuated animals went into the winter barns. Though this year's cutting of hay had not begun, there was enough of last year's hay and grain to keep them. Feeding the people was no great thing either. They began using the winter kitchens with the ease of long practice.

Despite this ease, this familiarity, there was disquiet and anxiety both among those who had arrived and those who had welcomed them. The burning of an estancia was not a familiar occurrence. It had happened before, but that had been long ago, in their great-grandparents' time. It was not something easy to comprehend or accept. When Persun Pollut brought news of the great trail toward the swamp-forest, anxiety deepened. Everyone knew the Hippae couldn't get through the forest, and yet . . . and yet, people wondered. They were uneasy, wondering if this event betokened mysterious dangers.

The unease spread even to Portside, where those occupied in serving and housing strangers became jittery. Saint Teresa and Ducky Johns were not immune to the common case of nerves. They met at the end of Pleasure Street and walked along Portside Road, Ducky bobbling and jiggling inside her great golden tent of a dress, Saint Teresa stalking beside her like a heron, long-legged and long-nosed to the point of caricature. He wore his usual garments: purple trousers tight at the knee but baggy elsewhere, and a swallow-tailed coat cut of jermot hide, a scaly leather imported through Semling from some desert planet at the end of nowhere. His bare cranium gleamed like steel in the blue lights of the port, and his great hands gestured as he spoke, never still for an instant.

"So . . . so what does it mean?" he asked. "Burning Opal Hill that way. There was no one there. . . ." His hands circled, illustrating a search from the air, then swooped away, conveying frustration.

"One person," Ducky Johns corrected him. "That fancy woman of the ambassador's is missing."

"One person, then. But the Hippae dragged fire through the gardens and burned it, all of it. It's burning now." His fingers flickered like flames, drawing the scene on the air.

Ducky Johns nodded, the nod setting up wavelike motion which traveled down from her ears through all the waiting flesh below, a tidal jiggle, ending only at her ankles, where her tiny feet served as a check valve. "It's why I wanted to talk with you, Teresa. The things are obviously raging. Furious. Out of all control. You knew the ambassador killed some of them."

"I heard. First time that's ever happened, from what I hear."

"So far as I know, yes. Darenfeld wounded one, years and years ago, before the Darenfeld estancia burned."

"I thought that was a summer fire. Lightning."

"So the bons say, but others say no. The bons pretended it was lightning and began to build grass gardens around themselves, but Roald Few says the Commons *Chronicle* called it what it was. Hippae, going rampageous."

He compressed thin lips into a tight line, more disturbed than he cared to admit. "Well, so! The bons are no concern of ours. If all of them got crisped tomorrow, it wouldn't make a whit of difference to custom, Ducky. They may think they're the pinnacle of creation, but we know different."

"Oh, it's not just them. It's this plague, too. We're hearing more and more of that."

"There's none here."

"So there isn't, which is strange on the face of it. I hear things. Asmir Tanlig has been around, asking this, asking that. Sebastian Mechanic has been around, digging here, digging there. Questions. Who's been sick. Who's died. Both of them work for the ambassador. So he's trying to find out something. I talked to Roald about it. He talked to some others, including some of us here in Portside who've heard what foreigners have to say. Seems there's plague everywhere but here. Hidden, though. Sanctity trying to keep the lid on it, but the word getting out, getting around."

"So? What are you saying, Ducky?"

"I'm saying if everybody dies out there, there'll be no custom here, old crane, old stork. That's what I'm saying. Then how will we live, you and me? To say nothing of it being damned lonely, us here with all the rest of the human population gone and those Hippae out there, being rampageous."

"They can't get in through the forest."

"So we're told. So we're told. And even if that's true, think of all humanity closed in in a space no bigger than Commons. It makes me claustrophobic, Teresa, indeed it does."

They had reached the end of Portside Road, where it ran off into ruts southward across the grazing land, and they turned as if by mutual consent to retrace their steps—more slowly on the return, for Ducky seldom walked such a distance.

Blue lamps cast runnels of luminescence on the ash-glass surface of the port. There were only two ships in, a sleek yacht in the dark shadow of a bulky warehouse and the *Star-Lily*, a fat Semling freighter squatting in a puddle of sapphire lume, its cargo bay gaping like a snoring mouth. In the puddle of light something moved, and Ducky put her hand on her companion's arm. "There," she said. "Teresa, did you see that?"

He had seen that. "No one working there this time of night."

"See to it, Teresa. Do. I can't move fast enough."

She spoke unnecessarily, for the heronlike legs of Saint Teresa had already taken him off in long, ground-eating strides across the cinereous surface of the port, moving like some tall hunting bird toward that flicker of movement. Ducky struggled after him, panting, her flesh bobbling and jiggling as though a thousand small springs inside were heterodyning against one another. Her companion had moved into shadow. She didn't see him, and then she did, one hand striking, head moving like a spearlike beak, the hand coming back with something pale and fishy wriggling in it. He turned and carried the thing toward her.

When he came close enough for her to see, she cried out in surprise. There it was, just like the last one. Another naked girl with no expression in her face, wriggling like a fish on a spear, not saying anything at all.

"Well," he said. "What do you think of that?"

"What's that in her hand?" Ducky asked. "What's she carrying, and what was she doing there?"

"Trying to get aboard," Saint Teresa said, holding the girl tight under one arm as he pried the thing from her tight fingers. He held it out, and Ducky leaned forward to look at it.

"It's a dead bat," she said. "All dried up. What was she carrying that for?"

They looked at the girl, at one another, full of questions and surmise. "You know who it is," Ducky said. "It's Diamante bon Damfels is who it is. The one they called Dimity. The one that vanished first thing this spring. It has to be."

He didn't contradict her. "Now what?" he asked at last.

"Now we'll take her to Roald Few," Ducky said. "As I should have taken the last one. Take her, and it, and ask Jelly to come along, and Jandra, and anybody else with any sense in their heads. I don't know what's happening here, old crane, but I don't like it, whatever it is."

In the Tree City of the Arbai night had come like a polite visitor, announcing itself with diffidence, moving slowly among the bridges and trellises, softly among the wraithlike inhabitants, quietly into each room to carpet every floor with shadow. Night had come gently; darkness had not come at all. Effulgent spheres lined each walkway and hung from each ceiling. They cast an opalescent glow, not enough light to work by and yet enough to see walls and floors and ramps, to know where one went, to see the faces of one's friends, to see the ghosts as they walked in and out.

Among the houses fronting upon the high platform, several were less frequented by phantoms. In one of these Tony and Marjorie had spread their beds and arranged their belongings. The two Brothers, the priest, and Sylvan had selected another. Once that was done, they had assembled on the open platform to eat together, sharing their own rations and the strange fruits Rillibee had garnered from the nearby trees. Several of the foxen had been close by for a brief time. The humans had seen shadows, heard voices reminiscent of the great cry, felt questions in their most intimate minds, tried to answer. Eventually the presences had gone. Now the humans knew they were alone.

"There is a lot I don't understand," Tony said, conveying what they all felt. There had been an interchange, but most of it had been more enigmatic and tantalizing than informative.

"There is much I have never understood," Brother Mainoa said. He looked very weary tonight, very old.

"These foxen are the children of the Hippae?" Father James asked. "They talked much of that."

"Not children," Brother Mainoa said. "No. No more than the butterfly is the child of the caterpillar."

"Another metamorphosis," Marjorie told them. "Hippae metamorphose into foxen."

"Some do," he assented. "Not all do."

"All once did," she insisted, sure of it. It was clear to her, though the means by which the knowledge had come was hard to define. She simply knew. "All the Hippae used to become foxen, long ago."

"All once did," he agreed. "And at that time, it was the foxen who laid the eggs."

Marjorie rubbed her head, trying to remember things she had learned long ago in school. "It must have been a mutation," she said. "Some of the Hippae must have mutated and began to reproduce precociously, while they were still in the Hippae stage. There are animals that do that even on Terra. Reproduce in their larval stage, I mean. But in order for that mutation to have survived, there must have been some reproductive advantage. . . ."

"It is in the Hippae stage that they use caverns. Perhaps the Hippae guarded their own eggs more assiduously," Father James offered. "Perhaps more of the Hippae eggs survived than did those of the foxen."

"And in time, Hippae did most of the reproduction. And not all of them metamorphosed into these creatures, these foxen, anymore. How many foxen are there?"

"Planet-wide?" Brother Mainoa shook his head. "Who knows? Every time the great cry is heard, these elder foxen know that a new one has been changed. They go out, tens and dozens of them, and try to find the new one—find it, welcome it, bring it into the forest where it will be safe. But if the Hippae find it first, they kill it while it is still weak and uncertain, or if it takes refuge in a copse, they get men on their backs and hunt it down."

"Don't the Hippae know that they themselves ..." Father James shook his head.

Brother Mainoa laughed bitterly. "They don't believe it. They don't believe that they change into foxen. They refuse to believe it. They think they remain always as they are until they die. Many of them do die. Don't you remember when you were a boy, Father? Did you ever think, then, that you would grow older?"

Sylvan moved restlessly along the braided railing, looking out into the night of the forest. "They must hate us," he said. "All the time they were talking to you, I kept thinking how they must hate us bons."

"Because you hunt them?" Tony asked.

"Yes. Because we bons hunt them. Because we help the Hippae hunt them."

"I don't think they blame you," Brother Mainoa said. "They blame themselves." He thought about this for a moment, then amended it. "At least, that's how the one I've been talking to feels. The others may feel differently."

"What do you call him?" Marjorie asked. "I can't come up with a label for him. Them."

"*First*," Brother Mainoa replied. "I call him *First*. Or *Him*, capitalized, as though He were God." He laughed weakly.

"It was they you were talking about when we had lunch together at Opal Hill," Father James said. "The foxen! It is they who were concerned with original sin."

Brother Mainoa sighed. "Yes. Though the reason I gave for their concern was not the real one. They have no pangs of conscience over eating the peepers. They have always done so. There are far more peepers than the world could hold if they all matured, and the foxen know that. They eat them as big fish eat little fish, with no concern for the relationship. No, what weighed upon them was the genocide of the Arbai. Some of them have acquired ideas of sin and guilt from our minds, and they do not know what to do with these concepts. It distresses them. Those that think about it. Not all of them do. Like us, they are variable. Like us, they argue, sometimes bitterly."

Father James turned toward him, curious. "They feel guilty because of the slaughter in the Arbai city?"

"No. Not merely *that* slaughter. I mean the genocide of the Arbai," Mainoa repeated. "All the Arbai. Everywhere. I don't know how it was done, but the Hippae killed them all."

"Everywhere?" Marjorie was incredulous. "On other worlds? Everywhere?"

"As the plague is killing us everywhere now," said Father James in sudden comprehension. "I think that's why Brother Mainoa brought us here."

"That's why," Brother Mainoa sighed again. "Because the foxen, at least some of the foxen, did not want it to happen again. They thought they had prevented its happening again. Don't ask me how, I don't know. Somehow, they were not careful enough, not attentive enough, and though there are things they have not or will not tell me, they have said it may already be too late."

"No," Marjorie said. "No. It cannot be too late. I will not accept that."

Brother Mainoa shrugged, his tired face crumpling. Father James reached out a hand.

"No," she said again with absolute certainty, thinking of Stella, out there somewhere, of Tony, of all those she had known and cared about all her life. Very small being or not, nameless or not, she would not tolerate this. "Whatever else we may believe, we may not believe it is too late."

15

At the Friary, while an aircar was readied and certain accoutrements were assembled (assassins, for the use of, Elder Brother Fuasoi thought to himself, grimacing at his own private joke) Fuasoi stewed and steamed in his lonely office, thinking of a thousand ways the plans of the Moldies might already have been forestalled. Or, if not already, then imminently. Perhaps Sanctity had found out about him and had sent people. Perhaps the Health Authority on Semling had become aware of Moldy plots. Perhaps Mainoa had talked to others; perhaps the ambassador knew.

He opened his desk drawer for the tenth time, searching for the book that wasn't there, Mainoa's book. Who had taken it? Had Jhamlees taken it? That totally Sanctified idiot? Had he? If he had, Jhamless would be messaging Sanctity about it. Messaging, getting messages back. Like a message from the Hierarch saying, open the secret armory and take the planet for Sanctity. A message like that.

Not that he knew there was a secret armory here in the Friary. Everyone said so; but then, everyone could be wrong. Suppose the Green Brothers did take the planet, wipe out the bons and the mounts and the hounds; so then what would they do with it?

They'd find a cure, that's what they'd do with it. Mainoa had seemed to think there was a cure here. They'd find it. Give them a little time. . . .

Fuasoi had assumed there was plenty of time to spread the virus. He had not hurried. Now Jhamlees might be onto him, and urgency overwhelmed him. Yes, Brothers Flumzee and Niayop and Sushlee and Thissayim and Lillamool should find that damned Mainoa and kill him—kill Mainoa and Lourai and anyone else who was with them. Yes, that should be done. At once. But there was one other thing that needed to happen at once: the distribution of the virus. In Commons. That's where it would do the most good. That's where people were packed most closely together. He had delayed unconscionably. He had diddled. Uncle Shales would not have been proud of him.

He took a small carrying bag from his cupboard, placed the packet of virus inside on top of a change of clothing, covered it with an additional robe which was all Shoethai would need, left his office, and went down hay-smelling corridors to the gravel court where he found Shoethai himself, just closing an engine housing.

"Is it ready?" the Elder Brother asked. He stood back and regarded the aircar with disfavor. It was one of the bigger ones, with two cabins, a large one up front and a private one behind, each opening to the outside. One of the smaller cars would have done as well and would have moved faster. Still, if it had been serviced. "Is it?" he repeated.

Shoethai grimaced, giggled, said it was. There was something almost gleeful in his manner, and the Elder Brother assumed that the thought of Mainoa's destruction pleased Shoethai. Well, and it should. The thought of anyone's destruction pleased Moldies. The more gone, the fewer left to go, so Moldies said.

"Where's Flumzee?"

Shoethai gestured to an alleyway from which Highbones was at that moment emerging, closely followed by four of his henchmen. When they saw the Elder Brother they stopped in confusion, tardily remembering to bow.

"I'm going with you," the Elder Brother announced.

Shoethai howled—only briefly, only a moment's howl, but enough to bring six pairs of eyes toward him. He groveled, curling his misshapen shoulders, so that his voice came from between his knees like bubbles rising in hot mud. "Elder Brother, you should not risk yourself. You have important work—"

"Which I'm about to do," Fuasoi said firmly. "After Flumzee and the others have found their quarry, you and I will take care of other urgent business."

"Me!" Shoethai squeaked. "Me!"

"You. You won't need anything. I've brought you an extra robe. Get in." He turned to Brother Flumzee. "You can drive this thing, I hope."

Highbones managed to bite down his glee and keep a serious expression on his face. "Certainly, Elder Brother. I am an excellent driver."

"You know where to go?"

"Shoethai said a place called Darenfeld's Coppice, northeast of Klive. I have a map. We're to look for a side trail there."

Fuasoi grunted assent. "Shoethai and I will take the back cabin." Shoethai seemed to be having one of his spasms, so Fuasoi took hold of him and thrust him up into the car, following him in and slamming the compartment door behind him.

The others cast quick, eager looks at one another as they assembled themselves in the front cabin, where Highbones sat at the controls with the ease of long imagination, if not actual practice. He had driven aircars now and then since coming to Grass. He had driven them often in his youth. Within moments they had risen high above the towers of the Friary and were on their way south.

"Can they hear us from back there?" Brother Niayop, Steeplehands, asked quietly.

Highbones laughed. "Not over the sound of the engines, Brother.

"Isn't there a speaker?"

Highbones pointed wordlessly. The dial on the console before him was in the OFF position. Highbones was trying to keep from showing excitement. His cohorts were starting to make enthusiastic noises, but he felt it behooved a leader to behave in a more dignified fashion, at least until it got time for the killing. Then there could be whooping and yelling and incitements of various kinds that they were used to. They'd never killed anybody old before. They'd never killed anybody directly before, not with their hands. Knocking someone off a tower or kicking them off—that didn't seem like murder. It seemed more like a game. He wasn't quite sure how they would manage killing women, though he knew he couldn't get the others—or himself—to do it right away. Elder Brother Fuasoi had told Shoethai there might be women. Shoethai had told Highbones, and Highbones and his friends had talked about that most of the night.

Highbones sat very still as he thought of women, not to disturb the hot throbbing that filled all the space in his groin and spilled over into his legs and up across the skin of his belly. He had had a woman before he had been sent to Sanctity. When he was fifteen, before they sent him. None since, but he remembered.

Her name had been Lisian. Lisian Fentrees. Her body had been white. Her hair had curled around her face, like clustered golden leaves. Her breasts had been soft and crowned with pink, with little slits at the tip that turned into nipples if he sucked on them.

They had spent all the time together that they could, all the time away from school or parents or religion.

She had said she loved him. He couldn't remember what he had said, but sometimes he thought he must have told her he loved her, too. Why would she have said it or gone on saying it, otherwise?

One morning he had wakened to a hand on his shoulder, had looked through half-opened eyes at a sun-blurred someone and had thought for a moment it was Lisian. It had the same whiteness, goldness, the same curve of face. The smell was wrong. It wasn't Lisian, it was his mother. "Get up, boy," she'd said. "You're going on a trip today." Nothing in her voice at all, no tears. As though it didn't matter.

They said ten years. The next ten years of his life pledged to Sanctity and no one had ever told him a word about it. Not until that day. *Didn't want us worryin' about it. Didn't want us thinkin' about it. Didn't want Dad upset.*

And not even a chance to say goodbye to Lisian. Lisian of the soft, warm, ahhhh . . .

Memory was as strong in him as reality. The throbbing spilled over into a spasm he couldn't control, and the car dipped and shimmied while the others howled and yelled at him. "Whooee, Highbones must be dankin' himself, look at that. Dank, dank, Highbones. Do it again, we wanta watch."

He snarled at them, striking out with one arm to knock Little Bridge off his seat, struggling against tears. "Shut up. I wasn't dankin'. I was . . . I was thinking what old Fuasoi said, about women."

Silence. Highbones had said he had a girl once, even though he wouldn't talk about her. Steeplehands had had women, so he said. None of the others had. Both the Bridges had been too young when they came to Sanctity, ten or eleven. And Ropeknots liked boys. Well, hell, they all liked boys. When that's what you had, that's what you did.

"Tell us about women," Long Bridge said. "Come on, Bones. Tell us about your girlfriend."

"Let Steep tell you," he snarled again, surreptitiously wiping at his face. "I'm busy." Darenfeld's Coppice was below them and he had found the side trail. The trail wasn't easy to follow, though. Long shadows crossed it and hid it from sight, even from above. When he could see it, it wound among grass hillocks and through copses, leading generally westward. Far ahead, a dark line on the horizon, the swamp-forest stretched away to the north and south. The trail led toward it.

Behind him, Steeplehands was describing women in urgent, prurient detail, dwelling upon orifices and the feel and lubrication thereof. Highbones tried not to listen. That wasn't it. What Steep was saying wasn't it. It was something else about women. Something he'd lost but wanted to remember.

The swamp forest was not far ahead of them now. Highbones scarcely saw it in his effort to recall what it was he'd lost, among old images, half-forgotten names. Something. He could almost put his mind on it!

The drive sputtered. Highbones frowned, came to himself with a start of panic, eyes darting across the dials in front of him. The car had been serviced just before they left. That monster Shoethai had seen to it. Fuasoi had seen to it.

It sputtered again, then whined. "Grab something," Highbones shouted. "We've got a problem."

He headed downward, faster than he knew to be safe, but if the thing zizzed out he wanted to be on the ground, near the trail. It sputtered, hissed, whined, then sputtered again. They dropped a hundred feet and Long howled in pain. "I bit my tongue—"

"You'll bite more than that if you don't hold on."

They slipped sideways, then recovered just long enough for Bones to set it down in a long, sliding skid through lashing grasses which ended with all of them thrown against the door, which broke open and spilled them out onto the bruised stems.

"Oh, God," whined Steep. "Oh, God."

"Shut up," commanded Highbones. "If the Hippae don't know we're here, don't go telling them we are." He stood up, feeling himself to make sure he was all there, not broken anywhere, not bleeding. Aside from a graze along his jaw, he was whole. "Rope, you all right? Long? Little?"

"All right, I guess."

"Fucking thing hit me right across my nose. . . ."

"Think I broke something."

Highbones slapped and snarled. "You didn't break anything. Lie down and your nose'll stop bleeding." When he was sure they were all accounted for, he turned back to the car and tried the door to the rear compartment. It was jammed, or locked from inside. He hammered on it, trying to make enough noise to rouse those inside yet not enough to rouse something else out in the grass. "Elder Brother!"

Nothing. No response.

He turned to the forward cabin and dug out the packs they had brought with them.

"Listen," said Little Bridge with a frightened look at the sun, low in the western sky. "If we're going to be here after dark, we oughta stay in the car. If some Hippae find us, there'd be some protection being in there."

"Swamp forest just ahead," said Highbones. "We're going there."

"Swamp forest! Are you crazy?"

"I said, we're going there. Anybody wants to stay here can stay. Anybody feels like trying to fix the car, that's up to you. I'm going to the forest. Hippae don't go in the forest."

"Neither do people," muttered Steeplehands. "Or they come out dead." He was careful not to say it loudly.

Highbones didn't answer. He was already halfway back to the trail they had been following when the car zizzed out. When he reached it, he turned to his right and started down it. Those who has passed this way had broken enough of the tall and tough grasses that it wasn't difficult to walk in the stubble. Though he didn't look back, within moments he heard the others blundering along behind him. He hoped they'd picked up their own packs; he didn't intend going back for them.

Inside the rear cabin, Shoethai came to himself slowly. Both he and the Elder Brother had been thrown against the door, or rather, thrown against the latch bar which held it closed. He looked upward through the viewport. Sky. Darkening sky.

"Elder Brother!"

Fuasoi put his hands under himself and pushed himself into an upright position. "What happened?"

"We . . . it . . . it came down."

"You serviced it!"

"We . . . I . . . I didn't know we'd be on it!"

"You did this?"

Shoethai was silent, crouched in a faceless huddle. The irony of it didn't escape Fuasoi. He laughed, one short bark of laughter. "Hated them, did you?" he asked, not expecting a response. "Thought you'd kill two birds with one stone—or more than that?" He received only a snivel in reply. "Let's get out of here. You know you may have just lost your chance in the next world, Shoethai. I'm not sure the Creator is going to look kindly on you."

Shoethai screamed in rage and threw himself at Fuasoi. The latch on the door jarred loose and spilled them out, Shoethai still screaming.

Fuasoi knocked his assailant aside and got to his feet. Shoethai cowered among the grasses, alternately sobbing and yelling. The carrying bag had fallen out with them. Fuasoi unfastened it and took out the package it contained. The virus. Well. He had intended to spread it about in Commons, but perhaps it would have to be trusted to the winds. He reached for his knife and slit the package.

And stopped. Coming through the grasses was a hound. A huge hound. Grinning at him.

Reflex action took over. He threw the package with all his strength and then tried to scramble back into the car. The package burst, spreading its dark, powdery contents over the approaching beast. Shoethai had time for one more howl.

From the crest of a long ridge, Highbones and the others heard howling behind them at the same moment they could look down on the stretching barricade of trees. The sound behind them was almost gleeful. For a time it stayed where it was, yammering. Highbones and the others did not remain where they were. As they ran, however, the sound grew nearer, coming on their trail. Highbones ran faster than he had known he could, hearing the thump and pant of Steeplehands and Long Bridge close behind him. The other two had fallen back. They had shorter legs. Little Bridge was still a kid.

"Wait," yelled Ropeknots. "Wait for us."

"Wait, hell," breathed Steeplehands, drawing slightly ahead.

Their feet hammered on the ground as the howling neared. Behind the leaders came one scream, then another. Whatever was chasing them stopped for a moment. Highbones and the two close behind him did not stop to see what it was.

In a moment the howling started again. Though it came very swiftly, it had not caught them by the time they splashed through the shallow mire at the edges of the forest. They stopped only when they came to the first deep pools gleaming with oily reflections in the dwine of the daylight.

"Now what?" Long Bridge demanded. "You want to go wading in there?"

"Not likely," said Highbones. His eyes were fixed on vine-draped trees towering from liquid depths. "Not likely." He laid a hand on the nearest vine and asked, "Will he climb?" as he swung himself up, feet pushing him along a spiraled vine-trunk and onto the first branch above their heads. "Will he?"

They stopped halfway up to look back the way they had come. The grass moved ominously, but there was nothing there to see. Of Little Bridge and Ropeknots, no sign. They waited, then Steeplehands said, "They're deaders, Bones. Just like on the towers. No different than that."

The three exchanged glances, then lofted themselves with the ease of long practice, moving effortlessly into the heights.

In his private quarters at the Friary, Administrator Jhamlees Zoe sought among a miscellany of papers for the packet which had come from Sanctity, from his old friend Cory Strange. He had sealed it up and hidden it to keep it safe from prying eyes. Now that he had seen Mainoa's book, he needed to read the letter again.

The packet had a security wrap on it, and Jhamlees had to stop several times to remember the proper sequences to prevent the thing from going off in his hands and taking his face with it. All this nonsense. Well, what was the office of Security and Acceptable Doctrine to do with itself, back there on Terra, if it did not engage in these senseless exercises. Coded cover letters. Explosive wraps.

Once he had burrowed his way into the packet, Jhamlees skimmed the pages, reminding himself that he was expected to inform his old friend if anything at all were discovered on Grass. Jhamlees referred to the enclosed itinerary with a pout of frustration. Much though he would have liked to seal his former friendship with the Hierarch, there was no point in attempting to send word about this Mainoa matter. The Hierarch was already on the last leg of his journey to Grass.

Jhamlees folded the letter and thrust it into his pocket. No more need to keep it. He'd dispose of it later. The rest of the packet—twelve pages of sanctimonious hash and the publicly announced itinerary of the Hierarch—could be left out where anyone could see it.

Advance word or no advance word, when the Hierarch arrived he would expect his friend Nods to know anything there was to be known. Mainoa had written as though those at Opal Hill knew something, or as though he, Mainoa, knew something. Question: Was there a cure? That's what the Hierarch would want to know! Brother Mainoa had gone off somewhere, so he couldn't be asked until and unless he was found. That left the only other one who might know. Roderigo Yrarier. Not even one of the Sanctified! A heretical Old Catholic, no better than a pagan!

Elder Brother Jhamlees summoned Yavi Foosh. "Find out where Ambassador Roderigo Yrarier is now. Arrange for me to visit him."

Yavi shuffled his feet, staring at the floor.

"Well?"

"Well, Elder Brother, I think he could be dead."

"Dead!"

"There was a great set-to at the bon Laupmons' place. Hippae and riders and all. Lots of them got killed. Hippae, too. This ambassador was in the middle of it. Way I hear it, his servants took him away to the hospital at the port, but he may be dead."

"Dead." Elder Brother Jhamlees sat down and frowned at the desktop with a sick, panicky feeling. Cory would not like that. "Well, if he isn't dead, I need to see him. Find out."

Yavi scuttled off to find out while Jhamlees thought bleakly how the new Hierarch would react to a message saying, "Dear Brother in Sanctity. The only two people who might know anything at all about this are probably dead." In his anything but amused contemplation of this possibility, Jhamlees forgot his intention to burn the Hierarch's letter.

Rigo came to himself among a whisper of machines. He tried to move and found he could not. His arms had been thrust inside two bulky mechanisms, one at either side of the narrow, barely padded bed he lay upon. Heal-alls, he told himself as he fought down panic. Another Heal-all had swallowed his legs. He tried to speak and could not. A mask was fastened over his nose and mouth.

Someone came, however, and peered at his eyes with an expression of gratification. After a moment the same someone took the mask away and demanded, "Do you know where you are?"

"Not sure," Rigo said in a slushy, bubbling voice. "Hospital, I suppose. At the port. I think I got trampled."

"Good, good." The figure turned away and gloated over the dials and flashing lights on the machines. A woman. Not much to look at, but definitely a woman. "Good," the woman said.

"Who?" Rigo asked. "Who brought me here?"

"Your man," the woman answered. "Or men. One or several."

"Is he here?"

"No. Good heavens, no. Had to go back and evacuate your house. Get the people out. He said something about the Hippae retaliating."

"Marjorie!" Rigo tried to sit upright.

"Now, now." Rigo was pushed into a recumbent position once more. "You aren't to worry. They'll get everyone out."

They couldn't get Marjorie out. She hadn't been there. Not Marjorie, nor Tony, nor Father Sandoval. Nor the two Brothers from the Arbai city, according to Tony's note; they hadn't been there either. All of them had gone away together. With Sylvan. At least according to the challenge delivered by bon Haunser for the Hippae, they had gone away with Sylvan.

Rigo groaned, trying to recall what had happened. The last clear memory was of that damned bon Haunser saying something about Marjorie and Sylvan. Sylvan who had gone away with her.

And with Tony, he reminded himself, and with a priest and two Brothers. Hardly a tête-à-tête. No, Marjorie had never had tête-à-têtes. Marjorie had never been unfaithful. Marjorie had never been guilty of any of the things he had accused her of. She had never refused him. Always let him come into her room, into her bed, whenever he'd wanted to. And now Marjorie was— Well, where was she?

"Is there any news of my wife?" he asked as the moment of clarity passed into a morass of threatened pain, great pain somewhere, being held back by a slender dike, a thin wall, a tissue which was fragile and beginning to leak.

"Hush," said the woman. "You can talk later." She fiddled with a dial, looking narrowly at Rigo's face as Rigo felt himself being irresistibly sent into sleep once more, to dream of Marjorie alone with Sylvan.

Marjorie was alone with Sylvan.

Brother Mainoa and Rillibee Chime were asleep. Rillibee had climbed to the top of a tall tree and had then come down again to tell them there was no way through the swamp forest to Commons. Not on the ground. Through the trees the way would be a little slow, but he could get there, he said, if there was any reason to go. Then he had lain down beside Brother Mainoa and fallen into recurrent dreams. From time to time Marjorie could hear his voice, raised in wordless ejaculations, wonder or complaint, perhaps both.

There were no foxen nearby. For a time, earlier, all of the humans had crouched in a house, arms folded protectively around their heads while the foxen disputed something among themselves. The dispute washed over them like waves of fire. After a time, they felt noticed by the foxen, and then there was a sense of departure. Almost as though one of them had said to another, "Oh, we're killing the little human creatures. We'd better go farther away." Brother Mainoa had seemed wearier than ever after they left, weighed down by some great burden of care.

"They won't tell me," he cried. "They know, but they won't tell me."

Marjorie could guess what it was they wouldn't tell. The foxen knew all about the plague, she was sure of it. They knew, but they wouldn't tell. And poor old Mainoa was so tired and distraught, she could not suggest that he try to talk to them more.

Tony and Father James had gone to explore the Tree City. Marjorie had thought Sylvan was going with them. She found he hadn't only when the others were well gone, too long gone for her to join them.

Sylvan had planned to remain behind. Now that Marjorie was away from her family, away from this husband she spoke of as though he were a barrier—now that she was away from that, he wanted to talk of love again. She would probably tell him to go away. He would tell her he had nowhere to go, and he would be charming. So he told himself. So he had been telling himself for some time.

Surprisingly, she didn't tell him to go away. Instead, she looked at him with a detachment he found almost chilling. "I find you very attractive, Sylvan. I found Rigo attractive, too, before we were married. It was only afterward that I found out we didn't fit together at all. I wonder if it would be like that with you."

What was there to say to that? "I don't know," he said haltingly. "I really don't know."

"He has never once allowed me inside his masculine skin," she said with a rueful smile. "He doesn't notice what I am, but only what I am not, which is whatever he may be wanting at any particular time. Eugenie does far better than I. He expects very little from her, and that helps. Then too, she is soft for him, like clay. She takes his impress and accepts it, like a reverse image, suiting herself to him." She frowned, thinking. "I tried that, at first. It didn't work at all. I cannot be that to him. I could have been something else, a friend perhaps, but that didn't fit his notion of what a wife should be, so we are not very good friends, Rigo and I." She turned to Sylvan, fixing him with a resolute glare. "I will never love anyone who is not first my friend, Sylvan. I wonder if you could be my friend."

"I would!"

"Well then, let us set about it!" She smiled at him, a humorless bowing of the lips. "First I must find my child. I have no choice but to do that, or kill myself trying. You can help me. If we accomplish that, then there is another task awaiting us. People are dying everywhere. We must try to find a solution. So, if you love me, let us talk with one another of what we have to do, but not of ourselves. We will be careful not to touch one another. Gradually, if we are successful and do not die, our natures will emerge and we may understand one another. Perhaps we could become friends."

"But ... but—"

She shook her head at him warningly. "If you're unwilling to do that, then you could show the love you claim to have by leaving me alone. I apologize for dragging you along with us, but I needed you to guide us. The apology is all I can offer. Until we find Stella, I can't spare the time for anything more, not even for argument."

She leaned on the railing, her hair falling forward around her face, a golden veil, masking her from him. Sometimes for a few moments she forgot Stella, only to remember her again with a spasm of intimate agony. Like backward childbirth. As though she were trying to take the child back, encompass it once again. Keep it safe. Suck it up into her womb once more. As obscene as it was impossible, despite the pain she felt. Still, it would do no more good to scream or cry or thrash about now than it would have done when she bore the child. It would do no good to grieve. It would do no good to try to distract herself with Sylvan either, though the thought had crossed her mind. She had wondered whether it would be the same with him as with Rigo. Whether it would be the same with all men as with Rigo. Awful, to live out one's life and never know! But no. As she had begun, so let her go on. At least she would not have to reproach herself later for that! "Stella," she said aloud, reminding herself.

Sylvan was abruptly angry at himself. If Stella had died, he wouldn't have expected Marjorie to be interested in lovemaking. Why had he thought she could be interested with Stella gone?

Lost in their separate worlds, neither was given the opportunity to reconcile them. Tony's voice called from among the glowing alleys. When he came closer they sensed that he and Father James were accompanied by First, by Him. In Marjorie's mind, the name announced itself. For Sylvan's benefit she said, "It's Brother Mainoa's friend.

"I see," he said, annoyed. He could barely detect the creatures. He could not hear them. He could not have an hour alone with Marjorie. He could not, seemingly, accomplish anything he desired.

"I think he's trying to tell me he's found Stella," Tony cried. "I can't be sure. Where's Brother Mainoa?"

"Here." The old man leaned from the door of a neighboring house. "Here, Tony. Ah . . ." He fell silent, one hand stretched toward the foxen like an antenna, feeling for meaning. "Yes," he said. "Your daughter. They've found her."

"Oh, God," she cried. It was a prayer. "Is she—?"

"Alive," he confirmed. "Alive but either asleep or unconscious. They haven't disturbed her."

"Shall we get the horses?"

"They suggest, if you have no objection, that they will take you."

Even in this extremity she remained concerned about the horses. "Will we be coming back here?"

Quiet, then Brother Mainoa gesturing. "Yes." He clutched at some passing pain in his side, shaking his head. "In fact, I think I'll stay here now, if you don't mind. You don't need me for this."

Father James, with a troubled look at Mainoa, chose to stay with him. The others crept apprehensively upon foxen backs and were carried away through the trees, along walkways and branches, moving away from the tree city into darkness, over moving water, under stars, coming at last to the edge of the forest. Foxen backs were wider than horse's backs—wider, muscled differently. There seemed to be no limit, no edges to those backs. It was not so much a matter of riding as of being carried, like children sitting upon a slowly rocking table. The message was clear. "We won't let you fall." After a time, they relaxed and let themselves be transported.

They sensed other foxen meeting them at the edge of the trees and escorting them along the swamp, not far but slow going as they detoured patches of bog and arms of the forest itself. Finally they came to a declivity where water ran, the first stream any of them had seen on Grass. It didn't run far, only into a wide pool from which it seeped invisibly away. Beside the water Stella lay in a nest of grass, curled up, barefooted, half unclothed, with her thumb in her mouth.

When Marjorie knelt beside Stella and touched her, the girl woke screaming, fighting, saying her own name over and over, "Stella, I'm Stella, Stella," writhing with such violence that Marjorie was thrust away. Rillibee grabbed the girl, hugged her, held her quiet. After a time the screaming stopped. Rillibee spoke to her softly, calmly. Tony touched her. She twitched, opening her mouth to scream once more. Tony drew back and she quivered but did not scream. She would not tolerate even Sylvan's touch, and each time Marjorie came near her, she went into frenzied spasms of screaming and weeping, her face contorted with guilt and pain and shame.

Though Rillibee, who was a stranger, could hold her, evidently she could not bear to be near anyone she knew. Marjorie turned away, pained at being rejected, ecstatic to have found her. At least Stella reacted. At least she knew her name. At least she could distinguish between those she knew and those she didn't. At least she wasn't like Janetta.

Sylvan laid a caressing hand on her shoulder. "Marjorie."

She drew herself up, made herself nod, made herself think and speak. There was no time for grieving or for pointless agitation. "If the foxen will carry you, I want you to carry her through the forest to Commons. She needs medical care, and the quickest way will be if the foxen can get her there through the trees. You go, Rillibee, because she seems to trust you. Tony, you go to arrange things. I'll go back to Brother Mainoa and Father James."

Sylvan said hopefully, "I'll come back with you."

"No," she said, looking him in the eyes, her mouth stern. "I want you to go with them, Sylvan. I said this to you before. I came to Grass for a reason, an important reason. The more I find out, the more important that reason becomes, but I keep getting sidetracked—by you, by Rigo, by Stella, by disappearances and alarms, cluttering up everything. All you do is distract me and bother me."

"Mother," said Tony. "Leaving you here—"

"Go, Tony. Stella is alive. I'm joyful about that, but we mustn't forget all the others. There is plague out there, and people dying of it. The foxen know things. Someone must find out what they know.

Brother Mainoa is old and tired, and Father James may need my help. I'll stay and find out what I can."

"After Stella's cared for, I'll come back," Tony said.

"Yes. Do. Either you or Rillibee. And let your father know what's happened if you can."

She turned and reached out in the direction of the foxen, thinking of Commons, across the forest. She pictured Tony going there, Tony and Stella and Sylvan and Rillibee. The picture solidified in her mind, became real, as clear as though she were seeing it, and she had a sudden headache. A purring sound came from the grasses. Foxen drew near. People were drawn upon broad backs once more, fished up like wreckage from the deep, Rillibee dragging Stella's limp body up with him while she whimpered like some small, hurt animal.

An uncertain number of foxen moved into the forest and disappeared. Marjorie felt herself summoned, and she climbed upon His back once again with a strange mixture of feelings: relief, grief, anger all mushed up together like an emotional goulash. Into her mind came both the picture and the feel of stroking hands. She leaned forward upon the endless expanse of hide and cried while the stroking went on. After a time the stroking changed into a firm patting, the feeling was of someone telling her to straighten up, behave herself. Marjorie felt herself saying, "Yes, Mother," in her mind.

Laughter. At least amusement.

"Yes, Father," she amended, slightly amused despite herself.

Beneath her His shoulders moved gently. Male. Indisputably male. Prancing, prowling. The gait, male. Head moving, so, so. Male. Claws sliding in their sheaths, fingers touching, delicate as needles. Male. She saw multitudes of shapes, not quite clearly, most of them male. The males were violet and plum and mauve and deep wine red. The females were smaller, more softly blue, though she could not see them, either. Male, he told her. I. "First." Male.

Yes, she assented. He was male. He had thought "First" at her with quotation marks around it. Not his name, then. Merely something Mainoa called him. In his own mind the symbol of his name had movement and color—a purple wildness, full of scarlet lightning, veiled with gray-blue cloud. Himself.

Pictures moved in her mind. She saw Mainoa, stout and green-clad, walking soberly among the foxen shapes. Around him an aura bloomed, a shadow gathered, pale light on a dark ground, the light growing dimmer. Still he walked, indomitable, his feet a counterpoint to the movement beneath her.

Mainoa, she thought. I like him, too.

A new vision. Marjorie among the multitude of foxen. Not herself, precisely, but an idealized Marjorie who danced on low turf amid a gathering of foxen, creatures without shape or limitation and yet indisputably themselves. They were dancing with their shadows as the sun either rose or set, the long shadows seeming to stretch almost to the horizon. Sinuous shadows. Sensuous shadows. She, Marjorie, among sinuous, sensuous shadows, dancing with the foxen.

They danced in pairs, male and female, weaving their shadows together, letting their shadows touch. Shadows, and minds, touching. The others danced in pairs. Marjorie danced with First, the sleeves of her shirt growing wide, like wings, flowing like a tail, her hair loose in a silky mane. A female. Dancing. She still could not see His vision of Himself, but she could see His vision of her.

You. Marjorie. Female. Gait. Motion. Color. Smell.

Perilous, she whispered inside herself. *Dangerous*.

Beneath her the muscles of his shoulders moved like fingers, touching her. Perilous. Yes. Dangerous. Yes. Mysterious. Wonderful. Awful. Mighty. His skin spoke to her as horses' skin had always spoken to her, conveying emotion, conveying intention. She lay upon his back as she had lain upon Quixote's, trusting— For one blinding instant she saw clearly, and the glory of sight stunned her into shocked withdrawal. She felt herself draw shudderingly away, refusing. Denying.

He sensed her denial. In the dance he stood on his hind legs and changed, becoming manlike, maned and tailed, not a man but manlike, mane and tail flowing, mixing with her hair as he drew her into a closer dance. The other foxen were paired, moving, part of it all, unintrusively part.

Joy. Movement in joy. One pair touching another pair. Like the pendants of a wind chime, striking one another, each moving, each striking, each sounding, but gently, barely touching, the minds striking, soft blows as from gigantic paws, gentle as leaves, sounds like bells, like soft horns blowing.

No words. Purring, roaring, growling from wide gullets where ivory fangs hung like stalactites of feeling into her, penetrating deep. Wide jaws closing, holding, gentle as a caress. She would not join the dance of her own will. She would be joined in it by His. She would not see Him. He would see her.

No thought at all. Sensation only. Floating on it as it billowed up beneath her like a great sail. No commitment. Merely sensation. Now. Only now.

Dangerous, he reminded her with laughter. Perilous.

A presence, hovering, ready to pounce, able to pounce. Herself the prey. Floating, as though on blood, warm, liquid, permeating, becoming air to breathe. Aware of him. The sensuous extrusion of claws. Ripple of muscle in a leg. Mass of shoulder, heave of gut, thunder of heart. Lightning trickling along nerves like golden wire.

Claws touched her, gently, drawing down her naked flesh like fingernails, sensation running behind them, shivering.

Perilous. Perilous.

The edge of his tongue touched her naked thigh, sliding like a narrow, flaming serpent into her crotch.

A flaming symbol with two parts which moved together to fuse with aching slowness into one. She could almost see them.

My name, He said. Your name. We.

The serpent raised her up and took her far away. She came to a door made of flame and He invited her in, but she was afraid and would not go. . . .

When she returned, she was lying on the short grass against his chest, between his forelegs, cushioned in the softness of his belly fur. His breath made wind sounds in her ear. Her face was wet, but she could not remember crying. Her hair was loose, spread around her like spilled silk.

He stood up and went away, leaving her there. She rose in the dark, glad it was dark so He could not see her face, hot with embarrassment as she realized He did not need to see her face. She fumbled with her clothes, thinking she needed to dress herself, realizing only then that she was dressed, that the nakedness lay within. Her mind. Changed. Something that had covered it stripped away. . . .

After a few moments, He came back, offering His shoulders again. She mounted and He carried her, discreetly, neatly, an egg in a basket, while the dance faded into memory. Something marvelous and awful. Something not quite completed.

Maenads, she thought. Dancing with the god. . . .

He was talking to her. Explaining. He said *names*, but she saw only a few females, obviously not as many as the males. Only a few of them capable of reproduction. Many of them deciding not to bother. Grieving over that. Now only melancholy. Dark brown-gray distress.

Hopelessness. The future opening like a sterile flower, its center empty. No seed.

How did the foxen know flowers? There were no flowers here on Grass.

Yours, He said. Your mind. Everything there. I took it all. . . .

A time of wonder. So he knew her. Really knew her.

We are guilty, He said. All should die, perhaps, He suggested. Expiation. Sin. Not original sin, maybe, but *sin*, nonetheless. The sound of the word in her ears. The sound of the word *wickedness*. Collective guilt. (A picture came into her mind of Father Sandoval, talking. Evidently Father Sandoval had thought of that diagnosis.) The foxen had let it happen. Not they, but others like them, long ago. She saw the pictures, foxen elsewhere while Hippae slaughtered the Arbai. Screams, blood; then, elsewhere, disbelief. Clearly. As though it had been yesterday. They were guilty, all the foxen.

Postcoital depression? Part of her mind giggled hysterically and was admonished by some other part. No. Real sadness.

It wasn't your fault, she said. *Not your fault*. She felt cold from the images. So much death. So much pain.

Why would she say that?

Because it's true, she thought. *Damned sure. Not your fault.*

But suppose some of us did it. When we were Hippae. Some of *us*.

Not your fault, she insisted. *When you were Hippae, you didn't know. Hippae have no morals. Hippae have no sense of sin. Like a child, playing with matches, burning down the house.*

More pictures. Time past. Hippae were better behaved long ago. Past memory. Before the mutation. Didn't kill things then. Not when foxen laid the eggs. A picture of a foxen bowed down with grief, head bent between the front paws, back arched in woe. Penitence.

Her fingers were busy with her hair, trying to braid it up. She thought, *Then you must go back. Make things the way they used to be. Some of you can still reproduce.*

So few. So very few.

Never mind how few. Don't waste your time on penitence or guilt. Solving the problem is better! It was true. She knew it was true. She should have known it was true years ago, back in Breedertown.

Lack of understanding.

She thought the kneeling figure, the foxen crouched in woe while Hippae pranced and bellowed. She crossed it out, negated it. She thought a standing figure, claws like sabers, a foxen rampant, laying eggs. *Better. Much better.*

This militancy fell as though into an umplumbable well, a vacancy. They had gone beyond that. They had decided they should no longer care about things of the world. They felt responsible without wanting to be responsive.

She cried, not knowing whether He had not heard her or whether she had merely been ignored as of no consequence. Changed as she was, she knew she should make Him hear, but there were others around and His thoughts were diluted and disarranged.

The night had gone on without their notice. Ahead and above hung glowing globes of Arbai light which they climbed toward. She heard the contented whicker of horses, grazing on their island below. She was very tired, so tired she could scarcely hold on. He knelt and rolled her off and went away.

"Marjorie?" She was looking up at Father James' concerned face. "Is Stella—"

"Alive," she said, licking her lips. Saying words felt strange, as though she were using certain organs for inappropriate ends. "She knows her name. I think she recognized us. I sent the others to take her to Commons."

"The foxen took them?"

She nodded. "Some of them. Then the others went away, all but . . . all but Him."

"First?"

She couldn't call Him that. Bless me, Father, for I have sinned. I have committed adultery. Bestiality? No. Not a man, not a beast. What? I am in love with— Am I in love with . . . ?

He said, "You've been a very long time. The night's half gone."

She blurted desperately, trying not to talk about what most concerned her, "I thought all that business about sin was just Brother Mainoa being a little contentious. It wasn't. The foxen are obsessed with it. They either have considered or are considering racial suicide out of penitence." Though it was not suicide merely to stand still, doing nothing. Or was it?

He nodded, helping her up and guiding her into the house she had selected, where she half sat, half fell onto her bedding. "You've picked that up, have you? Mainoa says so, too. There's no doubt the Hippae killed the Arbai. There's little doubt the Hippae are killing mankind. I don't know how. The foxen don't tell us how. It's something they're withholding. As though they're not sure whether we're worthy. . . .

"It's like playing charades. Or decoding a rebus. They show us pictures. They feel emotions. Once in a while, they actually show us a word. And difficult though it is with us, seemingly they communicate with us better than they do with the Hippae. They and the Hippae transmit or receive on different wavelengths or something."

It was no longer charades or rebuses to Marjorie. It was almost language. It could have been language if only she had gone on, entered in, if she had not drawn back there, at the final instant. How could she tell Father that? She could tell Mainoa, maybe. No one else. Tomorrow, maybe. "I think you're right, Father. Since the mutation they have not communicated with the Hippae, though I get a sense that in former ages, when the foxen laid the eggs, they exercised a lot of guidance toward their young."

"How long ago?" he wondered.

"Long. Before the Arbai. How long was that? Centuries. Millennia?"

"Too long for them to be able to remember, and yet they do."

"What would you call it, Father? Empathetic memory? Racial memory? Telepathic memory?" She ran her fingers over her hair, pulling the braid into looseness. "God, I'm so tired."

"Sleep. Are the others coming back?"

"When they can. Tomorrow, perhaps. There are answers here, if only we can lay our hands upon them. Tomorrow—tomorrow we have to make sense of all this."

He nodded, as weary as she. "Tomorrow we will, Marjorie. We will."

He had no idea what she had to make sense of. He had no conception of what she had almost done. Or actually had done. How much was enough to have done whatever it was? Was she still chaste? Or was she something else that she had no word for?

She could not tell anyone tomorrow, she knew. Maybe not ever.

Very early in the morning, while the sun hung barely below the horizon, Tony and his fellow travelers were deposited just below the port at the edge of the swamp forest. The foxen vanished into the trees, leaving their riders trying to remember what they had looked like, felt like. "Will you wait for us?" Tony called, trying to make a picture of the foxen waiting, high in a tree, dozing perhaps.

He bent in sudden pain. The picture was of foxen standing where they stood now while the sun moved slowly overhead. Rillibee was holding his head with one hand, eyes tight shut, as he clung to Stella with the other arm.

"You'll wait here for us," Tony gasped toward the forest, receiving a mental nod in reply.

"Tony, what is it?" Sylvan asked.

"If you could hear them, you wouldn't ask," said Rillibee. "They think we're deaf. They shout."

"I wish they could shout loud enough for me to hear them," Sylvan said.

"Then the rest of us would have our brains fried," Tony said irritably. While he had immediately warmed up to Rillibee, Tony wasn't at all sure he liked Sylvan, who had a habit of commanding courses of action. "We'll go over there." "We'll stop for a while."

Now Sylvan said, "Someone in the port will give us transport to Grass Mountain Road. We'll speak to the order officer there." He moved toward the port.

Though Tony felt arguing wasn't worth the energy it would take, he wanted to get Stella to a physician quickly. "The doctors are at the other end of town?" he asked.

Sylvan stopped, then flushed. "No. No, as a matter of fact, the hospital is just up this slope, near the Port Hotel."

Rillibee said, "Then we'll go there," admitting no argument. He picked Stella up and staggered up the slope toward the hospital.

"Can I help you carry her?" Tony asked.

Stella had slipped into a deep sleep, and Rillibee wondered if she would even know who held her. Still, he shook his head. He was unwilling to give up the burden to anyone else, though he had become exhausted by carrying it. Though he thought of her as a child, she was not a small girl. He had been holding her on the foxen for hours. She was his heart's desire, so he thought, without trying to figure out why.

"I'll manage," he said. "It's not much farther."

It was at the top of a considerable slope, a long climb for men already weary. They came at the place from the back, where blank walls confronted them on either side of a wide door. A white-jacketed person stuck his head out, saw them, and withdrew. Others came out, with a power-litter. Rillibee handed over his burden with the last of his strength, then leaned on one of the attendants to get himself inside.

"Who is she?" someone asked.

"Stella Yrarier," Tony said. "My sister."

"Ah!" Surprise. "Your father's here as well."

"Father! What happened?"

"Speak to the doctor. Doctor Bergrem. In that office. She's there now."

Minutes later Tony was staring down at his father's sleeping face.

"What's wrong with him?" He asked the doctor.

"Nothing too serious, luckily. We wouldn't be able to do systems cloning and replacement here the way they do elsewhere. We have no SCR equipment."

Cloning! Systems replacement! The mortality rate for systems replacement was high. Besides, Old Catholics were prohibited from using cloned systems, though there were always backsliders who had a system cloned and confessed it later.

The doctor frowned at him. "Don't get into a state, boy. I said not too serious. Some cuts and a bit of bruising on the brain. All that's taken care of. Some nerve injury, his legs. That's healing. All he needs to do is stay here and simmer quietly for a day or two more." The slight, snub-nosed woman hovered over dials, twitching at them. Her plentiful dark hair was drawn back in a tight bun and her body appeared almost sexless in the flapping coat.

"You've got him sedated," Tony commented.

"Machine sleep. He's too nervous a type to leave conscious for long. He frets."

That was one way of saying it, Tony thought with an ironic twist to his lips. Roderigo Yrarier frets. Or fumes. Or roars.

The doctor went on, "Your sister, now, that's something else. Mind reconstruction, I wouldn't doubt. The Hippae have been at her."

"You know about that!"

"Seen a bit of it when the bons come in with broken bones or bitten-off appendages. They don't respond normally, so I tell them I'm testing their reflexes when I'm actually looking at their heads. Strangeness there, usually, though I'm not allowed to do anything about it. Not with the bons. They choose to keep their warps and twists, however strange it makes them."

"We don't want Stella twisted!"

"Didn't think you did. Didn't think so for a moment. May not be able to straighten her totally, though. There's limits to what we can do."

"Should we ship her out?"

"Well, young man, at the moment I'd say she's safer here, warped or not, than she may be out there. You'd know all about that, wouldn't you?"

"What do you mean?" He stared, unwilling to understand.

"Plague," she said. "We're getting a pretty good idea of what's going on out there."

"Do you know anything about it? What causes it? Do you know if there's any here?"

"None here. That I can be almost sure of. Why didn't you ask us medical people? Didn't you think we'd be capable of doing anything? Me, for instance. I've got degrees in molecu-bio and virology from the University at Semling Prime. I studied immunology on Repentance. I could have been working on this." She turned an open, curious face toward him. "The word is you've been trying to find out in secret."

"It was secret," he whispered. "To keep the Moldies from knowing. If they knew . . ."

She considered this, her face turning slowly white as she realized what he meant. "They'd bring it here? Purposely?"

"If they found out, yes. If they once knew."

"My God, boy." She laughed bitterly. "Everybody knows."

16

Everyone knew, the doctor said, and it seemed she told only the truth. Everyone knew there was plague. Everyone knew there might be Moldies already on Grass. Everyone knew there was a trail half a mile wide out there in the grasses, ending next to the swamp forest, which all at once seemed a fragile and penetrable curtain rather than the impassable barrier they had always relied upon. Hysteria mounted as the talk gathered both volume and speculative intensity, here and there, about the town.

Among other topics was much discussion of whether Grass's seeming immunity to plague meant anything. Foremost among those who thought it did was Dr. Bergrem. She had seen one or two people arrive on ships with filthy gray lesions. After a week or two on Grass, they had departed cured. Once there had even been a man in a quarantine pod. . . .

Roald Few challenged the doctor to explain herself. "You mean more than that the disease isn't here, doctor. You mean it can't *come* here. Something here prevents it?"

To which she nodded and said she thought so, in her experience, from what she'd seen, turning to Tony and Rillibee for their opinion.

"No, that isn't it," Tony told them wearily. "It isn't that it can't come here. It isn't that no one gets it here. The disease started from here. Somehow. The foxen think."

This was a statement requiring more than a little explanation. Since when had the foxen been talking to people? And where were these foxen? Tony and Rillibee told what they knew to Roald and Mayor Alverd Bee while dozens of other people came and went. They tried to describe foxen, unconvincingly, and were greeted with skepticism, if not outright disbelief.

Ducky Johns and Saint Teresa were there with an outlandish scenario of their own: Diamante bon Damfels, sneaking around naked in the port. Diamante bon Damfels now occupying a room in the hospital next to ones already taken by her sister, Emeraude, who had been beaten, and by Amy and Rowena, who refused to return to Klive.

Sylvan, hearing this, went off to see his mother and sisters. Commoners looked after him, pityingly. A bon, here in Commons. Useless as a third leg on a goose.

"How did Diamante get here?" Tony demanded of the assembled group. "We've just come through the swamp forest, and if it's the same everywhere as the parts we saw, there is literally no way through! There are some islands near the far edge, and some near this edge, too, but in the middle it's deep water and tangles of low branches and vines everywhere you look, like an overgrown maze. If she wasn't a climber, like Rillibee here, or if the foxen didn't bring her, then how did she get here?"

"We've been asking ourselves that, sweet boy," said Ducky Johns. "Over and over. Haven't we, Teresa? And the only answer is there has to be another way in. One we haven't known about until now." Ducky's usual girlish flirtatiousness was held in abeyance by her anxiety.

"One we still don't know about," Teresa amended.

"Oh, yes we do, dear," Ducky contradicted. "We know it's there.

We just don't know exactly where. Unless these strange foxen creatures did bring her, which they may have done, for all we know!"

Rillibee heard all this through a curtain of exhaustion. He said, "I don't think the foxen brought her. Brother Mainoa would have known."

"Do I know this Brother Mainoa you keep speaking of?" asked Alverd Bee.

Rillibee reminded him who Brother Mainoa was.

Sylvan joined them again, his face white and drawn. Dimity was conscious, but did not know him. Emmy was unconscious, though she was getting better. Rowena was sleeping. Amy had talked with him. She had told him his father was dead, and he was wondering why he felt nothing.

Rillibee was telling the mayor about Mainoa's attempts to translate the Arbai documents.

"And you say they've translated something already?" Roald cried. He didn't sound astonished, merely wild with a kind of quavery excitement. His gray hair tufted around his ears like a spiky aureole; he cracked his knuckles between jabs at the tell-me link, clickety crack. The sound was like someone walking on nutshells. "I want to see that, just as soon as I can. Let me get on to Semling."

"Are you a linguist?" Sylvan asked him curiously, wondering why there would be any such thing on Grass.

"Oh, no, my boy," Roald said. "My living comes from the family supply business. At languages, I'm only an amateur." He said it without even looking at Sylvan, then asked Rillibee, "Who was Mainoa's contact on Semling?"

Thus dismissed, Sylvan sat down at a table nearby, resting his head on his arms as he considered the continuing bustle around him. Things were busier in Commons than he had assumed they would be. People were more intelligent and far more affluent than he would have thought. They had things even the estancias didn't have. Foods. Machines. More comfortable living arrangements. It made him feel insecure and foolish. Despite all his fury at Stavenger and the other members of the Obermun class, still he had accepted that the bons were superior to the commoners. Now he wondered if they really were—or if the bons were even equal to the commoners? Why had he thought Marjorie would welcome his attentions? What had he to offer her?

The thought struck him with sick embarrassment. He sought words he had read but seldom if ever used. "Parochial." "Provincial." "Narrow." True words. What was a bon among these people? None of the commoners were deferring to him. None of them were asking for his opinion. Once Rillibee and Tony had told everyone that Sylvan was deaf to the foxen, Commons had disdained him as though he were deaf—and mute—to them as well. He could have accepted their disdain more easily if they had been professionals, like the doctor, but they were only amateurs, like this old man talking translation with Rillibee. Mere hobbyists. People who had studied things that had nothing to do with their daily lives. And every one of them knew more than he did! He wanted desperately to be part of them, part of something. . . .

He heaved himself up and went to find something to drink.

Rillibee rose from his chair beside Roald. "You know everything I do, Elder Few. I must get back to the others. I can't stay here." He yawned again, thinking briefly of asking Tony to come back with him. No. Tony would want to stay until they knew something more about Stella. As for Sylvan—better that Sylvan stayed here. Marjorie hadn't wanted him back.

He went out of the place, still yawning, breaking into a staggering jog that carried him down the slope to the place the foxen waited. Something dragged at him, insisting upon his return. Perhaps the trees. Perhaps something more. Some need or purpose awaited him among the trees. If nothing else, then he would carry the news of the bon Damfels girl and of Rigo's injuries and of all that both those events implied.

In the room he left behind, the doctor and the two madams were trying to figure out why a naked, mindless girl should have been trying to get into a freighter. "Why was she carrying a dried bat? What does that mean?" Dr. Bergrem demanded of the group at large.

"Hippae," said Sylvan as he wandered by. "Hippae kick dried bats at each other. There are dried bats in Hippae caverns."

Now they were looking at him. Now, suddenly, he wasn't mute anymore. He explained, "It's a gesture of contempt, that's all. That's how the Hippae express contempt for one another, part of the challenge. Or at the end of a bout, to reinforce defeat, they kick dead bats at each other. A way of saying, 'You're vermin.' "

Lees Bergrem nodded. "I've heard that. Heard that the Hippae have a lot of symbolic behaviors. . . ."

Feeling foolishly grateful for their attention, Sylvan told them what little more he had learned about the Hippae when he was a child, wishing Mainoa were there to tell them more.

Midmorning found Mainoa with Marjorie and Father James on the spacious open platform of the Tree City. Brother Mainoa had been studying the material recorded in his tell-me link while Marjorie had explored and Father James had tried to talk to foxen, thanking God that he was present rather than Father Sandoval. Father Sandoval had no patience with the idea that there might be other intelligent races. Father James wondered what the Pope in Exile would think of the whole idea.

Marjorie hadn't tried to speak to the foxen. From time to time He had reached out and said something to her. She had accepted these bits of information, trying to keep her face from showing what happened to her each time He spoke, a fire along her nerves, an ecstatic surge, taste, smell, something. Now the three humans sat face to face, trying to put bits and pieces of knowledge and hypothesis together.

"The Arbai had machines that transported them," Marjorie said. She had finally understood that. "That thing on the dais in the center of town? That was really a transport machine. Machines like that moved the Arbai from one place to another."

Brother Mainoa sighed and rubbed his head. "I think you're right, Marjorie. Let's see, what have I picked up in the last few hours? There's been another message from Semling." He took out the tell-me and put it at the center of their space, tapping it with one hand.

"On the theory that things written immediately before the tragedy might be of most use to us, Semling put a high priority on translating a handwritten book I found in one of the houses some time ago. They've translated about eighty percent of it. It seems to be a diary. It gives an account of the author trying to teach a Hippae to write. The Hippae became frustrated and furious and killed two Arbai who were nearby. When the Hippae calmed down, the author remonstrated with it. He or she explained that killing intelligent beings was wrong, that the dead Arbai were mourned by their friends, and that the Hippae must never do it again."

Marjorie breathed. "Poor, naive, well-meaning fool."

"Do you mean that this Arbai person, this diarist, simply *told* the Hippae not to do it again?" Father James was incredulous. "Did he think the Hippae would care?"

Mainoa nodded sadly, rubbing at his shoulder and arm as though they hurt him.

Marjorie said, "When He . . . when the foxen think of the Arbai, they always put light around them, as we might picture angels."

Brother Mainoa wondered how the golden angels high on Sanctity's towers would look with Arbai fangs and scales. "Not as though they were holy, though, do you think, Marjorie? More as though they were untouchable."

Marjorie nodded. Yes. The vision had that feeling to it. Untouchable Arbai. Set upon pedestals. Unreachable.

"The Arbai could believe no evil of the Hippae?" Father James could not believe what he was hearing.

Mainoa nodded. "It wasn't that they couldn't believe evil of the Hippae. They couldn't believe in it, period. They seem to have had no concept of evil. There is no word for evil in the material I've received from Semling. There are words for mistakes, or things done inadvertently. There are words for accidents and pain and death, but no word for evil. The Arbai word for intelligent creatures has a root curve which means, according to the computers, 'avoiding error.' Since the Arbai considered the Hippae to be intelligent—after all, they'd taught them to write—they thought all they had to do was point out the error and the Hippae would avoid it."

"Of course it wasn't an error," Marjorie said. "The Hippae enjoyed the killing."

Father James demurred. "I have a hard time believing in that kind of mind. . . ."

Brother Mainoa sighed. "She's right, Father. They've translated the word the Hippae trampled into the cavern. It's an Arbai word, or rather a combination of three or more Arbai words. One of them means death, and one means outsiders or strangers, and one means joy. Semling gives a high probability to translating it as *joy-to-kill-strangers*."

"They think they have a right to kill everything but themselves?" Father James shook his head.

Marjorie laughed bitterly. "Oh, Father, is that so unusual? Look at our own poor homeworld. Didn't man think he had a right to kill everything but himself? Didn't he have fun doing it? Where are the great whales? Where are the elephants? Where are the bright birds who once lived in our own swamp-forests?"

Brother Mainoa said, "Well, they couldn't kill the ones who lived here in the tree city. The Hippae can't swim, they can't climb, so they couldn't kill the Arbai who were here."

"It must have been too late for the ones who lived here, nonetheless," Marjorie said, looking at the shadow lovers who had just returned to the bridge and leaned there in the sun, whispering to one another. Shadow lovers, perilously intent upon one another. Not seeing what was to come. "Perhaps they died when winter came. It was too late for all the others, out there on other worlds."

"The ones here in the city must have been immune to the disease," Father James said. "They could have gone underground. Why didn't they? We must be immune, too. All the people on Grass must be immune."

"Oh, yes," Marjorie said. "I'm sure we're immune, so long as we stay on Grass. It stands to reason the Arbai on Grass were immune, also. That's why the Hippae killed them as they did. But it doesn't help to know that! Nothing we've found out helps! Nothing tells us how it started. Nothing tells us how to cure it once it's started. I keep thinking of home. I have a sister back home. Rigo has a mother, a brother, we have nieces and nephews. I have friends!"

"Shhh," he said. "We know one way to cure it, Marjorie. Anyone who comes here—"

"We don't even know that," she contradicted. "Even if we could bring every living human from every populated world to Grass, we don't know whether they'd catch it again after they left. We don't know whether we will get it if we leave. We don't know how it is spread. The foxen know something that will help us, but they won't tell us! It's almost as though they're waiting for something. But what?" She looked up to confront a shadowed mass across the railing. There were eyes, for a moment. Something brushing through her mind. She shook her head angrily. "I have this dreadful feeling of hopelessness. As though it's already too late for all this. As though things have gone past the point of no return." Something had changed irrevocably. Some point had been passed. She was sure of that.

A foxen touched her mind with incorporeal hands. She heard a comforting voice saying, "Hush, dear, hush." She leaned her forehead on a vast shoulder which was nowhere near. The foxen danced in her mind, and she with them.

Abruptly the shoulder was withdrawn. She looked up. The foxen had gone.

In a moment she understood why. She heard human voices ringing over the susurrus of Arbai speech. It was too soon for Tony to be back. They were not voices she recognized.

"Listen," she said, turning to locate the sound.

Not far off in the trees someone saw her and young voices yodeled a paean of anticipation.

There was something threatening in that shout. Marjorie and the two old men retreated across the plaza, watching apprehensively as the three forms flung themselves through the trees, dropping upon the platform like apes.

"Brother Flumzee," said Brother Mainoa in a calm, weary voice. "I hadn't expected to see you here."

Brother Flumzee posed on the railing, one knee up, his arms folded loosely about it. "Call me Highbones," he chirruped. "Meet my friends. Steeplehands. Long Bridge. There were two more of us, but Little Bridge and Ropeknots got eaten by Hippae out there." He waved, indicating somewhere else. "Along with Elder Brother Fuasoi and his little friend Shoethai. Not that we're sure of that. We heard a lot of howling, but maybe they escaped."

"Why were you out there at all?" Brother Mainoa asked.

"They sent me for you, Brother." Highbones smiled. "They said you are no longer one of us. You are to be dispensed with."

"But you said Fuasoi was with you! And Shoethai!"

"We didn't expect them to come along. They were kind of, what would you say, last-minute additions. They were going to drop us off and then go somewhere else."

A shadow figure moved among the three climbers. Highbones beat at it, as though it were a swarm of gnats. "What the hell are these things?"

"Only pictures," said Marjorie. "Pictures of the people who once lived here."

Highbones turned his head, surveying the city. "Nice," he said. "A climber's place. Is there enough to eat so somebody could live here?"

"In summer," said Brother Mainoa. "Probably. Fruit. And nuts. There may be edible animals, too."

"Not in winter, hmm? Well, in winter we could go into town, couldn't we. Probably want to go there anyhow. Pick up some women. Bring them back here."

"You mean stay here?" Long Bridge asked. "After we do the thing, you mean stay here?"

"Why not?" Highbones asked. "You think of any better place for climbers than this?"

"I don't like these things." Long Bridge batted at the shadow forms moving before him. "I don't like these monsters all over me."

The two men had been listening and watching, noticing the tense muscles in the climbers' arms and legs, the strained lines of their necks and jaws. Brother Mainoa thought that all this talk meant nothing. The talk was only to make a space of time, to allow them to size up their opposition. And what was their opposition? An old man, a soft man, and a woman.

Brother Mainoa reached out toward the foxen. Nothing. No pictures. No words.

"Are you hungry?" Marjorie asked. "We have some food we can share with you."

"Oh, yes, we're hungry," leered Highbones. "Not for food, though. We brought enough food of our own." He ran his tongue along his lips, staring at her, letting his eyes dwell lasciviously on her. She shivered. "You look young and healthy," Highbones went on. "There was talk back there at the Friary about plague. You don't have plague, do you, pretty thing?"

"I could have," she said, struggling to keep her voice calm. "I suppose. There was plague on Terra when we left."

The two followers turned to Highbones, questions on their lips, but he silenced them with a gesture. "It's naughty to tell lies. If you got it there, you'd be dead by now. That's what everybody says."

"Sometimes it takes years to manifest itself," said Father James, "but the person still has it."

"What're you?" Highbones said with a laugh. "Dressed up like that? Some kind of servant? Mind your manners, servant. Nobody was talking to you."

"If Fuasoi sent you after me," Mainoa said thoughtfully, "he could have had only one reason. If he didn't want knowledge about the cause of the plague disseminated, then he must have been a Moldy."

Marjorie caught her breath. A Moldy here? Already? Had they been too late!

Highbones ignored the interchange. He put both feet onto the deck, stood up easily, stretching. "You boys ready?" he asked. "Each of you take one of the geezers. I get the woman first—"

"Highbones." The voice called from above them, from the sun spangle among the high branches. "Highbones the coward. Highbones the liar. Will he climb?"

Marjorie felt the breath go out of her. Rillibee. But only Rillibee. No other voices.

Highbones had turned, neck craning as he searched the high dazzle. "Lourai!" he shouted. "Where are you, you peeper!"

"Here," the voice called from above. "Where Highbones can't climb. Where Highbones can't reach."

"Keep them quiet," Highbones snarled, gesturing toward Marjorie and the old men. "Until I get back." He leapt upon the railing and outward, into the trees. "Wait for me, peeper. I'm coming to get you."

Marjorie's pack was just inside the door. There was a knife in it. She turned, moving toward it. Steeplehands dashed forward, intercepted her, and knocked her away from the door. She stumbled, reaching out a hand to catch herself. The low railing caught her at the back of her knees, and she went over, falling, seeing the sun-spangled foliage spin around her and hearing her own voice soaring until she suddenly didn't hear anything anymore.

"A very small being to see you, O God," the angelic servitor announced. The servitor looked very much like Father Sandoval except that he had wings. Marjorie paused in the vaulted and gauzy doorway to inspect them. They were not swans' wings, which she had expected, but translucent insect wings, like those of a giant dragonfly. Anatomically, they made more sense than bird wings, since they were in addition to, rather than in place of, the upper appendages. The angel glared at her.

"Yes, yes," said God patiently. "Come in."

God stood before a tall window draped in cloud. Outside were the gardens of Opal Hill, stretching away in vista upon vista. After a moment, Marjorie realized the garden was made of stars.

"How do you do," Marjorie heard herself saying. He looked like someone she knew. Smaller than she had thought He would be. Very bony about the face, with huge eyes, though the person she knew, whoever he was, had never worn his hair as long as God wore His, a dark curling about his shoulders, a white mane at his temples. "Welcome, very small being," He said, smiling. Light filled the universe. "Was something bothering you?"

"I can learn to accept that you do not know my name," Marjorie said. "Though it came as a shock—"

"Wait," He said. "I know the true names of everything. What do you mean I do not know your name?"

"I mean you don't know I'm Marjorie."

"Marjorie," he mouthed, as though He found the sound unfamiliar. "True, I did not know you were called Marjorie."

"It seems very harsh. Very cruel. To be a virus."

"I would not have said virus, but you believe it's cruel to be something that will spread?" he asked. "Even if that's what's needed?"

She nodded, ashamed.

"You must be having a difficult time. Very small beings do have difficult times. That's what I create them for. If there weren't difficult concepts to pull out of nothing and build into creation, One wouldn't need very small beings. The large parts almost make themselves." He gestured at the universe spinning beneath them. "Elementary chemistry, a little exceptional mathematics, and there it is, working away like a furnace. It's the details that take time to grow, to evolve, to become. The oil in the bearings, so to speak. What are you working on now?"

"I'm not sure," she said.

The angel in the doorway spoke impatiently. "The very small being is working on mercy, Sir. And justice. And guilt."

"Mercy? And Justice? Interesting concepts. Almost worthy of direct creation rather than letting them evolve. I wouldn't waste my time on guilt. Still, I have confidence you'll all work your way through the permutations to the proper ends. . . ."

"I don't have much confidence," she said. "A lot of what I've been taught isn't making sense."

"That's the nature of teaching. Something happens, and intelligence first apprehends it, then makes up a rule about it, then tries to pass the rule along. Very small beings invariably operate in that way. However, by the time the information is passed on, new things are happening that the old rule doesn't fit. Eventually intelligence learns to stop making rules and understand the flow."

"I was told that the eternal verities—"

"Like what?" God laughed. "If there were any, I should know! I have created a universe based on change, and a very small being speaks to me of eternal verities!"

"I didn't mean to offend. It's just, if there are no verities, how do we know what's true?"

"You don't offend. I don't create things that are offensive to me. As for truth, what's true is what's written. Every created thing bears my intention written in it. Rocks. Stars. Very small beings. Everything only runs one way naturally, the way I meant it to. The trouble is that very small beings write books that contradict the rocks, then say I wrote the books and the rocks are lies." He laughed. The universe trembled. "They invent rules of behavior that even angels can't obey, and they say I thought them up. Pride of authorship." He chuckled.

"They say, 'Oh, these words are eternal, so God must have written them.' "

"Your Awesomeness," said the angel from the door. "Your meeting to review the Arbai failure—"

"Ah, tsk," said God. "Now there's an example. I failed completely with that one. Tried something new, but they were too good to do any good, you know?"

"I've been told that's what you want," she said. "For us to be good!"

He patted her on the shoulder. "Too good is good for nothing. A chisel has to have an edge, my dear. Otherwise it simply stirs things around without ever cutting through to causes and realities. . . ."

"Your Awesomeness," the angel said again, testily. "Very small being, you're keeping God from his work."

"Remember," said God, "While it is true I did not know that *you* believe your name is Marjorie, I do know who *you* really are. . . ."

"Marjorie," the angel said.

"My God, Marjorie!" The hand on her shoulder shook her even more impatiently.

"Father James," she moaned, unsurprised. She was lying on her back, staring up at the sun-smeared foliage above her.

"I thought he'd killed you."

"He talked to me. He told me—"

"I thought that damned climber had killed you!"

She sat up. Her head hurt. She felt a sense of wrongness, of removal.

"You must have hit your head."

She remembered the confrontation on the platform, the railing. "Did that young man hit me?"

"He knocked you over the railing. You fell."

"Where is he? Where are they?"

"One of the foxen has them backed into an Arbai house. He came down out of the trees just as you fell, snarling like a thunderstorm. He's right out there in the open, but I still can't see him. Two of the others came with him. They carried me down to you."

She struggled to her feet, using a bulky root to pull herself up, staring in disbelief at the platform high above. "Falling all that way should have killed me."

"You dropped onto a springy branch. Then you slipped off that onto another one, lower down, and then finally fell into that pile of grass and brush," he said, pointing it out. "Like falling on a great mattress. Your guardian angel was watching out for you."

"How do we get back up?" she asked, not at all believing in guardian angels.

He pointed again. Two of the foxen waited beside the tree. Vague forms without edges; corporate intentions and foci, patterns in her mind.

"Did they help with the men?" she asked.

He shook his head. "The one up there didn't need help."

She stood looking at the two for a long moment, thinking it out. Dizziness overwhelmed her and she sagged against the tree, muttering "Rocks. Stars. Very small beings."

"You don't sound like yourself," he said.

"I'm not," she replied, managing to smile, her recent vision replaying itself in her mind. "Have you ever seen God, Father?"

The question distressed him. Her eyes were wide, staring, glassy. "I think you had a bit of concussion. You may even have a fracture, Marjorie. . . ."

"Maybe I've had a religious experience. An insight. People have them."

He could not argue with that, though he knew Father Sandoval would have. In Father Sandoval's opinion, religious experiences were something Old Catholics should eschew in the interest of balance and moderation. Once matters of faith had been firmly decided, religious experiences just confused people. Father James was less certain. He let Marjorie lean upon him as they staggered a few steps to the waiting foxen. One of them picked her up and carried her upward along slanting branches and scarcely visible vines to the plaza high above. She could feel foxen all about her, a weight of them in her mind, a thunder of thought, a tidal susurrus, like vast dragon-breathing in darkness.

"Good Lord," she whispered. "Where did they all come from?"

"They were already here," said Mainoa. "Watching us from the trees. They just came closer. Marjorie, are you all right?"

"She's not all right," fretted Father James. "She's talking strangely. Her eyes don't look right. . . ."

"I'm fine," she said absently, trying to stare at the assembled multitude, knowing it for multitude, but unable to distinguish the parts. "Why are they here?"

Brother Mainoa looked up at her, frowning in concentration. "They're trying to find something out. I don't know what it is."

A foxen bulk completely blocked the door. Marjorie received a clear picture of two human figures being dropped from a high branch. She drew a line across it. In the crowd behind her there was approval and disapproval. The picture changed to one of the two men being released. She drew a line across that as well. More approval and disapproval. Argument, obviously. The foxen did not agree on what ought to be done.

Her legs wobbled under her and she staggered. "Rillibee hasn't come back?

Brother Mainoa shook his head. "No. His voice went off that way." He pointed.

She approached the door of the house. The two climbers, their hands and feet tightly tied, glared back at her.

"Who sent you to kill Brother Mainoa?" she asked.

The two looked at one another. One shook his head. The other, Steeplehands, said sulkily, "Shoethai, actually. But the orders came from Elder Brother Fuasoi. He said Mainoa was a backslider."

She rubbed at the pain in her forehead. "Why did he think so?"

"Shoethai said it was some book of Mainoa's. Some book from the Arbai city."

"My journal," said Brother Mainoa. "I'm afraid I was careless. I must have left the new one where it could be found. We were in such a hurry to leave—"

"What were you writing about, Brother?" Marjorie asked.

"About the plague, and the Arbai, and the whole riddle."

"Ah," she said, turning back to the prisoners. "You, ah ... Long Bridge. You intended to rape me, you and the others, didn't you?"

Long Bridge stared at his feet, one nostril lifting. "We was going to have a try, sure. Why not? We didn't see those whatever-they-are hanging around, so why not."

"Did you think that was a ..." she struggled to find a word he might understand, "a smart thing to do? A good thing to do? What?"

"What are you?" he sneered. "You work for Doctrine? It was something we wanted to do, that's all."

"Did you care how I felt about it?"

"Women like it, no matter what they say. Everybody knows that."

She shuddered. "Were you going to kill me, then?"

"If we'd of felt like it, sure."

"Do women like that, too?"

He looked momentarily confused, licking his lips.

"Wouldn't it have bothered you? Killing me?"

Long Bridge did not answer. Steeplehands did. "We'd of been sorry, later, if we'd wanted you around and you was already dead," he mumbled.

"I see," she said. "But you wouldn't have been sorry for me?"

"Why?" Long Bridge asked angrily. "Why should we be sorry for you? Where was you when we got packed up and sent out here? Where was you when they took us away from our folks?"

Marjorie received a new picture of the two prisoners being dropped from a high tree. She drew a line across it in her mind, though more slowly than before. "What do all these foxen want, Brother Mainoa? What are they here for?"

"I think they want to see what you'll do," he answered.

Father James asked, "What *are* you doing?"

"I'm trying to figure something out," she said. "I'm trying to decide whether we can afford to be merciful. The Arbai were merciful, but when confronted with evil, mercy becomes an evil. It got the Arbai killed, and it could get us killed because these two might simply come back and murder us. The question is, are they evil? If they are, it doesn't matter how they got that way. Evil can be made, but not unmade. . . ."

"Forgiveness is a virtue," Father James said, realizing as he did so that the suggestion came from habit.

"No. That's too easy. If we forgive these two, we may actually cause another killing." She put her head between her hands, thinking. "Do we have the right to be fools if we want to? No. Not at someone else's expense."

He stared at her with a good deal of interest. "You've never spoken this way, Marjorie. Mercy is a tenet of our faith."

"Only because you don't think this life really matters, Father. God says it does."

"Marjorie!" he cried. "That's not true."

"All right," she cried in return. The sullen ache in her head was now a brooding violence inside her skull. "I don't mean *you*, Father James, I mean *you*, what you priests usually say. I say this life matters, and that means mercy is doing the best for them I can without allowing anyone else to suffer, including me! I won't make the Arbai mistake."

"Marjorie," he cried again, dismayed. He had had his own doubts and troubles, but to hear her talking wildly like this disturbed him deeply. She was almost violent, something she had never been, full of words that spilled from her mouth like grain from a ripped sack.

She turned to the imprisoned men. "I'm sorry. The only way I can see that we can be safe from you seems to be to allow the foxen to kill you."

"Oh, for God's sake, Lady," cried Steeplehands in dismay. "Take us into Commons and turn us over to the order officers there. We can't do nothing tied up like this."

She held her head, knowing it was a bad idea, but not knowing why. It was a very bad idea. She was sure of it. Inside her mind was an enormous question, waiting to be answered.

Father James was shaking his head anxiously, pleading with her. "Mainoa did tie them up very tightly. And we have to go to Commons eventually anyhow. We can turn them over to the order officers. They're probably no worse than half the port-rabble the order officers keep in check."

Marjorie nodded, though she wasn't convinced. This wasn't a good idea at all. This wasn't what a very small being should do. A very small being should scream danger and drop them from the highest tree. . . .

The foxen nearest them twitched, brooding shadow, hatching visions. Light and shadow spun across their minds, stripes of evanescent color, jittering.

"He's dissatisfied," Brother Mainoa offered.

"So am I," Marjorie said, her eyes wild with pain. "Listen to them. All of them. And only a few of them came forward to help us. Maybe they're like I've always been. Full of intellectual guilts and doubts, letting things happen, paying no attention to how I feel."

Her head was in agony. She received a picture of foxen traveling through the trees, going away. She drew a shiny circle around it in her mind. Yes. Why not? They might as well go away. "They're going away. We must wait here for Rillibee," she announced.

A cannon went off in her brain. She crawled to her bedding and lay down to let the quiet come up around her. Gradually the pain diminished. Outside in the trees, the foxen moved away. Pictures fled through her mind: their thoughts, their conversation. She let the symbols and sounds wash through her like waves, lulling her into a drowsy half-consciousness.

The sun had moved to midafternoon before they heard a "Halloo," off in the shadows, low among the trees.

A foxen breathed among the trees, close, threatening.

"Halloo," came the voice again, closer. The threat in the trees diminished.

Marjorie struggled to her feet and went out onto the platform. "Rillibee," she called.

He came into sight below them, moving wearily among the vines.

"You look tired out!" His bony face was pale. His eyes were circled with shadow, making them look enormous, like a night-dwelling creature.

"Long climb," he mumbled. "Long, long climb." He pulled himself upward, slowly upward, sliding over the railing at last in an exhausted heap. "Oh, I'm thankful for all that climbing at the Friary. All those spidery ladders, all those bridges. . . ."

"What happened?" Brother Mainoa asked.

"Highbones tried to catch me. He couldn't. I led him off into the forest, a long, long way. Then I hid from him, let him pass me, and came back. I'd have killed him if I could have figured out an easy way to do it. Bastard."

Marjorie touched his cheek. "We can go now. Back to Commons."

Rillibee shook his head. "No. Not yet. We need . . . we need the foxen. I'm sorry to have wasted so much time on Highbones, but I didn't know what else to do except get them away from here. I thought they'd all come. Highbones usually likes to outnumber his opponents. But you managed to deal with the others."

"One of the foxen did."

"Ah." He sagged wearily. "I have to tell you things, Marjorie. Opal Hill has been burned by the Hippae. There's a Hippae-hound trail half a mile wide leading toward the swamp-forest. The ambassador, your husband, is at the hospital. He's going to be all right, but it was a close thing. Stavenger bon Damfels is dead, him and a dozen or so bons. They've found the bon Damfels girl in there, at the port. Dimity. The one who vanished this spring. Just like they found Janetta. . . ."

"Both of them were taken by Hippae," Marjorie said in wonderment. "And both of them ended up at the port!"

Rillibee nodded. "Naked. Mindless. Everyone at Commons is frantic over it. Janetta and Dimity got in there somehow. They couldn't come through the trees unless the foxen carried them. If the foxen didn't carry them, then there's some other way in. Has to be. And if girls can get in, maybe Hippae can get in. We have to find how they got there—"

A troubled sound from the trees.

"Now they're upset," said Brother Mainoa, rubbing his head. "They're angry. The foxen have never carried anyone anywhere until they carried you and your companions, Rillibee. The foxen thought the town was safe. They had encouraged men to build the port there, where the Hippae couldn't get at it."

"Encouraged?" asked Marjorie.

"You know." Brother Mainoa sighed. "Encouraged. Influenced. As they do."

She felt the foxen retreating. "Where are they going?"

"They've gone to look for the way Rillibee says must be there. As they went they were thinking of migerers."

"Diggers? They suspect a tunnel, then."

"Something like that." Mainoa gave a weary shudder, putting his head into his hands. "Marjorie, at this moment, I'm a tired old man. I'm incapable of helping to look for tunnels."

Rillibee put his arms around the old man. "I'm a very tired young one, Brother. If the foxen are searching, let's let them do it. I need a little rest. Unless you think they need our help . . ."

"They'll do it," Brother Mainoa said. Whether they would or not, he could do no more. Marjorie crept back to her bed, feeling the pain ebb once more as she fell into sleep, empty this time of all foxen dreams. Rillibee lay sprawled like a child. Mainoa huddled into himself, snoring slightly. Father James sat by the railing, wondering what had really happened to Marjorie, what she had really seen or dreamed. Long Bridge and Steeplehands sulked and muttered to one another, chafing at their bonds.

Even before *First* returned late in the afternoon, they knew the way into Commons had been found. When He was yet some distance off, horses and riders swam into their minds, and they knew what He intended. Mounted once more, they were led in a circuitous route as they crossed quiet pools, forded dark streams, and rode down long, splashing alleys. Without a guide, it would have been impossible to find their way. Some pools were shallow water over sucking sands. Some were full of deadly sharp root knees. They knew, because the foxen showed them.

They came out onto the grass near the pool where they had found Stella. Near where she had lain, great sheaves of grass had been torn up, turf had been ripped away to expose a gaping tunnel mouth, wide and dug deep and mortared up as the Hippae caverns were. The grass had hidden it. When they had found Stella, all of them had been within yards of it without seeing it.

"Migerer work," said Brother Mainoa.

Somewhere a foxen cried out, a great, world-freezing cry.

"Devil's work," Mainoa amended. "So say our guides. This tunnel goes deep beneath the swamp. One of the foxen has been through it, all the way to the port."

It was not necessary to ask who had used it before. The tripartite hoofprints of the Hippae were everywhere inside it, everywhere except where the trickle of water had washed them away. "In," they were urged. "Through! Quickly!"

Marjorie, leading Don Quixote, went into the opening and was immediately soaked by the drip of murky water seeping through the soft stone above. The others trailed behind her, swearing softly at the dank air, the stench of droppings, the sog of the surface beneath their feet. The prisoners cursed and dragged at the ropes that held them. The tunnel top was not high enough for any of them to ride sitting up. It was barely high enough for Irish Lass to walk with her head down, her ears brushing the end of muddy roots which straggled through from above. The lights they carried lit their way, though inadequately. Horse and human feet splashed and sucked at the half-muck, half-rock beneath them.

"Foxen coming behind us," called Rillibee from his position at the rear. "I think. I feel them there. This tunnel isn't even tall enough for Hippae."

"High enough if they stalk," said Brother Mainoa. "Like great lions. One at a time. Slowly. But it was not made for them."

Within yards of the entrance the tunnel began to slope steeply down. The trickle of water, which had been running outward, reversed itself and began to flow in the direction of their travel. The horses sat back upon their haunches as the steep slope continued, whickering in protest. Something told them to go on, trilling at them, a summoning noise. The floor leveled and the water became deeper. They went on into darkness, water falling, water splashing, the darkness above them seeming to enfold them.

Marjorie flicked her light along the tunnel walls, finding numerous small holes where the walls met the water. "What are those?" she asked.

"I should think drain holes," replied Father James. "All this water has to go somewhere."

"Where? It can't run uphill!"

"We're actually in a hill," Brother Mainoa said, coughing. "All of Commons, including the swamp forest, lies in a rocky basin higher than the surrounding prairie. It's like a bowl on a table. If one drills holes in the bowl, the water will drain away."

"Do you think migerers dug all this?" she asked.

He coughed again, wrackingly. "I think so, yes. I think the Hippae told them to do it."

"Through rock?"

"Partly through rock. This looks like a fairly soft stratum. They can dig in soft stone. I've seen them."

"How much farther?" she wondered aloud.

After a time Brother Mainoa responded. "There's something just ahead."

What was just ahead was a side chamber of the tunnel, one made tight and dry and furnished with a pile of grasses. Marjorie used her light to examine the chamber. The floor was littered with scraps of underclothing, with two left boots, with a much-tattered Hunt jacket. "She was here," Marjorie said. "Janetta."

"And someone else." Brother Mainoa sighed, pointing at the boots. "Two left feet worth of someone. Janetta and Dimity bon Damfels, perhaps."

The tunnel was full of sound, trills and snarls and demands.

"He wants us to go on," said Brother Mainoa. "There is danger behind us."

They resumed to their splashing journey, fear lending speed to all of them. Marjorie looked at Don Quixote and wondered if he might not understand the foxen far better than she herself did. He moved alertly, as though summoned. All the horses did.

Far back in the tunnel, something screamed. The echoes went by them—*ee-yah, ee-yah, ee-yah*—ricocheting along the walls, fading into quiet.

"Hurry," something said in their minds. The Terran word pulsated at them, black letters on orange, large, plain capital letters, underlined, with an exclamation point. "HURRY!"

"What?" Marjorie whoofed. "What was that?"

"He does that sometimes," Mainoa breathed. "He's not much interested in written words, but sometimes he picks one up from me and broadcasts it."

Another picture, this one of all of them mounted and running. It had scarcely faded before they were all on horseback, lying flat while the horses trotted rapidly through the water, blindly moving into darkness as though moving in accordance with some guidance system known only to themselves. The prisoners, hastily thrown across Irish Lass, snarled and complained.

"Shut up, or we'll leave you for the Hippae," Rillibee commanded. The climbers fell silent.

Then there was rosy light, slightly above them and far ahead. The way sloped upward. The horses dug in with their rear legs, pushing. A foxen was silhouetted against the light, then gone. Then they too were out in the world once more. The tunnel emerged on a tiny island. Pools of water surrounded them. Ahead, the trees stopped and the land sloped up toward a red-flushed sunset. Illusory shapes prowled out of the tunnel behind them and took to the trees.

"Go," the word said, red on white, imperative. "Go!"

They went. The horses walked-swam to the edge of the trees and lunged up onto the long slope. The riders stared back, expecting horror to erupt behind them. Nothing. No sound. Perhaps the foxen had bought them time.

"I'll take these two to the order station," said Rillibee, tugging on the rope that bound the captives. He pointed up the hill. "That's the hospital. Where Stella and your husband are, next to the Port Hotel."

Marjorie urged Don Quixote up the slope, covering half of it before she realized that she was actually going to a place where Rigo was. Rigo. She said the word to herself. Nothing resonated. He was someone she knew, that was all. Normally the thought of him brought feelings: guilt and anxiety and frustration. Now she felt only curiosity, perhaps a slight sorrow, wondering how it would feel to see him after all that had happened.

The Port Hotel was packed with people, anonymous groups going here and there, anonymous faces turning to stare curiously at Marjorie and the others. Someone shouted. Someone else pointed. Then Sebastian Mechanic separated himself from the mass and came running toward them.

"Lady Marjorie," he cried. "Your son's here, and your daughter and husband."

She dismounted stiffly, wiping at her muddy face. "Rillibee told me," she said. "I need to see them. I need somewhere to wash." Then Persun Pollut was beside her, leading her in one direction while Sebastian and Asmir led the horses in another.

"Lady Westriding, I'm glad you're here." His heart lay in his eyes, but she did not see it there. "They'll take the horses to the barn. How can I help you?"

"Do you known where Rigo is?"

"In there." He pointed through a door to a crowd of people, seemingly all talking at once. "The doctor let him get up a few hours ago.

They're talking about the plague and whether the Hippae are going to get in and eat us all!"

"The plague!" She could see Rigo's lean form at the center of the mob. He sat in a chair, pale and haggard, but he seemed to be functioning. Still, to be talking about the plague!

"Everyone knows, ma'am. Your husband is there, trying to bring some order out of it all. . . ."

"I'll join them," Brother Mainoa said from behind them. "I have to tell them about that tunnel . . . something has to be done about it."

"And Stella?" Marjorie asked Persun.

"Through there," Persun pointed toward a hallway.

"I'll go with you," said Rillibee, as Brother Mainoa, leaning heavily on Father James's arm, went in to join the crowd.

Persun guided Marjorie and Rillibee along the building, into it through a small side door and down a corridor to a corner room which was almost filled by a humming box, a Heal-all.

"In there," Persun said.

She peered down through the transparent lid to see Stella lying below, slender wires and tubes connecting her to the box.

"Are you her mother?" The doctor had come in behind them.

Marjorie turned. "Yes. Is she? I mean, what do you. . . ."

The doctor gestured toward a chair. "I'm Doctor Lees Bergrem. I'm not entirely sure yet what the prognosis is. She's been here only a little more than a day. There was no . . . well, no lasting physical damage."

"They had done something to her . . . to her body?"

"Something. Something in the pleasure centers of the brain and nervous system, in the sexual connections to it. I'm not yet sure exactly what was done. Something perverse. Sexual pleasure seems to result from obeying commands. I think I can fix that part."

Marjorie didn't say anything. She waited.

"She may not remember everything. She may not be just the way she was. She may be more as she was as a child. . . ." The doctor shook her head. "You know about Janetta bon Maukerden? Had you heard that another one has been found? Diamante bon Damfels. It's as though they were wiped clean, except for that one circuit." She shook her head again. "Your daughter is more fortunate. She hadn't been disconnected yet. Even if she loses something, she'll have time to rebuild, relearn."

Marjorie didn't reply. What was there to say? She felt Rillibee's hand on her shoulder. "It'll be all right," he said. "I have a feeling."

She wondered if she should cry. What she felt was anger. Anger at

Rigo. Anger even at Stella herself. Rigo and Stella had done this with their foolishness. And the bons had done this. Forget the Hippae, malevolent though they were. It was human foolishness that had laid Stella in that box.

Mercy, a voice in her mind said softly. Justice. I wouldn't waste my time on guilt.

The doctor interrupted her thoughts. "You don't look at all well yourself. There's a knot on your head as big as an egg. Look here." And she began shining lights in Marjorie's eyes and hooking her up to machines. "Concussion," she said. "Let's set you right while you're here, before you try to do something about this mess and collapse. I'll send someone in to clean you up, as well. Do you have a change of clothes?"

Attendants came and went. There were basins of water and soft towels. Someone loaned her a shirt. Then Marjorie sat beside Stella's box, hooked-through tubes and wires to a box of her own. Gradually the vision she had had in the swamp-forest began to fade. She remembered it, but it lacked the clarity of immediate seeing. The words faded. What God had said to her faded. The doctor came back and sat beside her, talking quietly of her medical education on Semling, of her further education on Repentance, of the young people from Commons who had been recently trained as scientists and were working now on a puzzle Lees Bergrem herself was interested in.

"I know," said Marjorie. "I ordered your books."

The doctor flushed. "They really weren't written for the layman."

"I could tell. But I understood parts of some of them, anyhow."

The doctor asked about the swamp-forest, the foxen, and Marjorie answered, omitting her vision but telling about the assailants, telling more than she knew....

"Oh, I would have forgiven them before," she admitted. "Oh, yes. I'd have let them go. I'd have been afraid not to. For fear society or God would have judged me harshly. I'd have said pain in this life isn't that important. A few more murders. A few more rapes. In heaven they won't matter. That's what we've always said, isn't it, doctor. But God didn't say anything about that. He just said we should get on with our work...."

The doctor gave her a strange look and peered into her eyes.

Marjorie nodded. "They're always telling us what God has said in books. All my life I've had God's word in my pocket, and here He wrote it all somewhere else...."

"Shhh," said Dr. Bergrem, patting her on the arm. Marjorie relaxed and let it go. After a time the doctor went away, and there was nothing to listen to but her own breathing and the machines' humming. She thought of Dr. Bergrem's book. She thought about intelligence. She thought about Stella. Faintly she remembered the face of God, and almost as though she had read it in a fairy tale long ago, how Father Sandoval looked with dragonfly wings.

In the crowded room where Rigo sat, Brother Mainoa was being wearily firm, drawing on the last of his strength to insist upon action. "The tunnel has to be closed," he said. "At once. It's available as a way for the Hippae to invade Commons. We heard them behind us when we came in, no great numbers because the tunnel is too small for them to come through except one at a time, but still a few of them are enough to do great damage."

"Some of them came in behind you," said Alverd Bee, the mayor. "The minute you arrived and told us there was a way through, I sent two men to keep watch, and they report a handful of the beasts at the tunnel entrance."

"A dozen now could be a hundred by nightfall," Rigo said. "Brother Mainoa is right. That tunnel has to be destroyed."

"I wish I had some idea how to go about that," the mayor said, turning to his father-in-law. "Roald? Do you have any ideas?"

Roald fidgeted. "Alive, what the hell can you try? Blow it up with something. Flood it somehow. Get some kind of gate across it." He rubbed his head. "Hime Pollut is good at this kind of thing. Ask him."

Alverd went to find Hime Pollut. In a few moments he returned. "Hime thinks we ought to blow it up. He just doesn't know what we've got that'll do the job."

Rigo said, "Don't you have construction explosives, things you use to loosen up the rock when you have to expand the winter quarters? Or in mines? You have mines. Use that!"

"We've thought of that, Ambassador, but there are Hippae massed at this end of the tunnel. There's no way we can get in there close to blow it up without getting eaten first." Alverd chewed his lips, thinking.

"The other end—"

"The same, Ambassador. Hippae, at both ends. As soon as I heard about the ones at this end, I sent an aircar to see what was happening at the other end. The driver counted about a hundred of the beasts out in the grasses, with about a score or so guarding the tunnel entrance. Assuming they stay that way, still we've no way to get to the tunnel."

"Drop something from above?"

"What? We have a few explosives but no bombs. No—what do you call them—detonators. There are people here who could *build* bombs, if we had the materials, or make the materials, possibly, if we had the time. You and your friend here say there may not be time. If we could get into the swamp forest far enough, if we could locate the tunnel from above, and if we had days or weeks to work, we could drill into it and flood it. We don't have days or weeks. We have hours. Maybe. They've laid their plans. Your wife found their declaration of war trampled into that cavern. We've seen it. Brother Mainoa here has told us what it means. That word says they plan to come in here and slaughter us all, just as the Arbai were slaughtered. Fun and games for the Hippae, they say."

"Where does the tunnel come to the surface?" Rigo asked.

Brother Mainoa said, "On a little island among the trees at the bottom of this slope. The forest is narrowest here, on the east side of the port. Two or three Terran miles through, perhaps. Elsewhere it's wider, but on this side the land slopes up on either side of the swamp and narrows it to a neck. There's where the damned migerers dug. That's where they must have been digging for years. The tunnel has to go deep enough to have a good rock layer above or it'd be full of water. Who knows how long it's taken them!"

"Can you reach the entrance to the tunnel? Can you physically get to it?" Rigo asked Alverd Bee.

"We could if the Hippae weren't there, yes. But not with them there. Not with them rampaging around, coming after us," Alverd ran his fingers through his hair, pulled his lips back to reveal his teeth, furrowed his brow. "We don't have any armor, any kind of combat vehicle. The little runners we use around town, they're like pea pods. We could use aircars to drive them back inside the tunnel, just inside, but then they'd come out again when any one of us tried to lay explosives."

"If we enticed them away, you could go in close and blow up the entrance, block it."

"Entice them away how?" Alverd turned to regard Rigo with an expression of half hope, half suspicion.

"I don't know yet. Could you do it?"

"Maybe. Probably."

"Then get ready to do it."

"God, it seems pretty hopeless." Alverd shook his head.

Rigo glared up at him. "Those of us here on Grass may end up being the last of humanity, Mayor Bee. Assume that we are. How would you prefer to die? Waiting or fighting?"

Alverd showed his teeth again and went away. Rigo turned to Roald Few. "If we entice the creatures out, some of them may go around us. Can you get everyone down into the winter quarters and barricade the entrances? Can you arm people? If you have nothing else, arm them with laser knives, the kind Persun gave me."

"People can be armed, yes. But I think we have a line of defense to use before we're forced into winter quarters, Ambassador. We have the barrier at Gom. Let's put weapons there, first. Weapons and some courageous people."

"That could work. Get everyone behind that line. Evacuate the Commercial District and Portside. Get everyone into the winter quarters except those who are going to fight. Be sure the ships in port are shut up tight. If we get out of this, we may need them later. Where's your power station?"

"Below the town, in winter quarters. They'll have to get us first before they can get the power station."

And likely to do so, Rigo thought. Likely to do so. After a few moments of silence passed, Roald left him to his thoughts, which were all of death and destruction. It was easy to speak of enticement. Less easy to think of a way to do it. He went to the window and leaned in it, not seeing the bustle and confusion outside, not seeing anything but his own bloody images.

"Ambassador?"

"Yes, Sebastian."

"There's a Green Brother here to see you. The high mucky-muck. Head of that whole bunch."

"What's his name?"

"Jhamlees Zoe. Says he has to talk with you."

"I can spare him about three minutes."

"I told him you were all busy. Told him what about, too. There's a room over there with nobody in it. I'll bring him there."

The Elder Brother was peremptory. "Ambassador, I need to know what you know about the plague." Though the room was chilly, sweat stood at the roots of his hair and ran down behind his ears.

"Indeed," said Rigo. "On what authority?" He stared at the odd face before him.

"Sanctity's authority. They sent you. They told me to keep in touch."

"I wasn't given that information. I was told no one on Grass was to know anything about my mission here." Rigo watched a drop of sweat roll down the man's tiny nose and hang at the tip.

"I received word from the new Hierarch, Cory Strange. His message came on the same ship that brought you."

Rigo smiled mirthlessly. "So there's a new Hierarch. I wish he had taken office earlier, Brother Zoe. If he had, I wouldn't be involved in this mess. Well, your authority doesn't matter! Even if you have none at all, it doesn't matter. I could refuse to tell you, but you could find it out from anyone out there in the hotel in ten minutes. There is no plague on Grass. Which means, at least by implication, there is a cure here, but we don't know where. Or what. Or how. We don't know if people coming here are cured, and if so, permanently or only for a time. The answer is probably here on Grass. That's all we know."

The Elder Brother pulled a handkerchief from the pocket of his robe and wiped his face with it. "I ... I ... that is, I appreciate your giving me this information, Ambassador." He turned and left the room, almost running.

Rigo started after him, then stopped as he saw a folded piece of paper lying on the floor. It had fallen from the Brother's pocket when he pulled out his handkerchief. Rigo picked it up, smoothed it to see if it was important enough to send after the man.

"My dear old friend Nods," it began in a clear, quirky handwriting, narrow and clear as print.

Rigo read it all the way through in mounting disbelief, then read it again. "There is plague here, as there is everywhere else. ... It is not our desire that information about the cure be widely disseminated ... wiping out the heathen to leave worlds for Sanctity alone to populate ..."

"Rigo."

He turned to find her at his side. "Marjorie! They said you were with Stella." She looked very pale. Very tired.

"I stopped in her room. I couldn't really see her. She's boxed up in a huge Heal-all. Rillibee stayed there with her."

"How is she?"

"The doctor says she hopes for recovery. She was careful not to say full recovery. I gather some things were destroyed." Marjorie rubbed at her eyes.

He stood stiffly away from her, aware she had not reproached him and yet feeling reproached. He did not want to talk about their daughter, not yet. The paper cracked in his hand, reminding him. "You must look at this. The head of the Friary came to see me to ask about the plague. This thing fell out of his pocket." He thrust the letter at her.

She read, read again, turning a white face toward him at last. "Sanctity won't spread the cure even if we find one?"

"You read what I read. The man who signed that letter is the new Hierarch. Uncle Carlos may have been an apostate, but he wouldn't have been capable of this!"

"What are we going to do?"

"All I've done so far is wish I hadn't told the man anything. I don't know what to do next!"

She touched him gently on the shoulder. "One thing at a time, Rigo. That's all any of us can do."

"Very well. One thing at a time. There's an immediate threat from the Hippae at the tunnel. We'll probably end up having to kill all those damned Hippae. . . ."

"No!" she folded the letter and put it carefully in a flapped pocket of her jacket. "No! We can't kill them all. Not even most. They become other creatures. Important creatures. The foxen, Rigo. They're an intelligent race. Even the Hippae themselves are intelligent, in a way."

"We're going to have to kill some," he objected, thinking that Marjorie did not sound like herself. "No matter what they become. If we don't, we die ourselves. We have to make Commons secure from them, or everyone here will die, just as the Arbai did."

"Kill some," she agreed. "Yes. It will be necessary. But the fewest possible. That's what I came to tell you. I heard what you said about enticing them away. We must use the horses."

At first he wanted to laugh. When he had heard what she had to say, he wanted to cry. He objected, and she looked at him in firm decision, unlike herself. He could offer nothing better. Moved from mockery to despair, he stumbled out of the Port Hotel to make the preparations she had convinced him were necessary. Aircars could not get into the forest where the tunnel ended. At any threat from above, the Hippae would merely retreat into the swamp or the tunnel or both, as they had retreated from the aircar when Rigo had been wounded. If men were to destroy the tunnel, the Hippae would have to be enticed away. The Hippae hated the horses. They would use the horses.

"At least . . ." he said to himself, trying to laugh, "at least I'll never have to wear those damned bon boots or those fat-bottomed pants again!"

Not long after dawn they assembled in the great hay barn where the horses were stalled. They met without many words. What words had been necessary had already been carried from each to each, and they were all tired of words. Tired of words, afraid of action, yet determined nonetheless.

Rigo, pale but resolute, was saddling El Dia Octavo. Marjorie had chosen Don Quixote. Tony took Blue Star, and Sylvan, Her Majesty. Irish Lass, they had regretfully decided, was not quick enough. That left only Millefiori.

"I wish we had someone," Sylvan said, looking at the mare.

"We do," said Marjorie. She was very calm. Father Sandoval had suggested he hear her confession and give her absolution. She had told him there wasn't time. She wasn't sure she wanted to confess anything. She wasn't sure anything needed confession. Even if it did, she didn't think she would, or could, share it, because she hadn't figured it out yet. "Tony, we do have someone."

"Who?" he asked in surprise.

"Me," said a voice from the door. She stood there in the light from outside, very pale, dressed in her bon riding coat and a hastily re-modeled set of trousers. Rowena.

Sylvan gasped. "Mother!"

"I'm glad I have a child left to call me mother," she said coldly. "Have you seen Dimity, Sylvan?"

He bowed his head, for a moment unable to reply. "I've seen her, yes. I know what condition she's in. But it won't help her for you to do this," he murmured. "You're not well, not healed. . . ."

"I promised Marjorie my help if ever she should need it. She needs it. And who else will do it? A few hours ago Marjorie took me out and taught me how. It's nothing. Nothing compared to what I did all my girlhood, most of my Obermum life, even after you were born, Sylvan. Oh, I've enough experience riding to get through this, I think. Have you seen Emmy, Sylvan? She looks almost like Dimity. Though the doctors say she will heal, in time."

"Father did that," he said expressionlessly.

"I don't blame Stavenger," she said. "Why blame a dead man? I blame the Hippae. I blame who's responsible, and that has always been the Hippae."

"The bons and the foxen both deserve a share of blame," Marjorie said hotly. "The foxen let it happen. They allowed themselves a comfortable retirement. They let happen what would. Then, when it all went wrong, they chose to discuss it philosophically. When men came here, they learned new ideas of guilt and redemption and talked about that. They engaged in great theological arguments. They sent Brother Mainoa to find out if they could be forgiven. They talked of original sin, collective guilt. They're still doing it. They haven't learned that being penitent sometimes does no good at all." She pulled on a girth so furiously that Don Quixote whuffed in complaint.

"Mother," Tony said. "Don't."

"Damn it, Tony, they could help. They're great, powerful beasts, evolved to be so to protect themselves from something even more terrible that was long ago extinct. But they no longer do anything. They think. They discuss. They don't decide."

"I thought when they helped you, they had decided," Rigo said. She had told him about the climbers.

"Aaah," she growled, "Aaah. One of them helped me. By himself. I don't think even he would be much help against a dozen of the Hippae. Not alone. The rest of them are all sitting up there in the trees, thinking about it. Wondering what they might do if they ever decide to do anything. I made a mistake back there in the Tree City when I didn't kill those two climbers. I set a good example. They're all too ready to take a good example if it means they won't have to do anything and then take responsibility for it."

For the tenth time she checked her lance, a strong spear of light metal alloy with a trigger mounted on it which would turn on a big laser knife, one of the kind they had given their workmen for harvesting grasses. The knife was mounted at the tip of the lance and was counterbalanced by a weight in the butt end. Roalds' workmen had built the lances as well as the bucklers each of them wore, a kind of light breastplate with a hook under the left arm to hold the end of the lance down. The breasts and flanks of the horses were armored in similar fashion, with light plates strung on tough fabric, to keep the weight down. Rigo had remembered the breastplates from armor he had seen, armor dating from a time when lances had been monstrously heavy and had had to be carried dead level.

It didn't matter how level these were carried. Actually they would do more damage if they wobbled and swung. If they moved about a good deal, it would do maximum damage at the greatest distance. Still, the hook would help to control them and keep the tips from dipping or catching on the ground—for at least one charge. Marjorie hadn't really intended a charge. She had suggested a quick sally to bring the Hippae away from the tunnel mouth in pursuit, and then a long flight which would keep the Hippae away long enough for Alverd's men to blow up the tunnel. Rigo, having seen what knives would do to Hippae flesh, had suggested improving their chances with weapons. So each of them had a lance plus a knife in a pocket. Armed or not, after one charge horses and riders would probably be fleeing for their lives. If they survived that long.

There had been time for only a brief mounted practice with the lances. "Remember, horses are faster on the flat," Rigo had reminded them. "The Hippae will be faster running uphill. It's the way they're made. More like big cats than like horses. Their legs can give more thrusting power going up than going forward. We'll run on the flat, along the hill, slightly upward, not straight up. If we can make it to the gate at the order station, they'll let us through."

The gate seemed an impossible goal as they left the great hay barn and rode across the paved area that separated it from the Port Hotel, around the empty hotel and hospital, to the slope leading down to the marsh. Each of them studied it, finding the route they would take when the Hippae came after them. If they went north they would shortly be trapped against the implacable ridge of Gom. Besides, that's where Alverd's men were, waiting to move down to the tunnel as soon as the Hippae were decoyed away. So they would go south where they could run for miles in a wide arc, all the way around the grazing land to the ruts south of Portside Road and along Portside Road to Grass Mountain Road and the gate. The ground was the same wherever they would run. A grassy, weedy slope, uncultivated, scattered with rock and the break-leg holes of small migerish creatures. The sun was in their eyes. The marsh lay in shadow at the bottom of the slope, just outside the first fringe of trees. The Hippae were hidden. From time to time, the sound of their howling came up the hill. No one knew what they were waiting for.

"Ready?" asked Rigo.

Silence. He looked to either side to see them nodding, ready, unwilling to break the quiet with words. He kneed El Dia Octavo into a steady walk down the slope.

17

Marjorie thought: It always comes down to something like this, doesn't it. No matter what our consciences say, no matter how much doctrine we've been taught, no matter how many ethical considerations we've chewed and swallowed and tried to digest, it always comes down to us arming ourselves with weapons as deadly as we can manage and going out into combat. . . .

I should be frightened but it doesn't feel much different from competition, really. A high wall. Always the possibility of a fall, even a bad fall, even getting killed. Not the safest sport in the world. Still, it's only time and energy and staying on and trusting the horse. Thinking with the horse, not for him. . . .

I really don't have to think about anything except killing as many of them as I can. Killing them, and not worrying about the ethics until later. Forget that every Hippae at the bottom of the hill has the potential of becoming a foxen. A being more intelligent than I am. Every Hippae I kill or maim means one less like Him. Don't think about Him. Unthink Him. The whole thing was delirium, that's all. Imagination.

Where's the justice in this? If man had never come to Grass, nothing like this would have happened. If man and Arbai had never come. If no one ever went anywhere, nothing like this would happen. . . .

Except that it would. Some wild, malevolent virus would have found its way to us stay-at-homes. Something like the Hippae would come screaming through our windows, breaking down our doors, killing and raping and mutilating us.

Oh, Lord, I have been such a good girl! I have always attended mass, always gone to confession, always done my penance. I've done charity work. I've loved and cared for my children, no matter how hard they made it. I've tried my damnedest to love my husband. I thought about killing myself, but I repented that. I've lived a very acceptable, proper life at home, there. . . .

Piss on it.

I'd rather be here. Even if I die, I'd rather be here. If there's anything important for a very small being to do, it's fighting the plague. That's first. We've got to buy time to find the answer. The only thing that matters now is the plague. We've got to find the cure and make sure that Sanctity doesn't get it before someone else does. And if we do that, then . . . then there's something else. Oh, God, let Him talk to me. I want Him to talk to me.

Rigo thought: This damned lance doesn't balance right. It needs to be heavier at the butt so it'll swing with less strength. Maybe it's just that I feel lousy. Sick, weak. I should still be back there in a chair letting somebody put a blanket over my legs. Instead, I'm here. Where is here? How the hell did I get here? Well, no one forced me. I'm the only one of us who's ever fought a Hippae. I'm the only one who knows where to hit them. Legs first. Jaws second. Cut their legs out, their jaws off, let the damned, stinking things die.

I'm not healed yet. My legs don't feel right. My thighs feel soggy, like wet sponges. As though there were no muscle there. Someone may die out here today. Maybe me. Better me than Marjorie or Tony. They haven't played the fool, the way I have.

But if it's me, she'll be free. Free to do whatever she likes, go to whomever she likes. Sylvan. Look at him. Never ridden a horse before, but he looks like he was born riding. Well, it's not that different. The strengths are the same; legs, back.

If I get killed, will she go to him?

If she does, is it any worse than my having Eugenie? Poor Eugenie. Damn. I wish they'd saved her. Lovely Eugenie. Nothing in her head but how to make things pretty and taste good and smell good and feel good. No high aspirations. No high-minded innocence to offend against. No modesty to invade. No expectations to fall short of. No serious thoughts at all. Still, she deserved better than to die like that.

If she died. God. Maybe she didn't. Maybe the hounds took her, the Hippae took her, the way they took Stella. . . .

Don't think of that! The only thing that matters now is the plague. We've got to save Commons from being overrun, just for a while, until someone can come up with the answer. We will, will come up with an answer. Mankind will come up with an answer! Something always saves, us, just in the nick of time. God will intervene. There'll be time. Marjorie will turn back to me. She always has. Always, no matter what happens. . . .

Sylvan thought: You have to give him credit. Not a day out of bed, half killed by the mounts, and here he is. He keeps looking at me, letting his eyes slide across me. I know what he's thinking. If he gets killed, I get Marjorie. Fool. If he gets killed, Marjorie does what she pleases, and that doesn't include me. I don't know why. I've never had trouble with any woman I've ever wanted, but I'm no good with her. I'm the real fool. I thought she was like one of us. What's the Terran word? Pleasure-seeking. Hedonistic. Well, what else have we had to think of but pleasure? The damned Hippae haven't let us think of anything else. They've tapped into us and enslaved us and kept us right where they wanted us. . . .

Look at Marjorie! Like a queen! Regal and tall and rides that thing as though she were part of it. That thing! Ha-ha. Horse. Horse. They make soft noises when you pat them and they look at you kindly when you get on. This one, Her Majesty, she does what I ask her to. It's almost like loving a woman. Horse. Not Hippae.

Tony's watching me, too. He doesn't like me. I thought at first it was because of Marjorie, but that's not it. I offend him somehow. My manner. My bon manner. Maybe it was because I didn't take their plague seriously. I didn't know. Did I even think it mattered whether there was anything left of humanity, elsewhere? That's what the Hippae thought. They didn't care. If they thought it, we thought it. How long have they been doing our thinking for us? They don't want there to be another intelligent race. And they won't believe that they themselves become another intelligent race. Foxen. What was it Brother Mainoa said? We never believe we'll get old. The Hippae don't know what they have in them to be. They've stopped themselves, half grown. They've stopped themselves at adolescence. Brutal time, that. Hateful time. Not a child. Not grown. Full of strength and fury and no place to put it....

Well, they stopped us there, too. Marjorie looks at me the way she looks at Tony. As though I'm a boy. And when have I ever had the chance to be anything else....

Mother. Mother. You shouldn't be out here at all. Oh, Mother, do you really think this pays back for Dimity....

Tony thought: Let's get this over with and go home. If I die, I die, but if I don't die, let me go home. Let's leave these people, these crazy bons, let's go! Let me go through this hour, two hours, whatever it takes, then we'll go, I'll go, somehow. Let's get it over with. If I die ...

Rowena thought: Dimity. For Dimity. For Emmy. For Stavenger. For my other children, dead so long ago I've almost forgotten their names. For all of you. For all of us.

Sylvan. Oh, Sylvan. Whatever happens, remember that I love you, I love you all....

Don Quixote thought: She is riding. Trust her. Trust what she does. And listen, all of you. Listen for the voices.

At the foot of the hill they were separated from the Hippae at the tunnel entrance only by a few deep pools and a screen of foliage. Only Rigo rode all the way down, measuring the distance at a mental gallop. Then he turned back, summoning the others to a line that seemed an appropriate distance from the bottom. They wanted the slope of the hill to aid them, but there had to be space to turn along the hillside without being forced into the sucking pools at its foot. Silently Rigo checked his lance while the others did likewise, then began rattling the butt of his lance on his buckler, screaming insults at the same time. "Hippae fools. Mock horses. Stupid beasts." Not that they understood what he was saying, but they could pick the intent up from his mind.

"Genocides," shrieked Marjorie at the top of her lungs. "Ingrates! Malicious beasts! Curs!"

"Oh, wah, wah, wah, wah," screamed Tony, making as much noise as he could but incapable of thinking words.

"For Dimity," cried Rowena. "For Dimity, Dimity, Dimity."

"Cowards," trumpeted Sylvan. "Cowards. Animals. Peepers. Migerers. Muddy migerers with no more honor than a mole."

The Hippae came out of the screening brush in a rush, then stopped while those on the hill fell silent. The humans had expected Hippae. They had not expected them to have riders. Foremost among them was a great gray mount bearing someone they all knew on its back.

"Shevlok," breathed Rowena. "Oh, for the love of God, my son."

"It's not Shevlok," Sylvan spat at her. "Look at his face."

The face was a mask, empty as a broken bottle. There was nothing there. "You're fighting the beasts, not the riders," trumpeted Rigo. "Remember that. The mounts, not the riders!" He kneed El Dia Octavo into a trot. Behind him the others did likewise, falling into a diagonal line so that each would have room to charge and turn without endangering the ones behind.

Rigo counted as he rode. There were ten of the Hippae. The one bearing Shevlok's body was to the fore with three others beyond to Rigo's right. Well and good. The one in front would take the brunt, and better Rigo to attack that one than to expect the bon Damfels to do it. The other Hippae riders—who were they? He risked a quick glance. Lancel bon Laupmon. Three of the bon Maukerdens: Dimoth, Vince, and one whose name he had forgotten. He didn't know any of the others, or he didn't recognize them. The faces didn't look like faces at all. They had been transfigured into something merely symbolic. Something wholly possessed.

He was only a few feet from them when he felt them pushing at his mind, erasing his intent. He howled, the howl driving them out, away. He flicked the trigger to turn on the knife and signaled Octavo for a slow, collected canter. The gray Hippae reared high, and Octavo ran toward it, then turned to the right without hesitation as Rigo clipped off its front feet with the fiery lance. It hadn't expected that!

One. One, screaming, but down!

Octavo stretched his stride and galloped along the hillside, running swiftly as three of the Hippae came up from the swamp and tried to intercept him from the left. Cursing, Rigo lifted the tip of the lance from under his left arm, brought it across and anchored it in his right armpit, then stretched out his left arm to hold the lance perpendicular to the line of Octavo's movement. The humming flame caught the first interceptor low across its shoulders. Leg muscles severed; it fell as the other two screamed and turned away.

Two.

Sylvan was behind him, Her Majesty flying in the face of the Hippae, swift as a bird. He saw Rigo shift the lance and shifted his own almost simultaneously. The object was to get the creatures moving in pursuit, he reminded himself. Not necessarily to kill them yet. Now, if possible; eventually, yes, but not necessarily now. He jabbed the lance toward a green-mottled Hippae and heard it bellow in angry pain. Then he was past. He cast a quick glance across his shoulder and saw the green monster coming after him. Good. Well and good. He pointing the lance in the direction he was moving and leaned forward to whisper soft words in Her Majesty's ear. They were words he had whispered to lovers in time past. He saw nothing incongruous in urging Her Majesty on with them now.

Rowena was behind Sylvan, copying his tactics a little too late to make the wide turn he had made. It was only when her lance had chopped into the throat of a shrieking mud-colored creature that she remembered they had to flee. Millefiori had already decided it was time. Wheeling on her hind legs, she set out in pursuit of the other two while the mud-colored monster staggered behind them, screaming, being rapidly outdistanced by two other, uninjured Hippae.

Three, Marjorie thought to herself. Three down. Four in pursuit of the three horses, two of them at least slightly wounded. Three waiting for her, and for Tony. Little Tony. White-faced. The way he always got when he rode. Fearful. Not thinking about it.

"Anthony!" she screamed in his ear, "Follow me!"

She thumbed the lance on, sighted a line of travel that would take her in front of two of the remaining Hippae. The third one was hanging back, as though for an ambush. "Watch that one," she cried, pointing to the mottled wine-colored beast half screened by the trees.

Tony cried something in answer, she couldn't tell what. Then Quixote was crossing the path of the two, both charging at her, necks twisted to one side to bring the barbs to bear. She flipped the lance to her left as the others had done and raked them with the blade. Screams. Bellows. She turned Quixote up the hill and around.

Tony. He was facing the final Hippae, his lance dipping and swirling, the beast staying well back, out of range. Tony was too close. If he turned to flee, the other would have him!

She looked behind her. The two she had touched were not badly hurt. Surprised into inaction for the moment, but not badly hurt. She had touched their necks, not their legs. She pulled Quixote up and back, wheeling on his hind legs. "Come on," she cried to Quixote, riding directly at the monster confronting Tony. Beyond the beast was a patch of level ground.

Her heart was hammering so loudly that she could hear only it, nothing else, a pulse in her ears that drowned out the fall of hooves. She took the lance in her left hand, held it loosely. They came closer. "We're going to jump," she told Quixote. "We're going to jump over him, boy. Over him." Then there was no time to say anything. Quixote's haunches gathered under him; they were high, high over the monster's back and the lance was pointed down, down and back, then they had landed on the other side.

They were on a tiny island, only large enough for Quixote to stop on, stop and wheel and jump once more, back over the pool to the solid hillside. Tony was there, looking stupidly downward at the recumbent, slavering Hippae with the severed spine while two wounded ones stalked toward him.

Four.

"Anthony!" she cried as she went past. "Come, Blue Star!"

Horse heard her if rider did not. Quixote lunged up the hill, faster than the wounded Hippae, with Blue Star close behind. When they had gained a little distance, Marjorie turned to the south. Blue Star was even with her. She risked a look at Tony. He looked almost like Shevlok, his face white and expressionless. She drove Quixote at Blue Star's side so that they raced only inches apart, then leaned out and slapped Tony with her glove, and again.

He came to himself with a start, tears filling his eyes. "I couldn't think," he cried. "It got into me and didn't let me think."

"Don't let it!" she demanded. "Yell. Scream. Call it dirty names, but don't let it!"

Perhaps a half mile ahead of them on the hillside, Octavo and the two mares raced side by side with four of the Hippae in pursuit.

"Now," Marjorie cried, pointing ahead and to the right. "We're going to intercept them."

She leaned forward. Rigo, Sylvan, and Rowena were riding on the level line of the hill, around it, not up it. The full circuit of the sloping ground, back to the gate, would take two or three hours, riding at top speed the whole way. If she and Tony went slightly uphill and to the west, they should intercept the others a bit past the southernmost point of their arc. Quixote and Blue Star stretched out, galloping side by side like twins joined at the heart. Behind them came the two wounded Hippae, still screaming, still with their blank-faced riders aboard. They were not fast enough to be an immediate threat, but the laser knife had cauterized as it cut, so they were not being greatly weakened by blood loss, either.

"They're still trying to get into my head," Tony called. "So I'm thinking about going home."

She smiled at him, nodded encouragingly. Whatever worked. She herself could not feel them at all. She felt something, but not Hippae. Something else. Someone else.

"You didn't kill your bad individuals," Someone commented, quietly curious. "Why are you killing ours?"

"Because I could tie mine up and keep them from hurting anyone," she replied. "I can't do that with these creatures."

"You could figure something out," the voice suggested.

"No!" she said, angrily. "Everyone always says that. It isn't true. If you can figure something out, you do. If you don't, it's because you can't. Can't because you don't have the time, or the money, or the material. Can't because there isn't any way or any time or you're not smart enough."

A thought very like a sigh. A touch, like a caress.

"Damn it," she cried aloud. "Can't you see that theoretical answers are no answers at all! It has to be something you can *do*!"

Shocked silence. Tony was staring at her. "What was that?" he cried.

"Nothing," she muttered, concentrating on riding. "Nothing at all." The ground fled by beneath them. The leather of their saddles creaked.

Occasional bunches of tall grass whipped at them. Brush materialized before the horses' feet. Rocks and holes and hollows were there, were jumped, were gone. Behind them the wounded pair came on, howling. Time went by, swift but interminable. Time past was nothing, no matter how long. Time ahead was everything, no matter how brief. Tony's eyes were glazed with his effort to keep the Hippae from commanding him. Marjorie sat quietly, helping Quixote by her quiet. He would do all he could do for her without her bothering him. The arc of the hill against the sky seemed no closer, no matter how long they rode.

And then at last it was there. They came upon the height to see Rigo and the others to the south below them, coming around toward them to make the arc which would bring them back along the west side of the long hill on which Commons was built. The four Hippae still pursued Rigo and the other two riders, more closely than before. "Come on, Quixote," she cried, urging him down, wanting to let Rigo know she was there but judging the distance too great for him to hear her yet.

She looked at the point where the two lines of travel would intersect, laid her body along Quixote's neck, and urged him on. When they had halved the distance, she yodeled, seeing three heads come up.

Rigo looked over his shoulder, apprehending what Marjorie intended. She could come in behind the four Hippae pursuing Rigo, Rowena, and Sylvan. Rigo and the others could then turn and take them from the front while Marjorie and Tony attacked from behind. Which would have been an acceptable tactic except for the two other Hippae, just now coming over the hill behind Marjorie and Tony. Their presence would put her between two groups of them. He waved, pointing behind her.

She turned, saw what was coming, and cursed. She had thought the horses could outdistance the wounded beasts, but the Hippae had kept pace. That made the odds six Hippae to five humans. Even though four of the Hippae were slightly wounded, it wasn't good. Not good enough.

From the east came a great *crump*ing sound, a concussion of air, like thunder. The ground shivered. The two Hippae on the hill screamed in rage, realizing before Marjorie did what had happened. Alverd Bee's men had blown up the tunnel. *The* tunnel. For the first time, Marjorie realized that the tunnel had been too narrow and low to allow a sudden, full-scale invasion. If the Hippae had been planning their attack for long, there were probably other tunnels. There was that great trail out there in the grass. There had to be other tunnels. . . .

"We're looking," said Someone. "We haven't found any others yet." Which didn't mean there weren't any.

"Are you going to help?" she demanded. "Are you going to let us get killed doing this all by ourselves?"

There was no answer.

Rigo had heard the explosion. Now he leaned over Octavo's neck and urged him forward. Her Majesty and Millefiori fled along behind him, moving like the wind, opening the distance between them and the Hippae.

Marjorie turned more to the north. It would do no good to come up behind the other riders. Now they had simply to outrun their pursuers. Get to the stony ridges of Gom, get to the gate.

"If it were your people, I'd try to help," said Marjorie.

"Humans have been helping the Hippae kill foxen," came the answer, snappishly, not at all allusively, in clear words. Not the familiar voice, another one. "All along."

"You know damned well that's not so," she cried. "Humans have been *used* by Hippae to kill foxen. That's entirely different." At least partly a lie, too. Humans had been all too willing to lend themselves to that Hunt.

No answer.

They ran. Quixote was lathered, breathing harshly. It had been a long hill and the armor was heavy. Marjorie held the reins in her teeth, took her knife from her pocket, and cut the straps that held the armor, one around Quixote's breast, two on each side. The plates dropped off and the horse made a noise that sounded like a prayer. Tony saw what she was doing and did likewise.

Rigo had been watching. He nodded and called to the other two. Sylvan followed suit, as did Rigo himself. Rowena cried out in dismay. She had no knife. She had come last, and no one had thought to give her one.

As though distracted by this cry, Millefiori stumbled and fell. Rowena went rolling away, coming up wild-eyed. Then she was up, running toward the horse, mounting all in one fluid motion as Millefiori struggled to her feet, limping. Then the mare was running again, though awkwardly, slowly, with a wide space opening between Rowena and the others.

Sylvan saw. He turned Her Majesty and made a tight circle which brought him to his mother's side. He reached out, pulled her onto the saddle before him. Now Her Majesty was carrying double. She slowed. Millefiori slowed. Sylvan edged back to give his mother room. One of the Hippae leapt forward with stunning speed and gaping jaws, snatching him from Her Majesty's back. Another ran even with Millefiori, ready to leap. Rowena, face like death and mouth wide with an unheard howl, rode on.

Sylvan had vanished. Where he had been was nothing, no movement. Marjorie screamed in anger and pain, tears streaking her face. "I'll begin by burning the swamp forest. It won't burn easily, but we'll do it somehow. Then the grasses, all of them. That will take care of the plague and the Hippae. There'll be no more Hippae."

"What about us?" voices cried.

"What about you?" she snarled. "If you're no help, you're no help. You don't care about us. Why should we care about you?"

A whine. A snarl. A slap, as from one being to another being. Then, suddenly, there was something behind Millefiori, rising to confront the approaching Hippae. Mauve and plum and purple, a lash of tail and ripple of shoulders, a moving mirage of trembling air.

"If He has to do it alone," Marjorie cried, "I'll still burn the forest, even if I have to do it by myself."

"The ones behind us are gaining," Tony called. "Blue Star's exhausted."

"We're all exhausted," she cried, tears running down her face. Where Sylvan had been was a tumult of beasts. "Turn more toward the road." She looked behind her, then up at the sun. They'd been running for well over an hour. Perhaps two. Thirty miles, more or less, all of it over rough ground and a lot of it uphill. With another twelve or fifteen miles to cover before they got back to the gate. "If I die out here," she threatened, "my family will burn the forest, I swear to God they will."

"What's going on down there?" cried Tony. "The Hippae have stopped."

They had stopped. Stopped, turned, were running away. Not back the way they had come, unfortunately. Uphill. Toward Marjorie. "Foxen," Marjorie cried. "Not quite where I would have wanted them, but better than nothing, I suppose."

She was trying to feel philosphical about dying, not managing it, trying not be frightened, and not managing that, either. "Tony, we have to take out the two behind us before those others reach us."

He turned a stricken face upon her.

"We have to! If the other four reach us first, we'll have them all around us."

He nodded, biting his lip. She saw blood there, the only color in his face.

"Turn on your lance."

He'd forgotten about it. He thumbed it on, looking at the humming blade almost as though hypnotized.

"Tony! Pay attention." She motioned, showing him how she wanted him to circle—the two of them wide, in opposite directions, coming back to hit the wounded Hippae from both sides.

They broke from one another, circled tightly, and were running back toward the pursuing monsters before the Hippae understood what was happening. Then they, too, broke, one headed for each of the horses. Marjorie tried to forget about her son, concentrate on what she was doing. Lance well out in front, the blaze of its blade apparent even in the light of day.

There was a roar above her. She looked up to see Asmir Tanlig and Roald Few beckoning from an aircar, screaming at her. She lip-read. "We'll pick you up, pick you up."

Leave Quixote and Blue Star to face these beasts alone! She shook her head, waved them off, no. Only when the car rose did she realize what she had done. Oh, God, how silly. How silly. And yet . . .

The Hippae was before her, circling just out of reach, darting forward, then back. He could maneuver more quickly than Quixote could. Quixote kept his head toward the beast, dancing, as though he wore ballet shoes, as though he stood on tiptoe. Behind her she heard Tony yell. She didn't dare look. Again dance, dance. Then Quixote charged. She hadn't signaled him to do it. He simply did it. There was an opening, the lance found it, and they were dancing away again while the Hippae sagged before them, yammering at the sky, its neck half cut through.

Five, her mind exulted as she tried to find Tony. *Five*.

Six was standing over her son while Blue Star fled toward the distant gate as though she knew where it was, as though she had been told it meant safety. Great jaws wide, the crouching Hippae howled at the boy, ready to take off his face in one huge bite. Quixote raced forward, screaming. . . .

There was a furry blur on the Hippae's back. Another between the jaws and the boy. Another at its haunches, clawing at it. Three foxen. The screaming battle tumbled to one side and rolled toward the hill.

Tony lay still.

She dismounted and struggled to get him onto Quixote's back. The horse knelt to receive him, again without a signal to do so. Then Marjorie was up once more, holding her son before her, and they were running the way Blue Star had gone. Not really running. Moving, at least.

Down the hill, other foxen had taken on the other Hippae. Rowena was just behind Rigo. Millefiori came behind, limping badly.

"Now," thought Marjorie. "Now bring out your damned aircar or airtruck or what-have-you. Now."

And it was there, only a short distance from them all, with Persun Pollut driving it and Sebastian Mechanic dropping out a ramp for the horses.

"I knew you wouldn't leave the horses," Persun called as they came aboard. "I told Asmir you wouldn't, but Roald said you wouldn't be that silly."

Silly, she said to herself. Silly. As though that were the answer to a problem that had bothered her for a very long time. In her mind she sensed an enormous, unqualified approval.

Headquarters had been set up in the order station under James Jellico's watchful eye. A dozen eager volunteers offered to rub down the horses. Aside from Millefiori's bad leg they seemed to be all right. In one corner Dr. Bergrem was looking at Rowena with an expression of concern. Rowena had broken something in that fall. Her shoulder, maybe. Something inside her had broken as well. She sat still and white-faced, unresponsive. When Marjorie went to her, she was whispering Sylvan's name, over and over.

"We found him," Marjorie said. "We went out and found him, Rowena."

"What?" she asked. "How?"

"He's dead, Rowena. The fall broke his neck. They didn't touch him."

"He's not . . . oh, he's not—"

"No, Rowena," she cried. "He's not. We brought his body back to be buried."

She returned to Tony, who was sitting white-faced in a corner, slowly coming to himself. Beyond him she saw Brother Mainoa seated at the tell-me. Marjorie fumbled awkwardly at her pocket flap with hands that seemed frozen from their long grip upon lance and reins.

Her fingers were made of wood. Eventually she got the pocket open and the letter out.

She laid it before Brother Mainoa. "I think this should be sent to Semling," she said.

He read it, his face turning gray as the sense of it reached him. "Ah ... ah," he murmured. "Ah, yes ... but—"

"But?"

He rubbed his forehead, started to speak, stopped to think again. "If you spread this around now, there will be panic, rebellions, riots. Then, if we find a cure, the authorities will be so occupied with maintaining order, they won't be able to disseminate the cure. This letter shouldn't be made public until there's a cure, Marjorie."

"All right," she agreed. "But I'm concerned that it might not get out at all if we wait. Who knows what those—"

"Devils," he offered. "Sanctified devils. The Hierarch and his retinue."

"It's your faith. I didn't want to. . . ."

"It's what I was born to," he admitted. "What I was given to. That's not the same thing. No. This was written by someone unworthy of any faith, Marjorie."

She threw up her hands. "You know what I'm saying, Brother. What's-his-name, Zoe, may miss this letter at any time. May come looking for it. May take steps to stop its getting out."

"We'll make copies," Brother Mainoa offered. "Merely sending the text off-planet wouldn't do. The Hierarch could disclaim any such. Copies in his own hand, that's what's needed. And since this says the Hierarch is on his way here, we should get someone to take copies off-planet. There's a Semling freighter in port, ready to leave. The *Star-Lily*."

"How long to the nearest ... how long to Semling?"

"Two weeks, Grassian time."

"Thirty days," she murmured. "How wonderful if we could have a cure by then."

"We who?"

"The doctor here. She's remarkable, Brother Mainoa. She studied on Semling. She studied on Repentance. She's got some young helpers just back from school. She got interested in immunology, because of something she found here on Grass when she was a girl."

"Something?"

"A— I'm no scientist. She wrote a book about the stuff. It has a long name I've forgotten. It's a nutrient. Something our cells have to have in order to grow and reproduce. And here on Grass it exists in two forms, the usual one and one that's inverted. Nowhere else. Only here."

"When did she tell you this?"

"When I was visiting Stella. She was only talking to distract me, but she sounded so competent it gave me hope, some hope." She took the letter from him, stared at it, still finding it hard to believe. "I suppose you're right about this. If we don't find a cure, what difference does it make whether people know? But if we do? Then people need to know about this letter. People are entitled to know what Sanctity intended to do!"

"All right, Marjorie. We'll send copies off-planet, just in case. The *Star-Lily* still plans to leave tomorrow. Now that the tunnel is blown up, we'll ask Alverd Bee to get the crew and the warehousemen back over to the port to get it ready to lift."

"Tony," she said. "We'll send Tony." It would be a good idea to send Tony. He was too vulnerable to the Hippae. She had to get him away before he was tainted by them, as Stella was. Except . . . there might be plague on Semling. Which risk was greater? All risks were equal. All were life or death. "Tell the crew to be careful. There must be another tunnel. Why else that great Hippae trail leading here!"

He nodded, patting her hand. "If the men keep someone on watch and an aircar or two standing by, they should be safe enough. And, just in case the Hierarch starts looking for me—which he may do, if Zoe tells him about me—I'll hide myself away somewhere. I'll go back to the forest, that's what. Rillibee will come along to take care of me. If they come looking for me, tell them I went back into the forest. If they come looking for the letter, you never saw it. Rigo never saw it. When a cure is found, Tony will see that the letter is widely disseminated, just as the cure is."

Rillibee was beside them. "I'll go," he said. "I'll get Brother Mainoa up in a tree somewhere, and we'll wait until one of the foxen comes to get us."

She found herself trying to think of an excuse why she should go herself. She wanted to go herself. She wanted to be there, among the trees, not here with all these people. She looked around, seeking some reason, and turned back to find Rillibee already gone.

Damn. She felt unutterably sad but forbade herself to cry. "Does everyone accept that there's probably another tunnel?" she asked Roald Few, trying to distract herself.

"Oh, yes," Roald said. "Probably more than one. Probably not finished yet, or they'd be all over us."

"A tunnel could just as easily come in on this side of the wall," she whispered, looking around to be sure that no one else heard her. "It could come out below the town. Have you thought of that?"

Roald nodded wearily. "Lady Westriding, we've thought of that and of three or four other things that would be equally dreadful. People are beginning to talk about the winter quarters, how long they could hold them against a Hippae assault."

"So, if the tunnel isn't finished, what will the Hippae do next?"

"Burn the estancias," he replied. "Just as they did Opal Hill. That's one of the things we figured out while you were out there encitin' the Hippae. We all agreed. Given their nature, if they can't get in here yet, they'll start fires."

"Has anyone warned the estancias?"

He buried his head in his hands. "Nobody's had time! And who are they going to listen to? Obermum bon Damfels? They might believe her. They certainly won't believe me."

Marjorie went away to make copies of the letter, to get Tony onto the *Star-Lily*, and to find Rowena.

No one answered the tell-me at Klive. At the bon Laupmons', someone answered but declined to respond either to the information that Taronce had survived or that the estancia should be evacuated. At Stane, however, after learning that both Dimoth and Vince were dead, Geraldria bon Maukerden begged Rowena to send whatever help would come from Commoner Town to evacuate the house and village. Mayor Bee already had all available aircars and trucks going to all the villages, the bon Damfels village included.

"The damned bons can char on their own griddle if they want to," he snarled. "But we'll get our village people out."

It was too late to get them out of Klive. Even before the tunnel had been blown up, Hippae had attacked Klive. There were no people left alive there, not in the estancia, not in the village, except one man, Figor, found wandering among the charred houses, a laser knife in his hands.

When she heard the news, Rowena wept, wiping the tears away with her left hand. The right arm and shoulder were in a Heal-all, mending. "Emmy's here," she said. "Amy's here. Shevlok's here, alive in a way. Figor will be all right. But oh, I grieve for Sylvan. And my cousins. And old Aunt Jem."

No one had time to grieve with her. There had been a trail leading from Klive to the swamp forest. All the Hippae on Grass seemed to be congregating there.

The evacuation fleet shuttled back and forth across the prairies, continuing even after fires sprung up at Stane and at Jorum, the estancia of the bon Bindersen's. Obermun Kahrl and Obermum Lisian refused to leave the bon Bindersen estancia, but their children, Traven and Maude, left willingly enough with the people of the village and many others from the big house.

At the bon Haunser place, Eric joined the evacuees along with Jason, the Obermun's son. Felitia had died outside the bon Laupmon walls, during what Rigo had come to remember as "The Joust."

The bon Laupmon place was totally destroyed before the cars arrived, though the commoners had cut a fire break around the village and, armed with harvesting knives, were standing fast with their live-stock. At the bon Smaerloks', the drivers were told that the bons had gone hunting with the bon Tanligs. All of them, even the old folks. A vast crowd of hounds and mounts had showed up early on Hunt morning, and every occupant of the estancias had gone a-hunting. The only people left in the estancias were children. The children and the villagers were evacuated; a wide Hippae trail led from the estancias toward Commons.

The order station became the nerve center for Commons. From there one could see what went on at the port and receive messages from approaching ships. From there one could direct the defenses if Hippae came in through some other tunnel.

In the winter quarters below the order station a makeshift hospital was set up to house Rowena, Stella, Emmy, Shevlok, Figor, and a dozen others who had been badly injured before or during the evacuation. People with only superficial injuries were treated and dismissed. When the last of them had been attended to, Lees Bergrem insisted upon going back through the gates to the hospital with several of her assistants.

"Whether there's another tunnel or not, the equipment I need is at the hospital," she told Marjorie. "I may be in a position to do more about this plague thing than anyone else, but I have to get to my equipment. I can't let those Hippae keep me away."

"Do you have any ideas? Any line of attack?" Marjorie asked.

"Nothing. Not yet. I have a few ideas, but I'm not really onto a line of inquiry at this point!" She shook off Jelly's remonstrances and went, her helpers with her, all of them laden with food and drink and various esoteric supplies they had carried in when the Commercial District had been evacuated.

There was nothing else Marjorie could do. Tony was sleeping in the order station dormitory, ready to leave when the *Star-Lily* left—a matter of hours. Mainoa and Rillibee were in the forest. Persun and Sebastian were helping Mayor Bee get the evacuees settled and fortify the winter quarters.

There was nothing more that Marjorie could do. "Roald's offered us a room at his place in town," she told Rigo. "His wife, Kinny, is fixing us some supper. We can walk down. . . ."

He tottered to his feet with an apologetic grimace. "I'm not sure I can walk."

Persun overheard this and came forward. "I've got a little runner outside, sir. Room enough for you and Lady Westriding, if you don't mind being crowded. I have to go down to town anyhow."

Rigo smiled his thanks, and they rode in exhausted quiet to the Few summer quarters.

Kinny, with tears in her eyes, led them to a suite of comfortable rooms below. "We only lost one village," she said, weeping. "Only one out of seven. But everybody in town was related to someone there. Everyone's mourning Klive."

Marjorie herself could mourn Klive, mourn the waste of it.

Kinny went on, shaking her head in amazed, pained annoyance. "Those bons, already trying to take over, did you know?"

"No," said Rigo. "How do you mean, take over?"

"Oh, Ambassador, you wouldn't believe— Well now, let's see. It's Eric, brother to the dead Obermun Jerril bon Haunser, and Jason, Jerril's son. And it's Taronce bon Laupmon, nephew to Obermun Lancel that died, and Traven, that's the dead Obermun bon Bindersen's brother. The four of them. They've decided to take over Commons, for the time being." She laughed, angry and amused, both at once. "They told Roald they had elected themselves a council of four to run things. Roald and Alverd are tryin' to explain things to 'em. Not easy. Not with them."

"Did they think you would all take orders from them?" Rigo asked, amazed.

"They really did. Yes. Well, we always pretended to, when we went out to the estancias, you know. It pleased the bons, and it didn't do us any harm. But there's too much at stake here in Commons to let them meddle with it. They're so ignorant." She made a face and asked them if they were ready to eat something.

"I think so." Marjorie said with a sigh. "I can't remember when the last meal I had was. In the Tree City, I think."

"Oh, I want to hear about that! You folks take your time washing up, and supper'll be ready when you come up."

Kinny served them in the kitchen while she chattered about the Tree City and a dozen other things, interrupting herself to cry occasionally, then interrupting her tears to laugh about something she remembered. It was only when they had eaten and were sitting over cups of tea that she remembered. "Oh, Roald called while you were down below. He told me to tell you. There's a big ship coming in tomorrow. From Sanctity. Roald says the big high mucky-muck himself is on it. The what-do-you-call-him. The Hierarch."

"Is he going to let it orbit?" Rigo asked, his stomach clenching as he thought what such an arrival might mean.

Kinny shook her head. "Roald said tell you he doesn't want to, nor Mayor Bee. Question is, how would you keep it from sittin' up there if it wants to?"

Marjorie's imagination had leapt ahead, far ahead. "Rigo, we have to get Dr. Bergrem away from the hospital. It's right by the port. If that ship comes down. If Sanctity finds out what she's working on . . ."

He groaned as he got to his feet. "Let's go talk to Alverd Bee once more."

"What is 'Galaxy class'?" Mayor Bee wanted to know.

"It's a Sanctity ship," one of the port controllers said. "Called the *Israfel*. I've never seen one like it."

They were in the winter quarters of the order station. From the adjacent rooms came the moans of someone wounded and the wail of frightened babies. Someone bustled down the hall and the moans ceased. The babies went on crying.

The man at the tell-me paid no attention. "Warship," he said, staring at a diagram on the screen. "Sanctity navy. Big son-of-a-hound."

"It's a troop carrier," said Rigo, staring narrow-eyed across the operator's shoulder at the diagram. "And a battleship. Old. All their vessels are old."

"No matter how old, it carries a thousand men," the port controller agreed. "With real combat weapons."

"Dr. Bergrem has to go," Marjorie said. "On the *Star-Lily*. She can't stay here."

"Dr. Bergrem doesn't intend to go anywhere," said the woman's voice from behind them. "What is all this?"

The doctor divested herself of her cloak and sat down as though to stay awhile. "I was on my way into town to pick up some book I need, and I hear my name being taken in vain."

"Sanctity's new Hierarch is about to arrive," Marjorie told her. "Cory Strange. You don't want to be here when he gets here."

"Why in hell not?" The woman settled herself firmly into her chair. "Do you have a cure?"

"Not yet, no. But I think I've happened on a line of inquiry. If I just knew—"

"Then you must go," Rigo snapped.

The doctor flushed angrily.

"Shh," said Marjorie. "Dr. Bergrem, no one is trying to push you around. Read this." She took a copy of the note to Jhamlees Zoe from her pocket and handed it to the woman.

Lees Bergrem read it, then again. "I don't believe this!"

Rigo started to retort. Marjorie covered his lips with her fingers. "What don't you believe?"

"That anyone could— This must be faked. . . ." She looked into their faces, finding nothing there but apprehension. "But why would— Damn!" She handed the note to Alverd Bee.

"You have to go," Marjorie repeated. "You may be close to finding a cure, or something that will lead to a cure. You said so yourself. If you find the answer here, with that ship in port you'll never get a chance to tell anyone. A thousand troops can put us all under house arrest. We were going to send our son to Semling with copies of this letter. But you could disseminate it even better. You're known at the University there."

"You send me off-planet, I can't do any good at all," Lees Bergrem said. "I need tissue samples and soil samples. I need things that don't exist on Semling. Forget it."

Alverd Bee looked up from the note, his face strained and angry. "If you won't go off-planet, then we'll have to hide you somewhere, Lees. That means moving your equipment. Tell us fast what you need. We have about six hours to get you hidden and *Star-Lily* away. After that, it'll be too late."

"The new Hierarch won't know anything yet," Rigo said. "Jhamlees Zoe can't tell him anything until he lands on Grass."

"Jhamlees Zoe can't tell him anything, period," said Persun Pollut as he entered the room. "Sebastian and I've been out to the Friary to see if they'd changed their mind about being evacuated. The Hippae have hit the place. We saw the flames all the way from Klive. Half this piece of Grass is burning.

"So this Hierarch won't know," the doctor announced, turning around as though to renew the argument. "I've moved out of the hospital once already. We just got set up again. I can stay there. The Hierarch won't know what I'm doing."

"He won't care what you're doing," Marjorie pleaded. "Once he's here on Grass, you'll do what he says, or else. Dr. Bergrem, you haven't dealt with Sanctity. Rigo and I have. Believe me! Even their own people have few rights against Sanctity; unbelievers have none at all except what they can enforce for themselves. If the Hierarch chooses to deploy a thousand troopers, we couldn't enforce the coming of summer!"

"Oh, all right, all right. I'll hide! Tissue samples, Alverd. I need snips from whatever bons have survived. I'll send one of my people to get those. Samples from the children, too. I need soil samples. From in here and out there. Persun, come with me and I'll describe what I need. I'll pack up my stuff. It's heavy. Send some men over to load it."

And she was away.

"What about you two?" asked Alverd.

Rigo drew himself wearily to his feet. "There's nothing we can do just now. Tony's asleep down below, and there's no point in waking him until he needs to board the *Star-Lily*. I think we'll try to get some sleep. When the ship from Sanctity arrives, we need to be alert. At that time, some misdirection may be in order."

The *Israfel* bloomed like a star, and like a star remained in the heavens. One small shuttle came down to unload a small detachment of men commanded by a Seraph with six-winged angels on his shoulders. He was met by Mayor Bee.

"The Hierarch wishes to speak to Administrator Jhamlees Zoe at the Friary of the Green Brothers. We have been unsuccessful in reaching the administrator through your communications system."

Mayor Bee nodded sadly. "The Friary was wiped out by prairie fires," he said. "We're searching now for survivors."

There was a thoughtful silence. "The Hierarch may want to come down and verify this for himself."

"We evacuated the Port Hotel for the Hierarch's use," the Mayor agreed. "The fires have burned great stretches of grassland and seven villages. The town is full of refugees."

"The Hierarch may choose the town, nonetheless," said the Seraph.

"Well, certainly, if he wishes," said Mayor Bee, nodding. "Though there is sickness in the town which we assumed the Hierarch would wish to avoid."

The Seraph's expression did not change, though something wary came into his voice. "The office of the Hierarch will advise you. Any particular kind of sickness?"

"We're not sure what it is," said Mayor Bee. "People breaking out in sores. . . ." Rillibee had told him what it looked like. Rillibee had told them a good deal more than any of the commoners had wanted to know.

The small detachment made room for themselves at the empty hotel, but the Hierarch did not come down to Grass. Instead, he sent for Rigo. Marjorie insisted upon going along.

"For verisimilitude," she said. "We came here together. Let us support one another."

"I need you, Marjorie."

She gave him a thoughtful look. "You have never said that to me before, Rigo. Did you often say it to Eugenie?"

He flushed. "I may have."

She said wonderingly, "It's a different thing, being needed, from being wanted, which you often said to me, though that was long ago. I think the Seraph is waiting for us."

"Seraph," he snorted. "Why can't they call him a colonel or a general? Seraph!"

"We mustn't betray our biases! This Hierarch is not your uncle, and he may already be suspicious of us simply because we're outsiders."

The Hierarch betrayed no suspicion, though it would have been difficult to detect, since he greeted them from behind a transparent partition, calling their attention to it as though they could not see it for themselves. "My advisors," he said in an annoyingly satisfied though self-deprecating tone. "They won't allow me to expose myself to possible risk."

"Very wise," said Rigo.

"Is there risk here, Ambassador?" The Hierarch was clad in white robes with golden angels embroidered at the hem and in a wide border up the front. Their metallic wings threw a coruscant flicker around him, like an aureole. His face was ordinary. It had no feature more distinguished than the others. It was a face one could instantly forget. One would not forget the robes, however. The Hierarch repeated his question. "Are there deaths? Unexplained ones? Or deaths from plague?

"We don't know," said Rigo, remembering it was probable that the Hierarch had an analyzer on them. The least risk lay in disclaiming absolute knowledge. One could almost always do that truthfully.

"People do disappear on Grass," Marjorie offered honestly. "We've been trying to find out how, and why. It might help if we knew precisely what drew Sanctity's attention to Grass initially. The information we were given was not very specific."

The Hierarch gave her a long looking over, head to toe, as though assessing how well she would dress out for meat. It was not a look Marjorie had met before, and it chilled her. The Hierarch was not interested in her as woman or person, so much was clear.

"I will tell you precisely what we heard. A minor official at Sanctity was visiting his family. One of his visiting kinfolk worked as a port controller on Shafne. Sometimes this kinsman stopped in at a port tavern after work. On some unspecified occasion, he talked over his ale with a crewman from an unnamed freighter. The crewman said his friend, unnamed, had come down with some sores on his legs and arms just before the ship landed on Grass. The sick man was in a quarantine pod. The ship was on Grass an unspecified length of time. When it arrived at some farther destination, the man was cured."

"That's all?"

"Our official repeated this story to us when he returned from his visit to his family. Our computers say the likelihood is great that the unnamed crewman had plague, but we've been unable to verify the story. The man who told it to our official died of plague shortly after leaving Terra. We don't know where the alleged ship went from Grass. We have been unable to identify the ship or the crewman."

Rigo threw up his hands, indicating frustration. "Assuming the story is true, the cure could have come about here or elsewhere. Or he might not have had plague at all. Plague isn't the only thing that causes sores!" He let his voice and manner indicate frustration and fear. That was normal, and it would cover his agitation.

The Hierarch stared at them expressionlessly. "Have any survivors from the Friary been found?"

Rigo nodded. "A few, yes. Some are beginning to wander back to the site as they realize we'll be searching for them there."

"My old friend Nod—that is, Jhamlees Zoe?"

Rigo shook his head, unwilling to trust his voice. No. Jhamless Zoe hadn't turned up. If Rigo said that aloud it wouldn't take a machine to detect that he rejoiced in the fact.

The Hierarch nodded, as though someone had asked him a question. "I think we'll remain here for the time being. Zoe may yet turn up. Or you may find some more definite information."

In the shuttle, Marjorie asked, "Rigo, the crewman in the quarantine pod, assuming there was one, would have been given Grassian food and water and air, would he not?"

"Certainly." He nodded, indicating the men seated in front of them. "Quarantine pods allow nothing out, but materials do go in."

She chased an idea, worrying at it, but she asked no other questions.

They were escorted back to the order station by a handful of troopers. "There are definitely enough armed men on that ship to control the planet," Marjorie said to Roald Few.

"If they decide to do so," Rigo agreed.

"What do you think?" Roald asked, throwing a side long glance at his son-in-law, the Mayor.

"I think the Hierarch is doubtful," Rigo replied. "If I were the Hierarch, my next step would be to send the scientists down."

"Wouldn't he have told you that?" the mayor wanted to know.

Marjorie laughed, an unamused sound. "We aren't among the Sanctified, Mayor Bee. He doesn't like us, doesn't trust us. Probably he doesn't like or trust much of anyone. He'll get what he can from us, but he won't give us anything in return."

"Smart man," remarked Alverd. "Not to trust us Commons. We've no love for Sanctity. He's one should die of plague."

"When that letter of his becomes public, he may wish he had," Marjorie said. "Until then, we simply hang on and get in his way as much as possible."

They were given no further opportunity to impede the Hierarch. Sanctity scientists came down and occupied the hospital, setting up their own mysterious equipment.

"It doesn't matter what they find out," Marjorie reminded Rigo. "So long as Dr. Bergrem finds it, too."

"It would be better if she found it first," Rigo objected, taking Marjorie by the arm and leading her to a quiet corner. "You and I need to agree on what we will say if the Hierarch asks more questions. All of Commons needs to agree on what they will say." They discussed their strategy, at first alone, then with Roald and Alverd. When they had worn the subject thin, they returned to their rooms in the winter quarters, to more sleep and more of Kinny's cooking.

Late in the evening Rillibee came in from the swamp forest, waking the Yrariers. Marjorie came out of her room yawning, wrapped in a light robe, to find Rigo sitting up in his bed with Rillibee perched on the foot of it.

"I've come to get Father James," he said. "And the other Father, if he'll come back."

"What's going on, Rillibee?"

"I wish I knew exactly. The foxen are trying to figure something out. It's because of something you did, Marjorie. You talked to the foxen, didn't you?"

"During the . . . the episode out there. Yes."

"You didn't tell me that," Rigo said, almost angrily.

"It wasn't anything very real to me at the time," she said calmly. "I would have a hard time quoting the conversation. Mostly I was thinking words, but the foxen seemed to understand the threat I intended."

"It wasn't anything to do with a threat, I don't think. No. It was something else. Brother Mainoa is tearing what little hair he has left trying to figure it out. Whatever you did, it was the key to some change in their attitude. There are hundreds and hundreds of foxen in the forest, you know. All talking at one another, growling, yowling, thinking, sitting and looking at each other with their claws tap-tapping. It's like having shadow beasts projected all over you. You can't see them. You walk around them without knowing why. You hear them, and your mind tries to make wind noises out of it. After a while, you lie down and put your hands over your head, wishing they'd all go away. . . .

"Anyhow, they're having some major discussion. Something's going to happen. A foxen wants you, Marjorie, but I told him I didn't know if you could come. He'll settle for Father James."

Marjorie shook her head, longingly. "I mustn't leave here. If I were to vanish, the Hierarch could get very suspicious. He's got a thousand armed men, and he might not hesitate to destroy the swamp forest or the town or anything else he felt like. Father James will probably go with you, if he feels up to the trip."

"I'd like to take Stella, too," Rillibee said, looking at his feet.

Marjorie sighed and turned away. Stella was still at the temporary hospital, though no longer encased in a Heal-all. "Have you seen her, Rillibee?"

"I stopped there first."

"She's not . . . she's not like herself."

"She's like a child," Rillibee agreed. "A nice child."

"What use do you have for a nice child?" Rigo asked, his mouth in a grim line.

Rillibee drew himself up, a slight, wiry figure, somehow dignified in this circumstance by his very lack of stature and bulk. "I'm not interested in molesting her, if that's what you're imagining. She's in danger here. You all are. But you can choose what you'll do and she can't. I'd like to take Dimity, too. And Janetta. For the same reason. If the Hippae ruined them, maybe the foxen can help to heal them."

"Why not?" Marjorie said. "If Rowena and Geraldria are willing to have you take their daughters, why not? You'll have to ask them, but as far as I'm concerned, yes, take Stella."

"Marjorie!" Rigo was outraged.

"Oh, stop roaring at me, Rigo," she snapped in a voice he had never heard. "Think! You're doing it again, all these automatic responses of pride and masculinity."

"She's my daughter!"

"She's mine, too, and there's nothing in her head at all. She doesn't know me. She plays with a ball, bouncing it off a wall. What are you going to do with her? Take her back to Terra and hire a keeper for her?"

"This . . . this . . ." he pointed at Rillibee. "What?"

"This young man," she said, "who has been ill used by Sanctity, as we all have. This young man, who has certain talents and skills. What about him?"

"You trust him not to—"

"I trust him not to do anything to her nearly as bad as the Hippae have already done," she cried, "because you let them. I trust him to care for her better than we did, Rigo! Better than her father or her mother. I trust him to look after her."

Rillibee, who had tried to make himself inconspicuous during most of this, now asserted, "I will do for her what is best for her. From the moment I first saw her, I wanted only what was best for her. Right now there is only one good place left on Grass, and the Tree City is it. If there is trouble on Grass, it has not touched the trees."

Rigo did not reply. Marjorie could not see his face. She wasn't sure she wanted to see it, and she did not wish to argue it further with him. At the tell-me she reached Geraldria and Rowena, telling them of Rillibee's offer and advising them to accept it. When she turned, Rigo was there, and she said impatiently, "Yes?"

"Yes," he responded, as though granting a favor. "I'll accept this for now. It may be the best place for her for a time."

She tried to smile, not quite successfully. "I hope I am right about this, Rigo. I'd like to be right, a few times."

He didn't reply. Instead, he turned and left her, going back to his own room. Though she tried to get back to sleep, she could not. It was only hours later, near dawn, when the Seraph and his armed escort came for them, that she learned he had been as sleepless as herself.

They were given little time to dress. Perhaps it was only imagination, but it seemed they were treated with less courtesy than previously. When they were escorted into the Hierarch's presence, two other persons were already there. Rigo's hand tightened on Marjorie's arm as he saw the first. Her face grew momentarily rigid as she saw the second.

"Admit!" she cried in what she hoped was a glad-sounding voice. "Rigo, it's Admit Maukerden. I'm so glad you escaped the fires at Opal Hill. Sebastian and Persun went back time after time, but you weren't among the people they brought in."

"My name is Admit *bon* Maukerden," he said.

"A bon? Jerril bon Haunser told me he would provide a lateral," she exclaimed.

"I was assigned to find out what you were doing on Grass," he said. "The bons wanted to know what you were up to. As this one does, now." He gestured through the glass at the Hierarch. "He wants to know what you were up to."

"Well for heaven's sake," Marjorie cried, "tell him, Admit. Tell the Hierarch anything he wants to know."

"I am more interested in what this other one tells me," the Hierarch said silkily from behind his transparent partition.

The other one lounged on his chair like a lizard on a rock, his relaxed manner belied by his scratched and bruised face and arms. Highbones.

"Brother Flumzee?" Marjorie asked the Hierarch, her voice calm. "He and his friends intended to kill me in the swamp forest. What else does he tell you?" She looked at Highbones gravely.

He saw the look and remembered what it was he had forgotten about women. They pitied you sometimes. When you didn't even know why.

The Hierarch said in a silky voice, "He tells me that you were well acquainted with one of the Brothers, Brother Mainoa. He says that Brother Mainoa was thought to be a backslider. And that he knew something about plague."

"Did he really? What did he know, Brother Flumzee? Or do you still prefer to be called Highbones?"

"He knew something," Highbones shouted, hating what he saw in her face. "Fuasoi wanted him killed."

"What did he know?" asked the Hierarch. "It would be in your best interest, Lady Westriding, and you, Ambassador, to tell me everything the Brother knew, or thought he knew."

"We'll be glad to," Rigo said. "Though he himself would be able to tell you much more than we can—"

"He's alive?" The Heirarch snapped.

Marjorie replied calmly, "Well, of course. Highbones left his two friends to kill Mainoa and Brother Lourai, but they didn't succeed. I think Highbones hated Brother Lourai, and that was the reason for it."

"Fuasoi ordered Mainoa killed!" Highbones shouted.

"Well, I suppose that's possible," Marjorie continued, keeping her voice calm, though she was in a frenzy of concentration. "Since Brother Mainoa thought Fuasoi was a Moldy." She turned her face toward Rigo, nodding. She had never mentioned Brother Mainoa's speculation to him. She prayed Rigo would understand what she was trying to do.

The Hierarch, who had started the inquiry with a furious intensity, now looked stricken. "A Moldy?"

"Brother Mainoa thought so," Rigo said, following Marjorie's lead. "Because—"

"Because Fuasoi wouldn't have ordered Mainoa killed, otherwise," Marjorie concluded. "If he thought Mainoa *knew* something about the plague, the only reason to kill him would be if Fuasoi was a Moldy. Anyone who was *not* a Moldy would want Brother Mainoa alive, talking about what he knew." She looked at the Hierarch helpfully, feeling hysteria pushing at the back of her tongue.

"Moldies here, on Grass?" the Hierarch whispered, very pale, his mouth drawn into a rictus of horror. "Here?"

Rigo saw the man's terror and was thankful for it. "Well, Your Eminence," Rigo offered in a placating tone, "it was only a matter of time until they came here. Everyone knew that. Even Sender O'Neil told me that!"

The audience ended abruptly. They were outside the chamber, being escorted to the shuttle once more. Highbones wasn't with them. Admit *bon* Maukerden wasn't with them. Those two were taken away in some other direction.

"Where are they going?" Marjorie asked.

"Down to the port," the escort leader responded. "We'll hold them there in case the Hierarch wants them again."

Marjorie felt a surge of hope. If they had been believed, perhaps the Hierarch would depart. Perhaps this is all it would take! When Marjorie and Rigo reached the port, however, they were not allowed to return to the town. Instead they were taken to the empty Port Hotel and given a suite with a guard outside the door.

"Are we to stay here without food?" Marjorie demanded.

"Somebody'll bring it from the officer's mess," the guard said. "Hierarch wants you here where he can lay hands on you if he needs you."

When the door was shut behind them, Marjorie put her lips almost against Rigo's ear. "Anything we say here can probably be overheard."

He nodded. "I think Mainoa was right," he said loudly. "I think Brother what's-his-name was a Moldy. He probably had virus shipped in weeks ago. That's probably what the people in town have. I think we ought to get off this planet, Marjorie. As soon as possible." He shook his head at her tiredly. What more could they say or do than this mixture of half truth and part lies? If the Hierarch was frightened enough, perhaps his own fear would drive him away.

Rigo sat down, leaning back, eyes closed. Marjorie sat near him. The room was full of unsaid things and of the teasing memory of said ones. She looked at his exhausted face and felt an almost impersonal sorrow, like the feelings she had often had for the people of Breedertown. And she could help him no more than she had ever helped them.

Behind his slitted eyelids, Rigo wondered if it was too late. If too much had happened. Eugenie. Stella. His accusations against Marjorie. Stupid of him. He knew better. If he knew anything about her, he knew she had no appetites of that kind. Why had he accused her?

Because he had had to accuse her of something.

And now? Was it too late to forgive her for what she had never done?

18

In the Tree City of the Arbai two religious gentlemen sat in the mild breezes of evening, eating fruit which had been brought from the surrounding trees by foxen, one of whom had remained to join the feast.

"Like plums," said Father James. He had arrived at the city by foxen back in midmorning. Father Sandoval had refused to come. Brother Mainoa had come to the city earlier, an exhausting trip from which he had not yet recovered. Now the Brother reclined against the breast of a foxen, like a child in a shadowy chair, while Father James tried to convince himself yet again that the foxen were real—not dreams, not amorphous visions, not abstractions or delusions. Conviction was difficult when he couldn't really see them. He caught a glimpse of paw, or hand, a glimpse of eye, a shadowed fragment of leg or back. Trying to see the being entire was giving him eye strain and a headache. He turned aside, resolving not to bother. Soon everything would resolve itself, one way or another.

"Chameleons," Brother Mainoa whispered. "Psychic chameleons. The Hippae can do it too, though not as well."

Father James' lips trembled. "Don't you think the fruit is like plums?" he repeated, longing for something familiar. "Though perhaps the texture is more like a pear. Small, though."

"Ripening this early, they'd likely be small," Brother Mainoa offered in a breathy whisper. "The fruits of summer and fall are larger, even from these same trees." He sounded contented, though very weak.

"They fruit more than once during the season, then?"

"Oh, yes," Mainoa murmured. "They fruit continually until late fall."

Along a bridge leading from the plaza Janetta bon Maukerden was dancing, humming to herself. Dimity bon Damfels watched from the plaza, mouth open around a thumb, eyes remotely curious. Stella was with Rillibee in a room facing the plaza. The older men could hear his voice.

"Take the fruit in your hand, Stella. That's it. Now, have a bite. Good girl. Wipe your chin. *Good* girl. Have another bite. . . ."

"He's very patient," whispered Brother Mainoa.

"He would have to be," murmured Father James. "Three of them!"

"Poor unfortunates," Father James said. "We'll help him with them while we're here. It's the least we can do." He thought a moment, then added, "If we're here long enough."

A group of shadow Arbai came toward them, checkered them with arms and legs and shoulders, battered them with sibilant conversation, then moved on past. A swoop of scarlet and brilliant blue swept below them, from one tree to another, a colorful almost-bird, quite different from the Terran species, yet enough resembling them that one would think "parrot" on seeing them. Out on the bridge where Janetta danced, one of the shadow figures grasped a railing with shadow hands and squatted over the edge. The Arbai had been casual about elimination.

"It will be your choice," Brother Mainoa said in a weak whisper. "Your choice, Father. Whether to stay or go."

The priest protested. "We're not even sure we can live here! Food, for example. We're not sure these fruits will sustain our lives."

Brother Mainoa assured him, "The fruit plus grass seeds will be more than enough. Brother Laeroa has spent years determining the nutrient value of various grass seed combinations. After all, Father, on Terra many men lived on little else than wheat or rice or corn. They, too, are seeds of grass."

"Harvesting grass seed would mean going out into the prairies," Father James objected. "The Hippae wouldn't allow that."

"You could do it," said the Brother. "You'd have protection. . . ." He shut his eyes and seemed to drift off as he had been doing ever since they arrived.

"Though, come to think of it," said Father James, suddenly remembering farms he had visited as a child, "here in the swamp one could have ducks, and geese." He tried to summon a hearty chuckle, but what came out instead was a tremulous half sigh. The young priest had just remembered that the few humans on Grass might be all the humans there were. Whether one could have ducks or not, there might be nowhere else to go.

"Wipe your chin again," said Rillibee Chime. "Oh, Stella, that's such a good smart girl."

Janetta spun and hummed, then stopped momentarily and said, quite clearly, "Potty!" She hitched up her smock, grasped the railing, and squatted where she was on the bridge, her bottom over the edge in the same pose the shadow Arbai had adopted moments before.

"She can talk," said Father James unnecessarily, his face pink as he turned it away from Janetta's bare buttocks.

"She can learn," Brother Mainoa agreed, suddenly awake once more.

Father James sighed, his face turned resolutely away. "Let's hope she can learn to be a bit more modest."

Brother Mainoa smiled. "Or that we can learn to be—as, evidently, the Arbai were—less concerned with the flesh."

Father James felt a wave of sadness, a wash of emotion so intensely painful that it seemed physical. He suddenly saw Brother Mainoa through some other being's senses: a fragile friend, an evanescent kinsman who would not be concerned with the flesh at all for very much longer.

Someone was watching him. He looked up to see a pair of glowing, inhuman eyes, clearly fixed on his own. They were brimming with enormous, very human tears.

Shortly following the detention of the Yrariers, the Seraph in command of the Hierarch's troops took a few of his "saints" in battle dress—more to impress the populace than for any tactical reason—and made a sweep through the town and surrounding farms, searching, so the Seraph said, for someone named Brother Mainoa. Everyone had seen him at one unhelpful time or another. Several people knew where he slept. Others knew where he had been having supper hours before. No one knew where he was at that moment.

"He was depressed," an informer by the name of Persun Pollut told them with transparent honesty. "About all the Brothers getting burned up out at the Friary. It wouldn't surprise me if he'd gone down into the swamp forest. There've been several people done that recently." All of which was true. Though he pulled a mournful face and sighed at the Seraph, Persun couldn't wait to see the Tree City for himself.

The troop made a cursory search along the edge of the trees, sending a patrol some little way into the forest. Troopers returned soaked to the thighs saying they couldn't quite remember seeing anything. Spy eyes sent into the dim aisles of cloaking vines saw nothing either. Or, those who followed the spy eyes on helmet screens were sure they saw nothing, which amounted to the same thing. It was conceded among those who had inspected the swamp forest close up that if this Brother what's-his-name had gone in there, he was probably drowned and long gone.

Meantime, the troopers remaining in town were offered cakes and roast goose and flagons of beer and were treated to a good deal of garrulity which had nothing to do with what they were looking for. The search continued with increasing laxness and joviality while the day wandered inconclusively toward evening.

The Seraph was an old hand at appearing Sanctified, one who could and did spew catechetical references at every opportunity. In Commoner Town he found his views listened to with such flattering attention that he actually began to enjoy himself, though—as he told anyone who would listen—he would have felt more secure with a few hundred saints deployed, rather than a scant two score. According to these good people, there were hostiles on the planet, hostiles that had already built themselves one route under the forest.

"Haven't you any devices to detect digging?" he asked. "Any mechanisms that listen for tremors? That kind of thing?"

"Grass doesn't have tremors, not like that," Roald Few told him. "About the worst shaking we get is when the Hippae go dancing."

The Seraph shook his head, feeling expansive. "I'll bring some detectors down from the ship. Standard issue. We use them to locate sappers coming in under fortifications. They'll do the job for you here."

"Where do we put them?" Mayor Bee asked. "Here in the town?"

The Seraph drew a map on the tablecloth with his fingertip, thinking. "Out there, north of town, I'd say two-thirds of the way to the forest. About a dozen, in a semicircle. You can set the receiver up anywhere here in town. The order station'd be a good place. Then if anything starts to dig in, you'll know it!" He smiled beatifically, proud of himself for being helpful.

Alverd looked at Roald, receiving a look in return. So, they would know. Well and good. What in the hell would they do about it once they knew?

In the *Israfel*, high above all this confusion, the aged Hierarch fretted himself into a passion. The first time he had questioned the Yrariers he had been convinced the ambassador was misleading him, though the analyzers had said only maybe. The second time, however, the machines had declared Rigo and Marjorie to be truthful. Compared to Highbones and the Maukerden man—both liars (said the machines) from the moment of conception—the Yrariers had been certified honest and doing their best to be helpful. However, they weren't Sanctity people, and in the Hierarch's opinion they weren't terribly bright. This business about the Moldies. That couldn't be true. Sanctity had been too careful for it to be true. They had kept the plague so very quiet, so very hidden. The Yrariers must have misunderstood whatever this Brother Mainoa had said about Moldies.

The Hierarch considered this. The pair had been chosen by the former Hierarch because they were kin, because they were athletes. Not known for brains, athletes. That's where old Carlos had gone wrong. He should have sent someone cleverer. Someone slyer. And he should have done it long before instead of waiting until the last possible moment. There was no point in keeping the Yrariers locked up. And he, the Hierarch, would be safe enough in the specially modified isolation shuttle his people had built for him. Once he himself was on the ground, things would happen! Discoveries would occur! He knew it!

As he was about to depart, however, a bulletin arrived from the surface. Danger, the Seraph said. Not only the possibility of plague, but the presence of large, fierce beasts would make it dangerous for the Hierarch to descend. Hostile creatures might be planning to overrun the port.

The additional frustration was enough to send the Hierarch into one of his infrequent fits of screaming temper. Servitors who had barely survived previous such fits were moved to panicky action. After emergency ministrations by the Hierarch's personal physician, the Hierarch slept and everyone sighed in relief. He went on sleeping for days, and no one noticed or cared that no orders had been given for the Yrariers' release.

Persun Pollut, Sebastian Mechanic, and Roald Few took the Seraph's listening devices out into the meadows north of town to set them up. They were simple enough to install: slender tubes to be driven into the ground with a mechanical driver, long, whiskery devices to be dropped into the tubes, and transmitters to be screwed onto the tops.

"Foolproof," the Seraph had told them. "As they must be if inexperienced troopers are to use them. A-B-C. Pound it in, drop it in, screw it on."

Foolproof they might be. In the aggregate, heavy they also were. The men used an aircar to transport the dozen sets and the bulky driver that went with them. They started at the western end of the proposed arc, setting each device and then moving northward, parallel to the curve of the forest. Most of the day had passed by the time seven of the gadgets were in place, and they were bending the arc toward the east when Persun shaded his eyes with his arm and said, "Somebody in trouble up there."

When they stopped working, they could all hear it: the stutter of an engine, start and stop, the pauses like those in the breath of someone dying—so long between sounds one was sure no other sound would come—only to catch again into life.

Then they saw it, an aircar coming toward them, scarcely above the forest. It jerked and wobbled, approaching by fits and starts. When it had barely cleared the trees it fell, caught itself, then dropped, coming down hard midway between them and the swamp, not a hundred yards away.

Persun set out toward it at a run, with Sebastian close behind. Roald followed them more slowly. At first there was no sign of life in the fallen car, but then the door opened with a scream of tortured metal and a Green Brother emerged dazedly, holding his head. Others followed: six, eight, a dozen of them. They sank to the ground by the car, obviously exhausted.

Persun was the first to reach them. "My name's Pollut," he said. "We can get some cars out here to pick you up, since yours seems to be disabled."

The oldest among them struggled to his feet and held out an age-spotted hand. "I'm Elder Brother Laeroa. We stayed out near the Friary thinking we could pick up survivors. Obviously, we stayed too long. Our fuel was barely enough."

"I'm surprised to see any of you," Sebastian said. "The place was pretty well wiped out."

Laeroa wiped his face with trembling fingers. "When we heard of the attack on Opal Hill and the estancias, we suggested to Elder Brother Jhamlees Zoe that he evacuate the Friary. He said the Hippae had no quarrel with the Brothers. I tried to tell him the Hippae needed no excuse to kill." He tottered on his feet, and one of his fellows came forward to offer an arm. After a moment he went on in his precise voice, as though he spoke from a pulpit. "Zoe was always impatient with argument and impervious to reason. So these Brothers and I started sleeping in the aircar."

"You were in the car when the Hippae struck?"

"We were in the car when the fires started," said one of the younger Brothers. "We took off and went out into the grass a ways, thinking we'd pick up survivors later. I don't know how many days we've been out there, but we only found one man."

"We picked up a couple dozen of your people," Sebastian Mechanic said to them. "Young fellahs, most of 'em. They were wandering around pretty far out in the grass. There may be more. We been going out there every day to look. The Hippae aren't around there anymore. They're all around the swamp forest now."

"They can't get through, can they?" asked one of the men, obviously the one man the Brothers had rescued. His face was very pale and he carried what was left of one arm in a sling.

"Not so far as we know," said Sebastian, wanting to be comforting. "And if they did, we've got heavy doors down in the winter quarters and people down there already making weapons for us to use."

"Weapons," breathed one of the Brothers. "I had hoped—"

"You'd hoped we could talk to them?" asked Elder Brother Laeroa bitterly. "Forget it, Brother. I know you worked for the office of Doctrine, but forget it. I'm sure Jhamlees Zoe still retained his hope of converting the Hippae up to the moment they killed him. He's hoped for that ever since he came to Grass, no matter how many times we told him it would be like trying to convert tigers to vegetarianism."

Sebastian nodded agreement as he said, "Just be thankful the Hippae don't have claws like Terron tigers do. Otherwise, they'd be able to climb and we couldn't get away from 'em. Now, you start on up the slope there. I'll get on the tell-me and have somebody come pick you up."

The Brothers got wearily to their feet and started up the long meadow in a shuffling line. When Sebastian and Persun had seen that all of them could walk, they went to listen outside the car while Roald messaged for help.

"On their way," Roald said at last.

"Good," Sebastian murmured. "Some of 'em look like they couldn't walk more than a hundred yards or so."

"Thirty some-odd brothers left out of a thousand," Persun commented, as he went to install the next device.

"One thing we can be grateful for," the other replied. "There's nothin' left of the other nine hundred and some-odd to bury." He paused beside the mechanical driver. "Have you noticed how quiet it is?"

The two men stood looking around them. "The noise of the tube driver," Persun said. "It's frightened everything."

"The driver isn't that noisy. And we haven't been using it for the past little while."

"The noise of that aircar, then."

The silence persisted. The swamp forest, usually full of small croakings and rattles, the call of flick birds, the cry of leaf dwellers, was silent.

"Eerie," whispered Persun. "Something wrong. I can feel it." He started back toward the aircar, feeling in his pocket for his knife.

Behind him Sebastian moaned.

A head peered sightlessly at them from the edge of the trees. Blank eyes glared in their direction. Above the eyes, flesh was torn to expose the bone, which gleamed moistly white. The head wobbled on its neck, rising into view, shoulders, arms, then the hideous Hippae maw below. A rider on a mount! A rider dead or so nearly dead as made no difference. The corpselike mouth opened to emit a screaming rattle, and with that sound the edge of the forest erupted into life.

They burst into the open across a wide front, both riders and mounts screaming hate, defiance, death, and dismemberment. Persun turned back to grab Sebastian, who stood as one hypnotized.

Sebastian's only thought, before his body was ripped apart, was that their morning's labor had been too late.

Persun backed toward the aircar and swung the knife, a scream choked back. There had been another tunnel to the north. Teeth like razors raked his knife arm. His weapon clattered onto a rock. He clenched his jaw, readying himself for the final pain, his eyes staring into the blind dead eyes of the rider above him.

Something forced its way between him and the Hippae teeth. The aircar was hovering low beside him; Roald was shrieking at him. Hippae teeth darted toward him, then away. He threw himself backward into the open car, seeing, as he did so, that other cars hovered beside the pathetic line of green-robed Brothers, some staggering as they fled, some cut down and dead, some making it to the refuge of the cars, while all around them the Hippae howled and rampaged, their riders jerking and twitching as though they had been tied in position.

Persun tried not to look at what was left of Sebastian as they rose higher. Blood was dripping from his motionless fingers. His head was half out the aircar door. Packs of Hippae and hounds were already moving toward the town. Roald was screaming into the tell-me. Persun saw a Brother snapped in half. Others were shouting. All he could think of was that his fingers did not move. His carving fingers did not move. Beside him Roald cried out at something he saw, but Persun did not turn. His fingers did not move, and he thought it might have been better to have died.

While the Hippae in their hundreds overran the town from the north, battalions of migerers cut through the final few yards of a second tunnel on the south, one both taller and wider than the previous hole, an access route large enough to allow hosts of Hippae to move through it at a run. They came in waves, as they had come over the Arbai city long before; up from the forest toward the port, howling, ready to kill. There was no substantial opposition south of the wall. The handful of troopers at the port were inexperienced. They were taken by surprise and immediately overrun.

Even so, three or four of the quicker among them had time to arm themselves and get to upper levels of a ship maintenance gantry where the Hippae could not follow. Hippae died by the dozens in screaming disbelief, learning thereby to avoid the guns.

North of the wall the horn had been set off in response to Roald's alarm, and all Commons had fled to the winter quarters, sheltering behind doors already reinforced against attack, though not, most people feared, sufficiently so to stand against repeated battering by Hippae. At the sound of the alarm, James Jellico locked the tall gates. He also had the presence of mind to send runners to find the troopers who had been dallying among the friendly kitchens of town. Though Jelly didn't yet know where the threat was coming from, the dozen men with the Seraph at least had proper weapons. Possibly the Seraph could bring additional men and weapons from that ship above.

The hastily summoned Seraph chose the order station as his base and sensibly set about keeping danger at bay.

"Two men at every opening," he ordered, sweating at the sight of Hippae rampaging among the motionless bodies at the port. "Ninety-five degrees auto-fire coverage. Helmet lights on full fan. Night goggles. Auto on anything that moves."

"There's a dozen saints at the port," one of the troopers objected from a dry mouth. "They may try for the gate."

"There's fire from the upper levels of that structure, Cherub," the Seraph replied bleakly, pointing it out as though the trooper were blind. "If the men there have any intelligence at all, they'll stay where they are. They're safer there than we are here. If you see anything moving toward the gate, kill it. Communication silence except to report those things breaking in here. I've got to get reinforcements down." He knew it would take hours, even days. The *Israfel* had not been equipped with assault craft. Who could have thought they would be needed? They had only small shuttles, which would have to come down bringing ten men at a time, setting up a fire perimeter as they did so.

"Sir," said the Cherub again, "what about those people out in that hotel?"

"What people?" demanded James Jellico in surprise.

"The scientists that the Hierarch sent down," the Cherub replied. "And that ambassador. Him and his wife."

In the suite at the Port Hotel, Marjorie wakened at the first howls of the invading Hippae. Her windows faced the wrong way. She went through the room where Rigo lay in exhausted slumber to the window in the outside room. There were darting, wildly moving lights at the port. She saw Hippae lunging in and out of shadow. Without waking Rigo, she went to the door of the suite and opened it. The daytime guard had been replaced by another man.

"Trooper," she said. "Take a quick look out the window. Some very dangerous creatures are rampaging around out there."

He gestured her back, as though she were the dangerous one, she standing there in her crumpled clothing with no weapon at all, her hair falling untidily around her face. When he had seen, however, he looked confused, as though teetering among several desires.

"If we're going to stay here," she said, "we need to make ourselves as safe from those beasts as we can. We have to assume they'll come here eventually."

"How?" he asked. "What do you mean?"

"They can't climb ladders," she said. "But they aren't stupid. They may know or be able to figure out what lifts are. We need to turn off the power to the chutes. We're on the fourth level here. Without lifts, they probably can't get up here."

"Power controls are probably all the way down," he said.

"Then we'll have to go all the way down."

He divagated, starting toward the lift, then back.

"Come on, boy," she snapped. "I'm old enough to be your mother, so I can yell at you. Decide what you're going to do!"

He started to put his weapon down.

"Take it," she commanded. "They could get into the hotel while we're down below."

They fell into the down chute together, Marjorie complaining bitterly under her breath at the slowness of the thing. Luxury seemed to be equated with slow chutes. The Port Hotel held itself out as luxurious. They floated past the doors like dust motes, ending up five levels below the ground with a further five levels still beneath them indicated upon the board.

"Winter quarters down there," said Marjorie. "I'd forgotten there would be winter quarters."

"It must get really cold here, huh?" the guardsman wanted to know as he looked vaguely around himself.

"I have a feeling cold is only part of it," Marjorie answered. "Now where?"

He pointed. The power room was opposite the chute, a heavy metal door opening into a room full of consoles and bubble meters.

"We should probably shut it all down," said Marjorie.

"All? You won't have any water up there or anything. Besides, how'll we get back?"

"Climb the chute," she said succinctly. She moved down the console, reading labels. Main power control. Main pump. The main pump seemed to be on a separate circuit from the power control. It might be possible to leave them with water. She folded back the barrier and thrust the power control sharply across. The room went black.

"Damn," she snarled.

A blazing light came on in her eyes. "I should've had it on already," the trooper confessed, adjusting his helmet lamps. "Where do we climb back?"

"Up the chute," she said. "Up the emergency ladder."

They went back to the chute, leaning out over a well of chill dark to seize a cold metal rung. They climbed, Marjorie first, their ascent lighted by the trooper's lamp.

"That's a handy gadget," she commented between puffs as they neared the fourth level once more. "Your helmet, I mean. Does it see in the infrared?"

"Infrared," he agreed. "Plus about six other filter combinations. It can tell living stuff from dead stuff. And it's got a motion detector. And if you tie it to the armor arm controls, it's got automatic fire potential." He sounded proud of it, and Marjorie approved of his pride and confidence. He might need it. Their safety could depend on it.

"Now," she said when they had reached the fourth level, "you might as well come inside the suite. We'll close and lock the door behind us just in case something—anything—gets up here."

Rigo still slept. He looked drawn and worn.

"He'll be hungry when he wakes," she said. "We don't have any food here."

"Emergency rations," the boy said from behind her, tapping a long compartment down one armored thigh. "Enough for one man, ten days. Enough for the three of us for a while, at least. They don't taste like much, but the Cherubim tell us they're sustaining." He gestured at the sleeping man. "Has he been sick?"

She nodded. Yes. Rigo had been sick. All the riders had been sick.

"What's your name?" she asked him. "Are you Sanctified?"

He grinned proudly. "Favel Cobham, ma'am. And yes, I'm Sanctified, ma'am. The whole family. I got registered when I was born. I'm saved for eternity."

"Lucky you," she said, turning again to Rigo's bed. Here in the Port Hotel she and Rigo weren't saved for even this life if the Hippae got in. Tony was, maybe, if someone found a cure soon. And Stella. Remembering how Rillibee had looked at her, perhaps Stella was saved. If not for eternity, at least for a very small being's lifetime, which was all one could expect.

She went back to the window, looking across the battle to the huge barns against the wall. The horses! She could see the barn where they were stabled. It was stout, true, but not impenetrable. It was connected to the building they were in by the tunnel network. Everything was connected to everything else. Could she find her way there? She fumbled in her jacket pocket, finding the trip recorder that Brother Mainoa had returned to her.

"The Seraph, he had a few men in town," the trooper said.

"What will they do?" she wondered.

He shook his head. "The Seraph, he's what you'd call conservative, ma'am. I've heard the Cherubim say that, a few times. He'll wait until morning, then he'll prob'ly make a sweep from the wall with all the men moving on automatic fire. By that time, he'll have more men down from the ship."

"There's at least one tunnel where the Hippae came in," Marjorie said. "It'll have to be blown up, or flooded, or something."

"Do the people in the town know that?" he asked. When she nodded, he said, "Then they'll tell the Seraph and he'll take care of it. Maybe even tonight if he can get an assault hopper down. Seraph has an assault group moves with him, wherever he goes. Assault group's got all kinds of demolition stuff."

"Would he have taken a group like that into town?" she asked incredulously.

"Everywhere," he said soberly. "Everywhere he goes, even to the toilet. In case something happens while he's gone and he has trouble getting back to his command. Like a mutiny or something."

She shook her head, amazed. How insecure a Hierarch must feel to make a routine provision for mutiny.

"Mutiny?" asked an angry voice from the door. Rigo, stripped to his trousers, feet bare. "What's going on?"

Marjorie stood aside from the window to let him see.

"They've come through," she said. "This young man and I have turned off the power to the hotel," she said. "They won't be able to get up here unless there are some stairs I'm unaware of. By the same token, however, I'm afraid we're trapped. For the time being." She believed they might not outlive their entrapment, though she did not say so.

Rigo looked expressionlessly out the window. "Hippae," he said unnecessarily. "How many?"

"Enough to do a great deal of damage," Marjorie replied. "I quit counting at eighty some-odd, and there were still more arriving."

"If you'll wait outside," Rigo said to the trooper, "I'd like to talk to my wife."

"No," she said. "He can wait here. I don't want him out in the hall, where they might smell him or hear him. There might be another way up, and I don't want to attract them. If you want to talk, we'll talk in your room." She went before him, rumpled, uncombed, and yet stately. In the room where Rigo had slept, she sat in a chair and waited while he stalked about, three paces, three paces back.

"While you were away," he said, "I had an opportunity to discuss our situation with Father Sandoval. I think we need to talk about our future."

She felt sorrow mixed with a faint annoyance. It was so like him to pick a time when there might not be any future to discuss their future together. He had always picked times when there was no love to talk about love; times when there was no trust to talk about trust. As though love and trust were not feelings but only symbols or tools which could be manipulated to achieve a desired result. As though the words themselves were keys to open some mechanical lock. Twist love, love happens. Twist trust, trust occurs. Twist future ...

"What about our future?" she asked expressionlessly.

"Father Sandoval agrees with me that there will be a cure," he announced in his laying-down-the-law voice, as though his saying it made it fact. Well, Rigo's use of that voice had almost always produced the desired result. So he had spoken to his mother, his sisters, to Eugenie and the children, to Marjorie herself. If his voice hadn't worked, Father Sandoval's had, setting penances, invoking the power of the church. Now Rigo was going on, telling her what would hapen.

"Someone will find it. Now that we know the answer lies here, someone will find it, and it won't take long. The cure will be disseminated. We will stay here only until then. Then we must get back to our real lives, all four of us."

"We must what?" she asked, thinking of the monsters in the town, in the port. How could he simply ignore them? But then, how could he have ignored the fact that they were monsters before? "What must we do?"

"All four of us," he repeated. "Including Stella." His eyes were angry. Evidently Stella's going to the forest had rankled. "She'll take a lot of attention, but you needn't give up your charities or your riding. We can hire people to care for her."

"To care for her."

He made a grim line with his lips. "I know she'll require a lot of attention, Marjorie. The point I wanted to make is that it needn't be a burden on you. I know how much your work means to you, how important you think it is. Father Sandoval has pointed out that I shouldn't have argued with you about that in the past. It was wrong of me. You're entitled to have your own interests . . ."

She shook her head at him, slowly, disbelievingly. What was he saying? Did he think they could go back as they were before, as though nothing had happened? Would he find someone to replace Eugenie and then go on, as they had before? Would she go down to Breedertown, taking food, arranging transport? As it had been?

"Have you and Father Sandoval discussed how you will introduce Stella to your friends?" she asked. "Will you say, 'This is Stella, my idiot daughter. I allowed her to be mentally and sexually crippled on Grass in order to show off my manliness to people who meant nothing to me.' Something like that?"

His face turned dark with fury. "You have no right—"

She put up a hand, forbiddingly. "I have every right, Rigo. I'm her parent too. She's not yours alone to dispose of. She belongs to me, as well, and to herself. If you want to take Stella back to Terra, I suppose you can try. Somehow, I don't think you will easily remove her from where she is now. You would have great difficulty removing me. If you want to go back to the way things were, I can't stop you. I won't try. But you must not expect Stella or me to come along like dogs at your heels!"

"You're not thinking of staying here! What would you do here? Your work is at home. Our lives are at home."

"I would have agreed with you once. It's not true now."

"All those arguments you used to give me about your work at Breedertown? You're saying that was so much fluff? Lies?"

"I thought it was important then." Or made myself think so, she said to herself.

"And now you don't?"

"What difference does it make what I think? I'm not even sure what I think! And despite your assumption that the plague will be ended, we may die of it yet! Or the Hippae may kill us. This is no time to discuss what we will do *if*, what we will do *when*! We have no choices right now except to try to stay alive as best we can." She got up and went past him, laying a hand on his shoulder as she went, wanting to comfort him or herself. Now was not the time to have argued with him. If their lives were to end here, she would rather not have them end in rancor. What did it matter what he said now?

He went after her, finding her at the window with the trooper. Rigo, looking over her shoulder at scenes of fire and destruction, wondered why anyone would consider staying on Grass. The Hippae had found the scientists in the attached hospital and had dragged them out onto the weedy slope. Even when they were all dead, the Hippae rampaged among the bodies like bulls, trampling and bellowing.

Marjorie cursed in a quiet voice, tears running down her face. She had not known or remembered that there were other people in the port building. When she and the trooper had shut off the power, they could have brought the others up to safety. The sight of the rampaging creatures made her think again of the horses. She would not leave them to face this horror alone.

The two men were frozen at the window. She turned quietly and went out without their noticing. It would be a long climb down to the winter quarters and the tunnels which connected everything, as Persun Pollut had said, like the holes in a sponge.

Most of Commons managed to get behind the stout doors of winter quarters before the Hippae arrived. Most, not all. Those who were left above ground fought their way to such safety as they could find. Though most buildings in town were low, there were upper floors for refuge, stairways that could be held at least for a time. They had no weapons to oppose the Hippae and the hounds. While a knife could cut a leg or a jaw, a hound could come up from behind and take the arm that held the knife before the man knew the beast was there. Hounds could come up stairs like great cats. Bodies and parts of bodies began to accumulate in Commons streets. In the order station the Seraph sweated and swore, wishing he had ways of communicating with the defenders of the town.

"An aircar," James Jellico suggested. "You can fly overhead. Aircars have speakers."

"You do it," snapped the Seraph. "Tell them to get out of the streets onto roofs where we can pick them up. Tell them to stop dying uselessly until I can get my men down!"

So Jelly flew, and Asmir, and Alverd, and even old Roald, skimming the tops of the buildings as they bellowed at those below to get onto the rooftops.

"Climb," they shouted. "We'll pick you up."

Those who heard them swore and screamed and tried to get onto roofs while beasts darted at them from every doorway, lunged up at them from seemingly empty streets, materialized out of nothing in corners of walls. Always before, the Hippae had chosen to be seen. Now, in battle, they chose not to be seen until their teeth were fastened in their prey. Like chameleons, they faded against their backgrounds, their skins mottled the colors of brick or cobbles or plaster, only their teeth and the gleam of eyes betraying them, too often too late.

Those with the arrogance to be ridden could not disguise their eldritch riders, however. The sight of a shuddering corpselike figure coming head high along a wall was enough to warn that there was a beast beneath it. Roald, peering down from the aircar at this display, wondered what arcane motives led the Hippae to this horrid mockery of a Hunt? Why did they burden themselves with these useless excrescences? When the Hippae died, their riders rolled off, some of them alive, some barely alive, some already truly dead. Roald had picked up a few that looked like they might make it. Even the most alive among them did not know why they were there. Why were they there?

"I see more dead ones," Roald muttered to Alverd as they flew from rooftop to rooftop. "More dead Hippae."

"I know," Alverd marveled. "Who's killing them? Not the troopers. They're all tied up over at the order station."

"Us, I guess."

Alverd snorted. "Not likely, father-in-law. There's another dead one, at the corner down there. All torn apart."

"What's killing them, if we're not?"

"I don't know," he said. "Something. Something we can't see. Something with teeth."

From the lowest floor of the Port Hotel winter quarters, Marjorie worked her way through the network of tunnels toward the barn, which stood almost at the wall of Gom. The trip recorder could not guide her but it would keep her from becoming irretrievably lost. The barn was not far from the place where Hippae rampaged and killed. It would be difficult to get the horses out without being seen. However, if they could reach the swamp forest they might be safe. If they were seen, she would undoubtedly be slaughtered. She felt the anger of the Hippae, against her, personally. She was the one they hated. She had spied on them, gone into their cavern, ridden against them. They would not miss the chance to bring her down.

Even so, if she could get the horses out onto the slope, some of them would make it. She could get them moving in the right direction, at least. Once they reached the forest, First would take them, protect them. Gallant horses. They deserved better than this fangy death. They deserved meadows and foals and long days of grazing under the sun.

Her feet echoed on the stone. Dim lights picked out the junctures of one tunnel with another. When the trip recorder said she had come far enough in the proper direction, she began looking for a way up. The horses would be above her somewhere. Pray the barn had not yet attracted Hippae attention. Pray the horses were not injured, or dead.

No, said someone. *The horses are safe.*

She stopped, stunned into frozen immobility. That voice belonged to the wilderness, to the trees, not to these dry, dark corridors. When the shock passed, she turned toward the voice as a compass needle turns toward the north, quivering.

Here, it said. *Here.*

She crept toward the summons, upward along slanting corridors, up twisting flights of stairs, pulled like a fish on a line.

He was in the barn with the horses, lying across the door. She saw the troubled air, the miragelike wavering, the glint of tooth or eye. The horses chewed quietly, undisturbed. When she came in, Quixote whickered at her and she leaned against the wall, trembling. So. Was He the only one to get involved, or were there other foxen as well?

Why are you here? she asked.

I knew you would come here, He replied, in words, human words, clear as air.

She shook with the implications of that. *I could not abandon my friends,* she said.

I know, He said. *I knew before, but my people didn't believe in you.*

She asked, *Have they changed their minds?*

Yes. Because of these, He said. *Because of the horses.*

She saw herself on Quixote's back, menaced from front and rear, the aircar above her offering escape, saw herself refusing to go. The picture in her mind was larger than life, freighted with enormous import. She would not leave the horses.

Silly, she thought. *I thought so at the time.*

Silly, He agreed, using words again. *Important. Important to know one would risk herself for another not like herself. Important to know humans feel loyalty. Important to know friendship can extend from race to race.*

Were the Arbai your friends?

A negation. She saw Arbai involved with Hippae, working with Hippae while foxen prowled nearby and the Arbai studiously avoided seeing them. To the foxen, it seemed the Arbai preferred to teach at arm's length rather than communicate as the foxen did; she felt the fastidious withdrawal of the Arbai, their punctilious modesty of mind, similar to her own feelings, but carried so much further! They could not see evil, but they could perceive an invasion of privacy, and they rejected it. How familiar! How horrible!

He agreed. Nonetheless, He felt pity and guilt that they had died.

They died, she said. *Now we are dying. The Hippae are up there. They'll get into Commons and kill us.*

Already in Commons. But not many are dying. Not this time.

You're protecting us?

This time we know what is happening.

You didn't know what was happening before? she asked. *You didn't know what was happening to the Arbai?* It seemed impossible, and yet, would the foxen necessarily have known? The slaughter had been out on the prairie, away from the forest. . . .

He said, *Some hated humans because you hunted us. Some felt it was not our affair, not our concern, because you would not be our friends, no more than the Arbai. I told them Mainoa was friend. They said he was only one, a freak, unlike any other. I said no, there would be others. Then there was you. They say you, too, are freak, and I say there will be others yet. We have argued over it. Finally, we have compromised.* Humor. Almost laughter, yet with something sad and tentative in it. *We agree if you are truly my friend, I can tell you.*

Me?

If you will give your word. To be friend as Mainoa was friend. To be where I am.

She heard only the condition and assented to it at once. She had already decided to stay here. She would not take Stella away from here. At least the people here understood what had happened to her.

I will give my word, she said.

To be where I am?

Yes.

Even if that is not here?

Not here? Where would He be, if not here? She waited for explanation and got none. Something told her she would receive none. If she could only see His face. See His expression. . . .

We see one another, He told her. *We foxen.*

She flushed. Of course they saw one another, in their intimacy. As she could have seen them if she had let go of herself and joined them. As humans stripped away their day-to-day habiliments to come to their lovers naked, so foxen stripped away concealing illusion to perceive the reality. . . .

But she could not see Him now. If she accepted this condition, it would have to be blindly, like a ritual, like a marriage ceremony, swearing to forsake all others for this one, this enigma, with no more certainty than there had been before. Swearing to give up her central self for something else. She shivered. Oh, perilous.

Take it or leave it.

How could she? This is what Rigo had wanted, too, and she had tried, over and over, but could not. Because she had not known him, had not trusted him. . . .

Did she trust this one?

He had known where to find her. He had committed Himself and His people to saving her and her people. What else could He have done to be trustworthy? What else would she have him do?

She sighed, choking on the words, committing herself forever. "Yes. I *promise*."

He showed her then why and how the Arbai had died. Why men were dying.

When she understood, she leaned against Him, her mind whirling in a disorderly ferment of ideas, things she had heard, connections she had made. He did not interrupt her. At last things began to fall into place. She only partially understood, and yet the answer was there, close, like a treasure sparkling in a flowing stream, disclosing itself.

There is something you must get for me, she said. *Then I must go through these tunnels into town*. . . .

Marjorie came into the cavern where Lees Bergrem was huddled over a desk. For a time she stood in the corner, unseen, putting her thoughts together. Lees looked up, aware of being observed.

"Marjorie?" she asked. "I thought you were at the Port Hotel! I thought the Hippae had you trapped!"

"There's at least one tunnel under the wall. I came back through it," she said. "I had to talk to you."

"No time," the other said, turning back to her work. "No time to talk about anything."

"A cure," she said. "I think I know."

The doctor turned burning eyes. "Know? Just like that, you know?"

"Know something important," she said. "Two important things, really. Yes. Just like that."

"Tell me."

"First important thing: The Hippae killed the Arbai by kicking dead bats through their transporters. We don't have transporters, so the Hippae have been killing us by putting dead bats on our ships."

"Dead bats!" She pursed her lips, concentrating. "The bon Damfels man said that was symbolic behavior!"

"Oh, yes. It is symbolic. The problem is that we thought of it as purely symbolic. We should have remembered that symbols are often distillations of reality—that flags were once banners flown during battle. That a crucifix was once a real device for execution. Both are symbols of something that is or was once real."

"Real what?" Lees sat down, glaring at Marjorie. "Bats are real what?"

Marjorie rubbed her head, ruefully. "Real pains in the neck, originally. Real vermin. The Hippae kick dead ones at one another. I've seen them do it."

"We know that! Sylvan bon Damfels said it meant 'You're nothing but vermin.' "

"Yes. Originally, it would have meant 'You're nothing but vermin.' That's what it meant when the Hippae kicked dead bats at the Arbai, too. On Terra there were once animals that threw feces at strangers. The Hippae despise strangers. They think of all other creatures either as useful tools, like the migerers or the Huntsmen, or as things to be despised and, if possible, killed. The Arbai fell into that category, so the Hippae kicked dead bats at them, and at their houses, and at their transporter. It was pure chance that a bat happened to go through the transporter to somewhere else. At this end, it was only symbolic. At the other end, it meant plague. Death."

"The vector of infection. . . ."

"Yes. It happened. Somewhere, wherever the transporter was set for, Arbai died. And then the foolish Arbai here on Grass told the

Hippae what had happened. From that moment on, the gesture no longer meant 'You're vermin.' It meant 'You're dead.' Once the Hippae knew they could kill by putting bats through the transporter, they kept on repeating the act. It was not symbolic, it was real."

"Kept on—"

"Kicking dead bats through the transporter until all the Arbai were infected. It may not have taken long. Maybe only a day or a week. Whenever they weren't observed. The Arbai were so . . . so set in their thinking that they never thought to set a guard. I'm assuming the transporter must have worked like a voice-activated com-link. Whenever the network was in use, certain sets of terminals must have come on so that a bat kicked in at one terminal would have ended up far away. On Repentance? On Shafne? There are Arbai ruins both places. On a hundred worlds we've never seen? Wherever, however many, it worked. The Arbai died, everywhere. Hippae memorialized the event in their dances. A great victory. 'Fun to kill strangers.' They remembered it.

"When humans came to Grass, the Hippae would have repeated the act again, but we didn't have transporters, we had ships. Dead bats had worked with the Arbai, so the Hippae decided to put dead bats on our ships. Our ships, however, were inside the forest where the foxen had influenced us to put our port. The foxen had believed that if the port was inside the swamp forest, it would be safe. The foxen had enjoyed having the Arbai around. Though they would have liked direct contact, being telepathic they hadn't needed to have it. They had sought a kind of intellectual intimacy with the Arbai and been rebuffed, so they didn't try it with us. Instead, they regarded us as we might regard some intelligent, interesting, but unaffectionate pet, and they thought we would be safe enough. . . .

"They underestimated the Hippae. Perhaps they thought the Hippae wouldn't remember after all those centuries, but they did remember. They had codified their memory into dancing, into patterns. When men first arrived, the Hippae set the migerers to digging a tunnel, at first only a small one, one large enough to admit one human messenger at a time. Human messengers the Hippae had wiped clean except for a certain *impetus*, a certain programmed activity—"

"That's unbelievable!"

"It's quite believable because it was only a slight variation of their natural habit. Peepers have no such ability. Hounds have almost none. The Hippae have enough to affect the minds of those around them and bend those minds to their purposes. Think of what they do to the migerers and to the Huntsmen! When the Hippae change into foxen, the ability is multiplied a hundredfold. Hippae may not be truly intelligent. Evil and sly, yes, able to learn but incapable of true subtlety. They learned to kill by accident, but once having learned, they went on, and on. Everything they have done was merely a repetition of a pattern they already knew. . . ."

The doctor was very still, thinking. "You said you knew *two* important things."

"The other thing was about your books. I tried to read them. I'm not scientific. All I can remember is that one of them was about this nutrient, this protein building block. You said it was something we all needed. Most living cells. And you said it existed in two forms here on Grass, and only here. I got to wondering why. Why two forms here? And then I wondered, what if something here turned it around? What if something here on Grass turned around an essential nutrient? Something all our cells need and use. Something we couldn't use in a reversed form. . . ."

There was a long silence.

"I need a dead bat," said Lees Bergrem.

"I brought one," Marjorie said, reaching into her deep pocket. *First* had left the barn, had gone out onto the sloping lands to get it for her. She put the dried crumbling thing on Lees Bergrem's table. Then she sat down and put her head between her trembling knees and tried to think of nothing at all.

The two women stayed in the makeshift laboratory for two days. Above them in the town, battles were fought street by street, building by building. People died, though not so many as had at first been feared. There were allies no one could see. There were fighters no one could look at. Hippae were found dead, and no one remembered killing them. Then, too, since the Hierarch was not awake to countermand the Seraph's orders, troopers came down on the shuttle, a few at a time, to take over segments of Commons and man a slowly expanding perimeter. Demolition teams found the tunnels beneath the swamp forest and collapsed them into sodden ruin. No more Hippae came through. Those already inside hid, chameleonlike, to come screaming out of alleys, shrieking along walls. Sharing this much of the foxen invisibility, they found their way into houses and shops. Death came to Commons, death and blood and pain, but slow victory came also.

Roald Few missed death by inches, saved by something he could not describe. One of his sons died. Many of his friends were dead, or missing. A morgue was set up in the winter quarters. The first body there was Sylvan bon Damfels'. His was joined by a hundred others. In death he became what he could not manage in life: one with the Commons.

One by one the remaining Hippae were found and killed. Many were still hiding in the edges of the forest. Troopers ringed that perimeter, their heat-seeking weapons set on automatic fire. Within the trees, other beings found the Hippae, and none came out onto Commons ground again.

Toward the end of the battle, Favel Cobham climbed back down the chutes and restored power to the Port Hotel before going out to join his fellows. He had not been ordered to stop guarding the Yrar-iers, but neither had he been told to continue.

Rigo came out of the hotel later, when he saw the last of the troopers straggling back toward the port, and made his way toward the gate. In the port area, the men were already burying their dead and readying for departure.

"Going already?" Rigo asked a gray-haired Cherub with a wrinkled, cynical face.

"Lord and Master woke up and found out what happened to his tame scientists," the Cherub replied. "Found out what happened to the town, too. I guess he figures he might get gobbled up by something if we stay."

Rigo went on into Commons to ask if anyone had seen his wife. He was told to look where everyone was looking for missing kinsmen, in the morgue. He found her there, standing by Sylvan's body.

"Rowena asked me to come and arrange burial," she said. "She wants him to be buried out there, where Klive used to be."

"Wouldn't you have come anyhow?" he asked. "Didn't you care for him? Weren't you in love with him?" It was not what he had planned to say. He and Father Sandoval had agreed that recriminations were not appropriate. He had expected to find Marjorie's body and grieve over it. Thwarted of grief, thwarted of good intentions, this other emotion had happened.

She chose not to answer his question. Instead, she said, "Sebastian is dead too, Rigo. Kinny lost one of her children. Persun Pollut was almost killed. His arm is terribly hurt. He may never carve again."

He was shamed into silence, and angered for being shamed.

She walked toward the door, he following. "I've been working with

Lees Bergrem," she said, looking around to be sure she was not overheard. "She thinks we've found a cure. She already had some of the pieces. It can't be tested here on Grass. She's sent word to Semling. They can manufacture the cure, get some victims together, and test it."

"Manufacture?" he asked her, disbelieving. "Some kind of vaccine?"

She nodded, coming close to him, actually hugging him, an awkward, one-armed embrace, tears on her face. "Not a vaccine at all. Oh, Rigo. I really think we've found the answer."

He reached for her, but she had already turned away.

She would not say anything more until the people in Semling had received everything Lees Bergrem could send them. "Wait," she said to Rigo and Roald and Kinny. "Don't say anything to anyone until the word comes back. Don't get people's hopes up until we know for sure."

Marjorie and Lees Bergrem spent the third day since their discovery fretting together, stalking back and forth through the echoing room where they had worked. On this day the Semling victims would either improve or go on dying. At noon on the fourth day the word came from Semling. Within hours of being treated, all the victims had started to mend.

"Now." Marjorie was crying, tears flowing into the corners of her joyously curved mouth. "Now we can let everyone know." She went to the tell-me to call Brother Mainoa. Only then did she learn he had died in the lap of a foxen, days before. Only then did she understand a part of what *First* had tried to tell her.

19

"Our job is over," Marjorie said. "What we were sent to do is done." She and Rigo and Father Sandoval were sitting at a table at Mayor Bee's restaurant, drinking genuine Terran coffee. Around them the work of renewal went on. Renewal and burial. At the foot of the street, litter carriers went past, and Marjorie averted her eyes. She did not want to think any more about death.

"So you have said," Father Sandoval said in the aloof voice he had used to her recently. "I've seen no proof of it."

"I think I can explain it," she offered. They had scarcely spoken during the past few days. Father Sandoval had not forgiven her for going off like that, though, since a cure had seemingly resulted, he had not said much about it. He had not forgiven Father James, either. He and Rigo had been discussing the recalcitrants, Rigo's nephew, Rigo's wife. Their emotions were at war with their sense of what was fitting, and she wanted to help them both. She said, "I can at least tell you what Lees Bergrem told me, what she's telling everyone."

Father Sandoval set his cup down and twisted it on the tabletop, leaving a wet circle there when he picked it up again. He touched the circle with a fingertip, stretching it, breaking it.

"Perhaps that would be useful," he admitted.

She folded her hands in her lap, the way she had used to do as a child when called on to recite.

"Lees says that everything we've found in our universe has proven to share pretty much the same assortment of left-right molecules. She says there's no particular reason that we know of why some molecules are twisted one way and some are twisted the other, but they are, everywhere we've been. Some of these substances are essential to different forms of life, and one of these is a nutrient, L-alanine. L-alanine exists everywhere we've ever been. Human cells, most cells, can't get along without it.

"Here on Grass, however, a virus evolved which, as part of its process of reproduction, creates an enzyme, an *isomerase*, which converts L-alanine to D-alanine. L-alanine is the usual form. D-alanine is the mirror image, the isomer, and it is virtually nonexistent anywhere we know of. I'm quoting Lees exactly. She's said it a hundred times, so I know I've got it right." She stopped for a moment to drink, to watch Rigo watching her. He gestured vaguely, telling her to go on.

"After hundreds of thousands of years, the virus became widely dispersed here, in the living cells of all plants. As the plants died, the D form was released into the environment. Over time, here on Grass, the D form became as common as the L form. That's the important fact, Rigo. Here on Grass, both D-alanine and L-alanine are floating around, ubiquitous. We can't breathe or drink this coffee or eat anything grown here without taking in some of both—along with the virus.

"The minute we stepped off the ship from home, we were infected. The virus is in the air, in the dust, in the water. Lees says we probably had viruses in almost every cell of our bodies within minutes. The virus needs a co-factor in order to reproduce, however. A kind of activator. D-alanine is the co-factor. The viral protein binds to this co-factor, and then it converts L to D, very rapidly. However, the virus works both ways. It can also bind to L-alanine, and when it does, the viral protein converts D to L.

"Binding to D-alanine takes almost no time here on Grass because there's so much D-alanine around. Someplace like Terra, where there are maybe only a few accidental molecules, it could take a long, long time. That's why the plague was so slow to start elsewhere. It's also why there isn't any plague here on Grass. As soon as we started breathing on Grass, all our cells got supplied with D and L both.

"So, here on Grass, the virus inverts L, which we need in order to live, to D, which our bodies can't use. However, since both D and L are plentiful, it turns both forms around simultaneously, and each of our cells finds enough L-alanine to go on living. On other planets there was little or no D-alanine to start with. When L was reversed, only D was left, and the cells couldn't use it. When human cells died, the viruses escaped into neighboring cells in their immediately infective stage, and the process was repeated. People got sores that spread. Bandages, wash water, anything that touched the body served as a source of infection, and the dead cells provided the co-factor for newly infected cells."

"But not here," Rigo said stiffly.

"Not here. On Grass, both D-alanine and L-alanine are plentiful; our cells survive. The virus's life cycle is interrupted, the cells die naturally. People come here and get infected and go away, never knowing it...."

"And it was spread by bats?" Father Sandoval asked.

"Lees says the bats don't use alanine. It's only one of a number of amino acids, and the bats just don't use it. However, the blood of other animals has alanine in it. The bat doesn't need it, so the viruses and the co-factors exist in the bat's blood bladder. When bats die and dry, their insides are powdery with virus-rich material, as packed with viruses and with co-factors as a puffball is with spores. Dead blood-sucking bats are about as good a carrier as you could get."

"You haven't said what the cure is," Father Sandoval said, finding on Rigo's face an expression which reinforced his own mood, one of frustrated anger. One could not be angry that a cure had been found; one was, however, annoyed at the way it had been found.

"The cure?" She looked up, puzzled. "Well, of course, Father. I thought that was self-evident. All that's needed is to spread massive quantities of D-alanine around. Small doses are no good. If somebody gets small doses of D, it will bind to the enzyme and they'll die. But if they get massive amounts, more than is needed to bind, then there will be equal mixtures of L to D and D to L conversion. And, of course, Semling found that it was extremely easy to make. They just used the virus to manufacture it out of L-alanine."

Father Sandoval shook his head. "It sounds so simple the way you describe it. But the Arbai couldn't cure it, as wise as they were?" He would not believe in their wisdom, no matter what Father James had said. Furthermore, he felt the church would disbelieve in their wisdom as well. Doctrine, as he knew it, had no room for other children of God.

"Perhaps they died faster than we did. My informant doesn't know.

"Your informant?" Rigo said, his voice ugly. "A foxen! Horses weren't enough for you, Marjorie?"

She frowned at him warningly, repressing her sudden anger. "Don't, Rigo. If you are ambassador to Grass, you are ambassador to them, as well. They aren't animals."

"That is not for you to decide," the priest said, echoing her anger with a sullen fury of his own. "That is a question for the church, Marjorie. Not for you. They may be intelligent and still be animals. Your relationship with them may be a serious error. I caution you!"

"You what?" she asked, incredulous. "You what?"

"I caution you. On pain of excommunication, Marjorie. Do not continue in this mindless adulation of these creatures."

She looked at the priest, betraying nothing. His face was red, then white. His hand, resting upon the table, was clenched. Rigo looked much the same. They had been discussing her again. Talking over how she was to be controlled, no doubt. Her mind scuttered in its usual pattern of evasion, of compromise, then stopped as though it had run into a wall.

She had made a commitment.

She laughed.

"Does he speak for you, as well?" she asked Rigo.

He did not reply. His face was reply enough. He, too, flushed, livid with rage.

She rose from her chair, leaned forward. "You two . . ." she said calmly, "you two can go to hell." She turned and walked away, leaving them staring after her, their faces leaking anger until nothing was left except pallid amazement.

All Rigo could think of as he watched her back as she walked away was to wonder who she was thinking of now that Sylvan was dead.

"Father?"

They looked up to see Father James standing at their sides.

Father Sandoval nodded curtly.

"I've come to say goodbye," said the younger priest, with only a slight tremor.

"You recollect what I told you," Father Sandoval said through gritted teeth.

"Yes, Father. I deeply regret you cannot see my point of view. However, I feel you're wrong and my conscience will not allow—"

"Obedience would allow!"

The younger man shook his head and went on. "My conscience will not allow me to be swayed. I came in today to hear about the cure. Before Brother Mainoa died, he said he knew we would find it. The foxen, he said. They would help us. Mainoa was almost a hundred Terran years old, did you know? Well, why would you? A wonderful old man. He would have wanted to be here himself. . . ."

"You're going back to the forest? Despite what I've told you?"

"I am, yes. I believe I must stay here, Father. I agree with Marjorie that it may be the most important work we have to do."

Rigo's nostril lifted. "What work is that? More charities? Resettling the homeless Grassians? More widows and orphans?"

Father James shook his head, giving Rigo a perceptive, tilt-headed look. "No widows or orphans, Uncle Rigo. No. The foxen are the only other intelligent race man has ever found. I've already sent an inquiry to Shafne, to the Church in Exile. Despite what Father Sandoval says, I'm confident the Secretariat will think it important for us to find bonds of friendship with the foxen. Kinship, as it were. To find a way to share ourselves. Marjorie says that even small beings may be friends." He laughed, shrugging. "But then you know—"

"I don't know," he replied angrily. "She talks very little to me."

"Well," the young man reflected, "that's probably natural. You always talked very little to her, Uncle Rigo. She says she used to suffer from the Arbai disease."

"Arbai disease?"

"Terminal conscientiousness," he replied, his brow furrowed. "Scrupulousness of the kind that creates conditions making poverty and illness inevitable, then congratulates itself over feeding the poor and caring for the sick. Those are my words, not hers, and I may have it wrong. . . ."

He nodded, then walked away as Marjorie had done, leaving the two to discuss threats and confrontations, knowing as they did so that anything they might propose was as useless as what they had already done. Neither Marjorie nor Father James would change minds in the time before the ship for Terra left, even though both of them were to know by then that what they were doing was a good deal more complicated than they had assumed.

20

In the Tree City of the Arbai, spring gave way to an endless summer, and summer to an endless fall. The season moved slowly toward winter, day succeeding day in a kind of tranquil haze. The inhabitants of the city knew they must go down to winter quarters soon, but they delayed. Two, or perhaps more, were waiting for a certain occasion; others waited for no occasion at all. Sun still spangled the tops of the trees. The wind was only occasionally chill. On most days, it was warm enough to sit beside an open window with a book, or with a letter. . . .

"My dear Rigo," Marjorie wrote.

> You have written once more to ask that Tony and I return
> to Terra. Tony must answer for himself. I've written several
> times since you left, attempting to explain why I can't re-
> turn. It seems silly to use these same words over and over
> again when they meant nothing before. It is autumn here
> on Grass. That means years have gone by where you are.
> After all this time, I wonder why you even care.

She looked out the window of her house to see Rillibee Chime
drop down onto the plaza, returning from a climb among the treetops.
Other young Green Brothers were still up there. She could hear them
yodeling to one another. The older Brothers, including Elder Brother
Laeroa, were in their Chapter House, away among the trees. There
were still Green Brothers upon Grass, and would be. Who would make
grass gardens if the Brothers went away?

"All the leaves are curling or falling or withdrawing into the twigs,"
Rillibee called to her. "All the little things that live up there are going
down." He stopped beside Stella, who was reading on the plaza.
"Froggy things and all, burrowing down into the mud."

Stella looked up from her book. Her face was open and childlike,
yet it was not a child's. She was a young woman once more, though
a different woman than she had been. "Even the furry ones?"

"Those, too," he replied, leaning over to kiss her while she kissed
him back. From a window across the bridge two faces appeared, two
mouths making kissy noises, teasing, with a kind of feral abandon.
Like young dogs, tearing at something.

"You," Rillibee called. "Get back to your lessons."

Obediently, the two heads withdrew. "They're doing better," remarked Stella. "Janetta can read ten whole words, and Dimity almost
never takes her clothes off anymore."

"Your brother's a good teacher."

"Foxen are good teachers," she replied. "They don't make you learn
to read or talk human or anything. Dimity and Janetta can talk foxen
a little. I wish I could just talk foxen."

"Don't you want to be able to talk to your mother?"

Stella wrinkled her nose.

Marjorie stared at the mostly blank page on her lap-desk and
sighed silently. No. Even now, Stella did not particularly want to talk
to her mother, though she was much nicer about it than she had

once been. Soon there would be no mother to talk to, so there was no profit in regret.

"How about talk to me?" Rillibee asked.

"Yes," Stella caroled. "Yes, I want to talk to you."

"What do you want to do this afternoon?"

"Go say hello to Brother Mainoa. Pretty soon he'll be all by himself, so we'd better say hello now."

"That's true." Rillibee nodded, taking her hand as they set slowly off toward the bridge, stopping every step or two to exclaim at a creature or a leaf or a flower.

Marjorie returned to her letter.

> Thank you for bringing us current on what has happened at Sanctity. We had already heard that the Hierarch had been overthrown in absentia and that Sanctity itself has been invaded and largely destroyed. The last time Rillibee went to Commons, he was told that Sanctity is only a shell, that the angels upon the towers raise their trumpets to an empty sky. He also learned that all those in the Israfel perished of the plague on an unsettled planet where they'd fled for refuge. They must have carried the plague with them from Grass. I remember Favel Cobham and weep for him. He was a goodhearted boy.

"Stop." She heard Stella's voice.

Marjorie looked out. Rillibee had stopped obediently, just short of the bridge. "Why are we stopping?" he asked her.

"I want to see the Arbai lovers. They're coming along the bridge now."

The two humans on the bridge and the one in the house watched the inhuman lovers bending across the rail, curling into one another's arms, entwined. "What're their names?" Stella said in a stage whisper.

"You know their names as well as I do," Rillibee replied.

"Tell me!"

"The probably-a-boy's name is Ssanther. The probably-a-girl's name is Usswees."

"Arbai names."

"Yes. Arbai names."

Marjorie mouthed the well-known names to herself. Experts had come from Semling and Shafne to record the language spoken in this city and connect it to written words. According to them, the tiny projectors hidden among the trees would go on working for another century or more, throwing Arbai images into the city they had built and died in. Similar projectors had been found in the other city, buried in the ruined walls, lost under the soil, the source for the mysterious visions which had filled the ruins. Now that the specialists understood the language, Arbai artifacts were no longer so enigmatic. Scientists had even succeeded in restoring the Arbai transporters, at least from this end, though they had not been tested yet.

She turned back to her writing.

> Here on Grass, the foxen have determined to take charge of their lives. Several new villages have been built with solar-powered fences to keep peepers in and Hippae out. Those foxen who are still capable of doing so have begun laying eggs in these areas. The peepers that hatch from foxen eggs will be kept separately. Foxen will eat only those hatched from Hippae eggs. In time, through this purposeful predation, the malice of the Hippae may be abated.
>
> The Green Brothers have begun gardens around these villages. Where the gardens of Opal Hill once flourished, I have stood upon a newly sprouted first surface which may one day astonish the great Snipopean. The foxen agree that beauty must not be allowed to perish, that whatever else is done, beauty must be conserved lest we impoverish our destinies. Even Klive will be reborn.

Marjorie put down her stylus and rubbed at her cramped fingers as she continued to stare out the window, remembering Klive. Remembering Opal Hill. Such glory in the grass. Even Snipopean could not have told that glory, for he had not danced with the foxen. . . .

She came to herself with a start. She was merely filling pages, giving herself something to occupy the last few hours. Everything was done that she had to do. Her pack lay beside the door, its contents carefully selected. Who could have thought a promise would carry her so far.

Outside on the plaza, Stella tugged at Rillibee. "Come on," she said. The two of them went along the bridge toward its island end. In the flat green meadow at its base, at the foot of a tall fruit-bearing tree, Mainoa's grave lay, the herbage above it constantly littered with fruit and seeds and scraps of rind.

Marjorie rose, confronting one of the wall panels carved by Persun Pollut. The first one he had done with his left hand was crude, though full of harsh vitality. The later ones had gained in subtlety and ease of line. He was a great artist, Persun. Too great to stay here on Grass. Elsewhere, he could have a new right hand cloned for him. Well, soon the unwilling tether that held him on Grass would be untied. Then, perhaps he would go. . . .

Marjorie closed the lid of her writing desk, took it by its handle, and went after Stella and Rillibee. Around her the shadow Arbai moved and spoke. Their words had been translated. Their motives were understood. Confronted with evil, these had chosen to die. Marjorie mourned them, but could not regret them. They had been too good to do good. Someone had said that once. Rillibee, she thought. Rillibee, who loved Stella.

The two of them were sitting by Mainoa's grave mound when she came down the hill. "And how is Brother Mainoa today?" she asked.

Stella leaned forward to neaten the fragrant herbs, brushing away the litter. "He's going to be lonesome out here by himself."

"I don't think so," Marjorie said, turning slowly to take in all of the meadow: behind its protective fence, the twisted arch of the Arbai transporter, glowing with opalescent light; the blossoming reeds at the edge of the mire; the shaggy trees, towering into heights of heartbreak gold. She turned back to the young ones with a smile. "Not Brother Mainoa. He'll be very interested in everything that happens, all winter long. And the foxen will come talk to him. They come out above ground in the winter."

"What are you doing?" Rillibee asked her, indicating the desk she was carrying. "Writing a book?"

She shook her head ruefully, "Rigo has asked for explanations. Yet again."

"Father James says he may be trying to accumulate evidence in order to have your marriage set aside."

She looked thoughtful for a moment, then laughed. "I hadn't thought of that, but it's probable! Father Sandoval undoubtedly put him up to it. Perhaps the laws on Terra have changed and he would be allowed to father a new family. Well, in any case, this may be my last opportunity to try telling him about his former one." She shrugged, confronting Rillibee's look with a calm face.

"You're still determined to—"

"It isn't determination, Rillibee. I made a promise. I've always tried to keep my promises, when I could."

"Tell Daddy Rillibee and I are going to have a baby," said Stella. "Tell him that. We're going to name it Joshua. Or Miriam."

Two of Rillibee's magic names. Names he would hold sacred if all hell came against him. Now he would give the baby one of them, sending it out like a firefly into darkness. In time there would be others, lighting up nothingness with bright names, like the burning names of stars. Marjorie smiled, thinking that she would not tell Rigo that. He would not understand.

From above came a trill, a purr. Foxen. Marjorie trilled in answer. From the neighboring meadow, a horse whickered in reply.

"Did you see the new colt?" Stella asked suddenly.

Marjorie nodded. "This morning. Mother and baby doing well. All sixteen of the horses doing well, as a matter of fact. The foxen have been talking to the foals again. I keep getting these very percipient looks! Blue Star's new baby looks exactly like Don Quixote. Mayor Bee's terribly excited."

"The mayor gets the colt, does he?" Rillibee asked.

"Well, I promised. A few Hippae showed up at the interdict village near Klive, and the mayor wants to lead the expedition."

"In accordance with the plan," he said.

"In accordance with the plan," echoed Stella.

In accordance with the plan, thought Marjorie. She sat down and put the desk on her lap, looking at it with resignation. Father James was probably right. Rigo wanted written evidence of her dereliction, her apostasy.

"We'll let you get back to it," said Rillibee. "I'll go relieve Tony. He's been working with Dimity and Janetta. They'll never be right, Marjorie. Everyone knows that now. I don't know why Tony goes on. . . ."

"He's stubborn," Marjorie said. "Like me. Has he said anything?" she asked, a little anxiously. "About after . . . ?"

Rillibee nodded, frowning. "He's going back to Terra. He thought his father's request over carefully, and he's decided to return, at least for a while. Since he and Stella were the only children Rigo was allowed to have, Tony thinks going back, for a while at least, is only fair." He took her hand and pressed it, sharing her disappointment. Then he and Stella went away from her, up the green hill.

Marjorie sighed. She had hoped Tony would stay. In the winter, he would have lived closely in Commons, acquiring age, acquiring friends. In the spring Amy bon Damfels would be coming to the Tree City with Emmy and her mother. Marjorie had envisioned Amy and

Tony— Still, if he wanted to go back ... He was still very young. Perhaps he felt he needed at least one parent.

She opened the desk and started a new paragraph. If Rigo wanted proof she was crazy or ungodly or whatever, why not give it to him?

> You needn't refer to my religious duties, Rigo. I have not forgotten them....
>
> We came to Grass together, out of duty. On Terra I had become much accustomed to duty, much concerned with propriety. Even when I knew I was doing very little good with my visitations, I persisted, out of duty. It has recently occurred to me that I was not too different from the bons. As they rode the Hippae and were enslaved, so I rode custom and was enslaved. I was a very good child and woman. I was scrupulous in my behavior. I confessed regularly and followed my confessor's advice. I did good deeds, even feeling guilty because I sometimes broke men's laws of discipline to do what I thought of as God's laws of mercy. I was faithful to you because it was my duty, and I did what duty required because I thought God would be offended if I didn't.
>
> Here on Grass there was more duty. I found myself looking ahead to the time I could die and wouldn't have duty anymore. Here I was, barely forty, Terran, wanting to die so I could quit going through all these motions! So, I went out into the grasses one day, courting death, but what offered itself was not really death and the horror of that made me realize what I was doing.
>
> Duty simply was not enough. There had to be more than that!
>
> Father James suggested that perhaps we were viruses. I know now that he meant to be funny. He thinks I lack humor. I do. Everyone says so, even Tony. Because I do, I took his words seriously. Later I came to think we might be like other things, like white cells or neurotransmitters. Warriors or message carriers. Such cells have a purpose, or at least a *function* in the body they inhabit. They have evolved to have that function. So we, in the body which we inhabit, may have evolved or be evolving to have similar purpose or function, though we are, I believe, only very small beings....

Up among the leaves she heard Father James' voice raised in disputation with the foxen. Now that he was head of an official mission to the foxen, he did a lot of disputation and he always raised his voice when his logic was weak. Lately they had been discussing sins of the flesh and he had been raising his voice a lot. The foxen were not believers in sins of the flesh, and they offended the priest by quoting back at him the scripture he had once quoted to them.

Across the meadow one of Rillibee's red and blue pet parrots called over and over to itself, "Songbird Chime. Joshua Chime. Miriam Chime. Stella . . ."

Marjorie turned back to the pages once more.

When mankind thought that his was the only intelligence and earth was his only place, it was perhaps fitting to believe that *each* man had individual importance. We were all there was. Like frogs, each thinking its own puddle was the center of the universe, we believed that God worried over us each of us. Strange that we should realize Pride is a sin yet still be willing prey to such arrogance.

We had only to look around us to know how foolish the idea was. Where was the farmer who knew each of his seeds by name? Where was the beekeeper who labled his bees? Where was the herdsman who distinguished among individual blades of grass? Compared to the size of creation, what were we but very small beings, as bees are small, as seeds of corn are small, as blades of grass are small?

And yet corn becomes bread; bees make honey; grass is turned into flesh, or into gardens. Very small beings are important, not individually but for what they become, if they become. . . .

The Arbai failed because they did not become. Mankind almost failed. We squatted on Terra almost too long. We left only because we had ruined our planet and had to leave or die. Then, once we had swarmed far enough to find new homes, we let Sanctity stop us from going on. 'Fill up the worlds,' it said. 'Go no farther. Take no risks.' And we went no farther. We took no risks. We grew. We multiplied. We did not become. . . .

A trill came from behind her. She did not need to turn to know who was there. He touched her neck as delicately as a leaf fall, a claw barely extended, the tiniest prick.

"Now?" she breathed.

He dropped her pack on the ground beside her.

She wavered. "I haven't said goodbye to Tony, to Stella!"

Silence.

She had said goodbye. Every hour of the past season had been goodbye. Father James had given her his blessing only this morning. There was nothing left to say. He touched her once more.

"I must finish this," she said, bending above her letter.

> ... We did not become. We did not change.
>
> But change must come. Risk must come. God knows there are enough of us that we can afford some losses! Why else are we so many? And though the grass be numberless as stars, there must still be a first shoot set out to make a garden. ...

She had not said goodbye to Persun. Perhaps better that she not say goodbye. Considering everything. ...

> One of the foxen and I are going on a journey. No one knows whether we will arrive anywhere or be able to return. If we do not, someone else will, eventually. There are enough of us that we may go on trying, as long as it takes.

His claw touched her again, teasingly.

She sorted through the pages, setting them in order, knowing they wouldn't tell Rigo what he wanted to hear or even what she wanted to say. There was no time to write another letter, and what could she express otherwise? Perhaps, if things had been different along the way, Rigo would have been with her today. He had chosen to go back. She had chosen to go on. There was no blame in either choice.

She looked up at the city, seeing the wind-thrown shadows move among sun-dappled trees. The letter could be left here in the desk. Tony or Rillibee would find it and see that it was sent. She had never intended her departure to be ceremonial.

Now, He said like a trumpet. Now. There were others with Him, a great many others. Whether Marjorie had intended ceremony or not, the foxen had come to say farewell.

She wrote the last few words and signed her name, as she knew it, wondering whether Rigo would be relieved that she had gone or annoyed that she was past pursuit. What use would he make of these pages? She set the desk on Mainoa's grave. Duty was done, but there were still promises to keep.

They were all around her. She mounted the familiar mirage and arranged herself. A hundred yards away, the Arbai transporter glowed with bubble light, nacreous glimmers, a veil of mystery within the loop. There was only one way to test it: by going through. Decorum, she told herself as they approached. One should go toward one's destiny with decorum.

"Marjorie," she said aloud, voicing the last words she had written so she could hear how they sounded. He did not know her as Marjorie. This might be the last time she heard her name.

Marjorie,
by the grace of God, grass.
Amen.